Truthful LIARS

C.E. SAWYER

Truthful Liars

Copyright © 2016 by C.E. Sawyer

First Edition

Publisher: Five Suns Entertainment L.L.C.

St. Paul, Minnesota

Book design by Five Suns Entertainment L.L.C.

Photos by Adobe

Printed in the United States of America

Library of Congress Control Number: 2016918430

ISBN 978-0-9861417-2-0

ISBN 978-0-9861417-3-7 (ebook)

To Arin and Marissa With Love

Contents

Chapter 1

"You belong to me, baby, and don't you forget it."

Luca Nero smacked Robin Matthews' exposed round bottom as she got out of bed and grinned wickedly at the corresponding jiggle of her supple behind. He liked watching the angry pink splotch in the shape of his hand form on her fair skin.

"If only we could bottle up that ass and sell it," he murmured into his pillow as she glared down at him. He wound up for another slap and she shooed away his hand with a laugh. He eyed her like a tiger observing its prey as she bent over to pick up her tank top, which rested crumpled at her feet alongside the bed. She pulled the fabric easily over her mass of blond curls.

"I think you have me involved in enough money making schemes, don't you think?"

"*Enough* doesn't exist in my vocabulary."

"Speaking of *enough*, hasn't enough time passed for me to finally meet your brothers, your sister, or your father? Hell, I'd settle for anyone with the Nero name at this point," she scoffed as she buttoned the light fabric of her blouse over her fitted tank top.

He yawned, pulling the sheets around his waist and scratching his chiseled bare chest. She marveled that even after their hours of passionate and aerobic lovemaking, his jet black hair was still perfectly gelled without a strand of hair out of place. Despite a year of dating, they still were ravenous for each other and his appetite for her never seemed to waiver.

"You could meet my family, which sounds like a bore, *or*, you could walk that apple butt of yours over here and meet me under the sheets again," he coaxed. She tilted her head at him defiantly, but couldn't stay standoffish for long. One thing Luca Nero didn't lack was charm. He could melt ice off a glacier if he put his mind to it. Even his sleaziest of lines rolled off his tongue with delicate ease. His warm, brown eyes feigned innocence. His dimples acted as a playful mask covering his darker intentions. She'd seen his temper flare before, which made her think twice before disappointing him. She also knew he always carried his trusty Glock in a side holder whenever he left the house and had an arsenal of men on call. Luca Nero was undoubtedly a dangerous man. When it came to issues in the bedroom though, she knew she had leverage. She was the habit he couldn't break.

"I think three times is enough for now, don't you? Plus, I told you I have to stop by my place to get ready for an event later. You're the one who keeps telling me about the importance of maintaining appearances and that means keeping a legitimate job. As the event coordinator, I actually *need* to be there. *Shocker*." She found her heels strewn about the room and he groaned in defeat.

"Fine, but let's meet up later tonight after your shift. We have some business to discuss. We have a few things we need to accomplish, and then I can bring my baby to meet the family. It's all about timing." His eyes darkened briefly and Robin shrugged.

"Speaking of timing, I'm running late." She leaned over the bed and Luca propped himself on his forearms to land a kiss on her red lips. He snuck in a quick boob squeeze as she started pulling away.

"Hands off the merchandise," she giggled.

"I own the merchandise. You belong to me, baby, and don't you forget it."

Robin opened her door and walked into her sprawling Las Vegas apartment on the nineteenth floor of a luxury high-rise. She glanced briefly at the art print hanging by the entryway that her twin sister had bought her for Christmas three years ago, titled *Girl on Bridge*. It was Scarlet Matthews' favorite piece of art from the museum where she worked in Washington, D.C., her letter had stated when the gift arrived. It was too depressing for Robin's taste, but guilt over not seeing her sister for nearly ten years made her hang it behind her entry door. Though the twins never spoke, Scarlet never failed to send a Christmas gift each year with an offer to reconnect. Robin thought if she was the disappointing absentee twin, she could at least give Scarlet's gifts a place of honor in her home. They lived in separate worlds as far as Robin was concerned.

Her heels clicked across the wood floor as she carried her mail under her arm into the kitchen. She noticed a card propped on a white box tied with a black ribbon sitting in the middle of her kitchen island. She picked up the curious box with interest. She assumed the doorman delivered it for her while she was out. Her thoughts leapt to Luca and his tendency to lavish her with gifts.

A smile spread across her face as she allowed herself to feel spoiled. She pulled at the soft black ribbon with one hand and lifted the lid. The contents of the box made her gasp.

Inside was a dead bird. A robin, its chest with the signature reddish hue. The tips of its wings were blackened and burnt. Its neck was twisted in an unnatural way. She noticed the bird's dark beak was slightly open as if it was caught in mid-flight. She dropped the box and black ribbon on the floor in horror. The sickening smell of burnt feathers and ash rose into the air as the contents spilled. The curved neck and beak bounced a little against her wood floors. Her shaking hand still clasped the note in her right hand. Willing her hands to move, she opened the card carefully to reveal screaming red ink. One question was written in bold, red strokes.

How high can little Robin fly... without burning her wings?

Robin lurched toward the sink in her kitchen. She barely made it in time to vomit in the sink basin. She wiped her mouth with the back of her hand and silently scolded herself for having such a strong reaction. She forced her limbs to move forward to scoop up the dead robin into the box and tossed it in the trash. She glanced at the card one last time. She didn't recognize the handwriting.

She was no stranger to living on the edge. She believed risk led to reward even though sometimes she risked a lot for little reward. Yet, this mysterious gift left her ruffled and unsure of herself. She couldn't shake the lingering sense that this time she may have gotten in over her head. The feeling she was slowly sinking into the abyss started to settle around her like an old familiar friend. She felt the sensation of waves crashing over her head and she didn't have the ability to swim toward the surface. She thought of calling Luca but decided against it immediately. She knew she was safer drinking a bottle of lighter fluid than having Luca Nero view her as someone who could cause him trouble.

Her eyes lifted back to the *Girl on Bridge* print her sister gave her. The eerie image of the girl looking out at the crashing crimson waves stared back at her from the wall. The girl seemed to catch a vision of herself beneath the churning waters. Looking at the picture, Robin realized it was the first time in a long time that she missed her father. If he were alive, he would know what to do. He could decipher the meaning of the twisted gift. He was dead though, like the bird. He left Robin at home one night, seven years ago, when she was only 19, and both her father and his car were never seen again. She learned how to get along without him after that moment and she realized this time would be no different.

Her fingers trembling, Robin took a deep steady breath and pulled up the contacts on her cellphone for someone she thought she would never call again. She dialed the number and waited patiently. She dreaded making the call.

She knew any second the ringing would stop. She would then have to bridge the gap created from miles of space and years. She took a couple of deep shaky breaths. Her stomach lurched and seconds felt like hours as her heartbeat pounded in her ears. There was a brief silence as a voice came from the other end of the line.

"Hello, this is Scarlet. Hello?"

Chapter 2

"It is often the people we love the most, who hurt us the worst."

Scarlet Matthews bounded up the long staircase leading into the quaint Impressionist art museum. She fumbled with heavy metal keys that looked like they were pulled from the pages of history. Keys that should open Camelot's chambers instead of an art museum. She waited for the satisfying click of the unlocking steel and pushed open the heavy, wooden doors. Her heels made light tapping sounds on the marble floor as she rushed in, flicking on lights as she made her way to the back office. She enjoyed these moments of quiet to herself.

Now, at the age of twenty-six, she was the assistant to the museum curator. It was all she ever wanted to do with her art history degree. She opened the museum each morning and, as part of her morning ritual, she would take a couple minutes to gaze at her favorite painting. It reminded her each day why she remained in her role despite feeling unappreciated and overworked. The museum wasn't overly popular, which was reflected in her pay, nor was her position particularly coveted due to an overbearing boss with a bad reputation. The small museum was located a couple of blocks from the National Mall in Washington, D.C., away from the main traffic areas. She had submitted her résumé months ago to several of the most prestigious and popular galleries on the National Mall. She never received a response.

She paused in front of her favorite piece, appreciating the serenity of the vacant museum. She could hear her slow even breaths as she stood in the open viewing area. She wasn't sure why she liked the painting, *Girl on Bridge*, and couldn't answer why she preferred this piece out of their colorful inventory. She gazed at the careful features of the girl, standing at the edge of a metal railing. Angry reds peppered the clouds from an approaching storm that illuminated flecks in her hair. Her solemn face reflected in the crimson waves churning at her feet. Scarlet wasn't sure if the girl's expression was a result of the stealthy storm approaching her from a distance, or the raging waters below. Perhaps the girl wasn't thinking about either, but instead noticed her reflection staring back at her amidst the growing chaos. Almost like she had a twin.

Each morning, different questions flooded Scarlet's mind as she stood admiring the broad strokes and detailed layers. Was the girl heading home from a long day of work? Did she have a family who loved her, cherished her, and waited for her each night to cross that bridge? Did she live alone? Maybe she never intended to cross the bridge that night as her pensive eyes looked to the choppy waters below.

Art critics claimed the work's famous painter, Jacques Demeter, suffered from various maladies. Some even said he was certifiably insane, but Scarlet wasn't convinced. How could a man without his faculties create a vision transcending human emotion, a picture which looked and felt so incredibly *real*?

A familiar creaking of the heavy wooden door behind Scarlet alerted her that her boss, Janet Bearings, had arrived. Janet used to be an industry unto herself in the art world, until a nervous breakdown sent her reeling back into the shadows to become an art curator at the small museum. Fully recovered from her episode, she still demanded the same level of reverence despite the change in her status and situation. Scarlet scampered to the table in the corridor where she left her clipboard with her task list and agenda for the day. She ran a hand through her stick straight red hair, trying to smooth away any frizz before her meticulously groomed boss noticed a hair out of place.

"Morning Janet, how are you? Did you have a nice weekend?" Scarlet asked, quickly falling in line behind Janet's broad steps. Janet cavalierly took off her coat and threw it over her shoulder in Scarlet's general direction, and Scarlet lunged forward to catch the faux fur coat before it hit the ground.

"Ugh, it was such a nightmare. Dave had some of his friends over, what *bores*. You would think I would be rewarded for putting up with his nauseating friends, but no, not from Dave. Plus, I went to all this bother hiring a cleaning maid for the party, and then he has the gall to criticize me. Can you believe that? I slave away for his friends and yet he is never happy, never satisfied." Janet continued talking for another twenty minutes about everything she had to endure over her weekend. She never once asked Scarlet about herself, but after years of the same one-sided conversations, Scarlet didn't expect anything different.

Scarlet trailed Janet around the museum as Janet barked orders and asked questions. She half listened as they took their morning walks around the exhibits while she made a personal game of picking out things she would do differently if she was the head museum curator. "Have you thought about social marketing for the museum, Scarlet?" Janet asked and Scarlet mentally ticked another item on her checklist. *I would have the cleaning crew focus on the baseboards of the museum every other week. I don't know how they miss the stringy dust clumps that gather in the corners. We are displaying art on the walls, not gray fuzzy creations.*

"I know I ask you to wear a lot of hats around here, but I *cannot* emphasize enough the importance of finding innovative ways to incent the part-time staff to promote the museum through their own social channels. We need guerrilla marketing. Our budget is practically zilch this year," Janet spat the words and didn't wait for an answer as she continued. "Perhaps get some people to write on the sidewalks in the National Mall with chalk. Let's put together a new brochure to hand out on corners and make sure the staff is tweeting and posting on social media at least five times a week. Maybe they could cold call or email the list of attendees we had last year, asking when they are planning their next visit. We need to have our staff hit the phones. We need more foot traffic. How are we going to make that happen, Scarlet?"

Scarlet continued her internal musings while looking at her clipboard. *I would ask about my employees during our meetings and show I care about their lives and ambitions. Aligning the staff with exhibits or events that tie into their own interests will make them feel more motivated to promote the museum activities.* Scarlet's thoughts rattled around her brain as they walked. *I would replenish our artistic arrangements quarterly, and promote traveling art exhibits to pull in guests with a variety of different tastes.*

"Did you write that all down, Scarlet?"

"Yes, chalk and cold calls, got it," Scarlet said as she furiously scribbled doodles on her notepad.

"Okay great. Leave a proposal for me on all of those ideas we discussed before you leave today. Glad that's done because I have to tell you about what Dave's brother got into last week. You just *won't* believe it," she said, before addressing any of the important items on

Scarlet's list, which meant it would turn into another late night for Scarlet without the benefit of overtime pay. *I would hire employees I would enjoy being around, people I actually find interesting, and that way, I wouldn't have to fake interest every day. If I have to listen to one more story about Dave's brother, my eardrums might rupture in sheer rebellion.*

Guests started filtering into the museum as Janet spoke emphatically about Dave's family. The visitors wandered in, eyes sparkling as they looked at the perfectly presented works of art. Their minds twirled with possibilities and endless explanations for what the artists intended. Janet pulled Scarlet's arm past *Girl on Bridge* as she continued complaining.

Scarlet's eyes lingered on the solemn figure in the frame. After years of staring at the picture each morning, for the first time, Scarlet thought she recognized herself in the girl's face.

Leaving well after closing time, Scarlet skipped down the steep steps of the gallery. She checked her phone to see if she had any missed calls and noticed a voicemail in her inbox from a number she didn't recognize.

"Scarlet? Joan Simmons from the National Gallery of Art. I received your résumé and I think you could be a great fit for our team. Give me a call back if you would like to speak further about the opportunities we have open and if you are interested, we can set up an interview in a few weeks. Hope to hear from you soon." The message went on to leave contact details. Scarlet, after taking a quick look see if there was anyone around, did a happy dance. She threw her arms up toward the sky as she swirled around on the pavement outside the museum. Her face hurt from her wide smile, but it was a welcomed and joyous feeling. She was alone on the short street which fell quiet in the darkness of another busy day, but the stillness didn't damper her mood in the least. In fact, she couldn't remember a time when she felt more hopeful.

She looked up at the sky where only a few stars were visible from the glaring lights of the brightly lit mall area. She felt she was in a moment of fantastic change, and her life from this night on wouldn't be the same. She knew the voicemail could lead to a new and fabulous life. She hummed to herself when she got into her car, tapping the steering wheel with renewed energy. She couldn't wait to get home and tell her sister.

Scarlet unlocked the door to her second-story apartment and walked inside. It was already nine at night from getting out late and her forty-minute commute. She could hear noise from the back room, a scattering of papers and the smack of closing drawers, and she knew her twin sister must be home. Even though Robin moved in with Scarlet a good two months ago, it still felt surprising to have someone to come home to each night after years of living on her own.

"I'm home, Robin, whatcha up to?" Scarlet asked, putting her purse down on the kitchen table and hanging her keys on a hook.

"Nothing special. How was your day?" Robin said in the distance. Scarlet wrinkled her nose. If she had a dime for every time her sister said she wasn't doing anything, Scarlet could quit her job at the museum. Her sister liked her secrets.

"It was fine. I got stuck writing a long proposal for ridiculous marketing efforts for Janet. We didn't get to discuss any of my new ideas for the museum. If we don't attack some of the pressing items on my list tomorrow, I don't know what we are going to do. I did get a potential lead for a new job, though. I'm super excited. I have a good feeling about the interview. I just have to set it up. We are still on for movie night tonight, right?" Scarlet said as she laid out the rest of her work on the table to continue the laundry list of items for Janet. She watched as her identical twin ran out of her room to the bathroom.

"Yeah, yeah, you got it. Movie night. Congrats about the potential new job. I know you will get it," Robin said. She frantically moved from room to room in the quaint, two-bedroom apartment.

Robin's hurried movements suggested an active intent to leave the apartment, either forgetting or ignoring their plan to stay in for a low-key movie night. When Robin poked her head around the corner looking for her phone, Scarlet saw a fresh application of eyeshadow around her eyes. Scarlet sat on the couch curled under her favorite blanket as she scribbled notes in her notepad for work. Scarlet pensively thought back to her sister's call two months prior, when they first decided to move in together.

"Scarlet, I know I'm not the best sister. Hell, I know we've rarely seen each other during the last decade. I want that to *change*. I'm getting sick of Vegas, honest, and it's getting sick of me. Shouldn't two single girls like us experience the city together anyway? What if I came to live with you out there for a while, see how it goes? I could help with rent and do the dishes for us. We could have movie nights, stuffing our faces full of popcorn until we can't stand it anymore. We missed so much of that growing up. I won't take no for an answer. Come on Scarlet, you know it would be *magical*." Robin said with her typical confidence and charisma floating through the hard plastic of the cellphone and Scarlet couldn't help but smile.

"You seriously want to give up all the glamour of the Strip and live in a cookie cutter apartment in *Virginia*? I thought you would rather watch paint peel off the walls than to give up the lights and glam of Las Vegas? I'm thrilled you decided to finally reconnect, but I have to say

I'm a little shocked. Did you meet a guy? Is that what this is about? Let me guess, he lives in Washington, D. C. or New York, maybe the outskirts of Virginia?"

"No guy, promise. Maybe I need some normalcy for a change. Come on Sis, I get questioned for simply wanting to spend time with you? I was a crappy sister. Let me make it up to you. I'm giving you my best puppy face, you just can't see it. Do I need to get down on my hands and knees and beg?" Robin's voice was strained on the call. Her last few sentences came out in whooshes of exasperation, like she was holding in her breath until her final plea.

Scarlet wondered on the call if Robin was high on drugs. The new, forced enthusiasm for the simpler life felt unexpected and suspicious, but she let the notion pass. She secretly longed for quality time with her sister, wishing they had the same kindred bond as other sisters she knew. It wasn't easy after their mom died when they were five years old, in a fluke car accident. Her vehicle somehow careened off one of the winding roads, plummeting down the side of a steep cliff. Their father was never the same since the incident. He didn't seem to care about family anymore. With his fast Vegas career and little desire to raise two girls around his reckless lifestyle, he called his sister in Virginia to see if she was willing to help. His sister, Jo Matthews, never married and kept to herself on her spacious vineyard in Virginia. He thought throwing two energetic girls at her would be asking too much, so he made the decision to keep outgoing Robin in Vegas. Scarlet, the timid wallflower, moved across the country to live with Aunt Jo. His decision forever shaped both girls. Scarlet felt living with her caring aunt created a blissful childhood, but she feared Robin's upbringing wasn't as easy. Despite these nostalgic feelings to recapture missed youth, she couldn't fight the nagging feeling her sister was *lying* about her intentions from the start.

It was the same sickening doubt she felt now, sitting in the pit of her stomach like the hatching of a flu bug, nagging at her insides. She wondered if *normal* people doubted the ones they love. Did everyone have doubts, or was Scarlet's mistrust born from something more primal, the *instinct of a twin*?

"I'll be ready in ten minutes and then we can pop in that scary movie, can't wait," Robin called from the hallway of her bedroom. A vibrating noise rose from the end table. Robin's phone was lighting up, and bouncing on the polished red wood. Her tall, slender figure reappeared to retrieve her phone. She inspected the message, tapped a couple keys, and put it back down on the table. Her brow furrowed for a moment before she disappeared again into the bathroom.

"You don't have to get all dressed up for a movie, Robin. I was just going to put on some comfy clothes, like yoga pants and a sweatshirt. It's just me, no one else to impress," Scarlet said, baiting her sister to explain the obvious primping.

"Well, I'm craving some ice cream. I'm going to pick up a couple of those cute little containers from the grocery store. I want to have fuel for a proper night of scary movie mayhem. I'll put on sweats when I get back. I want to be prepared if I run into a cute guy at the checkout line. Never leave the house without mascara and a little lipstick, that's what I always say."

Lie. An obvious lie. Scarlet could hear her sister rummaging through her drawers, most likely looking for her favorite bright red lipstick. She thought it gave her the Marilyn Monroe glow, and she wouldn't go anywhere without it on her lips.

Hearing Robin running the sink in the bathroom, Scarlet, suspicious of all the words left unsaid between them, quietly tiptoed over to her sister's phone on the table and typed in a password. It proved an easy code to crack. The code was Robin's birthday - their shared birthday. Scarlet typed in the code, and pulled up the last text received on the phone.

The meet is set at 1974 Lincoln Street in the alley at 10:30. Bring the stuff and don't be late.

Scarlet's faced flushed red with the sting of betrayal. She placed the phone back on the table and took soft steps to her place on the couch. The somewhat ominous text seemed to confirm her suspicions. Scarlet toyed with this new information, rolling it around in her head like a malleable ball of clay.

Against her better judgment, she pried a little more. "I bought ice cream last week, no need to go out. Come on, let's put in the movie, it's already nine-thirty. You promised not to fall asleep this time and it will be midnight before the first one finishes. We have two sitting here."

Scarlet said the words, although there wasn't any ice cream in the freezer. A lie to catch a liar, she thought, and immediately felt guilty for her tactics. She heard more ruffling of clothing from Robin's room. She came rushing into the family room with her favorite lipstick in her hand and a compact mirror in the other.

"No offense, but I have certain flavors I drool over and it would make the night perfect if I could mix two together. Trust me. You'll thank me when you have a euphoric flavor experience later tonight while we are screaming our heads off during the gory bits. I'll be back in a flash, love you, bye." She rushed over and kissed Scarlet on her forehead and playfully tugged a red strand of her hair.

"During the movie, I want to talk to you about going back to your original blond like me. You look like a wallflower with that straight, red hair. Don't hide the *Marilyn*, Scarlet." She rushed out the front door, leaving Scarlet on the couch self-consciously pulling at her hair.

She sat quietly for a moment with the blanket over her legs and looked out the window. It wasn't much of a view, but the rent was right. It was a compact, second-story loft, recently renovated, with the owners living below. She rolled the soft and warm material of the blanket from the couch between her fingers, wondering what to do. She decided this was her chance to find out if her sister had a good reason for all the lies.

She pulled off the cozy blanket, caught a glimpse of herself in the mirror, and rubbed the smudge of lipstick off her forehead from Robin's kiss. She grabbed her bag and keys, and headed outside to follow her sister into the darkness.

Scarlet scribbled 1974 Lincoln Street on a pad of paper in her purse as soon as she got into her car. She put the address in the GPS in her phone, and noticed it was taking her from Alexandria, Virginia, to the outskirts of D.C. She clutched the wheel a little tighter as she entered the dangerous neighborhood.

She reached her destination and spotted Robin's car pulling into a dimly-lit alleyway sandwiched between dilapidated brick warehouse buildings with bars on the windows. She parked on the road leading to the alley and walked closely against the grimy red brick so her body was flush with the wall. She peered around the corner to avoid being seen. Robin's car was parked next to a flashy luxury sports car, which looked entirely out of place amidst the surrounding muck and graffiti-splattered buildings. She wiped her drippy nose, reacting to the pungent smell of garbage and mold.

Scarlet could see her sister's blond bouncy hair in the dark, as well as two men in suits. The trio made their way into a dimly lit back entrance of the warehouse. She heard Robin chatting with the two men as they walked in together. She thought she caught the names *Darius and Carlo*. Once the door shut, Scarlet inched closer. She hoped to get a better view through the window marred with silver bars. She slinked past the shiny silver car and caught a whiff of fresh polish from the spotless vehicle. She crouched beside the window for a better look.

The two men were clad in pinstriped suits. Their hair reflected the light of the flickering bulb handing in the room, a byproduct of massive amounts of hair gel. One of the men was bulbous and slightly red-faced, and the older man was considerably taller and slender with graying hair. They all stood around a single table with a couple of filing cabinets in the corner. She could hear Robin talking animatedly to the two men but their faces remained impassive. Scarlet couldn't make out the words. It was like watching an old movie reel, vivid action with indistinguishable sounds.

Robin passed a folder across the table. She rubbed her arm methodically with her left hand and adjusted her weight from one foot to the other. Even though Scarlet grew up across the country from Robin, the twins shared the same nervous tics.

The larger man began yelling. He tossed papers on the floor of the dimly lit office, and the conversation grew heated. His wild gestures hit the exposed bulb and it swung above the table casting shadows across the room. Scarlet held her breath as she watched the argument unfold. Robin held her hands up, shaking and wide-eyed. Scarlet stayed crouched in the darkness behind the window's ledge, unsure of what to do, and puzzled by the exchange. She continued to watch the scene, powerless to act, her hands balled tightly into white-knuckled fists.

The taller man pulled out something long and silver from under his coat. Robin reacted on the other side of the plain metal table, skittishly pointing at the pictures and documents she had brought them. The men looked angry and shook their heads. The taller man took a step toward Robin with a wild, unflinching look in his eye, and extended his arm. He held a shiny, long metal object. *Gun! He has a gun! Robin, what did you do?*

A muffled shot echoed through the thick brick walls. Robin's form crumpled to the ground. Scarlet's hands flung to her mouth, clenching hard around her lips, squeezing the scream back into her mouth. It took every fiber in her being to remain silent. Robin's still form laid on the ground. Her vacant eyes stared at Scarlet as a halo of red oozed onto the cement floor around her face.

Her blood looked copper red, the color of the breast-feathers of a fallen robin in the dim glow of the swinging light bulb. Scarlet struggled to process the horrific image before her. She thought the blood pouring from her twin sister was a simple shade of *Robin Red*. Saturnine poetry, ironically morbid, yet in her state of shock, it was the only thought to came to mind. Angry hot tears blurred her vision and her lip trembled. The rules of time and space seemed to dissipate around her as she felt enclosed in a fragile bubble of terror which could burst at any second. She forgot herself, looking at the reflection of her own face on the ground. *Robin red, my sister, do something! My God! It's my face looking back at me!* The girl on the cold cement floor was dolled up and her bloodied temple was surrounded by blond curls as opposed to straight, red hair, but it was her face that she witnessed hitting the floor with a thud as the bullet pierced Robin's skull.

The two men immediately went into action. The dark-haired man with beady eyes pulled out his cell phone. As the man spoke louder to overcome apparent inference on the other end, Scarlet clearly heard, "Sammy, we need a cleanup crew at the West End warehouse office."

Shuddering uncontrollably, Scarlet couldn't look away from her sister's empty stare. Her stomach lurched as she threw up on the gravel next to her feet. The noise of her retching next to the window caused Carlo, the taller, older man, to turn toward the window. Scarlet swore under her breath. She locked eyes with the man for an instant. She picked herself up off the gravel, and sprinted down the dark alley.

"Darius!" yelled Carlo, "There is someone in the alleyway, come on!" She heard footsteps behind her as she sprinted to her car, fumbling with the car keys as she reached the driver's side door. *Open the damn door, Scarlet! Stop shaking and put the key in, make your fingers work!*

Opening the door, she heard the men approaching her. The car roared to a start and she peeled away from the dark lot down to the adjacent side street. She heard light popping noises behind her car. *Gunshots? They are shooting at me? They want me dead...dead like Robin!* She expected to hear a loud pop from one of her tires indicating a direct hit, but she heard nothing. She dared to glance out of her rearview mirror to see if they were in pursuit and saw the two men standing shoulder to shoulder in the middle of the street, watching her drive away. One man held a gleaming silver object at his side, smoke wafting from the end of a long barrel.

A glimmer of light reflected in her mirror which made her look. *Shit, shit, shit!* her voice screamed in panicked yelps bouncing between her ears like ping pong balls. She saw one of them men with an object pointed at her. She knew what he held in his hands, *a cell phone*, and the flash she witnessed was him taking a photo of her car. With the right resources, he could develop and enlarge the photo of her license plate. If he had her license plate...*he could find her*.

Chapter 3

"Heart attacks...they'll kill yah."

Darius and Carlo returned to the warehouse office after the car disappeared. Both men stood over her lifeless body, looking down at her in silence. The dark red wound near Robin's temple was spilling crimson toward her pouty rouged lips. Her lifeless eyes stared blankly up at the two men. Carlo stood with one of his hands shoved into his pants' pockets while Darius stood scratching the back of his neck. They didn't think of her as Robin. They thought of her as the blond who had a funny thing for Marilyn Monroe who they met occasionally for information.

"Fuck, Carlo, you should have got in the car and tracked her down! Who was that chick anyway?" He continued scratching his head, his other hand on his large stomach.

"Me? You're *blaming me* for this nonsense? You shoot like shit so she got away, *idiot*. Plus, I'm the brains here, Darius. I used my ability to think on my feet and realized we both have smart phones, right? So let's be *smart*, and use them. I got a perfect shot of her car and all we have to do is enlarge the picture of her license plate and then *boom*, we got her. Probably some hot thing just out at the wrong place, wrong time. We find her, kill her, and we're good." He shook his head and pointed a lean finger at his friend's stomach.

"You're going to give yourself a heart attack. You have to learn to calm the fuck down. How do you expect to rise up in the family ranks if you can't stay cool? I'm supposed to train you to be a better soldier so you can become a captain in this family. You need to be able to think quickly so you can direct your guys. If you had your wits about you, and if you were in shape, you could have chased her down on foot and we wouldn't be in this mess. You can't even speak to me without *wheezing*. Think about your health, man. You're just over forty and you can't even breathe properly, it's ridiculous. You should be able to outrun me. Hell, I've got a good ten years on you but you're the one who can't keep up. Think long and hard about that, my friend. Heart attacks...they'll kill yah."

Carlo shook his head at his dimwitted partner. A burden bestowed upon him by other higher-ups within the family. Darius was the adopted son of one of the capo's sisters within the complex family organization. Carlo knew it was a favor to take him on and try to train him and he didn't mind having a favor owed to him by some of the more prestigious family members.

"Yeah, yeah, enough with that already. You are always on my case. Guessing I should call Sammy off? He was supposed to come over and do the regular clean up, but with a witness I think we have to take precautions. We can't do the normal grab and go, bleach the blood, and run. We need to speed up the disposal this time, and there can't be a trace," Darius said, only slightly wheezing between sentences.

"True. Sammy's got a guy we can use. Someone we call in for just these types of situations. Call Sammy and tell him you need the number for the Professor and then have Sammy come and do his typically white-out job. We need this placed cleaned top to bottom right away in case the girl is dumb enough to call the cops," Carlo said, hand still shoved in his pocket.

Darius rubbed the back of his neck agitatedly as his face started turning red. "The Professor? Why do they call him the Professor, Carlo? I don't want to sound like a freak asking for some crazy nickname and then Sammy doesn't know what I'm talking about, you know?"

"You're working yourself up again, Darius. You haven't heard about the Professor, because you don't know about him until you have to know about him and we haven't had to use him. I'm here to train you, right? Well, I'm training you now on who to use in this type of situation. I've been around the block a few more times than you, okay, now trust me and make the call so we can get this show on the road. I have a glass of scotch by my bedside calling my name and I want to get to it, so let's go already. I'm going to pack up my suitcase and load up what the girl brought us and by then, Sammy will be here. The boss isn't going to like what we found out about her as it is, I don't want him to get more pissed because we didn't take care of this mess."

"Okay, Carlo, fine, I'm calling him right now."

"Oh, and Darius?"

"Yeah?"

"One thing to know about the Professor. He doesn't like people who mess up. Seeing as how you were the one closest to the door but you can't run for shit, you let her get away. With that said, I don't think he is going to like you much. Let me do the talking, buddy, and whatever you do, don't piss him off." Carlo walked into the back room with the documents from Robin and began shoving everything he needed from the back office into his suitcase.

Left alone with Robin's dead body on the cold tile floor at his feet, the sting of Carlo's words made Darius' flushed face turned one shade redder.

Chapter 4

"Do you like the danger or do you like the power?"

FBI Agent Kelly Carter strode through the double doors of the Washington, D.C. field office. A grim line etched on her face, she barely nodded as she passed by her co-workers mumbling their morning pleasantries.

"Morning, Carter," said one.

"How was the weekend, Carter? Looks like you're on a mission this morning," said another.

She flashed a closed-mouth smile in response and kept walking. None of her colleagues referred to her by her first name, Kelly. It was always "Carter," an unmentioned nod to her bulldog personality and ferociousness. She ruled with an iron fist and demanded every ounce of the respect she received. There wasn't a soul who braved calling her Kelly unless explicitly given the right to do so by Carter herself. She liked the tough reputation. It made her job a hell of a lot easier if word of her temper arrived on scene before she did.

She lifted her handful of folders as a wave to those who chanced acknowledging her that morning. Settling into her desk, topped with folders and papers organized in her own style of logical chaos, she quickly started thinking about her day. She liked to start each morning with a habit formed early in her career by looking on the wall to the right of her desk at the framed photo of her mentors FBI Director William Webster and the then Federal Prosecutor, Rudolph Giuliani, at a press conference in the early eighties. They stood in front of a chart detailing the five crime families that made up La Cosa Nostra at the time, otherwise known as the American Mafia. Rudy Giuliani played an instrumental role in the indictment of eleven mafia leaders, and then went on to have a successful run as the mayor of New York City. She grew up with those names at the family dinner table every night since her father worked in the FBI. He respected them, so she, in turn, grew to idolize the men. Now in her early forties, she still insisted on having the picture hang in her office as a reminder of the long line of FBI members within her family.

Carter looked at Giuliani's determined face every morning she made it into the office. His direct stare motivated her. She admired his gumption to target a large crime syndicate. He successfully dismantled the leadership pool forever changing the nature of the mafia's existence. She envied his success, and used it as a reminder to push herself each and every day. She wanted to create her own story of excellence so another aspiring FBI agent or federal prosecutor would hang her picture in their office.

She felt good this morning. New photos had surfaced regarding the West Coast Italian mafia family led by its patriarch, Gabriel Nero. Her organized Crime Task Force focused on two major syndicates that still existed, the Neros on the West Coast and the Durantes on the East. It was always a good day when her team uncovered more information on the families' shady business ventures. She was convinced the Nero family business was the cover for international drug smuggling operations involving heroin, cocaine, and various other racketeering operations. Her team's undercover surveillance had finally garnered fresh results and a new face appeared in the mix of the Nero clan - a minx with bouncy, blond curls and magazine cover good looks who seemed connected with all the right players. Each new face and each new piece of data were pieces of a complex and convoluted jigsaw puzzle. The complexity and scope of the operation would make certain agents turn and run, but Kelly Carter always had a knack for games.

Carter opened the folder from the top of the stack and carefully pulled out the glossy and magnified photos from the surveillance her team ran the past month. Sipping her strong, black coffee as she sifted through the shiny stack of candid shots, she noticed some of the photos had the blond, always with the same shade of dark red lipstick, and in one photo, she was standing between two luxury cars. *Bingo!* Carter licked her lips.

The license plates were visible in one photo. The corner of her mouth curled up in satisfaction. *Finally, something I can work with on this damn case.* She hoped this plate would lead to something like following bread crumbs to the wicked candy house in the woods. Carter tapped her pen on her desk. Her thoughts were ravenous. She tasted blood, and, like any true bloodhound, she was energized by the hot lead.

She typed the license plate number into her computer and leaned back in her swivel chair. She could pace, but it would mean pulling her eyes away from the computer screen, and she wasn't about to do that. She thumbed the photos again taking another thoughtful sip of her coffee while staring into the eyes of the robin-red-lipped blond. Did she like the danger, or did she like the power? She wondered if the girl was in debt to the Nero family.

Staring into the eyes in the photo, it dawned on Carter this girl was out there somewhere, unaware she was being hunted down by the law. Carter was so close to finding this piece of the puzzle she could taste it, and it tasted slightly acidic, like her cup of strong coffee. She finally had a solid lead with the license plate number. This wasn't the typical lackluster results from our surveillance jobs. This break has legs. *This girl, whoever she is, could hold the key to uncover the truth about the Nero family. I can feel it in my bones. This red-lipped blond is our key.*

The computer continued to trace through the numbers. Each number was tied to a name and an address. Carter sensed that amidst the pile of faceless license plate numbers, she would find a match. Then, if the Gods allowed, she would find her mystery girl on the other side of the screen staring back at her.

Chapter 5

"Someone is always trying to kill somebody else."

Fenton sat down gingerly on his couch, tossing his keys, his wallet, his fake ID, and an assortment of plastic with fake names on the glass coffee table. and let out a sigh. *Finally, that damn job is done.* He hadn't been home in weeks due to his last assignment and his ribs were still sore from his last scuffle. A few minutes later, he stood up slowly and walked to his wall safe, expertly turning the dials, tick...tick... tick. It cranked open, revealing another metal lockbox atop a mound of large denomination bills banded together. He thumbed the dials to put in his code and placed the metal box on his coffee table, slowly sinking into the couch as he pushed his arm against his sore side to ease the pain.

With the metal box lid open, the first document in the pile of papers and photos was his birth certificate. Lars Robert Fenton, printed in bold flowing letters, with his baby footprints stamped on the worn paper. He liked pulling out the box every once in a while, typically right after completing a job, because it grounded him back in reality. His real name etched on the paper reminded him of who he was, and seeing it on the worn paper helped him remember who that guy was supposed to be. He was called Fenton by those he trusted, but they all assumed it was a nickname. He ran his finger over the words, Lars Robert Fenton, a stoic expression covering his face. He knew whenever he looked to his past, he had to approach it with strength, because he had no time to crumble...not even for an instant.

Behind his certificate was the yellowed photo of a smiling, strapping man in the prime of his years in a police dress uniform. The man's arm lightly dangled over a young boy's shoulder. There were only a couple photos in the box amidst the stack of fake IDs and medals from his time as a Marine, including the Medal of Honor, and the Purple Heart. He flipped the photo over and written in his mother's handwriting was the inscription, "Bobby Fenton and Lars Bobby Fenton, Jr." with the year, which put him at around ten years old. He grimaced as he lingered over their smiles, his boyish face wearing the same smile as his dad. He grew up as a spitting image of his dad.

The same man who died senselessly years ago in late March on the night Fenton's team won the championship college basketball game. While Fenton played point guard for his team, his dad lay dying in the street after getting shot by a dirty cop. Fenton was carried off the court on the shoulders of the squad, his most victorious night. He didn't hear about his father until much later after the cheers had died down.

He ran his thumb over the picture, then pulled a bottle of bourbon from under the couch and took a long swig, slamming it down on the coffee table without thought of the glass. The memory of that day caused Fenton to flip the photo back in the box with the certificate and slam the lid shut. He leaned back into the couch. He eyed the bottle warily. The anniversary of his father's death was rapidly approaching and it left him feeling off kilter each year.

He sat on the couch, muscles clenched and aching. His knuckles were bruised and slightly bloodied. Marks from his last job, protecting someone who wasn't particularly good or decent, but the money was phenomenal. *One more job, just one more job, and I quit. This time, I mean it.* He told himself on nights like tonight, nights when the memory of his father's death weighed on him, heavy on his chest and unyielding. He knew what would make him feel lighter, center him again: he would work one more gig, but for someone *deserving.* Someone who was simply pulled into something they had no control over, someone like Adrianna. The sweet-hearted widow who witnessed his dad's death and got shoveled off into witness protection because she came forward willing to testify. Someone like Adrianna who didn't ask for the world of trouble she walked into, but was brave enough to stand up so others wouldn't have to suffer. Someone like Adrianna who *should* be protected. *Maybe that will stop these damn night sweats,* he thought to himself, taking another pull from the bottle, and shuddering a little as it went down.

He was feeling a little better with the thought. It sounded like a good plan in his head. Protecting *"An Innocent,"* which is what he liked to call the decent and upright citizens who waltzed into bad luck by no fault of their own. He tried convincing himself if he took another job protecting someone who deserved a new chance at life, then the increasing pressure in his chest causing him shortness of breath sometimes would stop. Protecting the pure ones who dared to stand up against the evil of the world, but still had to go through hell and back to do the right thing. It happened every time. He would do a job, add loads of cash to his safe, and then he would get a familiar pesky, panicky feeling again. It was too easy to lose his way when he wasn't saving an *innocent* every few jobs. It was a tiring journey of paying respect to his father's memory by paying penance for what was the best night of his life while his dad died. It was his constant cross to bear. It was easier in the Marines. There was always someone who deserved protecting, but in the real world, the line of decency became a little more blurred.

Yes, I need a break, get my head straight. Then, one last job, an innocent, and everything will be fine he told himself as he rubbed his aching ribs and took another guzzle of bourbon. He certainly needed a break before his last case, just one more. Then with the cash he had stowed away, he could retire at the lake house and live a nice, comfy lifestyle. *Get away from flying bullets and bad guys always trying to kill somebody, oh yes, someone is always trying to kill somebody else. I need to get out of this racket, become a carpenter out by the lake house and get a job that doesn't require firing a weapon. Doesn't that sound nice?*

He sometimes wondered if he forgot what it was like to have a normal life with normal concerns. With his extensive black ops marine background, he made the perfect security consultant. The scenario was always different, but the essence of his role was the same: make sure the bad guys don't kill the particular *somebody* he's hired to protect. Staring down the barrel of a gun was simply an occupational hazard. He didn't mind when the client was innocent. Giving them a chance at the normal life made all the hazards worth it. He knew, deep down, he started to feel whole again when he successfully protected someone like Adrianna.

He knew the risks. He had the training and he could plan for every alternative but occasionally, there were surprises when dealing with the ranks of the wicked. Hiring someone like Fenton meant danger was imminent. He wasn't hired to work the easy cases. In those situations, to make sure the bad guys had one hell of a hard time killing that *somebody* on their list, Fenton had to be the one standing in their way.

Chapter 6

"Everything feels different in the daylight."

Scarlet didn't know where to go or what to do, so she just drove. Silent shocked tears left cold wet lines down her face as she nervously looked out of her rear view mirror every few seconds. *Can they find me? Are they coming after me? Oh, Robin, they shot Robin, my only sister, my twin sister, her face looking up at me in the window.* She used self-talk to make sure her trembling hands wouldn't fall from the wheel. She wanted to close her eyes and fall into the blackness, letting the car take her to wherever it needed her to go. She was still in shock. She felt an overwhelming feeling of numbness, like ice running through her veins, freezing every part of her that would function normally. She yearned for Aunt Jo, but didn't want to contact her until she had her until she had a sense of what happened, of what it all meant. She wondered what she could have done to stop the killing. The same images and questions replayed in her mind in a nauseating loop. Without the constant self-talk reminding herself to simply keep moving the car forward, she probably would have careened off the road, ending her night much like her sister's night ended - lifeless and wide-eyed.

It was difficult to tell if anyone was following her due to the dead of night darkness which absorbed everything. Whenever lights popped up behind her, she feared the worst. She tried taking side streets to lose any heavy traffic and her heart only slowed its thumping sprint on vacant streets when she could be sure no cars were behind her. Once she was convinced no one was following her after taking many diversionary routes, she went back to her second floor apartment. Safely parked, she ran into her place. With her heart racing, she slammed the door behind her, locking and bolting the door. She spun around in relief leaning against the closed door to face her empty apartment, looking at the same blanket she cozied up under a few hours earlier. She slid against the door to the floor, unable to look at the blanket. She put her head in her hands and rocked herself back and forth. The curtains started to glow with dawn's light. *Everything feels different in the daylight.* The light banished the darkness in her room, making it feel like everything was just a bad dream, but Scarlet knew she was awake.

When she could no longer handle simply sitting, she stood up and began pacing. She made the mistake of walking to Robin's room and saw the photos of Marilyn Monroe on the wall and her makeup case open from recent use. Her bed wasn't made and a couple outfits were on the floor. Her closet doors were open revealing the wide variety of exotic dresses and attire from her time in Las Vegas.

Scarlet slowly walked toward the open closet doors and reached out to touch the fabric of a particularly beautiful red sparkly dress. Its long fabric was elegant and refined, like it was meant for an important swanky event. The red dress shimmered slightly in her hand and Scarlet shuddered. It was as vibrant as Robin was, beautiful and bold. It was a dress to make a statement the minute she entered the room. Robin had the same effect. Waves of nausea and realization hit Scarlet. Her sister was dead and would never return to this room again.

Crushing panic and loneliness hit Scarlet like a tidal wave. *She left me, she left me, she left me!* The sobs came hard. The type of sobs making breathing impossible and her whole body convulsed with each wailing mournful sob. She thought she might pass out with the crippling inability to breathe. She stumbled out of Robin's room into the main living area, and fell into the couch, screaming into the pillows. *She left me, she left me, she left me!* Scarlet felt trapped by her own personal bubble of hell, as if the earth had opened up and swallowed her whole. She knew nothing else in those moments besides intense pain, anguish, and grief. She sat like that for a while, emptying herself of the horrible and overwhelming feeling of despair. She wanted to purge it from her body as she feared it would consume her.

When the exhaustion began to clear the fog brought her mourning her sister, she realized she had to act. Whoever killed Robin knew someone was there watching it happen and they have a picture of her license plate, which means they could be after her or searching for her. She willed herself to get off the bed and call 911. She tried steadying her breathing, knowing it would be difficult to speak between her crying fits.

"911 operator, please state your emergency," a sterile and unemotional voice said, sounding far away on the other end of the phone.

"Yes...I...I witnessed...my sister's...murder," Scarlet managed to say. She started recalling the series of events from that night.

"Where did this happen, what was the address of the incident, Miss?"

"Lincoln Street, in the alleyway. It was in the office building with bars on the window, I think it is part of a larger warehouse." She described the car she saw parked there and the two men with her sister.

"Did you happen to catch any names?" Scarlet wracked her brain, she knew she heard something. *What was it, what were the names? Think, Scarlet. A tall man and a short man. They were yelling, my sister said their names, what were they?* It was like itching a scab to think back to the scene only hours earlier, painfully vivid in her mind like an open wound. She closed her eyes briefly thinking of the alleyway and the two men. The rank smell of garbage, the shiny, buffed sports car, and the wafting of her sister's voice as she followed them into the building.

"Um, it was... Darius and Carlo, I think? Once they were inside I couldn't hear, but I heard those names when they entered the building."

"What was your sister's name again?" The operator asked, with a calm tone. They were trained for these types of manic calls, trained to remain professional in the midst of chaos.

"Robin. Robin Lilly Matthews. I'm her twin, Scarlet Matthews." Scarlet continued answering questions, where she lived, anything else she witnessed about the scene, and what went on beforehand. Scarlet explained she didn't know a lot about Robin's social circles prior to the move. The operator told her she would remain on the line with her while police officers were sent to her house and the scene of the crime. That was when Scarlet remembered another important detail.

"I forgot to say, the two men, the men that killed my sister... they know I was in the alley last night."

"What makes you say that?"

"When I ran to my car they ran after me and I could see a flash in my rear view mirror. The taller man, he was able to take a photo of the back of my car on his phone."

"Okay, I'm putting all of this information into the system. Stay put for right now, sweetie. The cops are on their way."

Chapter 7

"Feed the monster inside."

Carter bolted upright in her chair as the familiar ping indicated her computer finished running the license plates. She leaned forward to move the mouse and open up the results. What appeared on her screen would either lead to a tremendous break for her team, energizing her like five shots of espresso, or it would lead to heavy frustration to cloud her mood for weeks.

Many could not handle the rollercoaster of emotions that came with the job, but Carter used these extremes in stimulation to propel herself forward. She used these feelings to feed the monster inside called *power* and Carter had a voracious appetite for power in all forms.

She clicked open the folder revealing results for the plates. One of the luxury cars had Nevada plates and belonged to a Robin Lilly Matthews. Her driver's license popped open on the screen. It was the same blond girl from the photos taken from the Nero crime family stake out. She blinked rapidly. She wondered how one girl could be involved with two crime families on opposite sides of the country. Especially two families who hated each other and competed for business.

The other plate belonged to a Darius Durante, a lower member in the Durante crime family, who her team identified as a foot soldier in the Durante family business. Typically, the soldiers were the ones who had to get their hands dirty cleaning up messes for the business, making money through racketing schemes, or operating as the muscles to make sure debts were paid. The increase of his activity lately indicated he might be trying to make a move for a higher rank within the family, perhaps the highly-coveted captain position.

Carter grabbed the other photos of the blond from various surveillance stakeouts completed by her broader FBI task force and looked at the face of the woman whom she now could identify as Robin Matthews. Robin looked confident and collected standing next to soldiers from the Nero family.

The Nero family ran what Carter believed to be a prosperous drug smuggling and gambling operation out West near the Las Vegas area, while the Durante family operated on the East Coast near D.C. dealing with similar schemes. Despite being in the same line of work, the Italian mafia crime families were not allies. They operated as rivals always fighting over turf and influence just like any other business with competition. Carter had spent the majority of her career climbing the political ladder to run task forces, surveillance, and wire taps against what she considered the modern day La Cosa Nostra. She had minor mob busts in her background which propelled her into her current role, but she needed a major bust to strategically advance her career.

"Westbrook, come in here," Carter yelled through her office door. James Westbrook was one of the lead detectives on her staff. He didn't have a particularly imposing physique. He was all angles with a gaunt face, but he scored high marks all throughout his training and rose quickly within the FBI. He wasn't a talker, but got the job done. Good help was always hard to come by and not everyone warmed to Carter's icy exterior. James Westbrook successfully worked with Carter over the last couple of years leading to several arrests on high profile cases. He brought in enough good press for her to rely on him when she needed to. His partner, Nell Starr had a personality that reminded Carter of herself, but ten years younger. Starr had a bulldog mentality and was built short and strong. She could out bench most of the males on the taskforce and played rugby for most of her younger years. Her solid build contrasted Westbrook's lanky figure with Carter falling evenly in the middle. Considered attractive by most who met her, although they would never admit it, Carter balanced her two main team members at her slender five-ten form. Even though Starr worked with Carter longer, she still considered Westbrook the senior agent, because deep down she wondered if Starr was too soft to rise to the top of the ranks. It was the only area where the two women couldn't be more different. Starr and Westbrook made a strong team and were exactly who she wanted to use to help run point with these new developments.

Westbrook knocked briefly and paused at her door.

"I need you to track down everything you can on a Robin Matthews. Robin was previously living in Vegas, and was last seen by our surveillance team near us in the Washington, D.C. area. Find everything you can. I want to know what she's been up to the last few years. Who she talked to, what she ate, when she sneezed funny, whatever you can find. Grab Starr and dig into Darius Durante. I want to know how he knows Robin and everything we have on him from our East Coast taskforce. I want a full update on everything we have from our group in Washington on the Durante family, and a full briefing on the Nero family from the Vegas angle. Something is going on within these two crime families. I think Robin Matthews was smack dab in the middle of the whole thing. Get me the proof I need to move forward."

"Got it, boss." Westbrook strode out of the doorway back to the wide array of desks piled high with papers and folders. Despite the thriving computer age, old cases and surveillance from cross teams and old cases existed on paper, so the mounds of folders and physical documents were still in abundance in their line of work.

Carter spun her chair back to her computer screen. She was still on an active search for Robin Matthews when she noticed a 911 dispatch call pop up at the top of the results. The call was recorded in the system just hours ago with an alleged victim having the same name as the curly-haired blond Carter's team was tracking on the West Coast and recently appeared in Washington.

The call was recorded by the Alexandria, Virginia, dispatch team. The police were sent to investigate, and they took the witness downtown to get her statement for questioning. There was not a lot of detail on the witness in the system yet - no name or address - but that wasn't uncommon. They were still vetting the witness and securing her safety. Carter probably wouldn't see updated notes for a couple of hours. She could see the witness's original statement though, and Carter noticed in the notes that the witness said she heard two names- *Carlo and Darius.*

Carter licked her lips at her good fortune. She didn't believe in coincidence, and those two names lined up with two known soldiers in the Durante family. A man by that name had his car photographed next to the murdered girl. She typed the address listed by the witness, the possible scene of the crime. She crossed referenced it with all of the Durante and Nero known business locations. She licked her lips. The scene of the crime was next to a warehouse registered to the Durante family.

She needed to know more, but the challenge was the 911 call was being handled by the Alexandria police department. She knew the police chief of that precinct very well, and he owed her a favor. Carter picked up the phone about to call him, but then slammed down the receiver. *This is too big for a phone call.* Carter realized this was the first time in an extremely long time there was a *live witness* involved in a killing at the hands of the Durante crime family. She would go in person to speak to the police chief. It wasn't much of a drive and ensured she would come back with the prize. She coveted this case and she always went after what she wanted. She shoveled her folders and papers into her work bag and grabbed her long, gray trench coat off the back of her door. She strode purposefully from her office to the main room where the air was buzzing with agents on phones and the rustling of paperwork. She didn't pause, but yelled over her shoulder to her two top agents as she stalked toward the door.

"Westbrook, Starr, look alive. I'm going to Alexandria, Virginia. I have a case I'm going to snag for us and I won't come back without it. Keep digging on Matthews, the Nero family, and the Durante family. I want a full debrief when I get back. *I mean everything.* Keep your cells close. This day just got a whole lot more interesting."

Chapter 8

"Ash doesn't talk and last I checked, it leaves no fingerprints and no evidence."

The Professor looked at the two men, and shook his head. Despite his dark, inset eyes, which gave him a ghoulish appearance, he looked like the type of man who would wear a brown zip-up sweater and rake leaves in his backyard while he grandkids played. But, in his eyes there was pure blackness. A wolf in sheep's clothing. His reputation for disposing of bodies, quickly and cleanly with total discretion, earned him the utmost respect from boss Ugo Durante. Everyone who knew the Professor knew about his ties with the highest- ranking family member, which meant he was untouchable.

"Which one of you nobodies fucked up?" His voice was gravelly and monotone, his face emotionless.

"We did the job and then we heard a noise in the alley. By the time we stepped out to investigate and chase her down, the girl was already in her car. I got a photo of her license plate. We'll find her. Want to take the necessary precautions though, in case she tries to talk," Carlo said, clearing his throat, as Darius shifted his weight in his designer dress shoes.

"The big guy doesn't talk or is it the guilty don't have anything to say?" asked the Professor. "Carlo takes a photo, and what were you doing? Sitting in here with your thumb up your ass, ordering a pizza? You've got blood on your shoes, Doofus. Don't fuck up again. Put the body in this bag and let's put it in my trunk. Then, the three of us are taking a ride. Sammy's on his way for clean-up and I'm not getting any younger standing here, boys, so let's get a move on." The Professor walked out as quietly as he came in, leaving a body bag folded neatly on the metal table.

Darius and Carlo looked at each other, and then worked together to get Robin securely zipped up in the large, black, durable bag. It was industrial-grade material, made of thick, waterproof plastic, and sturdy enough to withstand the load of a dead body.

The Professor was waiting in the driver's seat as the two men shoved Robin in the trunk and grabbed their seats in the car. They sat in complete silence with Carlo and Darius watching the passing trees and highways, wondering where the peculiar, older man was taking them. Carlo swallowed hard and stifled a nervous cough. *What are the chances the Professor is going to take us someplace secluded and shoot us for our mistakes?* Carlo rarely found himself on the wrong side of the family's favor, but this time they had definitely screwed up. The family was forgiving, to an extent, unless they thought the act was unforgivable. He shook his head at his morbid thoughts. *Carlo, you're getting paranoid again. You're thinking crazy thoughts because the Professor just looks like that type of guy. His eyes would make anyone's skin crawl and with his specialty of quickly disposing of bodies, it is natural to think the worst - especially because he handles the type of disposal where a trace of the body will never be found...ever.*

They drove toward a small community college town nestled

in the heart of Virginia and pulled into a lot next to a biomedical engineering building. The Professor pulled out a laminated pass he flashed at the keypad for the underground ramp. He parked the car in front of large, double-wide doors. Darius looked concerned and was about to speak when the Professor held up his hand. Darius immediately shut his mouth.

"I deliver cadavers to the college. They are dissected by students and studied by professors to further their research. No one notices one more body, or parts of a body, especially in the incinerator. Ash doesn't talk and last I checked it leaves no fingerprints and no evidence. Follow me and bring the body." Carlo and Darius grabbed the body bag and followed the Professor into the basement entrance of the school's laboratory. The room was large and filled with metal cabinets and tables and looked like a sterile operating room. The Professor opened a large, metal, oven door and the men shoved the bag, body and all, into the incinerator. The Professor hit a few buttons on the computer panel next to the oven and a roaring fire lit up behind the metal casing.

"Well aren't I a monkey's uncle. Are you a Professor here?" Darius asked in surprise, reading the Professor's credentials on his badge with STAFF printed in large letters.

"Did I ask you to speak?" he said roughly to Darius. He spun toward Carlo and said acidly, "Did I ask this human doughnut to speak?" Carlo shook his head in exasperation. The Professor took two hunched over, yet menacing, steps toward Darius.

"You don't *speak* to me. You don't *know* me. You don't *look* at me. We've never met and you don't know me from the next guy on the street. You got that? You get that into your thick skull and don't make me remind you. I'll drop you both by your car at the warehouse and then you get the hell out of there. You weren't at the warehouse tonight, got it? You were playing cards at the nightclub Sneaky Benito's in D.C. all night, the boys there will vouch for you," he snarled, as grating as cement rubbing on metal. Benito Durante owned the club, and operated as the Captain to a large group of soldiers which included Carlo and Darius. Carlo swore under his breath. He knew Benito would find out about their situation if his guys were providing the alibi. He knew he should call him before he heard the news from someone else.

The ride back to their car was silent. They didn't go back into the warehouse, but a quick glimpse through the window indicated Sammy had already come and gone. The place sparkled as if it were brand new, certainly freshly polished and shined. There wouldn't be a trace of any of them in that office.

"So, that's the Professor. I finally meet the guy and he calls me a human doughnut," Darius said in a snarky tone.

"Yeah. That's the Professor. Go home, Darius. I have to call Benito," Carlo said, already dreading making the call. He thought about the bottle of scotch at home. He knew what waited for him at the bottom of that bottle and it was what he needed...the ability to forget everything about the day and what it meant for his future.

Chapter 9

"Easy to handle as a wild porcupine."

The ringing of Fenton's cell phone roused him from his tumultuous sleep. He eyed a half-empty bottle of bourbon on his coffee table. He sat up slowly, head pounding from a night of indulgence. He was off the clock, finally on a break from a couple of consecutive and taxing jobs. He told himself everyone deserves a little excess every once in a while, breaking free from his strict regimented diet he followed religiously while on the clock. He needed to be in peak physical performance to give him the best chance of protecting his clients. Mental and physical wellbeing was crucial and right now, he needed fine-tuning in both of those areas. He felt like hell and probably looked worse. He rubbed the stubble that had set in after days of not shaving and squinted his eyes briefly, trying to clear the fog as he answered his ringing cell.

"Hello," he said, his voice rough with fatigue. There was a pause on the other end of the line.

"Fenton, it's Carter. I think I have something that might interest you. Can we talk or are you on assignment?" Fenton rubbed his eyes.

Kelly Carter. He worked several jobs for her in the past and she was about as easy to handle as a wild porcupine. He rubbed his groggy eyes and wondered if he wanted to go down this rabbit hole again. Each job with her became increasingly complex and dangerous. As her ambitions grew, so did the scope of the assignments, but on the flip side, the money was always good. She typically didn't call him directly though. She would put out feelers through an encrypted portal online. Calling him meant she must have a hot lead. If nothing else, she succeeded in piquing his curiosity.

"I'm not on assignment currently. I just finished a job. I was planning on taking some time off though, Carter. I just got off several back-to-back jobs and could use the break. No guarantees I'll take the work, but I'll listen to what you've got."

"That's funny, Fenton, I didn't take you as the *resting* type. I'm on my way right now to take away a case from the local police department. I've latched onto something big, Fenton. I have a witness to a murder involving two soldiers from the Durante family. A *witness*. You know how long we have waited for someone to help us nab these guys? I'm talking potentially disrupting the balance between two notorious crime families. A girl was in the alley where a murder took place, she called it in, and she was close enough to even hear names. I don't have the case yet, but trust me, it's as good as mine. Are you in the Virginia or D.C. area?" He could hear in her voice that her mouth was curved in a satisfied smile. She knew something. She seemed too confident he was going to say yes to this job. He didn't know what was behind her certainty and it made him uncomfortable.

"I'm not far. You're going after them for a murder? What about the drug connections, smuggling, and illegal gambling?"

"You know me too well, Fenton. The girl who was murdered was linked to both families on the drug smuggling side. I can smell blood in the water on this one, Fenton. I need you."

"I don't know, Carter. I'm not in this for your political pursuits. Having a couple weeks off is looking pretty good right about now instead of chasing down a drug-smuggling ring with your band of thieves."

"Thieves? Oh, Fenton, what you must think of me and my team. How about this: I'll send what my team has gathered through our encrypted drop site. You can review the materials before you make a decision. I'll know more about our witness when we get there, but my gut is telling me she is completely innocent of this whole thing. Probably just some random schmuck at the wrong place at the wrong time. In a matter of minutes, this girl has become *someone*. She's in it now and I want her in my corner."

"Ever wonder what she was doing in that alleyway? Innocent people rarely end up on the wrong side of town with the bottom feeders of society, unless they are dirty."

"All I ask is you hold off on judgments until you have the full picture - at least promise me that much. Don't turn me down until you know the full story. My instincts are telling me she is clear on this one and Fenton...they got a picture of her car, so *they* are going to be able to find her."

There was a pregnant pause on the other end of the line. Fenton took a swig of the remaining drops of bourbon left in the lowball glass next to the half-empty bottle. The whole bottle was looking pretty good to him right now, but he hoped one swig would stop the pounding. A distracting throbbing between his ears intensified the sound of Carter's last words...*they got a picture of her car, so they are going to be able to find her.*

"Fine, send me what you've got, but no promises. I'll look it over, but that is all I'm guaranteeing."

"That is all I wanted to hear. You will be hearing from me. Until then, I'll have my people send you our files. Oh, and Fenton?"

"Yeah?"

"I know it's close to the anniversary of your father's death. He was a good man, but you can't let it eat you alive every year. I think this case will be just what you need to keep your mind off things. Believe me, I'm going to eventually get you on this case, but I need you clear-headed. That means, lay off the whiskey, will yah? You sound like shit." She hung up the phone.

Fenton slouched into the couch cushions, already thinking about the case. Carter was desperate if she called him directly and mentioned his father. *She wants you on this case badly, that's obvious, and if you've learned anything about Kelly Carter...that typically means trouble.*

Chapter 10

"I am here to make sure I'm the last person you talk to...ever."

Waiting for the cops was exasperating for Scarlet, but it was even worse when they arrived. She had to go through her story numerous times and they took photos of Robin's room, the bathroom, and their common areas. Robin's brush was still sitting on the sink, a few strands of blond hair clung to the bristles. Scarlet had to look away, fearing she would vomit at the feet of the policeman.

She felt powerless as the uniformed cops treated her place like a crime scene. Her mind was in such a fog from getting no sleep the night before she couldn't remember any of the police officers' names. She found herself studying her hands during their questions to avoid seeing their perplexed and disappointed faces when she had to explain why she had no idea who would do this to her sister. *How do I make them understand I don't even know my sister?*

"What do you mean, you don't know her very well? You're twins and you live together, right?" one skeptical female cop asked her, eyebrow arched in a judging way, as she scrutinized Scarlet. It was as if they thought she was lying or trying to protect her sister by hiding the truth. *The truth? Robin always had secrets.*

"Look, two months ago, after years of little to no contact, she called me asking to move in with me. I guess I thought we could become like real sisters. Yes, we have always had the bond many twins experience. I feel like I can judge her mood and can tell when she is lying, but that doesn't mean she confided in me. Robin always kept everyone at arm's length and I was no exception. I'm sorry I couldn't be of more help."

"Friends, acquaintances, business associates, enemies? You can't tell us anything about who she hung out with or who she surrounded herself with who could have committed this heinous act?"

"I know it sounds crazy, it makes her sound like she was a ghost...but I can't help you. She never mentioned anyone to me and I never met anyone she knew. We would hang out together on the weekends and I was introducing her to my friends. She did get a text that night, I mentioned it earlier, and the text was what made her go to that alley. She had a message from someone asking her to meet."

The cops tossed telling glances at one another as she spoke, exchanging looks as if she was a five-year-old girl and they had to tell her there wasn't a Santa Claus. It was that type of controlled pity she couldn't stand.

Scarlet was exhausted and when the uniformed police officers were finally satisfied she had given the same story consecutive times, they started packing up to leave.

"We are going to have a police officer stationed outside to keep an eye on things, okay? If you need anything, don't hesitate to ask. Here is a number to reach the police station if you notice anything suspicious. We will have a protection detail with you for the next couple of days at least, and once a detective is assigned to your case, they may decide to extend the rotation. Don't answer the door to anyone other than uniformed police officers. If someone does come snooping around, we want to make sure you're safe."

Scarlet retreated to the silence of her apartment. She was about to try to sleep, despite it being mid-day, when she heard a knock at the door. *What now?* she thought to herself.

She peered through the peephole and saw a dark-haired man wearing a police uniform. She opened the door a crack with it still bolted.

"I'm sorry, I'm really tired. Can we talk about the case more tomorrow?" she asked.

"I'm sorry, Miss, but I was told to come in and make sure the area is secure. We had a report a suspicious man was standing outside and I want to see if he has a good view into your place from the street. It shouldn't take long at all and then I'll be out of your hair."

"Okay, hold on." Scarlet unbolted the door. The police officer stepped in and locked the door behind him. He walked around, idly checking the windows.

"Did you say you were able to see the two men in the alley?" he asked nonchalantly.

"What? I thought I answered all of those questions earlier."

"Yeah, I'm sure you did. Come here a second. I want to show you the person we are keeping an eye on so you know who we are talking about." Scarlet walked over to stand next to the police officer. He pointed out the window and took a step back, giving her room to peer through the window pane as she squinted trying to find the figure.

"I don't see anyone..." As she started to turn she was blinded by the searing pain from a blunt object hitting her from behind. Everything went dark around her. When she came to, she was tied in a chair, bound tightly with thick rope. The police officer was sitting in front of her, tapping a long needle, which spurted a clear liquid. She blinked hard trying to clear her throbbing head. The constricting rope created jolts of pain up and down her limbs as her body screamed in protest.

"You're not a police officer, are you? You didn't come in here to secure my apartment or check on a suspicious man standing outside. How did you know about me? Who sent you?" Her throat felt like sandpaper.

He started prepping her arm for the needle, tying a long rubber string above her elbow to help her veins come to the surface. He inserted the point deep in her arm, causing her to wince. He looked at her face and gave a brief smile. When he was satisfied the needle was positioned properly, he rubbed his hands together with excitement.

"No, I'm not a police officer. Quite the opposite. My people are everywhere. *They* are the ones who sent me and they know all about you. I'm here to make sure you don't use your pretty little mouth to talk to pesky police officers anymore. In fact, I am here to make sure *I'm the last person you talk to...ever.*

Chapter 11

"Let the big kids play in the sandbox."

Carter had just parked at the police precinct in Alexandria, Virginia where she was about to storm into the police chief's office when her team called. "Holy shit, Westbrook! You got all of this from our West Coast task force?" she asked while tapping the center console of her car with a long fingernail. Westbrook and Starr were able to dig up a lot of dirt, which was going to make her power play with the police chief as easy as spotting a canary in a snow pile. She licked her lips in anticipation. She was almost disappointed as she had prepped herself for a verbal battle in Chief Elmhurst's office for the case, but Westbrook's update changed her approach.

"Yes, Robin Matthews not only was helping the Durantes run drugs, but she was actively working with the Nero crime family as well," Westbrook explained. "Her tie-in with the casinos in the area put her at every active drug bust that's happened in the past five years. She worked as an events coordinator on the Las Vegas Strip, which is how she met Luca Nero, and by all appearances, the two became intimately involved. That is how we think she was introduced to the Nero crime family. This smells like a double-cross job, boss — almost as if the Nero family planted her on the inside of the Durante family to help bring them down? Maybe they found out about her boy toy on the West Coast and they whacked her?"

"Great work, Westbrook. I want you to send everything you have to our drop site for Fenton to review."

"Boss, something else you should know," Westbrook's typically monotone voice warbled a bit as if he was anxious about the news he was going to report to her.

"I don't like the way that sounded. Out with it, Westbrook, if you're going to ruin my good mood, do it quick."

"No boss, but we may have gotten a little too lucky on this one. Good news for us, but bad news for our witness. The girl in the alley, the one who witnessed the death of Robin Lilly Matthews"

"Yeah?"

"The witness is Scarlet Sage Matthews."

"Matthews? You're telling me the witness is related to the deceased?"

"Not only related, boss, but a dead ringer for our dead girl. I'm talking identical twins. Scarlet has straight, red hair instead of curly blond, but everything else about them is a mirror image. Not only that, but all of our intelligence suggests the Nero family has no idea Robin was knocked out of the picture. The twin seems clean though, boss. Robin didn't move in with her until two months ago when she must have started connecting with the Durantes. Prior to that, it looks as if they had limited contact. I don't think the witness has any idea what her sister has been up to the past five years. Trust me boss, with all the data we were able to pull, that girl was busy working and burning both ends of the candle with both crime families. There is also no indication anyone knows she has a twin out there. The report indicates they found Robin's laptop in the apartment, but we need a password to break in, and her cell phone may have disappeared with the girl."

Carter realized she was holding her breath as Westbrook gave his details. Her wheels were turning, as if her brain was running a triathlon as she sat rigidly in her car. *Oh the possibilities. An identical twin, completely clean, with no knowledge of her sister's activities. A witness who saw the murder of her sister could be used to crack the code to break into her sister's laptop, which means this witness needs more than just police protection.*

"Westbrook, listen closely to me. I need you to send all of this to Fenton. I'm going to text him right now. We need him to go over there and meet with the girl. One whiff of this and he won't be able to turn it down. We need him, Westbrook, because if a fraction of this intelligence is legit, this girl is going to become real popular with the bad guys in town. We need this case, we need this girl, and we sure as hell need Fenton to make sure no one else can get to her. To this point we have failed in bringing the top tiers of La Cosa Nostra to trial, but this could be the big one, Westbrook...I can feel it. Keep me posted as you get more. I'm going to go in and get us a case."

"You got it, boss."

Carter ended the call and typed a secure message to Fenton. Once satisfied with the message, she hit send. A slow smile crept across her face as she knew just how to bait him. All she needed was to get him to visit the girl and have a quick conversation with her. He insisted on meeting the client prior to every job and even though she didn't yet have the case officially, the deal was as good as done in her mind. She needed Fenton to chew on this assignment early, because he always required a little deliberation, and she needed him to agree quickly. *Scarlet's life could depend on it.*

Carter strode swiftly into the precinct. She knew the way to Tom Elmhurst's office, and those in the office who recognized her didn't try to stop her. They knew better than to interfere when she came in because she came in for only one reason, to speak directly to Tom. Everyone else at the precinct steered clear — they didn't want to tangle with the bulldog. Tom had been Alexandria's police chief for the past fifteen years and Carter knew him well. She knocked with a loud, rattling thud as her knuckles hit the thick glass on his door.

Tom Elmhurst peered through his blinds when she knocked, his face darkened and his frown lines deepened. He rose and escorted his guest into his office and didn't look happy about the change of plans in the slightest.

"Tom, it's been way too long. Thanks for clearing your schedule," Carter beamed at him. She thrived off of contorting others to her will like little puppets.

"Carter, I would say it's a pleasure, but then again, I better not until I hear what you've come here to say. You drove all the way to see me, huh? I'm guessing your phone still works and your email isn't broken, so this must be a doozy of a case to come all this way to see my mean mug in person. Come on in and have a seat. Do I need to be sitting for this?" His sour expression matched his tone.

She smiled sweetly at him as she walked into his office decorated with mounds of paperwork and folders strewn about the room, covering any open surface. Once Carter sat down, she started explaining the evidence her task force put together on both crime families across the country.

"Everything you have is circumstantial, Carter. Blood was drawn on my streets and it's my team's job, not some fancy FBI office, to pick up the pieces. You don't have enough to justify my handing this over to you."

"We are not talking a simple murder here, Tom. I'm building evidence against two mob families involving violent, organized crime which we have documented and tracked for years. Our intelligence collection on this is massive. We are in a much better position to execute and tie together the interrelated pieces than your team. We need to work together. My task force could use your resources, and if pooled correctly, this could lead to huge busts for all involved. I am not trying to take your team out of the equation. On the contrary, we can help one another, but I need to run point."

"Is that so? Why exactly do *you* need to run point?"

"The Senate and House reviewed my task force's budget appropriations for this past year and approved specialized and selected programs and investigations to come through my team as needed. I have a dead girl who is tied with deep intelligence to two crime families. I also have a witness I can use to catch high-ranking members of the crime families. That witness is an essential part of the strategy for an undercover sting operation I want to run in the near future. My team runs point on all of our undercover work. I'm reporting to the Attorney General on this one and I need to detail all my findings to the highest authority. If you need more reasons, which you don't, the Director of National Intelligence is personally involved in reviewing findings from my team's task force." He squinted his eyes at her.

A sweet smile spread across her lips. "You're in over your head on this one, Tom. Let the big kids play in this sandbox. Trust me, you don't want this on you." Carter picked up the mug sitting in front of Tom and leaned back in her chair. His eyes became slits as he watched her take a long sip of his coffee. She knew how to handle him. She had to show him she had just as much gumption as any male who could walk into his office and in most cases, probably more.

"May I remind you, Chief Elmhurst, of that messy little business with Internal Affairs I helped you out of about six months ago? The horribly embarrassing little scandal? If the papers got a whiff of that little indiscretion, it would have been the end of your career. Who did you call? Remember? You came to me reeking of guilt. You had the fear that nestles deep within a man and starts to spread. I could see it resting beneath your features then and now it's etched into your skin from nights and years of marinating in the knowledge someone could find out about *you*." She watched as he swallowed hard, his neck muscles working overtime.

She put his mug down on his desk. "A dead hooker who had your number in her phone and the compromising photos — if that would have played out, I shudder to think what would have happened to your career. Your future ambitions, not to mention the embarrassment of having your good name dragged through the mud. You dream about it still, don't you, Tom? Bolting up out of bed drenched in a cold sweat, your heart racing until you realize you're under your nice, comfortable sheets under the safety of your own roof. My team stopped those dreams from becoming a reality... you're lucky it's only your nightmares you need to worry about."

"You're bringing that up, now, of all times?" he said through clenched teeth, his left eye twitching briefly at her last words. She could tell she was close. She was breaking him down. Just a few more hits and he would be right where she wanted him.

"Think about it. Think of your pleasant, comfy life. Then, think of it being ripped away from your shaking hands until your fingernail beds are raw and bleeding from trying to claw it back into your unsteady grip. I don't want to see you like that, Tom. More importantly, you don't want to see you like that. So let's make the deal, eh?" He blinked rapidly, teetering on the edge, ready to fall.

"What exactly do you need?" he asked.

"I said you owed me one and I need you to guarantee me I have the full and total cooperation of your team — no pushback, no questions. They report to me and are at my beck and call on this case. And, they better have smiles on their faces when I call. I could steamroll you, Tom. I could get this case easily without needing your permission. I'm talking with you as a courtesy and to ensure we get this taken care of quickly. I don't want to waste time going through all the typical red tape. It could be years, decades, before we have this chance again. That is what I need. I need your team on board and happy to play second fiddle in our little orchestra of justice. Then I'll consider the debt you owe me *half paid*. Don't misunderstand me. I'll come back for full payment in the near future. You can count on it."

"You want to cash in your favor, fine. Why did you help me back then anyway? To hold it over my head, to rub my face in it now? Why?"

"I'm not a sadist, as much as that may surprise you. I don't make a habit of torturing those who are simply trying to make the world a better place, no matter how messy it gets. I know you're not a bad man. I know you are an excellent cop and you run a good unit. Even the good ones break every once in a while, and you're one of the good ones. I like to have favors coming my way. Remember, this is just paid in half. I will collect on the rest and I expect you will be as eager to repay me then as you are now." It was a thinly veiled threat. It was Carter pissing on his post, letting him know this was her territory. She *owned* him.

He looked stunned, as if Carter had reached out with a velvet-gloved hand and smacked him twice across the face. Her words left him shell-shocked. It was the closest thing to a compliment anyone could expect from a woman like Carter. Perhaps it was a backhanded compliment, but something deep inside him felt slightly comforted because Carter thought he was a decent human.

There were so few decent humans, he thought to himself. It was hard to determine friends from enemies these days. It wouldn't help him to have Carter as an enemy and she had helped him before when he needed it most. What was another favor? One more and they would be squared. Perhaps then, he could drink his coffee in the comfort of his hectic office without the fear of her storming into his building, dipping her pursed lips into his coffee, and creating chaos and uncertainty with his staff. Perhaps then, she would finally be out of his sight and off his turf. Plus, he didn't need the reminder of what she did for him every time she showed her stormy face.

"What do you say, Tom? I can walk out of here right now and give you back your precinct. Just give me what I want and I'll leave," Carter tilted her head at him, patiently waiting for a response. It was like she could read his mind and he shuddered at the thought.

"Yeah, Carter, we've got a deal. The case is yours," he shook his head, not liking how the words tasted coming out of his mouth. Carter's mouth, on the other hand, curled up incrementally into what could only be considered a sinister sneer.

Chapter 12

"He had faith in one thing, his ability to motivate people."

Carlo futzed with his cufflinks nervously. He followed two large foot soldiers, cousins of his who moved up quickly in the ranks of the family business, down a long corridor leading to ornately decorated wooden doors. They pulled open the heavy doors to the private meeting room in the back of the restaurant. The heels of his dress shoes made echoing sounds as he walked on the marble floor toward a man with salt and pepper hair, leaning over a plate of pasta Bolognese with a glass of red wine. He was dabbing the corner of his mouth with a white cloth napkin.

"Carlo, it's been a long time. Please, come in, and have a seat," Ugo Durante said. The underboss, Romeo Durante, sat in a darkened corner but remained silent. Carlo nodded, accepting the boss' offer, and hesitantly sat down.

"I had a chat with the Professor," Ugo began. "The Professor and I go back a long time and I trust him. I trust him more than I trust a lot of members of my own family. Do you know what that means, Carlo? Do you know what that means when he calls me?"

"No, sir, no I don't," Carlo mumbled, even though he knew exactly what it meant. His typically confident and laissez-faire attitude had withered now under the intense scrutiny of Ugo and of Romeo, whom he could feel staring him down from the corner, which caused the feeling of little pin pricks on the back of his neck.

"When he calls, it means we have trouble, Carlo. Whatever he tells me, typically goes, because he is like a brother to me. Do you understand? I know some may...misunderstand his intent, but everything he does is for this family. He said we may have some trouble. He cleaned up a lot of my unhappiness with the matter, but I believe there is still an issue outstanding, is that correct?"

"An issue sir?"

"A complication, an unpleasant occurrence. In case I'm not speaking English, I mean a complication which needs to be rectified. Is that your understanding as well?"

"Well, sir, we are taking care of it. I happened to take a picture of the license plate of the girl in the alley. I have a man going after her now as we speak to take care of it. His orders are to find out what she knows and what she told the cops, if anything. We will go from there, sir, if that is agreeable?" Ugo Durante picked up his long-stemmed glass of deep, red wine, a sweet Italian Lambrusco he had been saving for a special occasion, which was fitting for tonight, as he was going to see what his cousin's sons could deliver. They held spots as foot soldiers in his operation, but mucking up his unblemished reputation was like spilling red wine on a white linen tablecloth. The wine would soak into the fabric until the stain became permanent, just like an unresolved problem could tarnish his family's name. He used the special wine on occasions when he had to decide if his family was strong enough to survive — not just simply correcting the error. Every second of the day was precious, and if it wasn't used to improve the previous second, then what was it good for? He wanted to make sure his family understood that philosophy, even if he had to beat it into them, even if he had to make examples out of a couple of lower-ranking family members so the others got the message. Even if it meant he had to *wipe out* the stain himself.

"What we are doing is not unlike art, Carlo. We have an intricate web of people who have specialties and these specialties are gifts like an artist has the gift to create beautiful sculptures. If the artist isn't given the proper mound of clay he was promised, he can't create the beautiful work of art he intended to create. If one component of the system breaks down, it creates a burden for the rest of the team to carry out their roles and responsibilities. I wanted to meet with you face to face to show you my complete faith in you and your abilities to correct this issue. This will be the last time we speak on this matter. The Professor, my dear friend, doesn't share in my confidence, but I'm giving you an opportunity to prove him wrong. You can give an update to Romeo and he will keep me informed. Fix this, and by doing so, restore the faith the family has in you. I wish you and yours all the best, Carlo." Ugo Durante waved a transfixed Carlo out of the room and Romeo the underboss walked him out of the two heavy wooden double doors into the hallway.

Ugo went back to enjoying his pasta drenched in red sauce and washed it down with a satisfying sip of wine. He wouldn't suffer from indigestion tonight. He would sleep like a baby, because after all the time he spent running this family, he had faith in his ability to *motivate* people. Whether or not Carlo could get the job done remained to be seen, but Ugo knew he would be able to motivate the *right* people to *correct this wrong*, one way or another.

Luca Nero took a long sip of the Recioto della Valpolicella wine that was set out for him to taste by one of his father's sommeliers kept on staff. He swirled the crimson liquid around lightly in the delicately adorned, long-stemmed glass, looking for the legs of the wine while inhaling the superb fragrance. He took a long sip and contemplated the forceful sweetness and intense flavor. He knew it was his father's favorite, made in the northeastern part of Italy, and even if it wasn't necessarily his personal choice, he knew disagreeing with his father on the matter would disappoint him.

"I think you're right, Father. This will be a perfect option for the reception. Wonderful choice, as always."

"I'm glad you think that, Luca. Please, choose one of the others from the list. I will have my chef fill in the rest of the drink menu based on pairings with our courses," said the patriarch, Gabriel Nero, with a wave of his hand.

"I think a Spanish Cava would be nice."

"Luca, we already have the perfect pairing of Champagne. Is there something else you would like instead?" his father said absentmindedly. Luca swallowed hard, forcing a string of profanities back down into the pit of his stomach. *Ignorant bastard!* Luca's angry thoughts seared through his mind leaving a trail of blistered agitation. He *knew* that Cava was not Champagne, but a sparkling wine. It annoyed Luca to no end his father told him to choose, only to dismiss his first choice based on his own misperceptions. Classic Gabriel Nero. Cava was his absolute favorite, and if his father got over his bullheadedness for a second to give it a try, he would see what Luca meant. Cava is drier than Prosecco, or typical Champagnes, and in the simplicity of the drink, lays its beauty. Depending on the variation, light flavors of apple or a crisp hint of toasty notes hits the palate. He even found the best location in Spain from which to purchase his Cavas, but he knew his father wouldn't be interested.

Even though Luca held the honored position of eldest son in the Nero family, first in the line of underbosses being groomed to take over the business for his father one day, his father refused to him see him as a capable successor. He constantly challenged Luca's opinions and suggestions for how the family business should be run and chose to fawn over Alonzo, the second eldest in the line of three boys. Somewhere along the way, Alonzo had become the most savage of Gabriel's three sons, but his father couldn't see it. His father mistook Alonzo's bestial nature for ambition and saw his bloodlust as passion.

Luca tilted his neck side to side in an effort to lessen the strain on his tightened shoulder muscles. He breathed in deeply, telling himself to remain calm. He had a plan in place and it was just a matter of time before he could unveil the fruits of his labor, which would surely put him in a different league than both his brothers and sister. *One day soon, I will prove to my father I have what it takes to run this family. I'll show him what I've been plotting when Robin brings me what she's promised to secure, and nothing will stop me from bringing the Durante family down piece by piece. Then, the Nero family can expand to the East and father will see I'm the only choice for successor. He wants passion for the family? I'll show him something better than passion — I'll show him what strategy and cunning can do. I'll show him what Robin brings to the equation, and he will be sorry he ever doubted me.*

"Maybe we should ask Alonzo what he would like to see from our wine selection chosen for the reception?" Gabriel Nero said as an afterthought, breaking Luca from his own sour thoughts toward his younger brother.

"No, father, we don't need Alonzo for this decision. You're absolutely right, let's not do the Cava. How about a nice Soave?"

"Yes, yes, a Soave would do quite nicely. We are getting close to finalizing our guest list. Is your employee coming? What is her name? Robin? Have you heard from her recently?"

"Yes, she is doing some work for me out East and I won't be able to reach her until she is back. I don't like her contacting me while she is out there as I know you value our privacy, Father. I make sure the way we communicate while she is completing her...business...is secure."

"I keep hearing about this top secret work you have her doing for the family. I don't like secrets, Luca. I should know how you are using her. You're not getting *close* with her, are you?"

"Close? Are you really asking me if she is my girlfriend? That is a little innocent sounding isn't it? We are together, but don't worry, I put business first."

"I would like you to end up with a nice girl from an influential family. Might as well bring something to a marriage as opposed to simply running events and promotions on the Strip — any girl could do that."

"*Not* any girl could do that, not in the way we would prefer it with the ability to move our product through the casinos. We have family money already. I'm more interested in *connections*, and that is where you will find Robin has a bounty of riches."

"When am I going to start to see the evidence of the opulence you claim Robin brings to the party?"

"Aptly put, father. Actually, at our reception gala coming up, I should have something more concrete to show you," Luca said as Alonzo walked into the family room holding another glass of wine he picked up from the kitchen staff. Alonzo was the tallest of the Nero children, his broad shoulders and square head made his mere figure intimidating even though his brutal reputation preceded him already. Alonzo sat lightly on an intricately embroidered and elegant armchair which cost more than an average person's salary. It fit the extravagance of the room and, after all, the Nero clan was anything but average. They were not even your typical mobster outfit. They were cultured, and they valued refinement in all areas of their business.

"Father, we should have a Cava at this event. This one is delightful," Alonzo said as an afterthought. The word Cava rolled off his tongue with ease, completely unaware of the conversation held between the two men just moments earlier.

"You think so, Alonzo? Okay, we can add it to our list," Gabriel nodded thoughtfully, and Luca said nothing, but stood silently, gritting his teeth as he gazed out the window of their family estate. He had to remind himself to loosen his maddened grip around the wine glass for fear he would shatter the glass in his hand as he focused his gaze at nothing in particular out the window. *Easy Luca, soon Robin will be here with the intelligence she gathered on the Durantes and then everything will change.*

Chapter 13

*"All the puzzle pieces were coming together and it was
creating a picture of doom."*

Fenton walked on the blustery street with his hands shoved
deep in his pockets. He couldn't believe Carter got him
out of his comfy home, a cozy bed where unfortunately, he
rarely spent consecutive nights. He was battered from his last job,
and mentally exhausted. With the anniversary of his Dad's death
coming up the end of March, he knew he was dangerously close
to going down a spiral of self-destructive behavior unless he could
keep himself occupied. He intended to paint the shabby walls of
his place for some time now. That he needed peace and quiet and a
break from violence and suspicion for a while. These long jobs were
wearing on him and when he was worn down and exhausted, it was
too easy to find himself at the end of a bottle or something worse.

That was what got him out of his cozy, quiet home – the fact
Carter had him hooked on the notion this case could be *different*.
Carter's claims about this girl, Scarlet, kept rolling around in his
head like marbles. His hands shook when he read the material

Carter's team sent over. He read through the new intel about Scarlet like it was a best seller. Not only was she the witness to a horrific crime, but she was also the twin sister of the deceased. Carter swore up and down Scarlet was one of those rare innocents who truly needed protection. All the puzzle pieces were coming together and it was creating a picture of doom for any witness in the case.

He checked the address he wrote on a slip of paper before shoving it back in his leather jacket's pocket. It was a brisk day. He had a light sweatshirt on under his leather coat, hood pulled up. He agreed to check her out, talk to her for a couple of minutes, and that would help him make a decision whether or not this was a case he wanted to learn more about. He knew they had a cop car stationed down the street, probably doing rounds every once in a while, a little bit of extra protection, but it wouldn't stop those who were truly *motivated*. If it wasn't him protecting her, Carter would have to get someone else. He was an excellent judge of character so he didn't need a lot of time with her to help him size her up. It was no small commitment when he took on one of these jobs. He weighed many factors and liked to take his time deciding whether or not to commit. Typically, he wasn't contacted unless the situation was dire to begin with, and that meant guaranteed danger. In his line of work, he had seen enough action for ten lifetimes.

Fenton gritted his teeth as he approached the duplex. It was a simple beige two story structure. He knew the girl lived upstairs, the owners, a young couple, lived downstairs. The duplex numbers were confusing though, and he wondered if packages and mail easily got mixed up between the two. If Carter hadn't mentioned she lived upstairs, he would have needed to flip a coin.

The downstairs door to the landlord's place was slightly ajar. The hair on the back of his neck went up immediately. *Something doesn't feel right.* He pulled out his sleek, black pistol from the back of his jeans and held it down close to his body. He slowly eased open the door and his whole body tensed as the chaos of the room came into view.

Furniture was overturned, and every cabinet and drawer was in disarray. A pair of legs as lifeless as a mannequin's stuck out from behind a large sofa. He walked around the room, listening closely for any noise or creek which could indicate an intruder was still in the home. A woman lay on the floor, sprawled behind the couch, shot through the chest. In the kitchen, he found the husband sitting at the kitchen table, two bullets in his chest as he sat slumped in the chair. The wood of the chair and the edge of the table were the only things holding him in place. *This can't be a coincidence. The inhabitants of the first floor of Scarlet's duplex magically end up dead? Perhaps the killer also became confused by the oddly-placed numbers outside the house and entered the wrong apartment?* His mind was racing. Both inhabitants were dead, but as he checked for a pulse on the woman she still felt warm. The blood was just starting to soak into the carpet around her body which meant it was recent. He thought the killer probably came into the wrong home, and killed everyone inside. Then, the killer checked in their drawers and cabinets for identifiers like mail or a driver's license to verify the address and confirmed they had the wrong location. At that point, the killer would know to head upstairs.

Fenton didn't have the luxury to pause to call the police. He went back outside to the porch and pushed open the door to Scarlet's stairway leading up to her second-floor home. It wasn't locked. There was no evidence of a break-in at the entryway, which either meant she didn't keep her door locked or she let someone inside.

He stealthily moved up the staircase to the door at the top and leaned his ear against the cool wood of the door. It was a habit. He always liked to listen before entering. He heard a faint noise from inside, a muffled whimper. That was enough, and his mind took him back to years of training and experience. He kicked open the door, but flattened his back against the outside entry way so as not to be seen. Bullets flew into the hallway past his head, a faint popping sound suggesting a silencer. There was at least one gunman inside. He crouched low and quickly maneuvered past the door, staying close to walls, until he was around the corner of the kitchen entrance.

He peered around the corner and saw a man in a police officer's uniform reloading a gun. A girl with long, red hair was tied up to a chair with duct tape over her mouth and a needle sticking out of her arm. Her green eyes were wide and panicked. What cut him somewhere deep inside was the flicker of *hope* that washed across her face with her mouth duct- taped and her eyebrows arched in a silent plea. Her gaze locked onto to his, and he felt his breath catch.

He hurried into the room. The gunman flinched and pulled his weapon toward Scarlet, causing Fenton to release a single shot into the gunman's firing arm. The force of the impact threw the police imposter onto the glass coffee table in the middle of the room. The table shattered it into wide, glass fragments, and one of shards pierced the intruder through his chest. The distinctive smoky smell of a fired gun filled the room. Fenton quickly grabbed the limp figure's gun and tossed it across the room. The man appeared unconscious, so Fenton directed his attention to Scarlet, carefully removing the duct tape from her wide lips. He had seen the photos of Robin, heavily made-up with her glamorous Hollywood style in Carter's documents. He could easily see Robin on the arm of a wealthy businessman at the table of a high stakes poker game for her promotions job in Vegas. Scarlet, on the other hand, was a classic beauty with soft, ginger hair which highlighted the juniper shade in her eyes. Her straight hair framed her face and hit below her shoulders in a relaxed, tomboyish way.

"Don't be afraid. I'm here, you're safe. Is there anyone else in the house? Was there more than one man?" Fenton asked as he carefully removed the half empty needle from Scarlet's arm and untied her arms and legs. She shook her head no, staring at him wide-eyed.

"Who are you?" she managed to whisper, her eyes were growing heavy as half of the needle's' contents started pulsing through her body.

"Call me Fenton. I'm someone who...protects people for a living. I was asked to come here and check on you. I'm glad I did. Did he tell you anything about what he was giving you? It is extremely important. Think back to everything he told you, Scarlet."

"Fenton...he's coming..." Her odd comment made him whirl around in time to see the bloodied police imposter on his feet again and lunging toward Fenton. Fenton moved like a cat, dodging the knife. Using the momentum from the lunge, he threw the imposter into the large window pane in Scarlet's living room. A loud crashing noise permeated the air as the glass shattered, sending the man flying through the second story window. *Stop him, Fenton! You need him. You have to find out who sent him to kill Scarlet.* Fenton grabbed the man's hand as he toppled through the window. His grasp met the cold steel of the blade clutched in the intruder's hand. Fenton yelped in surprise. The searing pain from grabbing the sharp knife shot up his arm, causing him to release his hold. The man hit the ground below with a dull thud. Fenton leaned over the broken window at the lifeless form, the finality of the moment searing into Fenton's brain like a badly-staged play.

Now there will be no answers, no clue as to who sent him, no end in sight for this wheel of horror which will only continue to swirl faster and faster for this poor girl. The man, the man with the answers, was now nothing more than a crumpled form amidst shiny pieces of glass spattered with tiny drops of angry, red blood.

There goes your only lead, Fenton, now what?

Chapter 14

"The gnawing terror became an ever-present companion."

The fear changed everything. She woke in an eggshell-colored hospital room without windows. Alone. She had a constant cotton taste in her mouth making it difficult to swallow. She didn't know how many hours had passed. Each breath was labored, as if invisible hands were closing around her neck, squeezing. She couldn't sleep. When her heavy lids finally shut, she would see her sister, smeared with blood, calling to her through a fog. Blurry faces would chase her in the darkness, emerging from every dank corner with their heavy feet splashing in shallow puddles closing in behind her. She would wake, shaky and disoriented, clinging to a thin sliver of sanity which threatened to dissipate with the realization her waking moments were more terrifying than her merciless dreams. As if her sister dying wasn't enough, now her waking nightmares included a handsome, dark-haired man in a pale blue police uniform, asking her to open the door. Once inside his conversation with her played like a Victorian phonograph in her dreams...

"What are you going to do with me?" she said to him,

once he had her sufficiently tied to the chair and was filling a long syringe with a clear liquid.

"You are refusing to answer my questions, Scarlet. Simple questions that require simple answers. I don't have time for games. With each answer you refuse to give me, I'm going to inject a little more of this special solution into your veins. Some prefer to use Valium cocktails or some other mix of household chemicals, but those seem so drab. Have you heard of Scopolamine, Scarlet? Otherwise known as the Devil's Breath? It's my personal favorite toxic substance. I've altered it a little, but I think you are going to like it."

"Scopolamine …" Her voice was barely above a whisper. Anything that might be known as the Devil's Breath couldn't be good, that much she knew. That was the problem with the unknown. Her mind took her to the worst outcome imaginable.

"Do you know what it is like…to have your skin feel like it's on fire, but you can't do anything about it? Your tongue feels too large for your mouth, too dry like you haven't had a drop of water in days? Have you ever had your eyes fully open and yet the images become blurry and unrecognizable? In slightly more complex terms, this handy little needle is going to deliver a liquid designed to paralyze your parasympathetic nervous systems. You can choose to tell me everything you know, or I can start to take away your nervous system functions one by one. The terror, the hallucinations, as you slowly lose your mind… it isn't a pretty way to go and you're such a pretty girl."

"That's going to kill me." She remembered saying as he tilted his head at her, a mocking answer to a silly comment.

"Well, if you tell me everything, maybe we can work something out. Nod if you agree, otherwise I'm putting duct tape on your mouth to make sure you don't try to get the neighbors involved. Oh wait, they're dead. Your cute neighbors, the ones who rent this little shithole to you, well, I had to have a little conversation with them. You see, I wasn't sure which apartment you lived in, and unlucky for them, I chose wrong. Still, better safe than sorry — can't have some nosy runner coming by and hear screams."

She blinked back tears as he applied the tape. She didn't want to give him the satisfaction of watching her break. The only way she could get back at him was to not say anything, but that would mean the worst possible outcome for her. She gulped and pinched her mouth shut to avoid tasting the tacky substance on the back of the tape. He tilted his head at her, one last silent question to see if she would cooperate? She shook her head no, blinking back a couple rebel tears, successfully holding them at bay. He slowly injected a little of the fluid. She could feel an angry warmth spread up her arm...

Luckily, Fenton arrived shortly after the minimal injection. The hospital staff didn't find large amounts of the drug in her system. Because they had the vial, they could test the substance to determine how he altered the drug to administer the proper antidote to her at the hospital, and luckily, they got her there before the convulsions started. She already had developed a fever without sweat, which was another telltale sign of the drug. She remembered groggily telling him something about the Devil's Breath, and the rest of her brief time with him was a bit of a blur. Scarlet remembered hearing the name Westbrook, another agent working for Carter, who showed up at the scene telling Fenton he would help clean up the landlord's apartment.

Fenton, a tough-as-nails, ex-Special Forces killing machine with a constant shadow across his eyes, had surprising grace and gentleness with the way he carried himself, which had Scarlet regarding him more as a dark angel who had saved her from a certain painful death than a rough around the edges, gun for hire. Broad shouldered, fiercely stormy gray eyes, and short chestnut hair and stubble which framed his square jaw in a shade lighter than his complexion demanded.

His was the first face she saw to break through the image of the waking nightmare. When he came into her place, gun drawn, he was dressed more like a criminal than a cop, wearing a black leather coat snugly covering a formidable form. Then again, the cop in the room was a criminal. Fenton was tall, easily six-five, and she guessed by the way he handled himself he was a star athlete at one time. Back before his face took on the hardened stare. She couldn't get him out of her mind. His look, the wiry, raw emotion which clung to him like a cloak.

Her reality seemed more like a postcard to her now. A snapshot from when things were simple and uncomplicated — back to a time when the most difficult decision in her life was whether or not to have spaghetti or a chicken salad sandwich for dinner. The new reality consisted of a constant burning behind her eyes, tears rising to the surface from the back of her head, her nightmarish dreams blending in with her waking moments. The gnawing terror became an ever-present companion for Scarlet, exhausting her with every shaky breath. If she were locked at the end of a long tunnel with no windows or doors, she would not have felt more alone than she did now. Locked in an emotional prison of fear.

How long had she been in the hospital? Hours? Days? She couldn't tell anymore. They took her phone and purse the moment she arrived at the hospital. The cell-like room they had her in was void of windows to the outside. There was one long pane of glass leading to an even longer hallway which was always stationed with guards. Whatever wing of the hospital they were holding her in was an area few ever saw and even fewer knew existed. No clocks and no devices which could be tracked like cell phones or computers. She was in a time capsule, and with the varying medications they had her on, she was in fitful bouts of occasional sleep. A few minor cuts from the flying glass and debris, markings on her wrists and ankles from the bindings, but it was what that small amount of liquid did to her insides which kept her in that room. The staff told her she was lucky. Few patients survive more than twenty-four hours, but those who did could hope for a full recovery.

She hadn't seen Fenton since he brought her in. At first, leaving her apartment she thought she could walk, but a few steps toward the door and she was collapsing into the secure hold of Fenton's arms. He carried her out the front door and into the light. He took her to the hospital, carried her in, but once inside, the staff pulled him in another direction. She faintly remembered him bloodied as well, his hawk-like gaze surveying the hospital scene for threats, telling the staff what he knew of what infected her and mentioning something about calling an individual by the name of Carter as they removed her from his capable arms. That was the last she saw of him as he was getting pulled by a nurse toward another corridor, never diverting his gaze from her until the swinging double doors in the emergency room blocked her view.

Since arriving at the hospital, police officers and agents were her only companions. Their stuffy interaction with her when words were exchanged was business, and not pleasure. They acted as if she were a lab rat they were there to observe. She feared she was getting closer to losing herself with each passing moment. Spending countless hours alone, straining her memory to recall what it felt like to laugh, to be carefree, to go to bed at night feeling safe, and what it felt like to dream about the future — a future free of bad guys toting guns, free of the visions of Robin's vacant stare, free to accomplish mundane daily activities like getting a coffee or grocery shopping without the lingering threat of getting murdered on the walk to her destination. It was as if a horrendous flu hit her, trapping her in a haze of aches and discomfort. She craved an end to the suffering, an end to the debilitating depression, the loneliness, the searing pain of losing an identical twin, the anxiety and constant worry.

She yearned for Aunt Jo, to tell her about Robin, but each time she asked, a police officer would inform her she was in a strict, no communication situation for her safety and they refused to return her cell phone. Her view of heaven in those moments of contemplation involved putting on pajamas and curling up to her aunt's bosom and crying like a baby in her arms as Aunt Jo rocked her back and forth. That view of heaven, as tainted as it was, was another wish which wouldn't be fulfilled. No one could know where she was, what she was doing, or that Robin was dead. Scarlet was forced to mourn in private, not allowed to contact friends or family to console her or share in her loss. She asked if she could contact the museum, to let Janet know she wouldn't be coming into work for a while, but she was simply met with a non-committal nod by uniformed police which simply told her it was getting taken care of on her behalf.

Her most constant companion was Kelly Carter, whom she understood took on her case and expected her to testify. They even brought in her sister's laptop to the hospital room, begging Scarlet to guess what her sister's password could be, which wasn't hard. Robin always used their birthday, October 10, or 1010, as her password. The girls would have enjoyed their twenty-seventh birthday this year. It was almost too much to think about when they asked for the code. This would have been the first year they could have celebrated together since they were little girls. Carter was almost foaming at the lips when Scarlet easily typed in the password and the laptop flushed with music indicating all systems engaged. She had Scarlet write down other potential passwords and emails accounts so they could log into her sister's email to access any messages which could help with the case. Carter also wanted access to all social media and bank sites, anything they could use to tie Robin back to the Neros or Durantes.

Scarlet was getting restless. When were they going to let her leave? When could she get back to her life? When could she apply for the new museum job, the job of her dreams? How would she explain this lapse of time to Janet? She was convinced those who used to be around her must think she literally disappeared off the face of the earth.

She found herself thinking of Fenton often. She had no reason to expect him, but it got to the point where each knock would have her sitting upright with anticipation in hopes to see his face again. The face of her dark angel. She brought it up to Carter once, nonchalantly, asking if she worked with him often. A small curve of a smile appeared on Carter's face for just an instant and then she wiped it away. She kept her answer short and noncommittal. Scarlet wondered secretly to herself if she shouldn't have brought up Fenton to Carter as she didn't know if she could trust her. Carter reminded Scarlet of the art insurance agent who came by the museum every once in a while. He had a knack for keeping mental notes of what piqued the interest of people he met in case he would *need* it for something later and Carter wore the same masked expression when she visited and interacted with those around her.

At first, Scarlet became worried with this notion, but eventually, she decided she didn't *care* if Carter had something to use against her — especially if it meant she may see Fenton again... and amidst the eggshell sterile hole of her current existence, it felt like a good trade.

Chapter 15

"Someone had to enter this girl's tortured world to bring her back to the surface or they could lose her forever."

Carter met with hospital staff for an update on Scarlet's situation. They were ready to release her as physically, she was fine, but Carter was more worried about her emotional state. Carter noticed Scarlet was starting to bite her nails, causing her fingers to bleed. She was becoming more like a caged animal than a young lady. On one visit, Carter saw the girl huddled in the corner of the drab hospital room, a wild look in her eyes.

Carter had seen numerous cases like this before, the death of a loved one, especially as close as twins, the added pressure of seeing the murder, and the burden of having to identify the culprits in court was enough to drive more than one witness into a mental institution. The wheels in her brain churning, strategizing, and always thinking five steps ahead. She had *plans* for her. Carter thought bleakly to herself Scarlet would be useless in this state for what she had in store. She knew someone had to enter this girl's tortured world to bring her back to the surface or they could lose her forever. She needed more from Scarlet, and fast, but each time she started to dig and ask for a little more, it was obvious the girl was shutting down and Carter risked losing her to a dark place within the girl's mind.

Carter was starting to doubt her position until the girl brought up Fenton. Her face lit up, she was alive again, not the hollowed shell she was becoming during their regular fact-finding conversations. After uncovering this anomaly in the girl's behavior, Carter knew her play. A new tactic to tap into what she was sure would be a goldmine.

A slow grin crept across Carter's face as she excused herself to the hallway away from the girl curled in a ball in the corner. She knew *just* the solution to her problem. She had a new plan of attack to get Scarlet to do whatever she asked...and he was only a phone call away.

Chapter 16

"I'm not paying you for your morality. I'm paying you for your skill."

"**I**f you don't care about the money, Fenton, what do you want?" Carter asked.

"I want out, one last job and I'm done. I vanish, with a new life."

"I could see what I could do, if you take on this case."

"Okay. I'll do it, but my way," Fenton's voice was gravelly over the phone, the exertion from the last few hours still grated on his lungs and vocal chords. There was a long pause on the other end of the phone as Carter stayed silent.

"You understand, Carter? None of this "cops down the road in cars" bullshit. You don't know how deep this thing runs, so I can't trust any of your people." There was another pause.

"Yes, he said they have people on the inside, but those could be idle threats. If there was an issue, it wouldn't be within my unit.

Maybe the local police?" she said hastily.

"They had to know someone to run the plates. We can't be too careful. I'm coming over so we can talk face to face. Stay where you are and make sure the armed guards stay at her door. I'll come find you." A click indicated Fenton hung up the phone without leaving room for Carter to reply.

He arrived at the hospital shortly after the call. He walked down the hallways loosening the bandages the medics put on his hands and wrists from the knife wounds and broken glass shards which cut into him during the struggle. He didn't like the way they constrained his movements and his ability to reach for his gun quickly. He wanted to rip them off, but knew he would be leaving droplets of blood everywhere if he did.

Entering the guarded wing of the hospital, he was escorted down the long narrow corridor to Scarlet's room. Carter was on a coffee run when he arrived, so he had some time to kill before she met him. As he paced the corridor, he found himself looking through the thick glass at Scarlet lying in the hospital bed in her room. Her room was in a restricted wing of the hospital to allow for better protection. She had a room at the end of a long corridor all to herself and guards stood post on all main entrances.

His throat tightened as she looked at her. *She looks so small next to all the large machines and gadgets hooked up to her.* He sighed as he studied her sleeping face. He could tell she was an innocent. He sensed it the moment he met her. Her cheeks were starting to get a hue of color again, a huge difference from when he found her — pale and almost unconscious. He could see the similarities in the twins from the photos Carter had sent him, but Scarlet's long flowing red locks framed her soft features, making her a natural beauty compared to her sister's loud blond ringlets and statement makeup. They were identical twins. Their facial features were the same, but everything else about them seemed different.

They were cut from different cloths, raised in completely different ways from Carter's report, and Scarlet had no clue what her sister had pulled her into.

He felt a tug inside of him, like someone tried sucker punching him, when he thought of her being completely innocent of all the trouble hurling toward her like water from a firehose. He was starting to feel angry about the incompetent way they handled her security to this point and was beginning to feel protective of her. He was starting to *want* this case and he knew that would put him in a compromising situation. He needed to stay aloof and in control to do the job. Feeling possessive of a case was not a good place to start, especially this early. He knew wanting the case would mean he'd be more likely to concede when he shouldn't and it put him at a distinct disadvantage when dealing with Carter. He shook his head slightly at his own deliberations. His thoughts and concern for this girl and her circumstances burned like small flames in the pit of his stomach, creating a fire he would have to control fast to handle Carter, if he could hold it together.

He was still pacing when Carter breezed past the guards at the end of the hallway flashing a pass at them as she did while balancing two huge coffees. Her long overcoat flowing out behind each stride, a steady tapping of sturdy heels on hospital tiling echoed in the hallway as she approached. She was leveling him with her eyes as she got closer, a sudden flicker of surprise crossing her face as she noticed the bandages, but she wiped the concern off her face as quickly as it appeared.

"I brought a peace offering. Wasn't sure how you take your coffee, so I assumed black would suffice. Before you start demanding things, let's keep in mind I brought you in on this, Fenton." Carter said in a warning tone, picking up their phone conversation right where it ended as he gladly took the large coffee from her.

"You brought me in because you know I'm the best. Let me do

my job, my way, or I walk. Thanks for the coffee. Black is just how I like it," Fenton said. Carter crossed her arms over her chest and tilted her head defiantly. He took a long sip as he thought about his play. *Lead with strength, and see if she budges.*

"There's the door, right behind those two armed gentlemen. No one is stopping you," Carter snapped back. Fenton's face hardened and his eyes narrowed. *Guess playing nice is out of the picture.*

"That innocent girl lying in bed, the one hooked up to all of those machines in there due to the incompetence of your people, will be dead before trial without me and you know it." A flicker of understanding flashed behind Carter's eyes as if she made a final chess move in a private game unfolding in their heads. Fenton wondered what strategic plot she was concocting, undoubtedly political, but he wasn't privy to her plan.

"Fine, Fenton. I'll agree to protect her *your way*, however you see fit, but I ask for something in return. If you think something I ask is too dangerous, you can voice your opinion, but I make the final call and then you fall in line, got it? That means when it is time, you keep your damn mouth shut and follow orders. Since you are so convinced that without you the girl is headed toward an imminent death, this should be an easy call."

"How do you plan to use her?" Fenton's eyes narrowed. He knew the game was afoot. *Carter relented too quickly, so there must be something larger at play, something Carter knows I won't like, something undoubtedly incredibly dangerous for Scarlet.*

"That's on a need to know basis and presently, you don't need to know. With your expertise you should be able to handle anything we throw your way. We are certainly paying you enough to protect royalty, so I wouldn't lose sleep over it. I'll let you know when we need her."

Fenton's eyes narrowed as Carter continued. "Let's get her

someplace safe first. Let me get with my team, review everything we have pulled together, and we will devise a strategy," she said. He turned to look at the sleeping girl through the window. He felt his resolve melting when he looked at her. There was a tender spot for this girl in him which started to swell, and he was nervous the growing feeling would eventually allow Carter to convince him of anything. Her commanding voice broke his train of thought.

"Whatever spell this girl has over you, make sure it doesn't interfere with the job. I'm not paying you for your morality. I'm paying you for your skill. Don't forget that." He nodded briefly, he knew what was at stake and he didn't need her reminding him.

"Does she understand what this means?" Fenton asked looking at Scarlet through the glass. "How her life will change because of this, what she is risking even thinking of coming forward?"

"I think she does, but she may need a little more prodding," said Carter. "We need to get her out of here, moved to a safe house or hotel with the proper security as we discuss next steps. Then I'll explain it to her and you can listen to make sure I'm painting the right type of picture. I'm giving you more access and input than I would give anyone else. I hope you realize that."

Fenton tugged at his bandages. He knew she was right, but it didn't help to settle the uneasy feelings which crept up the back of his neck. If she wanted him this badly, there was a reason, and he still couldn't see the full picture of what was motivating Carter to give such unprecedented freedom with what was certainly becoming one of her prized cases.

"May I have a couple minutes with her?" he asked, and Carter nodded.

"Okay, but make it quick. Here's a list of the possible hotels that pass our security clearance. You can choose which of these we move to as a temporary location." He took the slip of paper after eyeballing it quickly. He already knew which one he wanted, it was his business to have an intimate knowledge with the typical safe houses and hotels where they kept people before or after trials and before they safely transitioned the asset to witness protection.

Fenton looked through the glass again, a nurse was just finishing up her round and Scarlet was awake and sitting up. When the nurse left, he knocked quietly and stepped into the room. Scarlet gave him a warm smile, which made him clench his fists reflexively and swallow hard before approaching. *Damn, she looks too innocent for this place, for this mess.*

"Hi, Scarlet. I'm not sure you remember me, but..." he began, but she flashed him another warm smile which lit up her welcoming eyes. He felt his face redden as she stared at him with her emerald green eyes. He quickly looked down. He didn't like the warm sensation starting in the pit of his stomach leaving him feeling flushed and slightly out of breath.

"Of course I remember you, Fenton. I never had a chance to thank you. If you hadn't come in at that time, if Carter hadn't... thank you for saving me from that awful man. I could easily have met the same outcome as my sister, if it weren't for you. I wasn't sure I would see you again, but I'm so glad I have this chance to thank you properly. I owe you so much," she said and a genuine kindness radiated from her. Her bashful smile and gratefulness vanished when she noticed his wrapped hand. She touched his hand cautiously at first, then gently turned his hand delicately in her own. He shivered involuntarily from her touch. *Those green eyes again, they suck me in like a tornado. This can only lead to trouble, Fenton.*

"Are you okay? Was this from the glass or the knife?" she asked wide-eyed.

"It's just a scratch. I don't honestly remember how I got it, maybe a little of both? I tried to catch him as he...fell." He pulled away, moving his thickly bandaged hand behind his back. He noticed her eyes turn vacant as she was brought back to the memory.

"Scarlet?" She shook her head, pulling a long piece of red hair behind her ear.

"Sorry, it's hard to remember. I'm glad you came to see me. It is nice talking to someone who was there with me. I've explained it a number of times for the police, but I can't find the right words to describe what happened. The icy blackness in the back of his eyes. The twisted satisfaction on his face the moment I realized he wasn't a real cop. The way he looked at me when he injected that poison into my bloodstream. The police take their notes, getting all the details, but they don't *really* understand. Nothing I can tell them will make them actually *see*, actually *feel*, what it was like as the minutes passed by with such a monster in the room. What it was like playing his game." She chewed the inside of her lip for a bit and swallowed hard as she looked at him. Every word she said struck a chord of truth inside him. He did understand. His experience with the darkness of humanity extended well beyond the scene in her room. His thought he was meeting death many times before, and his experience extended well beyond the shores of the United States. He couldn't explain all of it to her, or to anyone for that matter.

"Yeah, I know what you mean," he replied. She smiled at him and played with the end of her blanket as she half-closed her eyes. He saw her blush again. A faint pink hue on her soft skin. He looked away.

"Did the police swarm my house after the man fell out of my window? Were there reporters flooding the streets?" she asked, wide-eyed.

"No. Luckily, Agent James Westbrook showed up right after the incident. He said Carter sent him to keep an eye on me. He told me he was going to keep the police and media away and would contain the scene to make sure it didn't turn into a circus. We don't need that type of press." She nodded as Fenton shifted in the chair.

"This isn't really, your kind of place, is it?" she asked. "Hospital rooms, especially those with no windows at the end of a long corridor. You seemed much more in your element in my apartment with that lunatic. Everything about you was confident and assured. I bet men would follow you into battle uphill both ways when you're like that. What's it like to know you're in complete control, even in utter chaos? Listen to me turning into a real chatterbox. I think the meds the nurse gave me may have just kicked in a little," she laughed. He thought her smile could light up a whole city. Her laugh was musical, like wind chimes on a breezy day. He couldn't help but laugh with her. He forgot how good it felt.

"Scarlet, after everything you've been through, you can be as much of a chatterbox as you like. You're right, this is not my kind of place, but I wanted to see for myself that you're okay." He noticed her hands tighten around the blanket in her lap. He almost put his hand over hers, but he brushed the thought away.

"This isn't over yet, is it? Those men I saw in the alley, the man who came to my place, they are not going to stop coming for me. She said my only option is to help put them away. Even if they were all locked up, they have friends who owe them favors. I still wouldn't be safe." Her wide raspberry lips fell into a frown as her eyebrows knotted in concern. Her jade eyes begged him for the truth.

He felt winded as she stared at him. He could feel her innocent features melting his insides and knotting his stomach. He gritted his teeth as he contemplated his response. If he was going to be in, he would be all in, no matter what that meant for him personally.

"Not if I can help it, Scarlet. If you agree, I would like to work with you. People hire me when they need protection. I've worked with Kelly Carter before on a lot of her cases. I've been in this line of work for a long time and I believe I can make a difference. Would you be okay with me taking on your case?" She beamed at him, albeit momentarily.

"Are you sure you want this case, Fenton? Carter was telling me about the Nero family and the Durante family. Every time we speak, there seems to be more people involved who could be interested in seeing me *dead*. You already sliced your hand because of me. Are you sure you want to sign up for this?" He felt a pain in his stomach and winced at the thought of becoming too soft, but he couldn't escape the fact he thought she looked entirely too beautiful to wear such a forlorn expression.

Because you're an angel, and you've done nothing to deserve this. Because I can't stop thinking about my dad as I approach the anniversary of his death and I need the distraction. Because I can't sleep at night, unless I'm helping someone who deserves better. Because I've killed more lives than I can count, so I need to save a couple to look myself in the mirror each morning. Because you're a better person than I am, so if one of us is going to get shot, it might as well be me.

Of all the reasons ran through his head as to why he wanted to take the job, none of them were reasons he could speak out loud. "You're making it sound like we've already lost. You can't give up." He sat down on the edge of her bed, he needed her to truly *hear* his message, hear it and believe it. Her eyes flickered, and he reached out a hand to brush away a stray eyelash fallen on her cheek, but he let his hand drop.

"My dad was a cop. He was killed by people like the Durantes and the Neros while on the job. There was one woman who witnessed the murder, Adrianna. She knew if she testified in my father's trial, she would have to go into witness protection, but she did it anyway because it was the right thing to do. She offered her testimony and my family was able to get closure. From that moment on, I knew I wanted to help other people feel protected. I was playing two sports in college on a full scholarship when my dad died. It was the night of the basketball championship. We won, but I lost my Dad the same night." He saw her flinch.

He took a deep breath. "Nothing else seemed to matter after that, Scarlet. I quit college and joined the Special Forces. All I knew was I wanted to fight the world, I had so much rage. Adrianna saved me in some ways. She was why after serving abroad I became a security consultant for the FBI and police. Adrianna made me want to help people in the way she helped my family. She helped my dad, even though it wasn't convenient and it was downright dangerous. If people like me don't exist, someone to keep you safe before going into witness protection, then the whole program fails. If the program fails, then people like the thugs who killed your sister get to bully witnesses into not saying anything. When the fear drives people away from doing the right thing, they win. I want to make sure those who have the courage to stand up against the monsters of this world, no matter how powerful, no matter how corrupt and dangerous, have the right of protection and safety. I want to rid you of any future doubts. My answer is yes, unequivocally, yes, I want to take your case. We can beat them at this and we will beat them, for you and for your sister." Her eyes widened at his response and he felt his stomach lurch.

"I'm sorry to hear about your father, Fenton. I know how you feel. Losing my dad was a confusing and angry time for me." She reached out and put her slender hand on his arm. The warmth of her touch lighting a fire within him.

"We will beat these killers for my sister, and for your Dad," her eyes gleamed. He could sense her mood shift from apprehension to trust. She squeezed his arm before letting go and her touch lingered with him long after she folded her hands back in her lap. *Wise words, Fenton, from a guy who drank himself to sleep last night.*

Make sure you can deliver on what you promised.

"Fenton, when I got here they took away my phone. I couldn't call family or my boss. I didn't tell my aunt about Robin earlier because I couldn't figure out how to tell her. Aunt Jo lives in vineyard country in Virginia. Will I be able to see her again if I have to go into witness protection? She is probably worried about me. I feel like I have not contacted her in so long."

"Can you write down her information for me, where she lives and her phone number? I'll make sure she is contacted. We will tackle those issues for you. We have a hotel we are going to put you up in for a while. I'll be there as well, with additional police protection, until we review your case in full and find a more suitable long-term place to stay before trial. Are you ready to get out of this stuffy hospital room?"

"Absolutely, I just don't know if I'm ready for what happens after we leave." She smiled meekly and he could tell she sounded more confident than she felt. *That makes two of us.*

Chapter 17

"I would rather die than disappoint you."

Romeo Durante, the underboss of Ugo Durante, sat with his back against a wall. He was the son of Ugo's brother who died of a heart attack shortly after Romeo was born. Not having any boys of his own, Ugo had raised Romeo like a son. At the age of thirty-seven, Romeo was often involved in the business dealings of the family and was being groomed to become the next boss. At the age of sixty-two, Ugo understood the importance of having a successor in line. Ugo's other brother, Benito, ran the nightclub Sneaky Benito's, which was often used as an alibi location for any members of the family. Benito ran many of the fronts for the family business, which was an important part of maintaining the appearance of having legitimate streams of income.

Romeo sat at his favorite table nestled in the corner of Gabby's, a popular steakhouse in the heart of Alexandria's historic warehouse district. It was a popular hangout for the Durante family as it was one of their many family-owned and run businesses and it was a restaurant with no windows, which was perfect for doing business.

Romeo always felt more comfortable in a place like Gabby's. He knew no one could get him there but out of habit, he always chose the table in the back corner and sat with his back against the wall. Those who practiced diligence were less likely to get whacked. He always made sure his back was to the wall with clear view of the door in any restaurant and café, which ensured a rival couldn't sneak up behind the table while he was handling family business. At Gabby's though, there was slim chance of anything bad happening. It was run by members of the Durante family or close associates — even wives and kids helped with day-to-day operations. He was enjoying a nice, buttery steak when Carlo and Pietro Durante walked into the restaurant. Pietro, son of Benito, was the *Capo*, the Captain or leader, of the main soldier crew that enforced the will of the Durante clan. Carlo was the best soldier in his group, but Romeo could tell by the look on Pietro's face Carlo's problem wasn't resolved.

Pietro adjusted his cuff links as the two men approached the table. Romeo was chewing on a piece of juicy steak and didn't look up. The two men stood patiently in front of his table. Without making eye contact, Romeo pointed at the two chairs in front of him with the tip of his steak knife. They pulled out the chairs, unbuttoning the last button of their suit coats, and sat quietly until Romeo finally put down his steak knife and fork. He dabbed the corners of his mouth with a blood red napkin and folded his hands across his broad chest as he leaned back in his chair. His dark eyes, black as soot, looked from one man to the other, deliberately, and with a slight tilt of his head he finally spoke.

"Pietro, I thank you for coming. Carlo, I know you are one of the best men Pietro has in his ranks, but we can all agree we have a problem. Ugo Durante is the man I do anything and everything for as he is like father to me. He uses fancy terms, compares things like problems to wine stains on a tablecloth – he speaks in a way to put pretty pictures in the mind. I don't talk like that. I speak plain, because that way, you won't misunderstand my meaning. We have a problem. While whacking a girl by the name of Robin in Carlo's employ, someone saw you. What is the update on the witness? I understand a girl was in the alley when it happened. Is it taken care of or do I need to worry about more indigestion on this?" Romeo looked at the two men as he smacked his lips. Carlo cleared his throat, but Pietro as Capo spoke first.

"I appreciate your speaking plainly, Romeo. We sent a guy, but it didn't get done," Pietro said, his deep voice rough from years of heavy cigar smoking. Without warning, Romeo slammed his fist on the table, shaking the water glasses in front of the men, causing both men sitting opposite Romeo to jump in their chairs.

"Ugo tells you to take care of it and you're two of my good guys, but it isn't *done*? It hasn't been taken care of? Was Ugo not *clear* enough or do I have to spell it out for you two? Why am I not sitting here enjoying my steak in peace, huh? What do you have to say for yourself, Carlo?" bellowed Romeo, smacking his lips as the two men began to show beads of perspiration around their temples.

The wait staff at Gabby's knew whenever Romeo had guests they were not to approach the table unless beckoned and they were familiar with his outbursts, so no one else in the restaurant showed any hint of surprise at the noise level from the corner of the restaurant. It was simply par for the course of doing business with the Durante family, and with Romeo. Carlo cleared his throat.

"I sent my best guy, we call him the Pig. He comes in dressed like a cop, and he gets people to talk. He was supposed to find out what she knew, what she saw, but more importantly, how much she's been flapping her lips. I know he got into her apartment, the uniform always works for him. The thing is, someone must have stopped him, because the Pig ended up as flattened bacon outside this girl's apartment. He fell out of her second-story window, splat. Now we can't find the girl, but we have some of our best men looking," Carlo said, and his eyes darted to Pietro.

Romeo tilted his head and licked his lips. "So we don't have *a* problem, we've got *big* problems. Did you mess this up originally Carlo or was it Darius?" Romeo spat as he spoke, his eyes turned a shade blacker and Pietro's eyebrow rose in response as he looked for a way to smooth things over.

"Darius let her get away," Pietro replied. "Carlo was the one who was smart enough to get her license plate so we could track her. This is a classic case of being on the run. I think the Pig showing up at her place of residence dressed as a cop scared her. It isn't surprising she hasn't been back to her place. Probably trying to be off the grid for a while. I have another specialist, called Percussion Pete because everyone he meets goes out with a *bang*. I know people in the system who can do some digging, find out what family is in the area — a mom, dad, sister, someone we can send Percussion Pete to deliver a message. That will bring her out of the woodwork and with any luck, we solve our problem as she tries to help someone she loves. Percussion Pete is the best explosives expert I know. He can weight a trigger with the best of them and his explosives come in all sizes and shapes — 'Made to order,' he likes to joke. It will take a little more time, I admit, because we have to smoke her out with the family connection, but it will be done. We won't hang you out to dry on this, Romeo," Pietro said. Romeo tilted his head, hands still neatly folded across his chest.

"May I ask, what was the reason to whack Robin? All I know is we got the order, and it was done," Carlo said and Pietro smiled.

"Yeah boss, you told me he didn't need to know, and like a good soldier, he sets out to whack her anyway. Perhaps it isn't his business to know now, either?" Pietro said as he lightly tapped Carlo on the shoulder as a warning. It was his way of reminding Carlo to remember his place in front of Romeo. To his relief, Romeo merely chuckled, smacking his lips with a grin.

"You're inquisitive, I get it. With this mess turning into a real heap, I guess you deserve an answer for your time on this. Another Capo was checking the footage of our security cameras at one of our warehouses, was looking at them for a completely unrelated reason, but he caught her listening at the office door as a conversation was taking place with me and one of our political friends on the other side. The information you gave me on the opportunity to get in on the casino action and back room gambling on the Strip didn't pan out when we started making inquiries. There were other reasons, but that one didn't sit right with me."

"You don't want to tell him the main reason, Romeo?" Pietro asked, a hint of anger at the thought flashed in his eyes.

"Yeah, may as well, since you want him to take care of it anyway. We also found out she was pumping Darius for information. I know he reports to you and I know he's family, but he is a blockhead. A few sprinkles short of a full doughnut if you know what I mean. Found out after a little tequila, our Darius gets a little chatty. He was telling her information about our safes and shipment schedules and who knows what else. Caught her logging into our bookings system with his password, don't know how she got it from him, but then again, that inebriated bastard is sloppy. She would bring him liquor and he would tell her anything she wanted to know." Carlo shifted in his seat.

"Now I'm not blaming you, Carlo. I know you can't physically be his shadow, but it has become apparent he is a hindrance to this family's operations. You just said he was the reason the girl got away as well. We have given him a lot of chances and his chances have run out," Romeo said matter-of-factly. Carlo sat wide-eyed and flustered, but he tried to remain composed.

"I knew he was a pain in the ass, but boss, I had no idea he was so clueless," Carlo said shaking his head.

"He is a vulnerability to this family and our business. He has exposed us. Even if we tried to correct the behavior, I don't think the intelligence is there to make it stick. Even if we demote him to an associate, he still knows too much. I was trying to do his father a favor, who is a close personal friend. I knew him before he married into the family. When they adopted Darius, he seemed a bit off even then. Family is family though, blood or not. Now you have to do me a favor, Carlo. I need you to take care of him," Romeo smacked his lips and the two other men exchanged glances.

"When? Now?" Carlo asked in surprise.

"Not right now. We have to wait for the right opportunity because it can't be tied back to us. His father knows the way we operate. We need to make it look like an outside job or he will be suspicious. Me talking about this with you, Carlo, means you're getting pulled closer into the inner circle of this family. You should be proud of that, yet, with more opportunity comes more responsibility. Can you handle knowing what you know, doing what needs to be done with Darius, and taking our secrets to the grave? Can we count on you to man up and step up in this family? Will you do this for the Durantes?" Romeo asked as he leaned forward with his elbows on the table to stare Carlo down with his bold, black eyes.

"Yes, yes of course. Whenever you need me to do it, it will get done. We will fix this whole Robin mess as well. I thank you for your trust in me and I thank God every day for this family. The Durante blood runs strong in me and I would rather die than disappoint you," Carlo said emphatically.

"Good, good. I'm glad to hear you say that, Carlo. You have made me very happy. Enough business for now," Romeo snapped his fingers, and a waitress came to the table.

"Give these two gentlemen a strong drink, whatever they like. I would like to toast with them before they leave." The waitress nodded as Romeo smacked his lips like there was extra wine on his tongue he was savoring. She brought over two glasses filled with rich and full- flavored brandy.

Romeo led the three of them in a toast and Carlo was relieved his hand only shook slightly as he sipped the drink. He was grateful the liquor started to warm his chilled insides as he sat across from the man with the unsettling inky black eyes. A man who was as comfortable issuing kill orders as he was ordering drinks. Carlo couldn't help but wonder if one of these days the order would be for him.

Chapter 18

"Do exactly as we say and we can bring them all down."

Carter and Fenton checked Scarlet in under a fake name at the hotel Fenton recommended. She was able to bring a small bag of belongings Carter's team pulled from her apartment. They managed to pull every family photo, home video, and random item of Robin's, and only pulled a random assortment of clothing and necessities for her. It wasn't what she would have chosen for herself, but they assured her they would make sure to get more of the items she wanted based on her requests. She bent over to grab her bag, but Fenton beat her to it. His warm hand grazing her skin, causing her to pause, her heart fluttering at the slight touch.

"Thanks," she said softly.

"No problem," he replied as she trailed after him into the hotel.

Fenton booked the room adjoining Scarlet's, and two of Carter's team, Agents James Westbrook and Nell Starr, were on call at different spots in the hotel. Carter started setting up a work station in Fenton's attached room. Carter immediately briefed Fenton on what they knew. Occasionally, Starr or Westbrook would come into Scarlet's room and asked pointed questions.

"Did Robin ever mention Luca Nero? Have you heard the name before?" Starr asked, with a doubting expression on her face. Scarlet shook her head. She was sick of trying to come up with new ways to say *no*.

"Scarlet, this is really important," said Westbrook. "Did your sister speak of an upcoming trip to Las Vegas? No? Are you sure? Did she mention a gala she was helping to host, or at least attend? No? Are you *sure*?" Westbrook scoffed at Scarlet as she bit her lip.

"Did your sister ever carry around a folder of documents, pictures or locations? Did you ever see her with a piece of paper with account numbers or numbers that didn't make sense at first glance?" Starr grilled her for hours, and then Westbrook would tag in to take over what felt like an interrogation. Whenever the door opened to the adjoined rooms, Scarlet saw Fenton and Carter hunched over a table full of documents and photos.

When Starr and Westbrook took a break to leave the hotel, Scarlet was thankful the hot seat questioning was done. Her head was spinning and she felt drained from the endless enquiry. She could hear Carter and Fenton debating something in the other room, but with the door shut, it was hard to hear what was being discussed.

Scarlet pushed her ear up to the door connecting the two suites. She knew she shouldn't listen in, but the air of secrecy lured her. A piece of her felt justified in her defiance after the endless questioning. She was starting to feel more like a prisoner instead of a witness. She heard muffled voices at first, and grabbed a clear glass from the nightstand to use as a magnification device. She felt silly as she mimicked a gag used in the movies, but thought it didn't hurt to try. She forced herself to focus on making silent, shallow breaths as the words became clearer through the glass against the door.

"Fenton, this has to happen. I have control of what we need to use her for in this case. I can't help it they were twins. I can't help it that with the dye job, it would be tough for even her parents to tell the difference between Scarlet and Robin. Those are the *facts*. This is the best opportunity to infiltrate La Cosa Nostra since Joseph Pistone. Remember him? Alias Donnie Brasco? He was an undercover FBI agent working on the inside for six years and he almost became a "made man" in the Colombo crime family, which would have brought him into their inner circle. The moment Robin pulled Scarlet into this mess, was the day she signed her own death warrant and that of her sister. What we can control is to help prevent this from happening to others and to get the drugs off the street so the fifteen-year-old down the block isn't getting ahold of white powder before she can drive a car. That is the priority. Don't lose sight of the bigger picture."

"What about protecting Scarlet? What about preventing the same fate which met her sister? I think you forgot that part when you mentioned your priorities," Fenton's voice was rough, like every muscle in his body was focused on only allowing a few, controlled words to escape his mouth.

"Fenton, always the bleeding heart, but that is what I love about you. I agree, her safety and her testimony are at the forefront of my mind, also. I'm sparing no expense when it comes to her protection, but with every investment, there also has to be a return. We wandered upon an opened treasure chest, and we can't walk away empty handed. We have girls that look *identical*, a gang of drug lords who don't know Robin is dead, and we have intelligence, including photos and case files we can use to prep her so she knows everything there is to know about the players. We won't send her in alone and we will use the highest quality surveillance when she goes in. We will be the voice in her head if she gets stuck." Fenton's reply was muffled so Scarlet couldn't hear, but his tone implied he wasn't pleased.

"Yes, there are security risks and reasons not to do this undercover operation, but there are more reasons to move forward. Therefore, the potential reward outweighs the risks." Scarlet heard a shuffling noise and the sound of footsteps on the other side of the door. She pulled back, forgetting for a moment she was still holding the glass from the nightstand, and replaced it on the table.

She sat down at the end of the bed, her hands resting on the sewn ridges of the comforter, her fingers tracing the threads. She heard a knock on the door which connected what felt like two separate worlds and she opened it. *Put a pleasant expression on your face so they won't suspect you overheard anything.*

Fenton walked in and sat on the edge of one of the tables in the suite, arms crossed, his face passive, but Scarlet detected a sour expression. Carter grabbed a chair and pulled it opposite of Scarlet's so they were face to face.

"Okay Scarlet, we have you as a witness to the murder of your sister. Bad news is there is no body, there is no trace of your sister ever being in the warehouse room where you witnessed the incident, not even a fingerprint linking her to the scene. This isn't terribly surprising. The Durante family has perfected the art of making people vanish over the years. All of their hits are nearly untraceable, but we have your eyewitness testimony, which is something. It doesn't take us very far though as we can only connect your sister with a couple of lower level thugs otherwise known as soldiers. Bottom line, I don't think we have a strong enough case based on what we have today to move forward. That being said, we recovered emails and communications on Robin's computer which link her with two powerful mob families, the Neros and the Durantes. We believe she was secretly working with both families in helping them to move drugs." Carter paused, looked briefly at Fenton who was continuing to lean, still as a statue, against the desk.

Carter took a deep breath. "From what we can gather, she was dating a man by the name of Luca Nero. He is the eldest son of the family patriarch, Gabriel Nero. The Neros run drugs and have an intricate web of organized crime throughout the casinos on the Las Vegas Strip. My task force in D.C. specializes in organized crime and drug trafficking, and we have been watching their operation for a long time. It is my belief each of the families monopolize the drug market on either coast. We think Luca pulled in Robin to work undercover in the Durante family as well, to provide him with information as a means to bring down the Durante family and take over more of their East Coast territory. All the information in the email correspondence indicates he is trying to unveil some of his findings to his father at a gala they are hosting in Vegas. I think that is what ultimately killed your sister — someone in the Durante clan caught wind of something making them suspicious enough to eliminate the threat." Scarlet shifted in her chair, and Carter leaned forward.

"I know I'm throwing a ton of information at you, and I know what I'm about to ask is a big request. My team is certain the Nero family has no idea your sister was taken out of the equation. They believe she is alive. Luca Nero has reached out via a secure connection to confirm their meeting's time and location. Typically, when she engaged with the Durante family, she used a separate phone and cut off communication with Luca until they could rendezvous at a location, which was always communicated over a secure, encrypted connection. He has reached out to make the confirmation, which we uncovered on your sister's laptop." Carter stopped again and leaned back briefly in her chair before exhaling loudly. She pulled her chair closer to Scarlet so they were practically knee to knee.

"Scarlet, you look identical to your sister, minus your hair coloring and style. The Neros think your sister is still alive. We need you to go undercover as your sister, in Las Vegas, to meet with Luca. If you meet with him, we are going to be able to build a more substantial case not only against the Nero family, but against the Durante family as well. We would prep you, of course, and Fenton would go with you to Vegas in addition to a small elite group of security professionals from my staff." Scarlet ran a shaky hand through her hair.

"This sounds crazy," Scarlet said.

"Scarlet, we would keep you safe. Luca is the key that ties this all together. We would conceal a microphone in your jewelry and plant you with a video recording device. We have your sister's communication, we know what type of relationship she had with the majority of the key players, and how she spoke with them. What we don't have is her cell phone she used with the Nero family, which we believe is in her locker in Vegas at the catering company where she worked. We can't recover the phone she used with the Durantes as we have to assume it disappeared with the body when they made her disappear. We would protect you through this whole endeavor up to the trial when we would need you to testify and until you are safely within witness protection. While you are out there, we would have you secure the contents of her locker. There could be valuable information inside." Scarlet blinked several times. She felt like she was dropped into some alternative reality. She couldn't wrap her brain around the weight of the request.

"Wait, wait just a second. You want me...to pretend to be...*my sister*? My sister who I barely knew? The one who kept *everything* from me? I mean, Carter, come on — you can't seriously be suggesting this? This is an insane idea. I don't even *know* Robin based on everything you just told me and you want me to convince a dangerous hoard of killers I'm her? You think this is actually going to work? I'm walking into the slaughterhouse and what will this even prove? I want out of this plan. Hasn't your task force gathered all the information you need? Why do I have to be a part of this?" Scarlet pushed herself off the chair, and ran a shaking hand through her straight copper locks, as she looked through the window. *No way, no way. They will have to get someone else. I won't do it. This is suicide.*

"Scarlet, will you sit back down please?" Carter's expression didn't change, and she said it as calmly as if they were discussing the weather.

"No, I will not sit back down. I don't think I want to sit right now," Scarlet snapped. Carter shot Fenton a look.

"Scarlet, unfortunately there is more to consider," said Fenton as he walked to a spot next to her. "I want to make sure you understand everything at stake," he said. His gravelly voice cut through her fog. His hand lingered on her arm, and she stopped moving, looking him squarely in the face. He seemed exhausted. She was already asking him for so much just trying to keep her from harm. His mood had changed since they moved to the hotel, he was becoming more indifferent toward her. She wondered if he already regretted taking on her case. She decided to listen, she knew she owed him for saving her. With his touch still a vivid thought in her mind, she begrudgingly sat back in the hard chair and stared coldly at Carter. Carter didn't flinch.

"We've had wire taps on these families for some time, but modern day crime families operate differently. Let me give you a quick history so you understand what I mean. Back when Rudy Giuliani was a Federal prosecutor, it was a different scene. There was The Commission, which was a governing body to make rules about how these five powerful crime families would work together. When Giuliani was able to pick off several key leaders within the families, they realized they had to work smarter. There were several huge arrests in the early nineties with John Joseph Gotti, Jr., his underboss Salvatore "Sammy the Bull" Gravano, and Gambino consigliere Frank "Frankie Loc" LoCascio. That trial was based heavily on FBI bugs and tapes from wiretaps, and thus, the mafia knew they had to change how they did business if they wanted to survive. We hear The Commission exists in some capacity today, but if that is the case, they are completely underground. After decades of arrests two families rose from the rubble and created empires, the Neros and the Durantes. Without a heavily invested Commission keeping order, these two families are more at odds with one another than with sharing business interests. We could see them either trying to merge or trying to destroy each other to monopolize the racketeering scene. We would need years of more wiretaps, bugs, and surveillance to get what you could walk in during a weekend or two and capture for us. It is that simple. You look just like her, she was already in with both families, and only one family knows she is dead. This is our only, and best play," Carter explained.

"Keep in mind, Scarlet, there is no way out of witness protection now. If your apartment proved nothing else, it proved the Durantes will continue to send people after you until you are no longer a threat. You're safer in the near-term pretending to be Robin, who they know is dead, than the witness they are trying to find and silence. We would hide you in plain sight as Robin. After this, you will go into witness protection. You want to see what they will do to you if they find you on your own?" Carter pulled a folder from her bag and started slamming down crime scene photos depicting images of brutal murders on the table next to Scarlet. Individuals missing hands, people shot point blank in the back of the head, and images where the remaining body is barely recognizable. She threw down photo after photo after photo. Scarlet's eyes burned.

"Is this really necessary, Carter?" Fenton growled.

"She has to understand, Fenton. When the Durante family kills you, there is no trace, but when they farm out the job to their gang of thugs, the gun for hire is sent to send a message. Like the fake cop they sent to your doorstep. He was going to do what, Scarlet? Inject you with a poison that by its very nature is a dangerous toxic substance which would send you into convulsions on the floor? If you told him what he wanted to hear, he would have slit your throat nicely and left you for the crime scene photos so all of their enemies as well as people like me, would know what matter of sins they are capable of committing. How do you think he got a cop uniform, perfect in every detail? How do you think they found your license plate and tracked you down? They have people on their payroll *everywhere*. There is no place you can run, and no place you can hide on your own. *You need us.*" Scarlet bit her lip and shuddered as Carter's words raced through her mind.

"Are you angry about that? Does that piss you off, Scarlet? Well, it *should*. I am not the enemy here. If you're angry, good. Get angry, but even better...get *even*. You have an opportunity that victims like you only dream of receiving. You have the perfect disguise...you have the perfect undercover alias...you have the perfect story to get you so close you can touch the bastards. Let me help you get them, not just a couple low level scum bags, but the whole lot of them. Because of them, you have to uproot your life, lose your sister, and lose your sense of self and security. What do they get? They get to run free in the meadows feeling the sun shine on their face. That isn't *justice*, that isn't *fair*. Let me help you make this *right*. You do exactly as we say and we can bring them all down. They are sitting in their ivory towers, eating their caviar and drinking their wine. They think they can toss people like you and your sister around as they see fit. Do you want to prove them wrong?" Carter leaned back in her chair, a smug scowl on her face.

"I don't know, Carter. I just don't know. I didn't ask for any of this," Scarlet said barely above a whisper. Fenton moved restlessly from his spot perched on the desk. He looked like he was about to interject when Carter held up a hand that silenced him.

"Can you give us a second, Fenton?" Carter asked. He looked uneasy, and paused as he debated following her request. She squinted her eyes at him, and he begrudgingly got up and went into the adjoining room. Once the door was shut, Carter leaned back in her chair and folder her arms. The look she gave Scarlet was piercing.

"You've lived alone here for quite a while before your sister joined you, so you're used to being by yourself. You were not close with your estranged father, in fact you rarely saw him," Carter laughed as she saw Scarlet's shocked expression.

"Yes, Scarlet, I do my research before taking a case and I dug into your background while looking into your sister. I like to know who I'm dealing with…always. I know you're passionate about art, particularly painting and sculpture. I've read some of the essays you completed in college on the subject, yes with the right resources I can track down even the most isolated activity you thought was lost forever. I also know the person in your life you care about the most is your Aunt Jo. You grew up with her and view her as a mother. She is the only family you feel you have, having lost your mother at such a young age, and then losing your father while you were at college. Aunt Jo was your rock, the person who helped you maintain balance and allowed you to feel loved and safe." Scarlet sat slack jawed as Carter continued telling Scarlet intimate details about her life she felt no one had the right or access to know. Carter raised an eyebrow and continued.

"I know how much your aunt means to you, Scarlet. We are going to have you in protective custody up to the moment of the trial, and after the trial, you are going directly into the witness protection program. Think about never seeing your aunt again, because that is the reality of the situation. There is to be no contact with her, as you are entering a new life." Carter watched as Scarlet swallowed hard, then continued.

"I can give you something I know you truly want, Scarlet. I can ensure you I can arrange a face to face with your Aunt Jo before going into witness protection. You have my word on that. I can promise you will be able to see your aunt one last time *if you play ball with us*. This is a one-time offer. What do you say?" Scarlet visibly sucked in a hard breath, and she thought she saw a momentary flash of a smile across Carter's stoic face, but it was gone as quickly as it came. Scarlet blinked hard, letting the fact marinate in her mind. *I may just have received an offer from Carter I can't refuse*. It was easy to see by Carter's face and her snide smile, she knew it too.

Chapter 19

"Enter a world of pretend."

Carter gritted her teeth. It was easy getting Scarlet to agree. Carter knew what buttons to push. Carter was growing impatient with Scarlet's unimpressive absorption of her teachings after several hours of work. She went to great pains with her team, specifically Starr and Westbrook, to make sure they combed Scarlet's place and Robin's laptop for any family-related video footage of Robin to help Scarlet transform into her new role. *Carter, be patient. Every reluctant witness started this way, until they realized she could provide them with something they wanted — something of value. Then they became the most malleable of subjects, like molding clay into a piece of beautiful pottery. I'm going to turn Scarlet into one of those pieces of sculpture she so ardently admires, whether she likes it or not.* Carter hid a smug smile. It was like she had a little secret she didn't want to share, her own private joke, for she knew she was the only one who could shed a ray of sunshine onto the pile of shit Scarlet had stepped into, and that sliver of knowledge was *power*. Power which would eventually lead to the outcome she desired, making Scarlet dance like a puppet on a string for the greater good of justice and Carter's prized case, *eventually*.

"Tell me who this is again," Carter said, holding up a picture of Luca Nero, the eldest of the underbosses in the Nero crime family, and Robin's boyfriend.

"Luca Nero," Scarlet said confidently. Carter held up other pictures of casino staff and event planners with whom Robin would have worked closely, and Scarlet stumbled.

"Again. Whenever you make a mistake, we are starting from the beginning. Who are these two?" Carter held up a picture showing the bodybuilder physique of Alonzo Nero, the second eldest in the Nero clan, and a picture of Manuele Nero, the youngest son. Scarlet got them correct as well. Carter could feel her neck muscles loosen whenever Scarlet answered correctly. They had reviewed the Nero family tree, all known associates, and Robin's colleagues what felt like a million times over.

"What are we going to do about Eleonora Nero?" Fenton's voice cut through Carter's concentration as she grabbed the next set of photos to quiz Scarlet.

"Look, we don't have a known picture of the daughter, she is a ghost. That being said, if we don't have a picture of her, and we couldn't find anything in Robin's files, then we have to assume Robin hasn't met her either. A good thing to fall back on, especially with females. If you don't recognize someone and you evoke a reaction from them making it appear you should know them, simply ask if they got a new haircut. Tell them they look fantastic, giggle, and brush off the fact you didn't recognize them. Downplay it with a joke, make fun of yourself, and seem uncomfortable," Carter explained, and Scarlet nodded as she made a mental note.

Carter's team was highly qualified on how to prep assets for undercover work. They knew how to take photos of essential targets at different angles and outfits to give the variety needed to help an undercover asset recognize the targets no matter what the situation. It never ceased to amaze her the data they could dig up on people with a couple of simple passwords and devices.

When Carter was fully satisfied Scarlet knew and could identify the key players in the sting, Carter was willing to move on. She knew they needed to focus on the next equally important stage of the transformation before heading to Vegas. It was the most important part of the plan, fooling those who knew Robin the best into believing Scarlet was Robin Lilly Matthews.

"Good work, Scarlet, but we have a lot of work to do with your dialect and intonation. Let's practice the script we gave you again, and go through the common phrases and words used in your role and with indicators you can use that tie-in with Robin's personality." Scarlet started reciting what they had practiced earlier, and Carter inwardly winced as she pulled out her notebook detailing Scarlet's transformational progress.

Carter squinted at her copiously handwritten notes. She wasn't putting enough inflection on certain words, her laugh was still slightly off because it wasn't as carefree as Robin's, and her walk still lacked the abundance of confidence which oozed from the Robin she saw on social media postings and home video footage. They had discussed the plan frontwards and back, and they couldn't move on to the next phase until they got this right, and time was mercilessly ticking by, mocking their efforts. *Step one: perfect manner of speech and walking like Robin.* Carter and her team were busy filling Scarlet's head with what Robin knew and how she knew it, from all the correspondence they found on her laptop. *Step two: physical transformation.* They were still at step one and there was no end in sight. Fenton, Carter, and Scarlet just went through what felt like the one hundredth attempt to a hold a conversation with Luca Nero, being played by Fenton, as Carter watched the show and critiqued as if it was a play on a New York stage.

"No, Scarlet. That isn't what Robin would say in response, because that is what *you* would say. You love this man, remember? You need to look at Fenton as if he is your one and only. A man you would risk your life for and double-cross an entire mob family because you want to please him. I need to see it in your eyes, you need to react the moment you see him. A little bit of a wider smile would help too. If Robin were to actually see Luca again, it would be a welcomed reunion. You are *Robin*, and that needs to emanate from every pore in your body without me or Fenton reminding you. This needs to become automatic, because when we are at the gala in Vegas, you are going to be the one alone in a room with him, not us. He needs to believe it. He needs to believe you. This means I need more concentration from you, Scarlet, *now*," Carter said frostily.

"I *am* concentrating. This just isn't working, and it seems like we have already gone through thousands of encrypted messages from my sister to these mobsters. I can't even see straight anymore," Scarlet huffed. She jumped up from the uncomfortably hard desk chair, which was a hideous addition to the room at the hotel's attempt to being modern and chic, but it lacked any padding or comfort, especially after countless hours of practice.

Come on Fenton, jump in here, this is why I hired you. I need you to control our subject. She shot Fenton a look, and he spoke up.

"The more you know the material, the more comfortable you will be going in there, Scarlet," he said. "That is why we are reviewing everything multiple times, so you have it memorized, as if you were the one who wrote the words. Don't give up now, you'll get there." Fenton's voice was low and controlled. Scarlet paced the room, her hands formed into fists balled tightly at her sides. Fenton stood in place, a polarizing stance to Scarlet's agitated movements, his arms folded across his chest like a statue compared to her flustered and shaky figure.

"Let's go through the home videos again. Scarlet, I need you to sound like Robin, walk like Robin, *breathe* like Robin," Carter began. "The meet is set, and if you're not there, if you're not Robin, then we are *screwed*." Carter leaned against the desk, only her eyes moving as she watched Scarlet pace from one end of the room to another.

"Yeah, well, I'm not my sister. I'm not Robin. No matter what we do, no matter how many hours of home footage you make me watch showing my *dead* sister open Christmas presents and graduate high school, and no matter how many phone recordings I listen to, it doesn't change the fact I'm not her. I'll *never* be her!" Scarlet spat the words.

Carter rose from her resting spot and moved closer to Scarlet, motioning for her to sit back down in the same chair she had occupied for the last several hours. Scarlet sat down begrudgingly, running a shaky hand through her hair in an attempt to brush it from her face. Carter's voice was deliberately soft and soothing.

"Were you ever in drama classes growing up, Scarlet? Have you ever gone out with girlfriends and pretended to be someone else for a night for fun? Have you ever gone to a restaurant and told the waiter it was your birthday when it wasn't, just to get the free cake? We need you to become an actress for a day, to enter a world of pretend. We are not trying to turn you into your sister permanently, it is simply a role you have to play for a while, like dress up on Halloween," Carter said.

"Maybe we should take a break," Fenton said in a cautious tone, and was about to continue as they were interrupted by a knock at the door. Agent Westbrook came into the room with a folder full of documents.

"You mentioned you wanted to review with Scarlet which pieces of information we give to Luca from the intelligence Robin was gathering on the Durante family? Is now a good time?" he asked, Carter knew he sensed the tension in the room.

"Yes, this is a good point to stop and review," Carter said tersely as she took the folder and started laying out all of the documents while explaining them one by one to Scarlet. Agent Westbrook cleared his throat. His gaunt face looked tauter than usual.

"Carter, you're not thinking of giving Luca Nero everything in this folder, are you?" asked Westbrook. "We can't control what he would do with it, or if he would take immediate action on the Durantes. We cannot reveal any information regarding the political ties we found with a couple of the laundering fronts and prominent politicians. We also shouldn't reveal the locations of the laundering sites in case that exposes the political figures tied in with those businesses. This information could put into motion actions we can't control." He looked at Carter and Fenton.

"If we were to give him everything, don't you think Luca would tell Robin his plans for this information?" asked Carter. "We would be able to step in and prevent any action from being taken."

"I don't think it is the safe play, boss," replied Westbrook. "We have to hold some of this to our chest. What if we say there was a snag, she couldn't print off all the documents because she thought someone was onto her or about to come into the room where she logged into their system? We could say we will have it all for him next time, there were simply complications."

"Doesn't that put Scarlet at risk, to send her in without all of the information they discussed? Speaking of control, we don't know how Luca would react to that news," Fenton chimed in, obviously uncomfortable with Agent Westbrook's sudden suggestion to course correct. Carter nodded in agreement, and Agent Westbrook's squinty-eyed expression turned into narrow slits of frustration.

"This opens us up to too much risk," Westbrook said. "Instead of all the information she promised him, which she can assure him she can bring him next time, she has a buyer ready to meet with someone of Luca's choosing. She has a source, maybe a soldier in the Durante family interested in vetting out the casino opportunities. He would find that valuable, another connection, another person, he could try to manipulate. Then, let's say, the contact's flight is canceled and it falls through. We can make something up, but it gives him more value than originally stated, without giving him all the dirt Robin was able to find, which puts this operation at risk. We can still get him on the conspiracy charges. Think of it this way: if Robin were to give him everything in that folder, what is to stop him from thinking she is no longer useful to him? What if we read their relationship wrong? What if he changed his mind, and considers her a liability — someone who can tie him to this data leak — and he whacks her. My plan actually keeps her *more* protected," Westbrook said emphatically, and Carter and Fenton exchanged glances.

"Okay, that could work. We will run it this way. I trust your opinion, Westbrook. Take some time to prep Robin on the documents we do want her to share, and I'll keep the rest in my hotel safe," Carter said.

"I can keep them with me, I would like to pore over the data a little more," Westbrook said.

"No, I want to dig into the pieces tying in with political pundits. We are hoping we get more on Robin's other cell in the locker in Vegas, but until then, I want to piece together a few things before I release these. Thanks for offering to do the leg work though, Westbrook," Carter said, and grabbed the documents they were excluding from the folder Scarlet would bring to Luca. Westbrook nodded curtly, and started educating Scarlet on the remaining documents and how to position them to Luca for the meet.

A couple hours passed when there was another knock on the door. Fenton looked through the peephole, then opened the door to find Agent Starr and a male with short, spiky, purple hair standing in the hallway. Carter rose immediately to greet the male, who was carrying two huge canvas bags. "Julian, thank you for coming on such short notice. This is Scarlet, she is the one you're going to be giving the makeover to today. You can come in and get set up."

"Who is ready for makeover magic? When I'm done with you, you're going to look better than Marilyn Monroe ever did. Who's excited?" Julian said with a slight lisp. Westbrook gathered his belongings and left with Agent Starr to go over the game plan and to prep for their trip to Vegas.

"Wow, tough crowd. You all look like you just came from a funeral," Julian said with a bubbly giggle.

"Yeah, if we can't get our shit together on this, we might be going to one," Carter mumbled under her breath to Fenton, who was the only one who would hear her brief moment of doubt. He stiffened, which gave her a slight sense of satisfaction. She needed him on edge. If he was overly cautious, he would be the most effective for her. It would be the only comment she made during the course of this sting which showed she questioned whether her plan would work, but there would only be one moment of hesitation. She *allowed* herself just one moment of weakness each case, and she prided herself on staying true to her personal pledge. She kept herself disciplined and focused, which was what she wanted, and she always got what she wanted.

Chapter 20

"Even the most luscious of apples can be rotten at its core."

Carlo sat in his vintage Riviera, a long and sleek vehicle popular in the sixties, a couple of blocks from Scarlet's aunt's property. He already scouted the back and every angle of the rolling vineyard, but couldn't find a single access point without risk. He didn't know what to expect when he pulled up. He was given orders to use the aunt to get to the girl, but to his dismay, he found a highly secure property. The entire chunk of land was fenced in with high-end security cameras and sensors at strategic points around the fence. The only way in was through the gated entrance, which also had cameras and a sophisticated access panel.

He drummed his fingers on the steering wheel. He didn't want to have to make the call to Pietro with bad news, but he also knew he had to keep his captain updated with his progress. His hand shook as he pulled his cell out and pulled up Pietro's number. He took a deep breath as he heard it ring on the other end.

"Carlo, I hope you are calling me with good news," said Pietro in his cigar-deepened voice.

"I wish I had some, boss. Even if I were to get through the gated entrance and past the cameras, the driveway up to the property is far too open. Past the grape plants, it is too easy to see someone approaching the house. I don't think this is the best place to do it. It looks as if all the stuff was recently installed, too, and is high quality. I'm sorry boss, but she is pretty much locked-down here. I don't have an answer for how we can penetrate the perimeter without getting caught. Do you think it is a coincidence all this security was added shortly after we got pictures of the girl?" Carlo asked. He was chewing the end of his thumbnail, wondering what Pietro would suggest as an alternative.

"Well, could be related, or maybe she has pesky kids in the neighborhood that step on her vines and try to break in to steal bottles of wine to have a good time. I don't know, and I don't really care, Carlo. The way Romeo is watching us on this one, it's like we grew a third eye or something, and we don't want this type of attention. One of my soldiers just did a job at a vacant property a couple miles away from there. You could use that location. Find a way to get her there, and then bait the girl. The next time we talk I need to hear progress on this, Carlo. What about Darius, did you take care of him yet?"

"No, boss. I've been putting all my time into this."

"Find a way to *split your time*, Carlo. You have two jobs to do, and if you do this, you will be a full-fledged captain. You've got my word on that. You have the ability to take care of two huge problems for this family. Do you want to be the hero or do you want to be dead? Romeo has run out of patience. He is fine with Darius taking the punishment for your past mistakes, but don't give him a reason to *change his mind*," Pietro's rough voice resonated loud and clear. Carlo shakily lit a cigarette. The puff of smoke floated from his Riviera, and the smoky tufts quickly dissipated into the breeze. Carlo took another deep breath and watched the smoke vanish into the sky. For the first time in a long time, he wished he could disappear as easily as the smoke, without a care in the world.

"You got it boss, I'll be the hero on this one. You can count on me," Carlo said, as he hung up the phone, threw his cigarette out the window, and drove away.

Eleonora Nero stood in the entryway of the lavish living room, a bemused expression on her face as she watched her brother Luca's knitted brows as he stood fuming by the window. His hand was shaking as he tried to remain poised while holding an elegant long-stemmed wine glass. Her father, Gabriel Nero, was fawning over Alonzo, which was typical, as he sat comfortably in an oversized arm chair. Eleonora stepped into the room and cleared her throat to announce her presence.

"Father, I thought you would be outside with Alonzo enjoying the nice day. I assumed you would both take advantage of the sun to shoot sporting clays with cousin Federico. I just saw him helping the lawn staff set up the course, and the way Federico was discussing the layout, I think he is going to give you a run for your money. The course is the most complex I have seen in a long time. Perhaps he wants to place bets with you, Alonzo, unless you're too sore at losing last time? I can tell him you would rather stay inside and sample wine if you prefer?" Her expression remained the same, although she was amused at Alonzo's raised eyebrows and flushed cheeks. *Foolish boy. I love knowing exactly what to say to evoke a reaction in my overly ambitious beast of a brother. I realized long ago all I need to get our father to commit to anything is to get Alonzo to agree first.*

"If Federico wants to hemorrhage money, I'm not going to stop him. I'll take him for everything he is worth. I've been prepping for this rematch. Father, will you join us?" Alonzo asked, folding his arms over his chest as he reclined in the plush maroon mohair arm rest. It was one of the several pieces that were created in the twenties and reupholstered to showcase the carved walnut feet, gold base trim and arms of the lavish club chair.

"Yes, I think we are done discussing preparations for the gala for now. You're absolutely right, Eleonora, it is much too nice a day to be cooped up inside. Luca, you'll relay to the staff what we discussed with the wines?"

"Absolutely. I'll take care of it," Luca said. Eleonora noticed a hard edge to his words. The two men left to gather their guns and equipment to challenge Federico. Once Eleonora was confident they were gone, she grabbed herself a glass of wine which was set out for tasting and approached her eldest brother Luca at the window.

"When are you going to make Father see your potential, Luca? He treats you more like a servant than his oldest son," Eleonora said slyly.

"I'm glad someone else sees it that way," he grumbled.

"Of course," she touched his arm as she took a thoughtful sip from her wine glass.

"You know you're my favorite, and I want to see you gain more influence. You and I both know Alonzo does not have the emotional intelligence or restraint to lead this family, yet everything he touches turns gold in our father's eyes. Please tell me you have a plan. In fact, I would like to help if I could." Her comment drew a large smile from Luca as he looked through the thick paned glass to the painstakingly landscaped grounds below.

"I think I have a good plan in place and I would love the support from you. I have an employee, Robin, who has been very busy on my behalf. If I tell you though, you have to swear an oath of secrecy. This can't come out before I'm ready," he said with a Cheshire cat type grin, the same type of mischievous smile which would be on a little boy's face if he stumbled across a hidden Christmas present early.

"Of course, who else would I even tell, Luca? Plus, your interests run parallel to my own, as you well know. I would much rather have you take over the family business than Alonzo. If he were to gain more influence or power in our family, the streets would run red with blood and there would be no peace. I'm happy with our comfortable lifestyle. I don't want to give that up, and you're the best person to expand and continue the family business in the manner in which we are accustomed." She took another sip of wine and tried to put on her most charming and trustworthy expression, even though the words that came out of her mouth were ripe with subterfuge. She liked the sweet yet sour taste they created.

"Okay, Robin has worked for me on the Las Vegas Strip for a while as an event planner for many of the casinos. She helps us push our products to the right type of buyers, especially cocaine. Her father was in over his head with gambling debts when I first met her, so originally, I got her to do whatever I wanted as part of his repayment plan when he was alive. I even convinced her to go undercover for me in a similar situation in the Durante family. Here is the beauty of my plan: they actually think she works for them, but in actuality, she is a rat gathering intelligence for me." He looked so pleased with himself Eleonora had to suck in her breath and remain collected so as to not show him her surprise.

"Is that so? Clever boy, you have been busy haven't you? What type of information is she getting for you? Once she paid off her father's debts, what would keep her working undercover for you with our rival organized crime family on the opposite coast? The bad blood between our two families runs deep. If they even had a whiff something like this was going on, I can't even imagine what they would do with her," she said innocently, even though she could imagine in detail what they would do to her, because it was the same thing she often fantasized doing to enemies if given the chance.

"She loves me, simple as that," Luca replied. "I took her from an employee, grateful to me for helping her father out of a jam before he died, to my lover. That has allowed me the control to convince her to put herself in the most difficult and dangerous situations. She has a file with all of the locations of their laundering sites and offices, and who their soldiers are so we can target them as necessary. We can hit the next several shipments of product where their main safes are located as well as their suppliers. We could take them down at the knees with this information. I can shut down their supply, which means I'm stopping the money, and target their family and where they keep the loot. They wouldn't be able to operate. They would lose too many key people, their slush fund of cash, and the means in which they make money. There was one final piece to the puzzle and I didn't want to reveal anything until I had the crown jewel, and she finally got it for me. With this crown jewel, I can present all of this information to our father, and it will prove I'm ready to take on the family business. It will also show I'm being gracious in allowing him to help me decide how to use this information to our advantage." Luca looked at his sister and smiled with great satisfaction.

"Does this girl think you are going to marry her? That is a lot of dangerous intelligence to gather simply out of a burning love for you. Come on, Luca, you're dealing with me here. You've told me all of this in confidence, yet you won't tell me about the crown jewel? I'm your one and only sister and I'm in your corner. Don't give me reason to mistrust you because you're not being completely open and honest with me," she purred the words.

"Eleonora, you know I want nothing more than to continue to nurture the trust you have in me. I have to talk to Robin when she gets here before I say anything, but you will be the first person I tell once I confirm she has what I need. You see, the Durantes have someone on the inside looking out for their interests. I don't want to say more than that until I have a chance to meet with Robin to look at the evidence she's compiled. I need it to be perfect before I mention it to anyone. As for marriage, if Robin pulls this off, hell, maybe I *will* marry her. You always said you wanted another strong female in this family. If she is able to uncover this piece of information creating our crown jewel political connection, we will have the whole family where we want them." Eleonora froze for a moment, absorbing the weight of his words. For an instant, she wondered if her own secrets could be pulled out of the shadows and into the light with Luca's gopher Robin digging into powerful crime family business. *Private business*? She let the idea wash away as quickly as it came. After all, what were the chances Robin was as good as Luca claimed?

"You think your pretty bird Robin found all of that out for you? Sounds ambitious, Luca. How do you know any of it is rooted in fact? She could be playing you, ever think of that? Plus, how would they let her get that close?"

"It is brilliant, Eleonora, I prepped her with information on the hotels we run our product through and compiled misinformation about how we are failing to make our commitments to buyers and our suppliers are unreliable. As far as they are concerned, there is a vacuum that needs to be filled and they want to slip in on the action. She offered to set up meetings through her connections, to expand their products on the Strip due to the high demand. I prepped her with fake schematics, hotels, casinos, and contacts which would help them get established and start pushing shipments out west. They also were drooling over some backroom gambling action in some of our casinos, and they were putty in her hands. She found a weakness, an ambitious up-and-coming soldier named Darius, whose father's connection puts him strategically in a position to eventually become a Captain. Robin realized quickly with her looks, and the right amount of booze, she could get anything she wanted from him — even managed to secure his password to access their internal shipping systems." Eleonora flinched. He had uncovered more than she expected.

"Don't worry so much, Eleonora. I don't want to blow this opportunity with our father. I'm smarter than that, so I'm waiting to comb through everything when I see her the night of the gala. If everything checks out like she said, then I'll have the conversation with our father. She just confirmed our meet, so as of right now, it seems like everything is coming together nicely. I appreciate your concern though. I didn't realize you were so invested in my wellbeing. It's very touching, but I can assure you everything is going as planned."

"What if one of the Durante family members wants to meet this high roller interested in pulling their supply into the casinos and backroom gambling rings? What if they want to set a meet? Have you thought about that?"

"Nah, I'll cross that bridge when I get to it. I could always send in one of our lower level soldiers to play the part or hire someone to do it. I could simply throw some money at that problem and I know I could make it disappear. We could fill them with so much misinformation their heads would spin. If I get everything I need, and convince Father I'm the man he is looking for to run this family, then we could hit them on all fronts before they even have time to book plane tickets."

"I want to meet her. I want to see the girl who has my brother smiling like I've never seen before," she said, forcing her voice to have inflections of awe and good-natured ribbing.

"I'm smiling because I'm closing in on certain *victory*. I'm inches away from locking in my position as future heir to this family. Not only that, but I'll be the son who gathered the most competitive dirt on our largest competitor running the east coast markets. Stay with me, Eleonora, and you can reap the benefits of my success as well. You want to meet Robin? I can arrange that. You would like her. She's got ambition, that's for sure. Any girl who pulls off the stunts she has deserves to meet my sister, right?" he flashed his pearly whites at her.

"Promise me one thing, Luca. Keep me close on this. You never know when an opportunity could present itself where you could need a little sisterly help." He nodded as he checked his extravagant watch. Only few of its kind were in existence and primarily found in Europe.

"You got it. I'd better get these wine requests to the staff before Father can change his mind again. Remember, this is our little secret."

"You don't have to worry about me, I won't dream of telling a soul," Eleonora said sweetly. Luca strode out of the room with a more purposeful stride than Eleonora had seen from him in a long time. She took another sip of wine, dissecting the flavors in her mind. She was drinking the Cava that Luca preferred, simply because she knew he would notice her drinking it, although it didn't fit her tastes in the least. She preferred Malbecs, which were similar to Merlots, but with more acidity and spice — just like her.

Eleonora played with a strand of long, cascading black hair which fell in soft waves around her shoulders and rested on her lightweight cashmere sweater as she contemplated everything Luca said. She was surprised it was so easy to get him to reveal more about Robin, and what value she was supposedly bringing to his little ploy. She could see an opportunity to inject her own agenda into this scheme, but she would need to be patient. It was easy to tell Luca she wouldn't tell a soul, because at this point, shedding light on his plans would not help her. There was enough risk involved that she didn't want to chance anyone pressing the brakes to slow down this speeding train. Even if she saw impending disaster, she wouldn't breathe a word. She needed Luca to go down in flames. She just didn't expect it to be this soon.

She left the rest of her glass of wine on the table and poured herself a nice Malbec. She smiled a little as she caught a glimpse of her reflection in a gold framed mirror across the room, and she winked to her reflection. She thought of herself as a vixen in disguise, masked with a voice as soft as silk and an expression as sweet as honey. To those who met her, she reminded them of an Arabian princess, her dark features coming from her strong Italian roots. They assumed her soft features meant she was the nurturing one in the family, and she allowed people to view her that way as she hid her cunning natural ability to manipulate. Her skills of understanding people, and how to influence them, put her far above any of her three brothers and made her as dangerous as she was beautiful. Not only was she the most strategic of the Nero heirs, she was the most Machiavellian of all her siblings, as she was the only one who managed to shroud her shrewdness and skill from everyone in the family.

She had managed to hide her ambitions and scheming behind her large oval eyes, her perfect features, and patient nature. She preferred their perceptions of her to be as simple as they were ignorant of her abilities. They thought her most valuable asset was to marry someone of even more power and social standing to aid the family, and they knew her exotic good looks and pristine upbringing would land her the most deserving suitor. They viewed her as their supportive, younger sister, who was a part of the family business, but only from afar. She would sit in on the meetings, but was careful when to give input, and occasionally, she would be left out of critical negotiations only to hear about them later from Luca or Manuele. To her brothers, Eleonora was the perfect woman, but what they didn't consider...is that even the most luscious of apples can be rotten at its core.

She tossed another soft wave of hair over her shoulder as she smiled sweetly at her own private joke. Luca saw himself as the heir apparent, but he was not their father's favorite. He rushed into plans which were not vetted to the extent they should be for flawless execution. His impatience and simmering anger would be what brought him down. Impatience leads to mistakes, and one thing the Nero family did not tolerate well was mistakes. Alonzo was their father's favorite, but his uneven temper and unnecessary bloodlust led to risky situations. He was easily lured into careless showmanship due to his massive ego and insatiable appetite to compete, which was his weakness. Then there was Manuele, the third and last son, but he was a drunkard. The only use Eleonora had for him was that he followed her like a puppy and lingered on every word she said. He was putty in her hands, and the perfect front for her to eventually run the family. *Eventually*. But it would require patience.

She had waited years for this chance, for the opportunities to move the chess pieces across the board in such a way to make her queen of this castle. The new developments with Robin fast tracked some of her plans. The girl who wouldn't disappear. Her plan was always to take care of Alonzo first. Then, once the strongest and most ruthless competitor was out of the way, Luca would be easy to take care of as well. Once her two brothers were gone, Manuele would be king of the Nero family. Manuele, her poor sniveling brother, weak in every possible facet, and in every way that mattered, somehow he ended up with the worst of everything, which suited her just fine, because it made him the perfect pawn so she could rule strongly behind him. He would be her arms, her legs, her mouthpiece. She would be the master and he would simply be the pawn. It was the ultimate irony. The one in the family who was considered only a pretty face, usurping all of her brothers to rule the family business.

All it took was patience. She licked her lips at the thought, for she knew as no one else did, her best personal quality was *patience*.

Chapter 21

"Think of something else. Basketball, football, guns, combat boots, anything."

Julian knocked on the door of the adjoining suite where Carter and Fenton were working. He was busy the last few hours working on Scarlet's appearance to completely transform her into Robin. Fenton heard the home movies playing in the background through the adjoining door, and he worried about Scarlet's emotional resolve watching images of her dead sister for hours on end. It was more than anyone should have to bear, to have to mimic the recently dead.

She is a strong girl, but even a strong flower wilts and falls to pieces in a hurricane. I hope she can keep it together. Snap out of it. Worrying about her feelings won't keep her safe, Fenton. Think about your dad. The feelings of her security team didn't help Adrianna testify, it was their strength and discipline which kept her protected. Turn off your emotions. You need to be more like a machine than a man. Think of your training, think of the killer's next steps. Don't think about her sweet smile and the way her hair smells like autumn. Make your dad proud, damn it, and stop thinking about her. Think about the case, or someone is going to get killed.

Julian's loud and boisterous voice broke through his thoughts. "She is ready for her big unveiling. Do you want her to come in here, or do you two wish to step into the other room? An Agent Starr and an Agent Westbrook, if I remembered their names correctly, brought a bunch of full-length mirrors into the other room so she could practice her walk. If you need pageant prep, you could have just asked me. I live and breathe pageants and am super happy to help. I hope you don't mind, I gave her tips and tricks for mirroring the girl in the videos she was watching. I think it sounds almost perfect now. I aim for perfection each and every time, and you only get one time to make a first impression with the judges. Kelly, you should have told me we were working with a beauty queen. You are always so secretive with the clients you give me," Julian said expressively with several wide hand gestures.

Fenton chuckled to himself as he noticed Carter turn beat red at the cavalier way Julian used her first name, as she was so used to her colleagues shaking in their boots simply being near her, let alone using her first name. Carter obviously didn't intimidate him in the least.

"I didn't want you to get too excited, Julian, and remember the confidentiality agreement you signed with us. Not a word of this to anyone. My level of secrecy was made quite clear when I hired you, and this particular instance is no exception," Carter said dispassionately.

"Of course, I had no idea the pageant world turned into such an underground thing. You're trying to get her to take them by surprise, right? I get it. It's very competitive. Come on in, I'll introduce you to your new and improved Robin. I also put her in one of the gowns you gave me to work with. There was one, this maroon-salmon color, it somewhat matches the name you picked out for her, so I thought it would be show stopper on any stage," Julian said with pride. He opened the door and led them into the attached hotel room. There were full-length mirrors propped in every corner of the room, and a couple by the main bathroom entrance.

"Okay, Robin. Come on out, and show us your stuff," Julian said exuberantly. Fenton took a seat on the edge of the desk in the room, half standing. The moment he saw Scarlet though, he wished he had chosen the chair.

Scarlet, looking like a carbon copy of Robin, walked out of the bathroom and stood in front of three full-length mirrors facing Carter, Fenton, and Julian. She was wearing a red shimmering dress, with a plunging neckline that emphasized her ample breasts. Her long, straight copper hair was cropped short and dyed a shiny golden blond. Fenton griped the sides of the desk for fear he would topple off his perch, and swallowed hard. He could feel his heart racing.

Holy hell. What color blond is that anyway? Not golden yellow, but blond like the sun streaming through the windows lighting up the room. It looks like she is surrounded by her own personal halo, like a saint. She can't go out like that. Sure we want her to be noticed, but hell, who wouldn't notice her now? My job just got a whole hell of a lot harder.

The elegant, long slimming gown looked like it was formed to her figure. Her pouty lips were Christmas red and dark eye shadow expertly applied made her emerald eyes glisten. She held him captive with her enticing gaze. Her tongue gently brushed the corner of her mouth. She sauntered a couple steps out in front of Carter and Fenton, finally perfecting Robin's confident stroll, and struck an aggressive pose with her hand perched lightly on her hip in a sassy stance. Fenton's whole body hardened in response to her every move.

"Welcome to the Vegas gala. I'm Robin. Thank you for coming. If you have any questions about the events we run on the Strip, or elite betting opportunities offered by the casinos, I can help get you situated. We have many exclusive events this week and I'm confident we have something you will find suitable. Our options range and we can accommodate even the most discerning of tastes," Scarlet said flawlessly, and Fenton caught himself blinking several times, transfixed by her transformation. Her voice was lower and smoother. Her words came out evenly spaced as if patience came along with the awareness that as Robin, she never had to worry about people losing interest in what she was saying. The sultry girl on the screen, the Robin they were working tirelessly to emulate, was now standing in front of them and it caused Fenton's mouth to instantly go dry. He looked over at Carter to see if she was equally as surprised, and he could see a hint of a smile behind her poker face.

"Robin, what if I need something special? What if I want to have a little fun at this gala?" Carter asked, testing Scarlet's imitation beyond her prepped statement. Julian smiled broadly, happily convinced he was the motivator to cause such an immense change.

"I always believe if you look the part, you feel the part. Go ahead, Scarlet," Julian said proudly.

"Well then, if you're looking to have a little fun, I'm your girl," Scarlet said, her jade eyes flashing and her red lips curving into a titillating and confident smile. Fenton felt like someone just jacked the heat up one hundred degrees in the room. He was ashamed to find himself turned on by this sudden transformation. He reminded himself any girl dressed to the nines like she was, and able to pull off this barely there, red sultry dress, would cause his body to react the same way.

It's just this dang cursed male anatomy. You can get past it.

Think of something else. Basketball, football, guns, combat boots, anything.

Carter continued to grill Scarlet. Despite Carter's battery of questions, Scarlet managed to stay perfectly in character with every response, and more importantly, kept the personality of Robin intact with each new question where she had to think on her feet. It was getting tougher for Fenton to focus, and he cursed under his breath.

"Congratulations, Scarlet. I think you have Robin nailed. Julian, you are a miracle worker," Carter said triumphantly, as she stood from her chair to move to Scarlet to inspect the makeover more closely. Fenton then saw the mask fall and the old Scarlet reemerge. The timid, quiet girl, self-conscious and unsure of herself, and the smile which returned was certainly more Scarlet than Robin. He realized with surprise he was even more attracted to her when the Scarlet he knew bubbled back to the surface. He noticed the mannerisms were that of the quiet and scared young lady he first met. It was as if she had taken the advice of playing a role on stage to heart and this was the actress behind the curtain now asking her theater instructor if her performance was on the mark for the night. It was the real her again, simply wearing a costume and a mask. The mask was not a mask though. It was a fearful girl going into the character of her dead sister, a superficial façade to save their case and potentially save her life. She had no idea how attractive her bravery was to him above all else — more than the makeup, more than the traffic-stopping, plunging cocktail gown, more than the sassy responses and seductress voice, more than the curly bob of hair that screamed to be pulled, more than the perky breasts that begged for attention in a siren's outfit, and more than the statement makeup and bright sultry lips. Even though he had no doubt Robin could make even the toughest of men melt, he had no interest in the Robin on the screen or in front of him recreated by a team. He was only interested in Scarlet and it was even more painfully clear with her apprehensive and awkwardness with a crowd of people fawning over her.

He found every ounce of her raw emotion endearing, and it pulled at his insides. He saw her steal a couple of glances at her reflection in the series of mirrors propped around the room, and with each glance, there was a glimmer of surprise when she didn't recognize the face looking back at her. He noticed her limbs trembling from the weight of the pressure she felt to perfect this act for them. The adrenaline from the show she put on was starting to melt away, leaving her quaking from its jolt. It was for all of those reasons he felt deeply for her. She tugged at his heartstrings in all the ways which left him slightly breathless and uncomfortable. He realized with dismay he wanted nothing else but to wrap his arms around her trembling figure and tell her everything would be okay, and comfort her until she wasn't shaking anymore. He ran a hand through his hair trying to brush away these inappropriate thoughts. She was the asset, his charge, and he couldn't let his feelings get in the way.

Turn off your damn feelings, man, whatever it takes. Maybe, if she couldn't stand me, it would make it easier. If being an ass means I can focus and keep her protected, then that's what I have to do.

Julian smiled at Scarlet broadly, pleased with how well she performed, and she smiled back. This metamorphosis mattered more to everyone in the room than Julian would ever know, more than he could ever fathom, but he would never find out why.

Fenton chewed the inside of his lip when he saw Scarlet look at him, the expression on her face a palpable mixture of consternation and foreboding, like a lamb preparing to walk into a lion's den. She looked entirely too vulnerable and it made him grip the edges of the desk as if the world were spinning, and he was afraid he would fall. As she looked up at him under her thick eye lashes, her face was a question, as if she was asking for his specific approval of her transformation. He rubbed the back of his neck uncomfortably and looked away.

Carter seemed to sense the electricity between them, and Fenton thought he glimpsed a small, satisfied smile flash across her pencil thin lips. He knew Carter would regard Scarlet's need for his approval as progress. It would mean they were one step closer to Scarlet obeying every one of his wishes and his wishes would ultimately be Carter's wishes. He promised himself he wouldn't let himself get distracted again by Scarlet. He would keep himself emotionally unavailable to her, no matter what.

"What do you think, Fenton?" Carter asked slyly.

"I don't think I'm the right person to ask," he said dryly, and saw Scarlet's face fall at his response.

"Come on, Fenton. Lighten up. Do you think she will pass for Robin?" Carter said, pushing him further.

"Yes, she'll do as Robin, almost an exact copy," he managed to say nonchalantly. Scarlet's face turned red as she was obviously expecting more. Carter scowled at him, and gave him a warning glance.

"I just prefer Scarlet, is all," he said in a low voice as he walked past Scarlet, and was rewarded with a smile lighting up her entire face. It made his insides turn to mush and all he wanted in that moment was to hold her in his arms and kiss those beautiful, plump lips. He reminded himself to ignore his thoughts. He moved to the opposite side of the room and perched himself on the end of the table, hoping the physical distance would help banish his growing feelings for her. He plastered a scowl on his face. *This is your new look, Fenton, get used to it.*

She was glowing in her red sequined gown, bright white teeth — a stark contrast to the deep hue of red lipstick, and emerald eyes glistening jubilantly as Julian continued to fawn over her. She cast a backwards glance at Fenton, and he could have sworn he saw her blush, which only tightened the coils wrapping around his heart. He dropped his gaze.

Carter started to usher Julian out of the room. He gave Robin a quick hug and a couple words of encouragement for the nonexistent pageant he thought they were preparing for, and moved to the hallway to settle payment with Carter. When she entered the room again, they started to talk logistics for going to Las Vegas.

"We are going to need you to fill out a psychological evaluation form for us. I often recommend it when I'm using people for undercover work who are not used to that type of high-pressured situation. I'll give you some time to fill in the questionnaire. Think through your answers, and I will have my internal team analyze the results." Carter noticed Scarlet's face scrunch with concern.

"Nothing to worry about, Scarlet," continued Carter. "I also took the liberty of utilizing Julian to help us rifle through Robin's clothing options from your apartment. With his input, we have a bag already packed for you for this first trip," she explained.

"A bag is already packed for me? Can I at least see what is inside? What do you mean by first trip?" Scarlet asked with hesitation, as she started to remove the large jeweled earrings with a hint of red, a perfect pairing for the flashy red dress which still adorned her body.

"Of course, I'll bring the bag over from the other room and you can take a look. There may, or may not, be the need for another trip to Vegas. I simply don't want to rule anything out at this time," Carter said dismissively, as she ducked into the adjoining room producing a large suitcase that Scarlet recognized as one of Robin's best pieces of luggage.

"Let me get the evaluation paperwork in order for you, one second," Carter said, and vanished into the other room again, leaving

Fenton and Scarlet with the overstuffed suitcase. Fenton raised an eyebrow as Scarlet carefully unzipped the long side and flipped open the canvas top. Inside, every outfit was in a separate plastic bag, complete with jewelry pairings and matching undergarments for each flashy combo. Scarlet sucked in a breath as she lifted bag after bag of showy gowns and seductive, yet more casual, evening outfits. Each bag showed a flash of lace with the different colors and styles of exotic matching bra and panty sets. Scarlet sighed as she held up a clear bag with a sage green dress inside complete with a plunging neckline and matching, barely-there, leopard print bra and panties. She flushed as she noticed Fenton keenly watching her.

"Welcome to Vegas, I guess, huh?" she said with a hint of a smile. Fenton grunted in reply. Carter walked back in, nodding with approval at the sight of the open and meticulously-ordered suitcase, and dropped a thick stack of papers on the desk in Scarlet's room.

"A little light paperwork for you tonight, Scarlet. I'm heading out. Fenton will, of course, be next door tonight if you need anything. Big flight tomorrow. I'll meet you in Vegas and we can prep your mic and equipment. It's show time. Just make sure to have that stack of papers completed in the morning and one of my agents will be by to collect it," Carter said as she tapped the huge stack of papers before waving a quick goodbye to gather her belongings in the other room. Scarlet and Fenton mumbled their goodbyes to her as she walked away.

"Yeah, welcome to Vegas is right," Fenton said looking at the mound of evaluation paperwork, and Scarlet winced.

"Well, I should let you get some sleep. Have a good night, Scarlet. Whoops, guess its Robin from here on out," he said with his arms folded. Scarlet turned toward him with a smile, and did her best Robin impersonation, giving him a wink and flashing her pearly whites. She looked like an exact replica of the Robin he saw in the photos. He was about to compliment her, but scolded himself again.

With a steely look on his face, he responded, "It's one thing to look the part, and another to act the part under pressure. Hope you're up for it," he said, and the hurt look that crossed her face winded him again. He left, going to his room and feeling like a scumbag his frosty remark to her.

It's for her own good, and for your sanity. She doesn't need to like you. She needs to trust you. Here's hoping she can keep it together, because if she lets her façade fall apart, then we are both as good as dead.

Chapter 22

"I may as well just book my room at the psychiatric facility now."

Scarlet boarded the plane, flawlessly walking through security as Robin, even though her nerves felt raw as she walked through the terminal. When Robin was murdered, her personal cell phone and purse were never recovered, which meant Carter's team at the FBI had to produce a new driver's license and credit cards all in Robin's name. Without a body, they made the police report confidential about her sister getting murdered, so if any curious outsider looked into whether or not Robin was alive or dead, they would find active credit cards and a person who looked to fit the part of Robin.

It felt surreal to Scarlet to have her first class ticket in hand in Robin's name. Looking at her belongings, it struck her that not a single object or piece of clothing was hers, it was all Robin's. Even the makeup in her bag, the purse she carried, the shoes she wore, the comb in her purse, nothing she had with her was actually something she would have chosen for herself. It was overkill perhaps, but when she tried to bring along a book she would enjoy reading, Carter dismissed the idea.

"Any thought of your previous life in this type of situation can be dangerous. Everything you see on this trip should make you feel like Robin, and Robin wouldn't read that book on the plane," Carter told her in a huff. After the conversation, Scarlet didn't ask to bring any of her own personal belongings with her. There was one item she managed to smuggle into the Robin purse at the last moment. It was something that had been tucked into a little pocket in her own purse that Agent Westbrook had retrieved from her duplex after her attack. It was a golden locket with the picture of her with Aunt Jo when she graduated college. Aunt Jo had a wide smile as she moved Scarlet's tassel away from her long straight red hair. Both had tears of joy in their eyes. It was a happy, candid shot which had quickly become her favorite. It was now her most prized possession, and she vowed to take it with her everywhere she went.

Fenton had prepped Scarlet before they got to the airport, saying he would be around and keeping an eye on her, but at a distance. He seemed different to her, cut off and curt, with his responses. She didn't know what changed from the day she talked with him at the hospital to now, but she definitely felt a shift, and it *bugged her*. She tried to clear her mind. She had more important things to worry about than why Fenton was turning into a bit of a bear. She busied herself with a magazine she bought from a vendor, one of the trashy gossip magazines she personally couldn't stand, but which Robin loved.

When she boarded the plane, she noticed Fenton a couple of rows behind her in first class. Their eyes locked for a moment, his face as stoic and hard as ever. She quickly looked away and went about her business as planned. She already knew which hotel to go to when she landed. He would have a larger adjoining room, which she would sleep in for safety at night, but they needed a room in her name to protect her cover. They explained to her, before she left, her room would be bugged and have hidden cameras as well. Agents Starr and Westbrook would see to that before they arrived. She continuously replayed the strategy in her mind on the flight. What they prepped her to say to Luca, how to say it, and all the other information they shoveled into her mind like coal stoking a speeding freight train, and she hoped it wouldn't eventually blow.

After the flight, she got into a cab followed by Fenton, to the hotel. She settled into the room, which was held in her name, and waited the appropriate amount of time before knocking on Fenton's door. He was located conveniently around the corner from her room. Agents Starr and Westbrook scouted the hotel before they arrived and found the blind spot for his hotel room door so she could come and go without any worry about surveillance. It was the hotel Fenton had picked, and it was laid out exactly as he described. When he opened the door, she thought his expression softened upon seeing her and was about to smile, but then his mood shifted. He glared at her, looking annoyed.

"I'm sorry, was I not supposed to come here now? I thought when we discussed the plan I was to meet you here as soon as we arrived. I can go back if this isn't the right time," she stammered, caught off guard by his peeved expression.

"No, it's fine. Come in. Let's get you set up with the mic." He had her sit on the bed and she could feel her palms beginning to sweat. She was shaking, not out of fear but how close he was crouched next to her. She could smell his masculine cologne, a soft woodsy scent with sweet undertones. She felt shy with his leaning over her in his simple black cotton tee clinging to a defined upper body. His skin was still tanned from his previous assignment revealing strong arms etched not from endless hours at the gym but from the physical demands of his dangerous job. She remembered the first time meeting him when his eyes locked with hers, guarding a quiet darkness, like an approaching storm. She caught herself staring at him, and looked away, trembling even more. She felt the brush of his skin against hers as he started placing the mic, wrapping his arm around her body to hide parts of the equipment. She jumped at his soft touch, the warmth of his hand radiating through her body.

"I can't put this on you if you're shaking," he said stiffly, and she reddened, biting her lip in shame.

He sighed. "Are you okay? If you're going to freak out, now is the time to do it. In here, not out there," he said, as he positioned the tiny camera in the elegant necklace he placed around her neck. She caught another glimpse of his eyes, and this time he lingered, scanning her face. Then with a confused expression, he stood back. She cleared her throat uncomfortably.

"I know it's silly," she began. "I think the adrenaline is making me crawl out of my skin or something. I'm fighting every urge I have to run out that door right now, and never look back. I can't though, because I have nowhere to go and no future if I turn back now. I have no choice but to embrace this attitude that I'm Robin in the flesh, and foster this feeling of ambivalence or anger if anyone were to doubt it. I need to push myself mentally to the other side of this tunnel and emerge as Robin, if there is anyway this is going to work. What happens if I go too deep? What happens if I compromise myself proving I'm her? If I don't pull this off, doing whatever it takes, there won't be a Scarlet to come back to anyway. Is that the way I should look at this, Fenton?"

She asked him plainly, with no preconceived notions of what he may say in return, with no judgements or anticipation. She felt odd saying the words. It didn't feel like her but, then again, nothing had felt familiar in the past several days.

He better not give me a snarky response. I need to hear something nice right now, even though he is the last person I should talk to if I want to hear something nice based on how he's responded lately.

He blinked and swallowed hard, leaning back in his chair, resting his hands on his knees. She thought she noticed his features change looking at her. She continued to stare at him in earnest, feeling the weight of what her question really meant. His eyes darkened as he came to some sort of inner conclusion, and she sensed him hesitate for a moment.

"I'm not the person to talk to about this, Scarlet," he said. She nodded.

"Look, I've got to take a walk or something. I can't stand being in this room another second."

"I can't let you leave."

"Then say something nice to me, say something to make me stay. I know this isn't your job, and I know I'm probably the least knowledgeable client you've ever had. I can tell you're annoyed with me, but please...can you just say something to me that will help me not crack? I know talking about emotions or weakness isn't your bag, but can you make an exception? Just this one time?" she said. She saw him flinch, his jaw clenched, and he scratched the back of his head debating something to himself.

"Okay. Um...jeez, Scarlet," he mumbled.

Screw this, I'm out of here. She shook her head, and grabbed her backpack. He moved in front of her path.

"Get out of my way. I have to leave," she said as she pushed past him toward the door. His strong hand caught her arm, causing her to whirl around to face him. This time the hardness was replaced with tenderness.

"Wait, Scarlet. Sit down." He took the backpack from her and led her back to a comfy chair. He took a deep breath, walking slowly around the room and explained

"Okay, survival often comes down to two basic instincts, fight or flight. In this situation, you can't run. There are terms and conditions you agreed to which involves this undercover work, which you know. That leaves only one choice: to fight. In some cases, it means you have to fight with yourself. I have known men and women who have done things to survive which they would never do in a normal situation, and in some cases, they have to do things they are not particularly proud to admit. I have to believe in the world's scale of judgement, there are things which won't be judged as harshly because isn't protecting your life one of the greatest charges we are given in this world? To be successful in this mission, you need everyone to think you're Robin to survive. If that means you have to go deep to the other side, so deep you're afraid you won't be able to find your way back again so even *you are convinced* you are Robin transformed, then that is what it takes to survive. You have to do what you have to do," he paused.

"That is your advice? To become certifiably insane because I need to believe I'm Robin? Great, I may as well just book my room at the psychiatric facility now. Maybe I can get a good view and my own bathroom. Thanks, Fenton, for nothing," she said, throwing her head back in the chair in exasperation, and running her hands through her curly mop of blond curls.

"Scarlet, these are the facts. I'm not here to candy coat reality for you. This may change you, Scarlet, and you have to know that. You may not be the same person you once were. You may never be the same, and you have to be okay with that before you make any decisions here today," he shot back.

"Is that why you are the way you are, cold, hard? Because you've gone through so many undercover assignments, you have to make sure you can't feel anything anymore?" He flinched at her stinging words.

"I try to get back to the core of who I am after each job, and you will do the same," He said gritting his teeth. His face hardened toward her and she noticed the set line of his brow, his steely gray eyes, the light stubble along his angular jaw, and even in the resting position, his training always gave him the appearance of a tiger lying in wait, ready to jump into action at a moment's notice. His fighter's physique, even while sitting, showed massive power, which she had seen in action in her apartment. He was everything she would have wanted if she were given the choice in who would protect her from a physicality standpoint, but it was abundantly clear he wanted nothing to do with this assignment. *Maybe he just wants nothing to do with me.*

Despite his sudden change in attitude toward her, she still felt guilty he was a part of this risky plan. She viewed him as a wild stallion that should be able to roam free and unburdened. The weight of cases like this showed around his eyes and mouth. There was a slight tightness there, and she wished to release him of the responsibility. She blinked hard before speaking, and took a deep breath.

"I don't think I can ever be the same anyway, with or without this undercover assignment. I know you're being blunt with the situation so I go to the extent needed to make this work. The moment I put on that dress, the red dress that Robin loved, I will become her. I won't be Scarlet in a red dress. I'll be Robin, in mind, body and spirit. I know that is what I have to do to survive no matter what it means for me," she said in barely a whisper. She saw his expression change again, and he rubbed the back of his neck deep in his own thoughts.

"I'll try to make this assignment as painless as possible for you, Fenton. Then you can get back to your real life." She tried to have the same unfeeling exterior as he did. *I won't let him see me break, or show this vulnerability again. He is a professional. Show him you can handle this responsibility.*

"You will have this earpiece in the whole time, Carter and I will give you prompts when you need them, so you won't be alone out there," Fenton said. He placed his hand on her arm, and the heat rushed through her limbs and up and down her spine. *Too bad the guy who has this type of effect on me, can't stand the fact he's stuck with me on this job.* She knew he meant his comment to be a confidence booster. What he didn't know, was she already felt alone.

After they tested the mic and camera in her sparkly necklace, they were ready to send her on her first task — to go to Robin's place of employment to retrieve the contents in her work locker. That is where they suspected her second phone was hidden. Scarlet took a cab to the events company located just off the Strip. Even though her hotel was technically in walking distance, it was easier for Westbrook and Starr to trail her in a surveillance vehicle this way and they didn't want to waste any extra time before the gala that night. She wore one of Julian's prepackaged outfits, a more casual, yet trendy, outfit better suited for daylight adventures. A pair of form-fitting jeans, a black blazer, and a slightly shimmery top, which could be dressed up or down for a night on the town or a relaxed day at the office. This outfit also came with apple red lipstick and large black shades.

She was prepped with the layout of the building on the interior. There would be swinging glass doors and a spiral staircase leading to an open office environment. Many of the other event planners wouldn't be in on a weekend day like this, especially with many evening events taking place up and down the Vegas Strip. She didn't expect to see too many people, but she knew names and faces if she were to run into anyone. Carter and Fenton were also in her ear in case she would get into any trouble.

She found the employee entrance to the break room, which led to another back room with rows of lockers.

"Remember Scarlet, Robin's locker is two hundred and three."

"Got it," Scarlet said under her breath, and started punching in the code that the team found in Robin's computer where she kept a list of active passwords and important numbers. She dialed the four-digit code, then yanked on the lock, but it didn't budge.

"Why isn't the locker code working?" she mumbled, just loud enough for the mic to pick up.

"Try it again, perhaps it didn't catch or is picky. Try dialing it very slowly this time," Carter's voice buzzed in her ear, and even though she said it with her typical confidence, Scarlet could detect an edge of worry. Scarlet plugged in the numbers again, and still the locker wouldn't open. The door to the locker space swung open behind her, and Scarlet swung around to see a smiley brunette walk into the room.

"Hi, Robin. Great to see you, I was wondering when you would be back. How did all the classes go out East? You just finished a quick semester, right?" the girl chirped. Scarlet's breath caught, and she froze.

Carter and Fenton were watching the live footage from a surveillance van a couple blocks away, and they could see the girl's warm expression start to waiver with concern as she regarded Scarlet with curiosity.

Scarlet heard Fenton's voice echo in her ear. "Easy, Scarlet. Pull it together, mind, body and spirit. Or was that just talk?" *What a punk, using my own words against me. Well I'll show him, I've got this.*

"Hi, Amy. Sorry, you really startled me for a second. I thought no one else would be in today. Ah, you know how it goes, more partying than actual school work gets done, but it was good. I was just grabbing a couple things before the event tonight. Once the event starts, you don't get a second to breathe, so I wanted to stop in quick now before I get pulled in a million directions. You know how it goes. I just totally forgot my combination to this stupid lock. I need some caffeine or maybe something stronger," Scarlet gave her best carefree Robin laugh, and Amy lit up in response.

"Yeah, I hear yah. They had us change them right before you left to go out east, so it doesn't surprise me you forgot. What a pain, right? You would think picking our own codes would be easier, but I forgot my passwords and locker combos all the time. Don't even sweat it. Hope it comes back to you. I just wanted to poke my head in and say hi. I have an event tonight too, so got to run. Great seeing you though, Robin!" Amy waved and smiled as she headed back to the main office from the employee locker room. Scarlet gave a sigh of relief.

"Good cover, sounds like the code just changed and Robin didn't update her new one in her computer. Any guesses as to what it could be?" Carter's voice came through the microphone sitting on the inside of Scarlet's ear.

"Huh, maybe her month and birthday, nope. Maybe the last four digits of her phone... no. Year we were born? Got it." Scarlet slid open the lock, and pulled the locker handle up to swing open the locker door.

Inside, she found clothing, badges, make up, a mirror, and a gym bag at the bottom of the locker. She opened it quickly to see the contents. She quietly voiced what she was seeing as well in case the mini video feed in her necklace wasn't catching the images.

"Cell phone, another laptop, and a file folder with more photos and documents. I think we hit the jackpot, more than we expected right?" Scarlet asked hopefully.

"Absolutely, clear out the whole locker and put it in the gym bag. Let's get you back to the hotel." Scarlet put everything in the bag and was walking down the spiral staircase when the front doors opened.

Walking through the doors to stand in the middle of the shiny tile floor was a suit-clad, hair-gelled, wide-smiled Luca Nero, in the flesh.

"Well are you just going to stand there, or are you going to say something? This might be the first time my girl is speechless, and you're wearing my favorite lipstick, Robin red. I told you with your looks and the way you pull off red, we could start an empire of products, but I guess we have enough business ventures going already, now don't we?" Luca Nero said, his voice smooth and deeply rich, like melting butter on a warm piece of bread.

"Robin, you're Robin! Say something." Carter's words commanded in Scarlet's head.

"Luca," Scarlet said breathlessly, and the moment she said his name like Robin would say his name she saw him in an entirely different light. Handsome by anyone's standards, hearing her say his name made him smile like a model in a cologne ad. Perfectly-formed teeth, dark features, and meticulously well-groomed. He manifested a dangerous edge with his direct gaze, but yet there was a playful charming side as well. Scarlet's legs carried her down the stairs, drawn to him as if he were calling her, and was rewarded with another grin as he picked her up and whirled her in circles. She laughed, as only Robin could laugh, carefree and giddy.

"Luca, put me down, anyone could see us," she laughed.

"Since when do you care about what people see? I've missed you," he said, leaning in and kissing her with a smoldering passionate kiss, lightly biting her lower lip.

Locking lips with Luca Nero, shit, what do I do? What do I do? Pretend he is someone else. Anyone else...like Fenton, Scarlet's inner voice yelled, and she gave him a fiery kiss back.

"I've missed you too, but what are you doing here? I thought we were meeting up at the gala tonight?"

"I had one of my associates keep an eye on your office today. I wanted to see you before the gala. I couldn't wait. He called me when you walked in, so I came out to personally welcome you back." He moved a hand possessively to her face, and cupped her neck in his hand.

"Did you get everything we discussed?" he said roughly, the scent of him wafting into her nostrils. His cologne was a powerful blend of manly fragrances, a commanding mix, just like every movement and glance commanded power as he stood in front of her.

"I had a complication. I can show you all of it later, but to make up for what I missed I have something extra I brought as well. I don't want to ruin the surprise, though. It will make more sense when I can lay everything out for you. I know you will be pleased though, Luca. We are well on our way, and you will be able to move forward with your plan," she purred at him and his eyes flashed. Another strong hand came up around the other side of her neck and he applied light pressure as he rubbed his thumbs over her ruby red lips while tightly holding her neck and jaw.

"I certainly hope you didn't disappoint me, Robin. Knowing your tenacity, you found a way to get me much of what we discussed, and I have to admit, I'm intrigued about this surprise. I can hardly wait. Make sure to wear your red dress, my beauty. If you brought me what I asked for, I would like to introduce you to a couple people tonight and I want you looking your best. You only get one chance to make a first impression, and you have certainly left an impression on me. This isn't the place to discuss more in detail of course. Make sure to meet me tonight at our arranged meeting spot. Don't keep me waiting, Robin. This better be one hell of a surprise, because you know how much I hate disappointment." He kissed her roughly, and walked back out into the Las Vegas heat.

Scarlet stood in the middle of the grand entryway, winded, and gasping for air. It took every ounce of her strength not to collapse on the floor, but her legs miraculously took her outside to where she hailed a cab.

"Don't say anything until you get to your hotel room, and don't go to Fenton's room. Go to your own room first. Obviously, he is having you watched and we don't want to draw any suspicion," Carter's voice echoed in her earpiece.

Scarlet said nothing, keeping her hands in tight fists the whole cab ride back to the hotel. Carter didn't say anything else either, even though both Carter and Fenton could clearly see Scarlet's hands visibly shaking through the camera lens.

Carter left the surveillance room to meet with Starr and Westbrook, finalizing details for the gala event that night. When Scarlet knocked on Fenton's door, he was in his room alone.

He opened the door, and Scarlet entered still wearing Robin's dark sunglasses, and wordlessly walked into the room to stand by his window.

"You did fine, Scarlet. We didn't expect him to show up at the event center, but the good news is you got your first meet out of the way. We will need you to run though the charts of faces and names again for tonight and we should use every moment we can for practice." Fenton crossed his arms, watching her from across the room, but leaving the distance between them. She nodded without a sound. She simply stared out the window and chewed the end of one of her long red fingernails. He moved a couple steps closer to her.

"Scarlet?" His eyes followed her, dissecting any nonverbal cues he could. She turned.

"You sounded just like her," he began, and was about to say something else, but she stared at him coldly.

"That is because *I am her*. I am Robin, remember? Whatever it takes," she said. Fenton reached out and removed the large dark sunglasses, revealing red puffy forest green eyes. He scanned her face, and she was pulled in to his gaze, before quickly snatching the glasses back.

"Are you going to talk to me, Scarlet? Or are you going to pout," he said. She shot him a cold glance, the red of her eyes burrowing into him.

"Carter told me about your background, and about reading people. I don't need to tell you anything, right? You can probably read it all over my face," she said as she curled into a ball in a chair in the corner of the room. He continued to stare at her in silence.

"I'm sure you have better things to do than babysit me. I release you. Go do whatever you do somewhere else," she said.

"Look, Scarlet, I'm tough with you because I have to be. I know it was rough out there today for you, and I'm not judging you. I know you have to be brave outside of these walls, but you don't have to be brave in here with me," he said, just loud enough for her to hear. She buried her head in her hands. He brought her a blanket, pulling it around her shoulders.

She hid her face in the blanket, sobbing openly. He sat on the edge of the bed, in silence, arms folded. When she stood up, she was slightly off balance, and he held out an arm to steady her.

"What can I get you?" he asked.

"Nothing, I'm fine."

"Yeah, you look fine."

"I don't need condescending comments like that, Fenton."

"What do you need?"

"You're not my shrink."

"No, but I need you to be solid out there. That's my job. It won't do either of us any good if guns are pulled and someone gets shot."

"Don't remind me. I feel like I'm going to be sick."

"Take deep breaths, in and out. You're getting all worked up, and are going to hyperventilate if you're not careful.

"I'm working myself up? What a misogynistic thing to say. Yeah, it's all me. It has nothing to do with the fact I have to pretend to be in love with the devil's spawn. Has nothing at all to do with the fact that whenever I look in the mirror, I see my dead sister staring back at me. Nope, it's just me, working myself up, just a typical girl."

"That's not what I meant, Scarlet, you're being dramatic. I just don't want you to make it worse for yourself. That's it."

"Worse for myself? There you go again," she said, as she tried to storm off to the bathroom her blanket caught the chair causing her to trip forward. Fenton reached out to stop her from tumbling to the ground. He held both her arms securely in his strong arms, and she looked up at him in surprise, breath ragged.

"Easy, Scarlet. I'm not the enemy," he said barely above a whisper, looking down at her.

"Yeah, maybe."

"I need you to trust me, Scarlet, I'm here to make sure you're safe. Period. Even if it means taking a bullet for you. I'm going to be tough on you, because I want to avoid that outcome. I'm disciplined, so I'm going to ask a lot from you, but at the end of the day, it is only to keep you safe. That being said, I'm also human, and I understand what you're going through. If I could turn the tables, if I could take your place out there, I would. I know you have no reason to believe me, I know you think I'm a bit of a jerk, but I would do it in a heartbeat." He was still holding her steady, and she wordlessly sunk into him, resting her head on his chest. He stood paralyzed for a moment, but then his arms wrapped around her as well, their heartbeats melding into one synchronized rhythm as she clung to him.

She clung to him as if to pull herself from some oubliette of loneliness and despair. She clung to him as if he were the only person left in the world, as if holding him tightly would stop time from marching forward and she would forever be protected in this pocket of the present — safe from what the future would hold.

He held her until her tears stopped and the periodic sobs disappeared.

She knew Fenton would turn back into the man of few words, cold and deliberate, focused and unfeeling, but for a moment in his arms, she felt protected. For a fleeting moment, she felt he actually cared and that would be the feeling she would use to propel her forward further into the darkness.

She eventually left the hotel room, as wordlessly as she came in, to put on the obligatory red dress which was Luca's favorite in preparation for a gala she wished would never happen.

Chapter 23

"Great, another person in the picture we know nothing about."

A knock at their adjoining door told Carter Agent Starr was finished prepping Scarlet with the correct surveillance equipment for the night. Carter flashed a look at the monitors on her desk, and she was starting to see a live feed from the necklace around Scarlet's neck, which displayed the hotel room. Fenton rose from his chair to open the door. *Am I going crazy, or does he look nervous?*

"We are all set, Carter," Agent Starr said, entering the room. "Agent Westbrook and I will be in the room on the main floor watching as well. We have our headsets and gear set up, and Westbrook just texted me he is getting the feed and visuals loud and clear. We will start recording as soon as she enters the main ballroom area of the gala." Carter nodded and Agent Starr mouthed "Good luck" to Scarlet as she left to go to her post.

Scarlet walked in the room and Carter couldn't help but beam back at her. The wide grin on Carter's face was nothing short of pride and accomplishment. She didn't think it could be done and she had her moments of doubt, but undeniably there was Robin standing before them. Of course, having professional hair and makeup with Julian didn't hurt, but she thought Scarlet had never looked so radiant.

Julian was right about one thing: she certainly could pass as being a beauty pageant contestant competing for a national crown. Out of the corner of her eye, Carter snuck a glimpse of Fenton and he seemed a shade paler than usual, his expression carefully blank.

"You certainly fit the part, Scarlet," said Carter. "We are ready. You will head down to the gala, and when Luca is ready to discuss the documents, you will just need to go to the front desk and ask for the large envelope which is in the hotel safe. Remember, your safe word is Espresso. You could say you would love a shot of espresso, or you could really use a shot of espresso, and once we hear the word, we would know to send an agent in because you're in trouble. The only other way we would send someone in is if we noticed physical danger, otherwise we will go in at your command. Of course, we will have eyes and ears on you the whole time, and will feed you information or lines if you get stuck. You'll do just fine, Scarlet. We have prepped for this event and you're ready. Do you have any questions for us before you head down?"

"No, nothing else comes to mind. Let's get this over with," Scarlet said, and mustered a smile.

"Make us proud out there, and don't forget how to steer the conversation like we discussed. There are certain confirmations we need Luca, and other family members, to say on camera for this to be useful evidence for our case. Make sure you're careful, we need you to have your wits about you. If you need to drink in a situation, ask the bartender for soda water with a lime in a clear glass. It will look like you're drinking a cocktail." Carter was satisfied when Scarlet nodded, and Fenton walked her to the door. Carter pulled her headset on and told Starr and Westbrook the asset was in the hallway, preparing them for her imminent arrival at the grand staircase leading down to the ballroom, which was the entrance of the Nero family gala. Fenton came back to the table and put on his headset and took his seat next to Carter.

"We will be live in a couple minutes. You think our girl is ready to do this?" she asked Fenton.

"I can't imagine what this is like for her, especially with how she looked tonight. Geez, it was like seeing Robin alive again from their home videos. I'm still concerned about a couple of the details, but by judging with how well she did with Luca at their first meeting, I think if she can stay strong, she could pull this off. The only problem is this isn't just Luca in a room, this is a crowd of people and the high-powered Nero crime family. I'm worried about how Luca is going to take the news that we don't have all the documents, and worried about the hordes of people we need to fool tonight," he said.

"Well, that's what I'm paying you for, Fenton. I'm paying you to worry, because that's when you're the sharpest. You've shown me time and time again since I first met you ten years ago when you were deep undercover. I know you haven't forgotten your first assignment. You proved to me then you are the best. Worry about the logistics, and I'll take care of the execution. Here we go. She is coming up to the stairs, no turning back now," Carter said as she felt the familiar rush of adrenaline hitting her bloodstream and giving her an extra edge of alertness. She lived for these kinds of moments, because if everything went as planned, she would be one step closer to bringing down members of one of the most powerful crime families in existence. She could imagine her name in gold letters on a plaque hanging at FBI quarters, and shaking hands with her superiors and everyone who ever doubted she could make a difference. This wouldn't simply make a little splash if she pulled this off. It would create a tsunami which would rock this nation from coast to coast, and she would be the one at the top of it, riding the glorious waves.

Carter watched the camera as Scarlet descended the large, winding staircase to the luxuriously decorated interior of the enormous hotel. Lights and gold decorations warmed the expansive entryway, and a huge diamond chandelier crowned the room.

Fenton coughed as he gripped the edge of the table. His knuckles turned white. She chose not to comment on his ridged posture. She had worked a number of undercover and private security jobs with him. She couldn't remember another job where he was this on edge.

A vast array of people dressed in their finest cocktail attire started to come into view on their screen. Scarlet paused on the stairs, observing the immense crowd.

"It's okay, Scarlet, it's a big turnout, but without Luca on your arm, those in the room may only recognize you as part of the event staff. You don't have to talk to anyone else right now, just keep an eye out for Luca. The others can wait," Carter said in a reassuring tone in the microphone.

Scarlet started making her way through the crowd and the lavishly dressed women and men parted for her like the Red Sea. Fenton and Carter could see people's reactions as the hidden camera caught their expressions. She was stunning, the belle of the ball, and women and men alike noticed her as she walked by. Even though the room was filled with attractive young people, there was an enigmatic spark to Scarlet, a luminous glow moving radiantly, yet resolutely, through the crowd. Luca came into view as the crowd parted.

Luca's jet black hair was slicked back with gel, and he wore a white tailored suit with black cuffs. It was a modern look, flattering his broad shoulders and fit form. The stark contrast emphasized his olive skin and dark coloring. They could hear Scarlet inhale quickly, obviously struck by how handsome Luca looked.

"I wonder if he smells as good as he looks. No wonder Robin fell for this guy," Carter said to Fenton as she watched the scene unfold on a little table top television monitor and covered her mic so it would be a private comment. Fenton only glared back. *Jealous much, Fenton? Geez, lighten up.*

"Robin, my dear, you look simply ravishing. How could a guy get so lucky?" Luca said in a voice as smooth as silk, and kissed her lightly on the cheek.

"Luca, you clean up rather well yourself. That suit looks like it was made just for you," Scarlet purred back at him.

"That's because it *was* made just for me. Only the best for my first night out with my girl since returning to this great Strip of ours," he said, and Scarlet laughed in response.

"Let me grab you a drink and then we can get the business out of the way so we can enjoy ourselves. I have some people I want to introduce you to as well. What can I get you from the bar?" He placed his hand lightly on her back, moving closer and guiding her to a spot off the main floor.

"Surprise me," she said in a low voice, and he smiled. As he was grabbing their drinks, Scarlet pivoted in her spot to catch a wider view of the room for Carter and Fenton. They began to notice other members of the Nero family the task force had been watching closely the past several years. Alonzo Nero, Gabriel Nero, Federico Nero, and some of the other capos and successful foot soldiers mixed in with the rich and famous. The rest were invitees who were lucky enough to receive the highly sought-after invite from a family known for their opulence and affluence in the community, and most notably known for their lavish parties in true Vegas fashion up and down the Strip. Some of their high rollers were at the party as well, those who gambled at their tables, or knew people of power who aided the family in some way.

From the TV screen on the table, Carter and Fenton watch as Luca glided back to Scarlet and handed her a long stemmed glass of champagne.

"Something sweet for my sweet," he said with a wink, and she took it with ease, her hand shaking at the bottom of the screen as they watched, but she quickly managed to control her nerves and move with Luca off the ballroom floor to a hallway taking them to the front desk.

"The lady would like to retrieve a package from the hotel safe, if you would, under the name Robin Matthews," Luca said to the hotel concierge, who bobbed his head and bowed.

"Yes, of course, Mr. Nero. Right away, sir," he said, and jumped to retrieve the package. He came back with a long envelope wrapped in thick packing tape to dissuade anyone from even attempting to open its contents.

"By the way Patrick, I've said it before, *Mr. Nero* is my father. You can call me Luca."

"Yes, sir. Very good, sir. I'll try to remember, sir," Patrick said with a big smile. Carter, watching the scene, shot a glance at Fenton. He was looking at the screen with a furious expression on his face, like a rabid dog ready to pounce.

"Lighten up, Fenton. He hasn't even tried anything yet. Hell, I'm even starting to like the guy. Charm and class, suave and debonair – looks like he walked right out of a spy thriller, and nice to the staff at his family's hotel to boot. Where's the Jekyll to this guy's Mr. Hyde routine?" Carter mused.

"Just give it time. Even a tiger can look like an innocent kitty cat until you throw a piece of meat in its path. Our girl is unfortunately the prey. I don't feel comfortable about this, Carter," Fenton answered as he leaned back in his chair and rubbed the back of his neck. Carter noticed he was starting to look tired.

"Have you been sleeping, Fenton? I've been keeping close tabs on the girl's wellbeing, making sure she can keep it together. I don't have to start looking out for you too now, do I?" she asked, half kidding.

"Nah, I'm fine. I'll be better when this little skit is over and she is back in her hotel room, alone," he replied. Carter was about to press him, but Luca and Scarlet were headed to a back room behind the front desk, where Luca punched in a code to enter a private elevator. The elevator quickly took them to the top floor, which opened to a huge, lavish office space with a rich oval wooden conference table. The room was lit with a soft, bluish glow, and the floor to ceiling windows showcased the lights of the Strip, which added all the extra light they could possibly want. There was a bar in the room with diamond-encrusted crystal decanters, filled with every top shelf liquor imaginable. The room completely encapsulated the Vegas life with rich colors and flashy designs. Scarlet stepped out of the elevator, and Luca described the design of the conference room with an eminent Vegas designer when Carter noticed a shadow in the background.

"There is someone in the corner of the room, do you see that?" Carter asked Fenton under her breath.

"Scarlet, there is someone else in the room," Fenton said in a low voice into the microphone, so Scarlet could hear.

"Jeez, Fenton. That was just meant for you, I don't want to freak her out," Carter hissed, covering her mic.

"That's part of my job, if there is someone else in the room lurking in the shadows you better believe I'm going to tell her about it. I have half a mind to storm up there myself," he spat.

"Cool your jets, cowboy. You don't have the elevator code, remember? Plus, we don't know who it is yet. If you, or one of my agents, goes charging up there, this whole gig is up, do you understand? All of this work, all of this time, all of the preparation — for nothing. Keep in mind, if this falls through, our deal is off. Remember our deal? Plus, she has the safe word. Let her do her job," Carter replied back cheekily.

"Luca, I think someone else is here with us," Scarlet said, breaking up the conversation between Carter and Fenton, and Luca stopped his explanation of the room décor and met her concern with a smooth smile.

"I was going to wait to introduce you. She was simply being polite in letting me finish the quick tour. I invited my sister, Eleonora to join us, to review the treasures you worked so hard to secure. Eleonora, I would like you to meet Robin," Luca said and gestured for her to step forward. Drink in a hand, a voluptuous, raven-haired beauty stepped forward in a sparkling blue dress similar in style to Robin's. She was adorned in jewels, and her dark Italian coloring matched Luca's. Her raven-colored eyes were lightened a little with shimmery eye shadow and only her high heels made a sound as she approached the table toward them.

"That's Eleonora, we finally have a visual on her," Carter gasped.

"Great, another person in the picture we know nothing about," Fenton growled back.

"Such a pleasure to finally meet you, Eleonora. I hope what I have to share is up to your expectations as well," Scarlet said pleasantly.

"My brother speaks fondly of you, Robin. I hope we can become fast friends. I have to admit, I'm curious to see what you've brought us here today." She smiled back, but the warmth of the smile did not reach her eyes, which seemed to have a cold edge as she scanned

Robin's face.

"Let's get right down to it then," Luca said, as he ripped open the packaging and started to display the documents Carter's team worked hard to sift through and explain in detail to Scarlet.

The hotel room where Carter and Fenton sat was eerily still, as if both stopped breathing when Luca asked Scarlet to go through the materials. Carter cast a sideways glance and raised an eyebrow as Scarlet confidently went through the documents' details — names of several key foot soldiers in the Durante family who did the dirty work and ran money-making schemes for the family. She also laid out documents detailing shipment schedules.

Powerful information for the Nero family, because if they wanted to do some damage they could take out some of the key soldiers, or have them watched to get a better sense of their business. If they chose to try to infiltrate the family from the inside, it would be helpful to get one of the soldiers to turn, which would be a real prize as crime families operated heavily on loyalty. The Neros could target major shipments and take the supplies, which would impact the Durante family's abilities to make good on their shipment promises while hitting their bottom line.

Some of the documents entailed several safe locations where large amounts of money were stored in various locations on the East Coast, even though they held large amounts of money in foreign bank accounts, they still needed liquid assets readily at hand and there were several key locations where that money and gold were stored. *Disrupt the money, and any organization could crumble.*

Scarlet flawlessly explained all of this, but faltered a little when she confessed she was unable to get the political figures names off the computer in time, as well as their money laundering sites.

"Can I talk to you a second over here, Robin?" Luca said, his face scrunched in concern. Carter and Fenton watched the video screen, which showed Luca pulling Scarlet away from the table where Eleonora stood reviewing the papers.

"What do you mean you couldn't get the politicians' names? I need to know which senators have the docks and unions in their back pockets. There are too many names tied to the committee on commerce, science, and transportation to guess who has influence. I need to know if there is someone on the appropriations committee, maybe they are able to maneuver behind the scenes motivated by threats to redistribute funds. They could even sit on the committee of foreign relations. We know they have a couple key players knee-deep in the politics game, and you didn't bring me anything? That was the crown jewel that would cause my father to bow before me." Luca's typical calm demeanor was starting to crack as he scanned Scarlet's face. Fenton was starting to tense watching Luca unravel, just as Carter jabbed him in the ribs and pointed at the screen.

"Do you see Eleonora in the background? Scarlet is looking right at Luca, but the camera is still catching his sister. She is taking *pictures* of the documents with her cell phone. There is something going on here, Fenton. I just don't know what yet. Eleonora has remained off the grid within the family. We haven't caught her on any previous surveillance or stakeouts. We need to make sure we contain the information. We anticipated Scarlet acting as Robin would ensure we would be alerted to any action taken by the family through Luca. We want to avoid collateral damage, but if another member of the family has the information, this is going to become more difficult to contain the situation," Carter said breathlessly.

"Remember the backup plan, Scarlet. The positive spin we put on missing some of the information," Fenton prompted into the microphone. Scarlet picked up the cue, and started to go into the made-up scenario that Carter's team devised about the Durantes wanting to send a high-ranking leader to meet and discuss the business opportunities at the casinos.

"They are incredibly interested, so much so, they are willing to send one of their advisors to meet with someone of your choosing to discuss in more detail. This is another tool you can use against them," Scarlet explained, and Eleonora perked up overhearing their conversation.

"Interesting turn of events, Luca. You don't have everything you were looking for, but I think your girl still did a wonderful job. She already explained she was at risk to be discovered and that wouldn't have done anyone any good, don't you agree? Come on brother, have another drink and let's go and enjoy the rest of the party. Robin, it was absolutely a pleasure, but I must be getting back to our guests. I suggest you do the same, Luca," Eleonora said evenly, and seemed anxious to get back to the main ballroom area.

"I'll be fine, Eleonora. I'm calm as can be. You head back, we will be out shortly," he said in response, and Eleonora left to return to the party.

"Are you happy with what I retrieved for you, Luca?" she asked.

"Yes, but I still need the names of the politicians they are working with as well as their money laundering sites. We will have plenty of time to discuss what we do with all of this information once I have a chance to review everything in more detail. I have a little something for you for all of your hard work. Come here." He grabbed her hand and walked her into the adjoining room. There on the glass table were too long lines of white powder. Carter flinched at the sight of the drugs.

"Go ahead, Robin. Here is part of your reward." He motioned to her to take a sniff of a line of cocaine on the table.

"Luca, you were going to introduce me to your father and other important people tonight. Something could come up from an event standpoint I need to deal with, so I think it's better if I stay clear-headed," she said, thrown by the sight of the drugs in front of her.

Luca's eyes darkened.

"The Robin I know couldn't resist a slide down the white way. What's the matter with you? You didn't bring everything we agreed on, you've been acting strange all day, and now you're passing on your favorite poison? You haven't called me 'Baby' once since you've been back. It's like you didn't even miss me. Is there something you're not telling me, Robin? Did you get pinched by the Durantes? Did they turn you against me?" His voice turned into a snarl as his accusations became more serious. He gripped both of Scarlet's arms, tight enough to leave whitish imprints on them which quickly turned red after she squirmed away. Carter knew she had to jump in and say something.

"React like a girlfriend, Scarlet. Get offended, become irate, but more importantly become pissed at how he is treating you after everything you've done for him. *Do it* Scarlet, he will respond to strength," Carter said into the microphone, as she kept a hand on Fenton's shoulder. He looked like he was about to charge out of the room after them.

"How dare you say that to me? You want to know what is wrong? I got this close to getting caught, this close!" She said shoving her fingers into his face to emphasize the inch of distance with her finger and thumb.

"I've been on edge since then, I admit. Everything could have ended for me, it would have been over, you understand? My life flashed before my eyes, and I barely escaped. Then, after everything I risked to bring you what I could, shedding blood, sweat, and tears along the way, it's still not good enough for you. You have your sister lurking in a corner of the room, you didn't even tell me she would be here, and now I get interrogated. Yes, I want to snort both of those lines right now, but I'm not going to. You know why? I'm already a nervous wreck. If I add drugs to the mix, I'm afraid I'll jump right out of my skin. I'm supposed to meet members of your family on top of it all, which is enough pressure for any girl under normal circumstances. I've missed you like crazy, Baby, but I've been sick knowing I let you down. Won't your father be pleased with everything we have here? Your disappointment is crystal clear. It's written on your face, and it's a little tough to handle. I must have been away from you too long this time. I feel like everything is half a step away from where it should be with us. I know it's important to you to impress your father, but you're jeopardizing us in the process, and that's one hell of a bad feeling," Scarlet fumed, and Luca's face softened.

"Aw, Baby, I'm not disappointed in you. You did me proud. We just need a little more, and then it will be perfect. Here, just have a little, and you'll feel better." He dipped his finger in the white substance and held it out for her to sniff.

"Luca, I can't," she began, but he put the scoop of white powder over his teeth and pulled Scarlet's face forward with both hands for a passionate kiss. She muffled moans of surprise as he continued to hold her lips to his, kissing deeper, until finally releasing her. She pulled back, and he wore a wide grin on his face.

"You just need to loosen up a little, baby. Let's go back down to the party. I want to introduce you to some people. We can discuss this more later." He pulled his arm around her neck, and led her back to the private elevator to go downstairs. Fenton's chest heaved and the irate expression on his face made him look like he was going to kill the first person he saw.

Carter watched the screen as Scarlet wiped her hand over her lip. A white residue remained on her hand. There was nothing either of them could do about it, but they both knew Scarlet was most likely already feeling the effects of Luca's poisonous kiss.

Chapter 24

"Men have lost fingers for less."

Carlo pulled into the lot of a hole-in-the-wall breakfast joint, next to a small doughnut shop. There were a couple of small shops off a two-lane highway, where truckers and travelers stopped, but not many others. The paint was chipping from the buildings, and the staff looked as worn as the buildings themselves — both in need of repair. Carlo grabbed a box of doughnuts from a disgruntled woman in her fifties, anxiously waiting her next cigarette break, and wearing a faded apron and scuffed white sneakers. Bringing the box unopened back to his car, he sat in the driver's seat and waited. He soon saw Darius's old clunker pull into the lot. He rolled down his window.

"You ready to grab breakfast?" Darius said, with an eager smile on his face which created an extra roundness to his cheeks.

"Change of plans, hop in."

"Change of plans? Why did you make me drive out to this diner if you aren't going to let me get breakfast? I could have just met you at the office instead," he said and got out of his car, his face turning an angry red.

"Come off it, Darius. I got you doughnuts. We just got a job, so we have to run. Quit your whining and get in."

"Okay, Carlo." The mention of doughnuts perked him up again, and he squeezed himself into the passenger seat. He pulled back the top displaying a colorful assortment of doughnuts oozing jelly at the sides. Carlo was pleased the treat accomplished exactly what he was hoping for, a quiet ride to the long alleyway where he stopped the car.

"What are we doing here, Carlo?"

"I got word a working girl had some news for us. Insight into a business opportunity for the family. She said she would wait behind those two dumpsters. She already has cops picking her up whenever they see her for selling her services, so she wanted to stay hidden until we arrive. Why don't you walk over there and see if she is waiting for us?" Carlo said.

"Really? I'm just finishing this doughnut."

"For fuck's sake, bring the doughnut with you and hurry up. I don't have all day," Carlo said. Darius pulled himself out of the car, carrying an oily raspberry doughnut with sprinkles, and Carlo quietly got out after him. Darius strode up to the dumpsters and peered around both large metal bins.

"I don't see nothing, Carlo. Maybe we are too early?"

"Look around that one again, I think I see something," Carlo said, pulling out his silver barreled gun with silencer attached. Darius turned his back to Carlo, peering around the corner. Carlo aimed his gun and slowly pulled the trigger.

Darius crumpled to the ground, his face smooshing into the

pavement. His mouth was open, filled with doughnut remnants, and sprinkles layered the pavement. Carlo knew he would shoot him in the back of the head, like a dog, because from the point of view of the family, Darius had betrayed them. He needed to learn to keep his mouth shut, so that was the way he would die, with his mouth filled with his last meal and never seeing what was coming for him.

"Take care buddy. Hope you enjoyed the doughnuts," Carlo said as he stared down at his old trainee. He holstered his gun and walked back to his car alone. He pulled out his cellphone and found Percussion Pete in his contacts.

"Pete? How the hell are yah? Yeah, fine, thanks. Say, I've got a job for you. I think your unique skill set is exactly what is needed on this one. If I can meet you on price would you be in? Okay great, Pete, I'll be in touch soon." Carlo's thoughts went back to the high security vineyard, and then to the vacant lot — a lot perfectly designed for the type of work he would need to do, to secure his place in the family — an abandoned lot where no one would be around to hear someone scream.

Eleonora Nero kept a watchful gaze around the ballroom floor as she was looking for someone in particular, but she wanted to keep a low profile. Eventually, she found who she was seeking – her brother Alonzo, schmoozing a group of glamorously-attired women wearing more precious stones and diamonds than most people see in their lifetime. She wrote a note on a hotel napkin, and told a waiter to bring the message to her brother.

"I don't care if he tells you he is busy, tell him it is an urgent message, and he needs to read it immediately," Eleonora said in a low, raspy voice to a wide-eyed waiter who couldn't believe she just pushed a hundred-dollar bill into his hand for the small request.

"Yes, Miss, right away, Miss," he stumbled on his words, and she smiled back politely. She didn't even want to risk the chance of anyone seeing her speak to Alonzo before their meet. She leaned against an intricately decorated pillar in the ballroom, her blue dazzling dress in perfect contrast to her crow black hair, with her favorite white ice diamonds delicately sitting around her neck. She watched in amusement as Alonzo tried to brush the waiter off, but the waiter stood his ground as Eleonora had asked. Alonzo was forced to look at the note in the napkin or risk unnecessarily making a scene in front of his giggly female guests.

Meet me in the back office in 10 minutes and don't be late, unless you are willing to make the biggest mistake of your life- Eleonora

She knew it was a risky note, but Alonzo only responded to risky situations. Otherwise, it was tough to get her oversized gladiator brother to take notice. He was too busy either enforcing his will or enjoying his precious gym time and steroid use. In his mind, bigger was always better, and more was not quite enough. He was a man of extremes, which was what she counted on with her carefully-devised plan. She made her way slowly to the back office, grabbing another glistening glass of wine from one of the many wait staff on the way. She perched herself on the edge of a desk, and waited, forcing her heart to stop pounding loudly for fear it would give her away.

When Alonzo busted through the door, his face was slightly flushed, which meant he was enjoying the spirits of the night. She wondered if alcohol was the only thing he dabbled in that evening. The irises of his eyes looked larger than normal for the lighting of the room, but she wouldn't let it concern her. If he was on cocaine or another substance, it would only *help* aid her plan.

"You have some nerve interrupting me while I was entertaining, Eleonora. You're lucky you are my only sister. Men have lost fingers for less," he growled. The charming façade he had on moments earlier in the crowd of smiling faces was gone, and the real beast below the mask appeared in front of her now.

"You will eat your words in one second, my dear brother. Before I tell you why you *love* me, and before you start *kissing* the ground I walk on, you need to promise me one thing: You cannot say a word of this to anyone else. The moment you leave this room, this conversation never took place despite how angered you may be, and if you choose to take action, you must do it yourself. You cannot send anyone in your place because it would leave us all open for risk. Those are my terms. If you disagree, you will regret your decision tomorrow, and, as I mentioned earlier, it will be the biggest mistake you have made in your entire life. That being said, my dearest brother, it is *your* decision to make. If you agree to my terms, I will fill you in on a surprisingly juicy secret which will forever solidify *you* as the heir to this family's throne." She could see him licking his lips as he listened carefully to her words, but her selling wasn't done yet.

"*But,* I want your assurance I will have a position of power in this family when you take control. When I tell you what I know, you will see clearly my allegiance is to you, and what a useful allegiance it will turn out to be for both of us. If you do not agree, or you do not believe me, then I will leave here not telling you a single word of what I know and you will wake up tomorrow morning having lost all the power you once held in this family. Do we have a deal, or should I go back and enjoy myself at the party?" She raised an eyebrow at him as she calmly took a sip of her wine. She was challenging him in the only way she knew how. It was a constant game of poker, and she had to play her opponent. He crossed his arms and a slow smile spread across his blockish head. She knew she had piqued his interest.

"Well, Eleonora, I have to admit, you put it in such a way I am entirely too curious to walk out of this room now. Your requests are interesting. I could try to force the information out of you, but I have a feeling that wouldn't do either of us any good. Your payment for this information is your security and position of power within the family. Telling me about information which could either *ruin* or *make* me does not come without a price. Yet, I cannot fault you for that my lovely sister, because it only shows you have place in this business because that is how a *businessman* thinks. It is not an entirely unreasonable request. You have my word on our dead mother's grave I will agree and abide by all of your terms. Keep in mind though, Eleonora, if this information disappoints or if you have led me astray in some way, I will come after you with such vengeance you will wish I would have killed you here today instead of facing what I would have in store for you." He lifted his palms up with a smile, as a gesture of agreement and encouragement for her to tell her story.

"Ha, dear brother. Just like a shrewd businessman. I would never knowingly walk into a deal with the devil, unless I knew what I had was greater than any possible hellfire he could bring down on me." She smiled back at him sweetly.

"Very good, Eleonora. We will make a good pairing, you and I. What is this life changing news that was worth pulling me away from such a titillating party?" he chuckled, his lips turning into a smiling sneer.

"Our brother, Luca, has been a busy and naughty boy," Eleonora began, and filled her brother in on all the details regarding the information he was gathering from an inside source within the Durante crime family. A story that pulled in mostly truths, she only lied about Robin because it didn't help her plan.

"If you don't believe me dear brother, I took photos on my phone of some of the documents he showed me directly. Not only that, but he has more information coming by a messenger *directly* from the Durante crime family, and he is meeting this person at two in the morning after the party *tonight*," she said emphatically, the lies spewing from her mouth easier than the truth ever did.

"Let me explain, Alonzo. Luca's plan is to show all of the information he gathered on our rivals to Father to secure his place in this family. He even suckered a member of the Durante family into a meeting tonight. He is going to find out which political figures they work with who help push less-restricted shipping regulations in exchange for getting into the casino racket. The Durantes have no idea he gathered all this other information on their family such as when their shipments come in, where their safes are, access to information on their personal computers such as intel as to who works for them and where. I am giving you the opportunity brother, and with my help you will be able to present all of this information to Father instead of Luca. I can stall Luca and you can meet with the contact tonight instead. When Luca finally leaves, you would have already gathered the last remaining pieces and I'll grab the file. While Luca is sitting there in the dark wondering why the Durante contact is detained, you can approach Father with all of this information before Luca even knows what is going on." She looked at him and he was listening, an intrigued expression on his face.

"Father will be so impressed he will insist you start running the family. He will also want to make sure you are a large part of the decision-making process regarding what to do with this wealth of information against our main competitor. You, in our father's eyes, *single-handedly* changed the future and nature of this family's business. There will undoubtedly be some bloodshed when you decide how to attack them, but we both know you are the man for that task, not Luca."

"What if Luca claims we stole the information?"

"If Luca tries to rat you out, I can verify your story, and it would be his word against yours and Father would always take your side. Plus, Luca won't have this new information. He won't have the folder with all the other information he gathered because I'll snag it when he leaves, so the evidence won't support his allegation he was the one behind this genius plan. You can't lose, but you have to act quickly because I know the location of the meet. If you want me to distract Luca, I need to know now to put the plan into action."

He nodded.

"Was I not accurate in saying you would love me after you heard everything I had to tell you? Am I not the best sister ever? But, keep in mind dear brother, you promised not to say anything to anyone, even though your blood is boiling at Luca's plan to take you out of the picture. You simply need to go to the meet, and from that meet, everything will beautifully fall into place." Eleonora took another slow sip of her wine, her eyes twinkling as her brother looked at her in awe.

She delighted in her private knowledge the fake meet she just told him was too easy to sell, nuggets of truth rooted in complete nonsense. There was a newfound respect in the way he looked at her.

It's nice to see that type of respect from my apish brother. It is certainly a shame I won't be able to see that look in his eyes for years to come.

"I keep my promises, Eleonora. You did good telling me this and I will reward you. You will be revered as a queen in this family. It is just past midnight and I need to prepare for this meeting."

"I have the location and instructions written on this piece of paper. Follow them exactly, because that is how the Durante contact will know it is safe to approach you. Don't breathe a word of this to anyone. Everyone else must think you are still at the party. The party will easily run well into the daylight hours, and you will be back before anyone knows you're gone."

"Okay, I will contact you when I get there."

"No, don't contact me until you have the new information and the meet is complete. That way I will know it is safe to let Luca leave. That is the only way we can ensure he is detained long enough for our plan to work."

"I think we have a bright future in front of us, Eleonora. Enjoy the party, and make sure Luca stays here."

"Oh I wouldn't dream of letting him leave. Godspeed, Alonzo," Eleonora said, and a slow and confident grin spread across her face.

At two in the morning, Alonzo pulled into a lookout spot only thirty minutes away from the Las Vegas Strip near Red Rock Canyon. There he parked and got out of the car, the headlights illuminating his body against the steep cliff below. Across the street behind a large boulder, a man crouched behind the rock carefully hidden from view. He peered through his scope at the large figure, cocked his rifle, and squeezed the trigger. Alonzo, illuminated by the lights of the car, fell backwards from the force of the blow and toppled over the cliff's edge to the rocky ground below. Even though he fell a considerable distance, and the impact would have killed him immediately, he was dead before he ever hit the ground.

Meanwhile, Eleonora, with a bright smile on her face, was back at the party, arm in arm with Scarlet and Luca, as they talked with family and friends.

Carter and Fenton furiously scrawled notes about every person they caught on camera and those associated with the Nero family. It was a veritable gold mine, especially when Luca whispered in Scarlet's ear telling her what they *really* did for the family. There was every manor of criminal behavior, like the colors of a rainbow, from laundering to stealing, to massaging business interests, to insider trading, to blackmail. All of it caught on camera and audio by Scarlet.

As the party continued into the daylight hours, Eleonora put a light hand on Scarlet's arm.

"I'm going to make a quick trip to the washroom to freshen up. Care to join me, Robin? Luca, you don't mind if I steal her away do you?" she said with a sickly sweet smile.

"No, not at all, two of my favorite girls should enjoy some girl time together." He flashed his pearly whites and Scarlet was dragged away before she could respond. Once in the lavish gold decorated women's wash room, Eleonora pulled out a compact container and dabbed her face with her makeup. Scarlet started to do the same.

"You make such a lovely couple, you and my brother. It is nice to see him happy. He isn't always the easiest to deal with of course, but I'm sure you know that. Why, what a lovely hand bag you have, may I see it?" Eleonora said, grabbing the clutch before Scarlet could respond.

"What a great designer, one of my favorites as well," she said as she peered in the inside, not caring about intruding on Scarlet's privacy. She paused, and with a wide smile she pulled out the locket, after opening the picture while it was still hidden in the purse.

"Is this you, Robin? Who is this woman with you? I thought I heard your mother died when you were young?" Scarlet grabbed the locket, shutting it, and noticed Eleonora's curious expression.

"Just a professor who was special to me, that's all. I actually totally forgot I had it in there. I don't use this clutch very often you see. I thought I lost it long ago, how silly. I better get back to Luca, I know there are still more people he would like me to meet. See you out there, okay?" Eleonora raised an eyebrow as Scarlet turned to leave. Meanwhile, Carter fumed behind the table.

"I told her nothing personal, and then she pulls a stunt like this.

If she wasn't still out there I would give her a piece of my mind right now. We can't afford mistakes like that, what a rookie blunder!" Carter raged, and Fenton held out his hands as a warning.

"You can't rip her apart right now, Carter, she is under enough stress. I'm sure it will be fine, she played it off. Think of what you've asked her to do — you can't blame her for keeping a locket of her aunt during this stressful undercover assignment. Cut her some slack," Fenton said, and Carter exhaled loudly in frustrated acceptance of his argument.

Soon after the restroom debacle, Luca approached Scarlet.

"We have some important people we need to meet with. I'll need to be with my father during some of these dealings. It's early in the morning, why don't you go back to your hotel room and get some sleep. We can connect tomorrow after I've taken care of all of this," he said with a smile. He lived for the family business. It ran through him as passionately as the blood in his veins.

"If you're sure that's what you want. I am a little tired, because your kiss is wearing off," she said and he winked back at her. Eleonora approached them, saying she was going to call it a night as well.

"Where is Alonzo, have you seen him, Eleonora? Father and I would like him to help us with some business." By that they all knew he meant their *father* wanted Alonzo present.

"No, I haven't seen him since earlier at the party. You know him, he is probably entertaining one of his female friends somewhere privately," she said. Luca shook his head in annoyance.

"Well, his loss. If you see him, pass along the word. I'll be with Father and his guests the rest of the night. Night, Robin." He kissed Scarlet on the cheek, and she pulled his face forward with her hands and affectionately kissed him. Fenton looked away from the screen.

"Goodnight, Baby," she said, as she let her hand drop to linger in his for a moment, before letting her slightly shaky legs carry her back to her hotel room. Even though she had been awake for hours, she knew she would not be able to sleep. Carter spoke in her ear first.

"You did well, Scarlet. That could have gone a number of different ways, but you held your own. I'm proud of you. You can disconnect your microphone and camera as Agent Starr showed you earlier and we can connect tomorrow. Get some rest." Carter said, and started packing up her stuff. It had been a long night, but the material they received that night was invaluable.

"Get some sleep as well, Fenton. You look like hell. I need you sharp for the rest of this weekend. Tomorrow is another big day and I need you, big guy," she said while patting him on the arm.

Once Carter left for the night, Fenton tried his microphone, out of a hunch.

"Are you okay, Scarlet? You there?" he said, feeling she could hear him on the other end, but there was only silence.

Chapter 25

"I hate myself sometimes."

Fenton knocked on her door, and stopped to listen. He couldn't hear anything through the door. He pulled out the extra key card he received for Scarlet's room. When he entered the dimly lit room and saw her huddled in the oversized chair in the corner, he paused. A small lamp was casting a glimmer of light across her face, showing lines of dried tears and dark rivulets from her mascara on her face. He couldn't have prepared himself even if he tried for how he found her. *Almost as if she was waiting for me.*

The expression on her face burned an image into his brain, and he actually wondered if he would ever be able to forget the way she looked at him. It was the loss of innocence, the loss of something pure and untouched, like pristine wildflowers in a meadow now stomped into a bent mess. Something which was once whole and wonderful about her spirit, now sat before him broken and trembling.

Was I a part of what did this to her? Should I have stopped all of this madness somehow? He wished more than anything he could turn back the hands of the clock a few hours. He wished he could have gone in her place, but he knew those types of thoughts were pointless. Her look made him yearn for her even more, wanting to protect her and shield her from all the darkness which seemed to be caving in, but he promised himself to stay disciplined when it came to her.

She twirled a bottle of bourbon in her hand, brought in by one of the agents in case she needed to entertain in her room for the undercover act, and she took a swig. He walked over, and held out his hand. She passed the bottle to him.

"Not very lady like, drinking from the bottle," he said. "Let me get you a glass, we can make you a proper drink." She narrowed her eyes at him, and he poured her a shot's worth. She took it from him without speaking, the liquid emptying quickly as she downed the liquor in one gulp. The quickness of the movement caught him off guard.

He was about to leave her room, when her hand touched his arm. It was as if a bolt of lightning connected with his flesh. He turned around, thinking she could be feeling faint or ill. She was standing before him in a light satin nightgown they had found in Robin's closet, and he could feel her hot breath on his chest. Her wide, sage eyes peered into his, and before he knew it, her soft, supple raspberry lips were brushing his own. A wondrously freeing, forbidden lust roared inside him from her inviting kiss. She awoke something deep within him, like waking a sleeping bear from his winter slumber, and made him feel alive inside. He moved his hands to the small of her back, soft beneath the satin material. His reaction to her, unlocking a piece of him, felt right even though he knew for him it was wrong. He could still taste her lingering on his lips, when she pulled away, more frightened by the anticipation of how he could react. She pushed herself up on her tippy toes and kissed him again, deeper this time, sucking his lower lip, with her hands moving to the back of his neck, and her soft caress turning his insides to jelly. He kissed back with hungry, aching kisses. He wrapped his arms completely around her, lifting her as her legs wrapped effortlessly around his waist. He could feel his body harden. Her breath was hot against his neck, kissing, and sucking against his skin. He was blinded by the sensation, wanting nothing more than to ravage her. She looked up at him, a question behind her eyes.

When she saw his eyes darken with surprise, and then soften, a slow smile crossed her lips. He shook his head, as if trying to wipe away the instant fog flooding his mind the moment their lips connected. *Stop this, Fenton. Stop this before it turns into something you can no longer control.*

"Scarlet, we can't do this. It's been a long day for you and you're not feeling like yourself right now. I'll be right down the hall." He put her back down on the ground, and unwound her legs from around his waist. He tried saying it in a dismissive tone, but he was not entirely convincing.

He started to walk away and she grabbed his hand, causing him to turn toward her. Her face was flushed as her eyes met his.

"Stay with me," she whispered. *Oh fuck yeah! I'll do more than stay with you. I'll never let anyone get to you.* He shook his head, trying to banish these thoughts from his mind.

"This is a bad idea. If one of the Neros come looking for you here, I can't be in this room with you. Plus, all of my focus needs to be on protecting you. No distractions." She looked wounded as he told her.

"I am thinking clearly. These last few hours have helped me think more clearly. Yes, I'm not used to being this forward, but I'm getting used to doing things I'm not accustomed to. The thought of you, the thought of seeing you after this, was the only thing to get me past these last few hours. When I kissed him, *I was thinking of you*, and maybe it was wrong, but it worked. Maybe you don't feel anything for me at all, but you kissed me back just then, I could tell. You're not a machine, you are a man, and if you have a life outside of the job, it doesn't mean people will die," she said with her eyes, as wide as saucers, beseeching him.

She was thinking of me, when she kissed him? That fiery kiss which made me want to rip his gelled head clean off through the screen, was for me? The thought of that scumbag's lips touching hers, I thought I was going to lose it right there in front of Carter. What are you saying? Discipline, man, it doesn't matter anyway. She's getting too close to you. You need to push her away if you want to protect her.

"You and I, Scarlet, it can't happen. Get it out of your head. I don't feel that way about you," he said, his words tasting like acid. It took every ounce of his strength to say the poisoning words which went against every fiber in his being. *Lies, all lies.* He had to look away when the shock of his words covered her face like a shadow. Her penetrating stare felt like it was burning a hole through his heart. She was cold toward him now, removed. *Good, that is the way it should be. Good...then why doesn't it feel better?*

"That's a super attitude you've got there, Fenton, you know that? Thanks for your bluntness, I won't make the same mistake again," she said bitterly.

"That's the cocaine talking, from when your fake boyfriend shoved his tongue down your throat," he shot back, regretting it the moment the words came out of his mouth.

"Wow, I knew you could be an ass, Fenton, but you've outdone yourself tonight. I was simply asking you to stay. I can't sleep." He looked down at his feet, feeling like a horrible person for what he was doing to her. He pulled a box out of his back pocket.

"Here, I brought you a light herbal sleep aid to help. Nothing that will leave you feeling drowsy or make it difficult to wake up in case someone comes looking for you, but it helps most of my clients. It's why I stopped by." He knew it was another lie.

She looked at him like he sprouted another arm, and instead of responding, she poured herself another glass of bourbon. He left the box of sleeping pills on her nightstand.

"I'll let myself out," he said cautiously.

"Yeah, you do that. Don't let the door hit you on your way out," She spat back at him, and downed the rest of her glass of bourbon. He left her room, feeling worse than he felt in a long time — a horrible, sticky, powerlessness, a feeling like he was alone in the world but couldn't stand to be stuck with himself.

It's bad tonight. Almost as bad as the night dad died. He went back to his hotel room, and breaking one of his main rules of the job, raided the mini bar. *Discipline.*

Chapter 26

"You hide such ugly secrets behind such a pretty face."

When Scarlet woke, she had several missed texts from Luca asking her to join him in his suite. After turning on the video monitor and audio, and touching base with Carter about their plan for the day, she went up to Luca's hotel room wearing one of Julian's more glamorous prepared outfits. It was a knee-length fashionista dress, which she dressed down with a leather coat. When she was let into the suite, it was a room filled with chaos. Luca was pacing, holding his head in his hand, wearing dress slacks, tailored shirt, and a blazer. He rushed toward her, kissing her on the cheek. Scarlet noticed his father Gabriel, Eleonora, and Manuele in the room as well.

"No one knows where Alonzo is. We have our staff out looking right now, and we're trying to track him by his cell phone," he said in a rush, and Scarlet nodded.

"What can I do?" she asked.

"His partying and disregard for our business has created

problems for my father. During our negotiations last night, he could have played a useful role, but instead he was out gallivanting with his female admirers. Now we can't find him. Father is not pleased, but I may go ahead and share with him the documents you gave me. This might be the perfect time. Come with me." He looked like an excited school boy, about ready to clinch his victory over his brother.

"Father, at this time, where Alonzo is showing his lack of respect for this family, I've got something to tell you about what I've been spending my time doing," Luca said, as he led Scarlet near the window where his father stood with a disgruntled look on his face.

"Leave us please. Eleonora and Manuele, you can stay. The rest of you stay close though, in case I need any of you," Gabriel said to excuse all the other members of the family who were in the room waiting for orders. Luca started going into detail as to what he had gathered on the Durantes, and Gabriel listened with great interest. Once Luca had explained the immense position of power this put the family in, and about the extra information they would soon have once they could get her back to the East Coast to pull the remaining pieces off their system, Gabriel stood slowly and pulled Luca into a fatherly embrace.

"This is very impressive, son, very impressive. You are stepping up in this family. Alonzo missed essential meetings last night, which I told him were imperative, and he disappears, disappointing me greatly. While you, busy at work, bring this wealth of information. Let's go to lunch, the three of us, and discuss your future." Luca beamed back at his father and squeezed Scarlet's hand. Eleonora was standing in the corner of the room, glaring at the exchange, and Manuele's eyes looked red as if he didn't get a wink of sleep the night before.

Carter and Fenton were amazed at the smorgasbord of information they were able to gather at lunch from the audio and video feed coming from Scarlet's necklace. Gabriel talked about intimate details regarding their racketeering operations, including loansharking, illegal gambling, heroin and cocaine distribution, tax evasion, bribery, and conspiracy to commit murder. It was a treasure trove of bad deeds, which he nonchalantly talked about with Luca, and Scarlet sat in silence nodding. Carter was salivating at the mouth. The lunch could not have gone better if she planned the whole thing herself, until Federico Nero came rushing into the restaurant shattering the perfect picture. He leaned forward whispering in Gabriel Nero's ear. The Boss of the Nero family bowed his head listening, and then a look of complete rage filled his features as he grabbed Federico by the tie.

"When did this happen?" he roared, and Federico whispered in response.

"What is the matter, Father?" Luca asked.

"They found Alonzo's car near Red Rock Canyon, just beyond the Calico Hills overlook. He was whacked, shot in the head, and he fell off the edge. They killed my son! We have to find out who did this, Luca. We have to find them, and destroy them. Do you think this is the work of the Durantes? Do you think they ordered this hit? It is even more important now than ever to bring them down. We need the rest of the information. You said Robin could go back and find out who they are working with so we can take them out at the knees?" Gabriel demanded, pain and anger welling in his eyes.

"Yes, yes, we will get you whatever you need," Luca said.

"I'm so sorry, Luca," Scarlet whispered, and Luca squeezed her arm with a nod. The lunch was over, and the group headed back to the hotel, with Luca telling Scarlet he needed to be with his family to discuss the matter more in depth. Eleonora's eyes were wet and she shook her head in shock, "I have a fundraising event at the high-end boutique in the city to promote our casino. How am I going to face them now?" she whimpered, and Luca gave her a quick hug as

Gabriel chimed in.

"It's best to keep up appearances right now because we don't know who is behind this and who knows about it. Take Robin with you for comfort. Can you still attend the event? It's important we don't deviate from our regular routine or let on we know anything until we have a chance to investigate on our own." Eleonora wiped her eyes and nodded solemnly. Luca pulled Scarlet aside.

"You should make flight arrangements soon to go back to Virginia to hack into the Durante computer system again to gather the rest of the intelligence for Father. It's more important now than ever. I'm sorry we haven't had a lot of time together since you've been back, but that will change soon. I need to get a couple things settled with my father, but then I want to see you. I am not trying to neglect you, I promise," Luca explained, kissing Scarlet and grabbing her rear end to give it a squeeze to emphasize what he meant.

"Don't give it a second thought, Luca. I know you need to be with your family right now, and I completely understand. Keep me posted if I can do anything else to help. Otherwise I'll wait to hear from you. I have plenty of work to keep me busy in the meantime," she said sweetly.

"You're doing everything you can already. Do you mind going with Eleonora to the event while I sort out these details with Father? I'm sure she would find your presence comforting," Luca asked as Eleonora continued to wipe her eyes.

"Of course, and Eleonora my condolences for your loss," Scarlet said as Eleonora nodded, and promptly linked her arm with Scarlet's.

Eleonora's driver took the ladies to a trendy boutique located below ground with a lavish entrance. Signs adorned the entryway promoting the casino, and women were dressed in skimpy cocktail gowns as they paraded around the interior for a mini fashion show as wealthy onlookers applauded and wrote checks for the cause.

Scarlet could tell her cellphone reception was breaking up as they walked down the grand silver staircase, fashion icons and signatures adorning the walls.

"Can you hear me, Scarlet? The feed...breaking up...can you..." Carter's voiced muffled into static, and then silence. Scarlet swallowed hard as she continued into the lower levels of the fashion hot spot. Two huge bouncer-type men stood by the door, policing those who tried to enter, only letting in the most elite clientele. They knew Eleonora as one of the main hosts of the event, and let Scarlet pass as her guest. Inside was a mixture of botanical gardens and high fashion, and the scent of fresh flowers filled the air as props next to the costly merchandise.

Most of the items Scarlet touched were at the low end, five hundred dollars for a patterned blouse, and several thousand for leather pants and designer jeans. At one point, Eleonora excused herself to take a couple of phone calls outside, which sparingly took a good ninety minutes, and when she returned, she was in even greater spirits than ever. Her mood seemed to shift, which was bizarre to Scarlet this soon after hearing the news she lost her brother. Eleonora was radiating happiness when she returned from whatever business she needed to attend to above ground where she could receive decent cell service. Scarlet had kept herself busy in Eleonora's absence, mindlessly picking up dresses, and admiring the fashion show with the rest of the guests. Scarlet found one of the dresses from the show and held it in her hands as a staff member came around with a silver tray of caviar and crackers. Eleonora came back, and looked over Scarlet's shoulder at the dress.

"Hold up the gown so I can see what it would look like on you. Yes, I like that. Oh, Robin. Robin, so pretty like a *little bird*. I wasn't sure what to think of you at first, but now I'm starting to get a good picture," she smiled sweetly, as Scarlet turned her head to meet her gaze.

"That color matches your complexion. You have such nice skin, and such a pretty face. You hide such *ugly* secrets behind such a pretty face, don't you my dear?" she said with a wicked smile. Scarlet took a step back in surprise.

"What do you mean by that, Eleonora?" she asked.

"Oh, you know, being so close with my brother and all, you must be able to hold your share of secrets to be around a man like him," she winked, brushing off her jabbing remark.

"I'm actually feeling pretty tired. I don't want to hold you back from handling the event. I may just head back to the hotel. Do you mind?" Eleonora gave Scarlet an icy smile.

"Oh yes, dear. You go ahead. I'll have to keep my driver though. Do you mind taking a cab or car service back?"

"No, I don't mind at all," Scarlet replied, happy to be dismissed from this bizarre afternoon. "I'll see you soon. Again, my condolences to you and your family."

"Thank you. Oh, and Robin, I hope you sleep well. You know us girls, we would look just like death without our beauty sleep," Eleonora said. Scarlet nodded as she headed out to hail a cab.

When safely in the vehicle, Scarlet tried her reception again.

"Can you hear me?" she said under her breath, low enough for the cab driver not to hear.

"Yes, you are back and we are receiving you. How did everything go with Eleonora?" Carter asked. Scarlet took out her cell to pretend like she was talking into her device in case the cab driver got suspicious.

"I know I can't say a lot right now, but she was acting strange toward me," Scarlet confessed.

"Okay, I'll send Fenton over for a full debrief and you can hand over your surveillance equipment. Head back to your room and get some rest. It's been a long night and day for you, with little sleep. Take a nap, shower, relax, and we can reconvene tonight. We will book you on a flight soon. With Alonzo getting murdered, we don't want to keep you under much longer. Plus, everyone in the Nero family expects you to head back to the East Coast to complete the job. We still can't get into the computer or cell you recovered from the locker. We need to bring those devices back to our main office in D.C. to have our team of experts break past the security to access the contents. We will have you out of this within twenty-four hours, so hold tight. The end is in sight. Great work today," Carter said, and Scarlet turned off her equipment.

Back at the hotel, she heard a knock at her door, and saw Fenton standing outside her room. She opened the door.

"Hey."

"All my equipment is in this bag. Take it and go please, I don't feel like talking." She shoved a duffle bag filled with the surveillance equipment and leftover files she found around the room.

"Carter said we should debrief, talk about what happened with Eleonora."

"Later, Fenton. I'm tired."

"I don't think she meant it as a suggestion."

"Are you always this obnoxious? You're really taking this jerk thing to a whole new level aren't you? Look at my face, do you think I care? Just leave me alone." She slammed the door in his face, almost catching his foot in the process.

Scarlet fell onto her bed, mentally exhausted. She half expected to hear Fenton knock at her door again, waited a couple seconds, and then exhaled slowly when she realized he wasn't coming back.

She closed her eyes for a moment, trying to remember what it felt like to breathe normally, with a heartbeat which didn't feel like a freight train barreling down the tracks. A curt knock at the door forced her eyes open again.

"I'm not here," she called. *That will teach him.*

"Room service. Some of our best hotel dishes, compliments of the Nero family." She couldn't help but smile a little. Luca must have ordered it for her. She pulled herself up from the bed and went to the door, peering through the eye hole she saw a man standing in a white staff uniform with a cart and trays. She noticed with curiosity his bow tie design, there were little images of sweets on it, which was the one pop of color in his white ensemble.

She opened the door and he wheeled the cart in to the middle of her room. Following him in she was curious what Luca ordered for her. When he walked past her she noticed he smelled sweet, like watermelon and lime gumdrops doused in sugar. It was a peculiar smell for a man's cologne, and she was about to ask him what he was wearing when his abnormally high voice disrupted her thoughts.

"Please have a seat miss, and I will explain all the options prepared for you today," the man said gallantly, in a nasally high voice, pointing at a chair he pulled out for her with his white-gloved hand. She noticed a black rose on the tray with the covered dishes, which she thought was peculiar. She sat down, and he removed one of the large, silver plate covers. Underneath, rested a long silver gun, which he grabbed and promptly pointed at her face.

"Stay right where you are, miss. Here is a piece of rope. Tie your legs to the chair please, and then clasp your hands together. Do it quickly." She noticed then a faint scar running from his eye down to the corner of his mouth. His dark Italian complexion hid the ugly scar well at first, but now with a weapon pointed at her she realized he was not part of the wait staff. She did as she was told, her mouth going dry.

"Who are you? What are you going to do to me?" she asked, a metallic taste filling her mouth as she could feel her body reacting to the terror with cold sweats.

"Why, my dear girl. When I'm sent to a job, it typically means one of two things. I'm known by my associates as the Confectionist, and I have a specific skill set. If I'm called in, then there is either a problem which needs resolving, or there is information which needs revealing. All I know is you arrived into town, and then Alonzo Nero shows up dead. Quite the delicious coincidence, wouldn't you say?" he said with a bright smile, placing the gun on the table when he was satisfied she was cuffed properly. He pulled out a rope from under another tray, and tied her around the chair so she couldn't kick or try to wiggle off the hard surface. Scarlet wracked her brain for a plan, and any way to increase her chances of survival. Her thoughts went to her sister, eyes wide, blood pouring from her blond hair. *I'm Robin, I'm Robin, I'm Robin...I'm Luca Nero's girlfriend, who does this guy think he is?*

"I had nothing to do with that, nothing at all. Who sent you? I'm Luca Nero's girlfriend, and I'm doing a very important job for him. When he finds out about this, you are going to wish you never set foot in this room," Scarlet spat at him, hoping her anger and forced confidence would cause him to think twice about whatever he had planned for her.

"Luca doesn't know I'm here, and my employer assured me he will never find out. I have a little magical device that jams signals, so all security cameras went static when I got within range, so clear your mind of any wild fantasies that someone will discover I'm here. I'm sorry, Sweetie, but I follow the sweet smell of money and there is quite a bit of money on your pretty little head. All I know is you have secrets, and I'm here to uncover those secrets. Layer by layer, bit by bit, inch by inch, cell by cell — the good news is you can decide."

"I can decide what?"

"You can decide how much pain you feel here today. I have to admit though, part of me hopes you don't cooperate, because I love to see pretty girls squirm. It's like watching the sweet exterior of a chocolate bunny melt and twist until there is nothing left but a brown sticky mess." He uncovered another silver shiny tray, revealing knives of various sizes, several vials of clear liquids, needles of varying lengths, and a pair of pliers. He pulled a large, clear drop cloth from under the cart.

"Why do they call you the Confectionist?" she dared to ask. His eyes widened, and he smiled as he started filling each of the three needles with liquids from each vial. On the bottle were the descriptions, rapid-acting, intermediate acting, and long acting. Another vial had the word glucagon. He took a needle filled with the rapid-acting formula, and injected a small amount into Scarlet.

"Well, my dear girl, what a sweet question. I'm a perfectionist, I don't leave a drop of blood behind, and when I do need to leave a body, I stage it in such a way it is almost impossible to conclude it was anything but suicide. Tell me when you start to feel this injection. Perhaps you will be more willing to talk in about ten minutes or so," he said as he winked at her. Her eyes filled with watery tears, and he continued.

"You must be wondering about the colorful word Confectionist, aren't you? I can't resist a sweet treat, and I am obsessed with sugar of any kind. I especially like the effect it has on the body, you see. I think insulin is the greatest discovery of all time. Do you know about insulin? Well, it is my favorite thing to talk about. It's a hormone produced by your pancreas, and that hormone, in essence, allows your body to utilize sugar from carbohydrates in the food you eat. Those who suffer from diabetes need insulin shots to help their body regulate blood sugar levels, but what is even more interesting is the effect is has on a body which doesn't need insulin. Quick and effective really, in getting people to tell their little secrets. Enough of this stuff will send you into insulin shock, or hypoglycemia, which can lead to death. I have several types with me, each reacting at different speeds. You would be amazed how effective it is to pump a full vial of the long-acting insulin into someone's system, and explain in about ninety minutes, they will either be dead or cooperate." Scarlet squirmed, and he smiled.

"If they cooperate, I could inject them with glucagon, which counteracts the effects of the insulin. It gives them time to think about their life, you see, when I have that type of time to play with. Now, you're probably wondering why I need to go to all the trouble of bringing this tray of treats along, knives, insulin, and needles. You would be surprised, but it often doesn't matter how sweet I am to people, and they, in turn, are sour with me and refuse to tell me what I need to know. Are you one of those people? I think you might be. Ah, well, it doesn't matter. I have another savory goody with me on this tray, and it is just a matter of time when you'll tell me everything about Alonzo's death," he said, tilting his head at her. Scarlet started to feel her body perspiring. She was getting the chills and shaking in her chair. Her heart was starting to race in her chest, and her vision was becoming cloudy.

"What if I really had nothing to do with Alonzo's disappearance or death? What if, whoever sent you, is trying to set me up?" Scarlet asked, trembling in her chair as she watched him work. He shook his head with a smirk, and started injecting more of the insulin from the first needle as his eyes gleamed.

"Well, that wouldn't do. That wouldn't do at all. My employer told me if you don't talk about Alonzo and how you had him whacked, then I'm supposed to make it a very long and uncomfortable night for you. Don't worry, once you get a little more of the taste of this syrup in your veins, you will want to talk to me. It just takes a little time, and honey, I've got nothing but time," he assured her. Her lips were starting to tingle now from the effects of the insulin, and a wave of lightheadedness hit her. She had to shake her head to try to clear her vision and she could feel her body reacting to the poison hitting her bloodstream.

One single tear slid down Scarlet's face as he placed the tarp around her chair with a wicked smile. He winked at her as he picked up the syringe from the cart, and started toward her, the end of the needle oozing with insulin.

Chapter 27

"Leave your questions at the door."

Carlo leaned up against the back wall of a small café. He sipped his third cappuccino of the morning, letting the warm liquid slip down his throat, providing a warm courage he previously lacked. He discretely pulled out a flask from his jacket, pouring in two fingers of the scotch he brought with him. He couldn't afford to appear shaken in front of his boss, when shaky was all he was feeling these days. It didn't help when his nights were filled with restless sleep, the image of Darius haunting his waking thoughts and his vivid dreams. He knew it was a problem he had to shake, or else he could lose his sanity. He knew guys who cracked, broke under the pressure, and turned into slobbering psychotic messes. *I'm not going to be one of the horror stories. I'm too smart to crack. Get your head on straight, Carlo and forget about Darius, the poor schmuck. It's just part of the job, it wasn't personal, it was just business.*

Pietro walked in the front door, scanned the café, and nodded toward Carlo. The two men hugged, and pulled their chairs out to sit down.

"Carlo, I appreciate what you did for the family. I know it can't be easy. Darius was a trainee in your care. I know we forced you to take him on to begin with, and that was a mistake, but I want you to know Romeo and I view this as a wrong that was righted because of you. You did right by the family, Carlo. You did right by me. How are you holding up?"

"Fine, Pietro, just fine. I appreciate you asking, but I've never been better. You need a coffee or anything?" Carlo took another long hard pull from the dainty coffee mug filled with the spiked cappuccino.

"Nope, I already had my morning coffee so I'm set. Okay, I wanted to make sure. I know some guys when they have to whack one of their closest friends, trainees, buddies, or family members, they need some time afterwards. If you are fine, that's good to hear, and I don't see any reason why we can't move forward. Now about this girl business. Were you able to contact your man?"

"Percussion Pete is game if we can provide him what he needs from a payment standpoint. His explosives are delicate, and setting it up properly is a dangerous job."

"Yes, I understand. We will pay him what it takes. It needs to lead to a clean fire which won't ever lead back to us."

"He understands. I just need to figure out how to get the aunt lured to the location, and then how to get to the girl."

"The aunt has to lead us to the girl. We can't find her without the aunt pulling her out of hiding. I was talking with Romeo about this predicament, told him the news about Darius, and he was very pleased — pleased enough to help us. I have instructions here for what you need the aunt to do to pull out the girl." Pietro slid a piece of paper across the small café table. Carlo read it quickly, and raised his eyebrows in confusion.

"I don't understand. How will this get her to come? Sending a letter with this information in it, to *her old apartment?* She hasn't stepped foot back in her apartment since the Pig botched the job, and fell out the window."

"This is the way Romeo wants it to be done, so this is how we execute. Leave your questions at the door. You have to trust the family has your best interests in mind. Plus, we don't have any other options. Romeo thinks this will work, so this is what we need to do. If you knew where she was, we wouldn't have to work through the aunt to find her. It is because we lost her in the first place she was able to go into hiding."

"Yeah, I get it. Okay, I'm going to make sure everything is ready at the property. You said it is deserted?"

"Yes, it's an old farmhouse on the outskirts of town. It's a recent foreclosure my contact told me about that's hidden by a thick ring of trees. Perfect spot for a murder. What are your next steps, Carlo?"

"Next steps? Guess I have to become a little better acquainted with this Aunt Jo I've heard so much about. I have a feeling if she thinks her little girl is in trouble, she will do whatever it takes, and go wherever is needed to protect her. Consider it already done, Pietro." He gave a confident smile, the smile he was working on mustering the whole hour he sat there before the meet, knocking back several cappuccinos with a little extra flavoring from his flask. His smile was a full *scotch smile,* the happiness which comes only on the other side of dulling senses and drowning fears, but it was better than no smile at all.

Pietro smiled back with pride, the two men hugged, and Carlo left on his own. He lit a cigarette by his car and looked around. There were a couple of people walking around on the streets glancing toward him occasionally, and he thought he saw Darius's face on each one. *Keep it together Carlo, keep it together man. Now is not the time to break, not when there is work to do.*

He took another swig from his flask, blinked hard several times until Darius's face disappeared, and he got in his car. He looked over to the passenger seat, and saw a couple candy sprinkles in the seat from the box of doughnuts he gave Darius. He almost choked on his own tongue seeing the multi-colored sprinkles. It was a half sob, half cough, which made him take another gulp of scotch from his flask. He picked up each individual sprinkle one by one in his fingers, opened the door, and stomped them into dust on the ground before driving away.

Eleonora returned from the event at the boutique. She was exhilarated by the events of the past few days, and intoxicated with happiness. Things were falling together for her beautifully. Alonzo was out of the picture due to some careful planning and cunning, and now she only had to move a few more chess pieces and she would be set for a lifetime of luxury and power.

She walked into the expansive family home, perched on a hill, surrounded by the best security money could buy. She felt safe and protected. She could not think of a better spot to hide while destroying the family within the family walls. It was all too perfect, and a little too much fun. She put down her bags from shopping, content with the fact her driver and the shop clerks were her alibi while Robin was being murdered in her hotel room. There could be no questioning where she was, no question she wouldn't be able to answer in a way to satisfy even the gravest of skeptics. She found Manuele, long hair pulled back in a bun, dark circles under his eyes as he looked out the window. He looked over at her when she entered the room, his eyes lit up seeing her, but he shoved his hands in his pockets and lowered his head expecting her wrath.

"Is everything set that we discussed? You found someone you trust? I had to step in last time you disappointed me, Manuele. Alonzo could have walked away unscathed, and those heaping coals of blame would have been on your head. You could have ruined our chances. I told you to stay at the resort that night, I told you to send one of the soldiers we vetted as trustworthy, but no, you completely deviated from the plan wanting to do it yourself. After everything we've gone through with your drinking, you expected to have a steady aim against your brother? Did the booze give you courage, you *idiot*, to run a plan and think you could successfully execute the kill? I would cut off your ears right here and now to help you remember to *hear me* better next time. You know you deserve even worse, but you are lucky we are in our family home, and I need your *ears* brother. I thought you would betray me, so I sent someone else, and good thing I did. I am granting you mercy with the understanding if you cross me again, I can't protect you from the consequences. I will let you keep your ears for now, but remember, if you fail to listen again dear brother, you don't deserve to keep them. That's a promise." She leaned in close to him, inhaling deeply to smell the musky cologne she bought him.

"I'm sorry, Eleonora. I wanted nothing more than to please you. Thinking of all the years Alonzo treated me like dirt, dragging me behind his wake, pulling me through the ashes of his destruction, thinking of the pain he inflicted on me, I wanted nothing more than to pull the trigger myself. I've fixed the problem, I only want to please you," he mumbled, as she pulled him into a hug.

"Shush, I know. I'm the only one who is here to protect you. I'm the only one who always saw amazing potential in you, and soon, brother, you will have your reward. I'll make sure everything works for us, because I love you, brother, and I know you would lay down your life for me and for your loyalty, you will receive all the reward you could imagine. You need to show me your love by listening and obeying me. Do you understand? Give me a kiss." She turned her cheek so he could kiss her, hesitantly, his eyes gleaming with appreciation of her mercy.

"I will do whatever you ask, Eleonora," he said, a glazed look forming over his eyes from the mixture of alcohol and prescription pills.

"Okay, I'm glad to hear that. Now I have to say this, because I love you, and I want to make sure you fully understand for your own good. If you disobey me again, your handsome face won't even be recognizable to *family*. I may have to take those precious lips of yours so you can't taste the sweet taste of liquor anymore — the poison that clouds your mind — maybe then you would be of use to me. Do you understand me, brother?" She kissed his forehead, cupping his head in her hands so she could look him fully in the eyes. They were watery and his lip was trembling.

"Yes, I'm so sorry, Eleonora, I only want to do what you ask," he blubbered to her.

"Yes, yes, I know. I only want what is best for you, so I have to be tough on you and discipline you to make you better. I know what you can be and I am the only one who sees this potential in you. I saved you from the brink of death many times. You owe me *your life*. If you do as I say, then I will give you the life of your dreams, understood?" she said gingerly to him, and kissed him lightly on the lips, brushing away a couple of his stray tears like a mother would. "Now, who is your most trusted man? Have you set everything up for us?"

"Yes, I've contacted my most trusted hitman who goes by the nickname the Confectionist. He is already carrying out our orders."

"Good. I need to find Luca, and have the conversation we talked about. I won't be contacting you from now until then. Don't text me anything either to make sure we don't leave a trace on this. Make me proud, Manuele. I'll handle Luca. I already have a perfect plan in mind for how we can get him out of the way." She winked at him, and left her brother.

Eleonora hummed to herself as she headed toward the back of the mansion to find her next target. The next person standing between her and power was Luca.

Chapter 28

"Get everyone out of Vegas, before a little leak turns into a shipwreck."

Kelly Carter was on the phone with her taskforce. She was sending all the evidence they gathered across secure lines to start matching faces and names with intelligence her team had already gathered. It was like fitting together a large jigsaw puzzle, and she knew the undercover operation with Scarlet would be instrumental in filling in the gaps and getting that much closer to a conviction. She licked her lips in anticipation, she was excited. It was the thrill of the chase, the conviction of being right, and the thirst for criminal blood giving her an all-time high. She couldn't manufacture that type of high with drugs or booze, so she didn't even try. The occasional glass of red wine was all she allowed herself to keep the hunger sharp for the next win on the job.

She was eager to get back east. They had scheduled one more debrief with Scarlet this evening after she rested, and then Carter would be heading to her private airplane with her team to get back to the main headquarters office to start making sense of everything.

She heard a knock at her door while she was packing, and noticed Agent Westbrook standing outside. She let him in, his face looking steely and pale.

"What's wrong, Westbrook? I don't like the look on your face," Carter said. Working with him on numerous cases, she could tell when he was on edge. Even though his typical demeanor was far from sunny, she could tell there was an extra shade of darkness looming over him.

"I have news you are not going to like. Just remember, don't shoot the messenger," he said. He stood stiffly with his hands in his pockets.

"Out with it Westbrook, what do you have for me?"

"I was able to get into Robin's computer, but it looks like a lot of key information was erased. I'm trying to recover the information, but I think there may be some damage to the integrity of the photos. I'm doing the best I can, but I need to go back to headquarters where I have access to all my equipment and the broader team. I was thinking I would try to head out tonight, if you are okay with that?"

"Permission granted, but I want to come with you. I have a hunch this computer and cell phone hold key information for us. She would not have taken such pains to safeguard these devices if she didn't have sensitive material on them. It doesn't make sense why she would try to destroy and remove information herself though. I would have guessed the computer was her insurance plan. Evidence of wrongdoing she could use as collateral if someone came after her. It doesn't add up," Carter mused, unable to hide her frustration.

"You don't have to come along, really, I'll be fine trying to decrypt and recover everything on my own," Agent Westbrook stammered, but Carter was adamant.

"This case is my white whale. I'm going to be hands-on through this whole thing. Nothing personal, Westbrook. I just can't stomach letting that device out of my sight. Remember, the Neros and Durantes have people on their payroll everywhere. One can't be too careful. Plus, I want to go back to the lab myself and get in touch with the rest of the team. It will be easier if I'm there at the center of the action. Is that it, Westbrook?" she asked, and he shook his head gravely.

"I don't know what happened, but the video feed from when Scarlet was showing the evidence to Eleonora and Luca is corrupt. We don't have a good picture and the audio cuts out periodically throughout the recording. With the corrupted file, we can't tie Eleonora's name to the scene. The picture and voiceover are indistinguishable." He rubbed the back of his neck. Carter slammed her fist down on the table, fury flooded her eyes and her nostrils flared.

"Are you kidding me, Westbrook? How in the hell did that happen? You were watching the feed, recording our only copy, and you never noticed any interference? That is one of the most pivotal moments of this entire undercover operation. We need to tie Eleonora and Luca to the scene!" Carter fumed, pacing the room, throwing an empty plastic water cup into a nearby wall. It made a satisfying smack, but it didn't alleviate Carter's temper.

"I don't know what happened. I'm going to bring the video and audio feed back with me to Washington to try to repair the damage. I'm guessing something interfered with the signal or feed, but we didn't notice it real-time, so it could just be an issue with the recording. I might be able to work some magic on it," he began, but Carter stopped him.

"No, I want Starr to try to repair our undercover footage. You have enough to do with the laptop contents. I'll take Robin's cell we found in the locker and I have just the person in mind to retrieve messages from the device — a contractor I work with periodically on the side," Carter said, and Westbrook looked like he was going to protest again.

"That's it, Westbrook. I've made up my mind. You're dismissed. Fill in Starr and have her call me. I'll let Fenton know there has been a change of plans, and I'm heading out tonight. We can debrief with Scarlet back in D.C. We will make this right, Westbrook. We can still make this right." She thought her words would comfort him, but he looked more miserable than ever. She didn't want to admit it, but even after all their hard work and a somewhat flawless undercover operation, things were starting to crumble around her. Key footage and audio could be lost forever. Audio and visual files which are indiscernible are not admissible in court. The laptop was corrupted, they were at a dead end with the phone, and Alonzo was murdered while they were running their sting. Her temples started to throb as she thought about the fallout from all the mistakes popping up in her operation.

What happened to running a tight ship, Carter? What started out as a successful sting operation now has more holes in it than a little league player's socks. This flagship is now starting to take on water like the damn Titanic.

It was all the more reason to pull the plug and get everyone out of Vegas, before a little leak turns into an all-out shipwreck.

Carter called Fenton, and filled him in on all the news from Westbrook.

"I'm sorry, Fenton, but I have to head back to try to save the evidence we gathered. Plus, I need to get a team on the case of who killed Alonzo. There could be massive fallout from that type of upheaval, and I need to make sure we have the right wiretaps in place to prevent mass murder. Especially if it appears the Durantes had anything to do with it. Are you okay finishing this up by yourself?

We moved up your commercial flights, so you are on the red-eye flight tonight. We need to make sure if anyone checks it out we have Scarlet on a commercial flight instead of a private airplane which might raise their suspicions. That being said, we don't want to risk her leaving during the day when she is more exposed."

"Yes, I understand. I have an exit route planned I just checked about an hour ago. I'll take her out through the basement and past the kitchen, and I'll check it again to make sure the route is secured. It should be just fine. Good luck with everything on your end. I'm sure you will be able to save it, Carter. You have the best team in the country assembled and a host of technical wizards at your disposal. If there is even a shred of it left, they will find it, I'm sure of it," he said confidently, his words meant to reassure.

"I appreciate that. Get her out of here and get off the grid, but stay in touch through our secure portal. I know you want to protect the girl, but I may need her, especially if we can't use some of what we already gathered. I need to be able to reach you in case..." she reminded him.

"Yes, I know. Stay safe, Carter." His voice sounded far away, deep and assured.

"Funny, you took the words right out of my mouth," she sighed as she hung up the phone. She felt guilty leaving before the asset and her bodyguard were out of harm's way, but she didn't feel she had a choice. She had to protect everything she worked so hard to build, and her sights were set firmly on her end goals.

She was in striking distance, and nothing would stop her from her most prized kill. She thought of a picture of her in front of a chart at a press conference, smiling and victorious at the end of this long and tedious process, gaily answering questions about how she pulled off one of the largest sting operations within the world of organized crime. That is, *if* she could salvage her case from the wreckage. She sighed, thinking about the possible future. She wanted it so bad she could taste it, and it tasted glorious.

Chapter 29

"How do I wipe these beastly images from my mind?"

Fenton started prepping his bags for their red-eye flight. He checked the duffle bag Scarlet gave him to do a quick inventory of the items when he noticed the sleeping pills shoved in the bag as well. *Shoot, she will probably want these. She needs rest and whether she hates me or not right now, these will help her. Better put on your armor. Round two of Fenton vs. Scarlet is about to begin.* He took a deep breath and decided to take the bottle to her room.

As he approached her door, he heard a quiet whimper. The he heard an odd male voice unlike any he heard on the tape footage they captured from Scarlet's undercover work. The hair on the back of his neck stood up as he heard the man's voice again, and this time, he was certain he didn't recognize the voice on the other side of the door. *Someone is in Scarlet's room.* His training kicked in. His breath shallow, he slowly drew his gun, the familiar cold metal fitting perfectly with his hand like a glove.

He pulled the card out for her room slowly, gently sliding it through the scanner, a green light appeared on the panel, and he slowly moved the door handle to not make a sound. He cracked the door, peering in, and saw a man standing over Scarlet wearing a white staff uniform. He could see her visibly tied to the chair. He noticed a gun on the table, as well as a number of torture instruments.

He didn't have to think through each step, his body and instincts reacted, calculating through his training how many steps and movements it would take for the perpetrator to reach the gun, while also assessing other ways to incapacitate the danger without using bullets. *Bullets flying in a hotel room would only hurt the undercover operation, and put Scarlet in more danger.*

He shoved through the door, gun drawn. The Confectionist turned around stunned, not expecting the sudden arrival of a stranger during his operation. He pushed the table with all his strength in Fenton's direction when he saw Fenton running toward him, sending the contents on the table scattering to the floor. Fenton knocked the syringe out of the Confectionist's hand with a swift punch. As both men exchanged blows, Fenton grabbed the Confectionist by the collar and spun him away from Scarlet, slamming his head down on a nearby dresser.

The Confectionist hit the ground, but managed to grab a knife which landed near the furniture on the floor. He madly stabbed and swiped the blade at Fenton and managed to swipe Fenton's chest before Fenton contorted his body over the desk at the last moment, so the knife merely cut a hole through his shirt, leaving a gash which started bleeding through the blue cotton.

He was able to thrust out with his legs, kicking the Confectionist, who tripped over the tipped cart and stumbled backwards. Fenton leapt on top of him, landing several hard punches near his jaw, eventually knocking the perpetrator out cold.

Fenton rushed to Scarlet, and touched her face. Her eyes were glossed over, as she fought a wave of unconsciousness threatening to pull her under.

"Scarlet, Scarlet, talk to me!" he growled, noticing her skin felt clammy and cold, her whole body trembling in the chair. He frantically untied her hands and feet from the chair.

"I need glucagon, counteract the insulin..." she said, and he understood looking at the label on the vials of liquids and seeing needles strewn about the room. From his time in the service, he was well aware of any ailment his comrades could have going into battle. He knew how to administer injections, especially for a young kid new to the service who could accidentally overdose on their insulin shots. He quickly grabbed an empty syringe and filled it with a moderate amount of the counteracting drug, and shot it into Scarlet's leg. Her eyes widened in surprise.

"Are you okay? Shit, how did this happen?" he asked, cupping her head in his hands and her eyes cleared a little. She seemed to register him crouching in front of her now, she was about to speak as she noticed sudden movement out of the corner of her eye.

"Fenton, watch out!" she managed to say, but the Confectionist already smashed a vase over Fenton's head as he was turning toward the criminal, causing him to collapse backwards. The man stood over him, sneering, and started to bend over to finish his work. Scarlet, more aware of her surroundings, noticed a full needle by her feet, and crawled toward it. Noticing her movement, he grabbed the back of her shirt to spin her around, and backhanded her face with a furious slap sending her sprawling across the room.

He was on her again, holding her down, threatening to end her right there, hands around her neck squeezing her windpipe so she felt like she was in a room with all the air sucked out of it. Her hands were grasping, grasping for something she could use. She felt the insulin needle she reached for earlier, grabbed it, and stuck it in his chest, pushing in the full vial of liquid. His eyes glossed over as he fell off of her. He sat slumped up against her bed.

"You're not a very sweet girl are you?" he said to her, one last smile flickering across his lips, and then his eyes rolled back in his head as he breathed his last breath.

Fenton pulled himself off the floor, noticing the Confectionist immobile by Scarlet's feet. He drew himself up, and took the pulse of the man, and felt nothing. *He's dead.* He looked over at Scarlet, wide-eyed and terrified, and he crouched next to her.

"What happened, Scarlet?"

"I killed him! He was going to kill you. I grabbed a needle, but he hit me, then he was choking me— choking me until I couldn't breathe, and I was going to lose consciousness, but I found the needle that fell from my hand in the scuffle. I was able to grab it, and stabbed it in his chest, and injected all the insulin from the vial. I didn't expect it to work immediately, but he slumped onto me right away. I think he is *dead.* I killed him, Fenton. I killed him, but I didn't mean to, I just wanted him to stop. Oh my God, I'm a murderer!" Tears were streaking down her beautiful face as the words rushed out of her in a panic. She was unraveling in front of him, piece by piece, and he surveyed the scene one last time before making up his plan to protect her. Fenton's eyes scanned the body, noticing the placement of the needle. Scarlet had managed to inject the insulin directly into his heart.

"Okay, listen carefully to me. Forget this ever happened. I'm going to say I killed him. Do you understand? I'm going to call Carter, tell her *I did this*, and have her send a clean-up team. There was a scuffle, and I grabbed what I had at my disposal before he could get to this gun. I grabbed the needle and injected him. End of story. I'm going to take the rest of this, the vials with your fingerprints and throw them in the dumpster outside the kitchen area. You are going to move to my room though, and don't talk to anyone. I'm going to take care of this, this won't even touch you, you understand? Scarlet, look at me, tell me you understand," His steely determined voice cut through her confusion.

"Why would you do that? I don't understand why you would take the blame for me," she asked, barely above an audible whisper.

"Just do as I say, erase this from your mind. I did this, remember, I did this. Don't argue. It's time for you to get going." He cupped her face gently, then blinked and pulled away. *Don't get out of character now Fenton. Especially when you have her at the right distance from you emotionally.* He noticed her whole body quivered at his touch.

"What do I tell Luca? I'm supposed to meet him," she asked.

"Don't say anything to him. We don't know who sent the hit for you. It could be Luca for all we know. It will be safer for whoever set this up to believe you're dead — at least for the time being, okay?"

She nodded, her eyes frantically taking in the room, in shock.

Fenton grabbed the body under the arms and dragged him into the closet along with the cart. He then took all of the needles and vials, and anything which could link back to Scarlet into the bag he grabbed from the trash basket.

"Can you walk?" he asked as he came toward her, trash bag in hand.

"I think so, maybe." She tried getting to her feet, and he grabbed her arm, putting it securely around his waist. He laced his arm around her body to steady her as she moved with him to the door. He was cautious exiting her room, making sure no one was in the hallway to see the two of them leaving. He then helped her to his room, having her lie on his bed.

"Listen carefully, and do exactly as I say. I'm going to drop this in the dumpster, and then I'll be right back. Don't let anyone in while I'm gone and don't answer the phone, got it? He said sternly, and she nodded in agreement.

He made his way to the dumpster outside, getting rid of any evidence to go against the story he was about to tell Carter. He took a deep breath, and dialed her number.

Lie, Fenton. Lie like you've never done before. Make it sound convincing. The last thing Scarlet needs is a murder tied to her name. You don't want to compromise her position. She deserves a chance at a real life after this, and I'm going to make sure it happens.

After Carter listened to his version of events, she had questions she wanted answered. "Do you think her cover is blown? Do we know who sent him? Do you think it was Luca? Perhaps he thinks she is expendable now, but he still wanted her to complete the job for him so it doesn't add up. We need to figure out who else wanted her out of the way," Carter said, over the sounds of the airplane engine revving in the background.

"I know. I'm instructing her not to contact Luca for now, in case. We want whoever set this up to think she is dead until we can piece some of this together. I'm going to talk to her about it when I get back to the room. As planned, once we touch down in D.C. I want to take her straight away to the safe house. I will probably have the team grab some of her original clothing, and pack what we need. I don't know what this will do to her. She will obviously be shaken up. I think a change of scenery is what she needs, and I know just the place," he said.

"Okay, keep me posted when you have a theory. You said the body is in her closet, right? I'll send a team over right away. We will run his prints and see if we get any hits. Perhaps we even have a record of him from our various surveillance operations. I'll send a message to you as soon as we have the material off the laptop and phone as well. I know you like to take those cheap burner cell phones when you go off the grid, but Fenton, stay in close communication with me. We are not out of the woods yet," Carter warned, but he knew what she was afraid to admit.

"Yeah, well a manic witness won't do you any good either. She needs rest, Carter, and I'm going to make sure she gets it," he said sternly.

"Don't forget our deal, Fenton."

"I couldn't if it tried."

"That's my guy. Safe travels, and Godspeed." Carter hung up, and Fenton headed back into the hotel to see Scarlet, the adrenaline finally starting to dissipate. He was nervous though, wondering what state he would find his witness in when he returned after such a traumatic ordeal. He stopped at a vending machine and picked up a candy bar, and took a deep breath before turning the knob to his hotel suite.

He saw her in the corner, wide-eyed and terrified, and it churned his insides. He had to fight every urge to run toward her, sweeping her into his arms, telling her she would be safe with him. He shook his head, trying to brush away the thoughts like cobwebs.

"I need you to pack everything and get ready. Here, eat this. Should help balance out your sugar levels a little more." He handed her the candy bar and she took it gladly.

"Fenton..."

"There is nothing else to discuss, just do as you're told," he said sternly, and she bit her lip at the reprimand.

"I killed that man," she said barely above a whisper.

"No, Scarlet. What did I say earlier? I killed him, remember? It is going to be important for you to keep this story straight." He folded his arms, he was taking the desperate feeling of seeing her hurting and funneling it into anger. He could hardly look at her without melting, and he needed to stay strong. She sniffled in the corner.

"Did you hear me? You need to get ready."

"Yes, sir," she mumbled.

"Sometimes bad things happen, Scarlet, even when you are trying to do something good. Wash this from your mind. I'm going to walk the route to the underground parking garage. We have a red-eye flight later tonight and I want us to sneak out of here in the cover of nightfall, to make sure no one sees us. I have a walkway cleared through the kitchen, but I want to double-check the path once more."

She grabbed his hand as she was about to walk away, and when he looked into those large green eyes which pleaded with him to stay. She could hardly speak, her lip was trembling and her body was moving in sporadic little spasms from the emotional toll the heaving sobs took on her.

"Fenton, I feel...hollow inside. I have become someone I don't even know. There is darkness inside me. How do I wipe these beastly images from my mind? How do I make his wicked laugh and his candy smell leave my thoughts? Robin has taken over my body, and now the Confectionist has my mind. I don't know how to live like this, all of these lies, all of this evil. It's invading me from the inside out, trying to turn me into something unrecognizable. I feel *nothing*. I don't remember what it feels like to be Scarlet. I don't remember who that girl was and how she felt, because this darkness in me is eating up everything standing in its way like a tornado. Can't you make it stop? I need it to *stop,* Fenton, help me. Help me!" She reached for his hand, noticing a little scar on his hand. She looked at it for a moment and then dropped his hand when she realized what she was doing.

His eyes closed at the soft touch of her skin. It heated every square inch of his body, and he wanted to lean in and kiss her deeply, passionately. It crushed him to see her like this, vulnerable, looking to him to reassure her and make her feel whole again. It was that pesky possessive feeling again, when she touched him, when she looked at him as if he was the only one she could see. The urge within him to make her happy was strong. He wanted nothing more than to help her feel comfortable and safe. He yearned to see her smile, a real, unadulterated smile, not forced or disingenuous. He was becoming too invested in her feelings and mood, all of the nuances which should come second to keeping her alive, and he knew it.

Conflicting feelings and uncertainty weren't normal for him and he didn't like it. It muddled his thoughts and kept him burning for her, those insatiable flames in the pit of his stomach were constant embers now. She had too much control over him, she was re-wiring his insides. The spell she cast over him was spinning his insides so tightly that the coils were reconnecting and twisting in new ways, keeping him off balance. She had entirely too much in common with him. She was beautifully broken, withered and burdened, yet somehow more resilient and stronger than ever.

He scolded himself for taking this last job with an innocent who struggled through many of the same trials and tribulations. Empathy was dangerous. His thoughts were becoming more like mush when she affected him in this way, which meant he was endangering her, and the job, because he wasn't focused on the right things one hundred percent of the time.

"Scarlet, I don't know how to help you. I'm here to keep you safe, that's all," he said softly, knowing full well his words were lies, and it took every ounce of strength not to comfort her in her time of need. He saw her eyes change, he rebuffed her yet again, and she walked toward the window.

He decided taking a look around the exit route one more time would help keep him distracted. *Any distraction will help.* He turned to go, pausing at the door. Every fiber of his being wanted him to turn around, and go back to her. He knew if he turned and saw her face, exposed and needing him, he wouldn't be able to leave. He took a deep breath, cursed to himself, and walked out the door without looking back.

Chapter 30

"I'm walking to my death, this is the day."

Several hours later, Scarlet and Fenton safely landed back in Washington, D.C and temporarily got a hotel room while Fenton arranged the last minute plans to take her to the safety of his lake house. Scarlet paced in the small hotel room, the chaos of the last few days creating a constant buzz in her ears like flies circling a garbage can in the summertime.

Scarlet heard a knock at her door. She assumed it was Fenton, but felt she wasn't ready to face him again. Peering through the peephole, she saw Agent James Westbrook stood outside her door with a stack of envelopes instead. She opened the door.

"Agent Westbrook, I didn't expect you at the hotel. To what do I owe the pleasure?" she said with a quick smile.

"I know you're heading out soon with Fenton to an undisclosed location, so I thought you may want to go through your mail before you leave. We've held it for you, but since we don't know how long you're going to be gone and you can't go back to your apartment, I thought I would stop by with what I have while you're still in town. I probably shouldn't be bothering you with this right now, but I know if it were me, I would get a little comfort seeing a couple of things from my old life." He dropped the stack of mail on her table.

"Um, thanks. That was nice of you. I appreciate it."

"Know when you're heading out, or in which general vicinity he is taking you yet?" he asked.

She gave a quick shrug. "Nope, I think Fenton is focused on making sure everything is a secret, even to me I guess." She was used to being in the dark when it came to the case, or even what the next day would bring.

"Yeah, he is cautious that way. Well, I'll let you get back to packing, and I'm sure you want some time to dig in. Good luck, Scarlet."

"Thanks, I guess I'll see you when I get back?"

"See you then."

She wasn't excited to look at her mail at all. She imagined the stack filled with bills for things she no longer used, a request to interview for her dream job that would never be, cards from family she would never see again, or promotions for stores which soon would be states away from wherever they relocated her. For a moment she debated throwing the whole stack unseen into the trash.

As she picked up the pile, ready to dispose of everything, the top letter got to her sense of curiosity. It was addressed to her in her aunt's handwriting. Placing the pile back on the table, she nervously opened the envelope. She could only imagine how angry and worried Aunt Jo must be with her for discontinuing all communication. A surge of guilt washed over Scarlet as she pulled out the letter.

Scarlet, I'm sorry to have to write this to you. A couple men came to see me today, and they need to speak with you. I'm with them, at the address below, please come as soon as you can. They told me if the police or anyone else gets involved, they will kill me. I love you more than anything, your Aunt Jo. (DC)

Scarlet slumped into a chair. She felt entirely responsible. Waves of nausea hit her hard, and she went running to the bathroom to throw up. She knew what DC meant, it was her aunt's clever way of telling her without the people holding her hostage knowing, *don't come*. She was teaching her aunt to text and Aunt Jo loved using letters instead of typing out the full sentence. She would often text CO for come over, or DC for don't come. When she needed help at the vineyard she would text DC Sat, CO Sun. It was smart, she probably told the men it was her term of endearment for their life close to the District of Columbia, but Scarlet knew her Aunt would rather die than put her in danger. *I'm not going to let that happen. I am not going to let one more person die because of me.*

She cleaned herself up, packing a bag with a couple of pocket knives she found in Fenton's bag, and anything else she could find she could use to defend herself around the small hotel room. She pulled out the bulky yellow pages book she found stuffed in the tiny bedside table of the hotel to locate the address and found a bus line to bring her somewhat close. She would have to walk the rest of the way without any other form of transportation. She knew Fenton was getting the last of the supplies for the trip, and wasn't in his room attached to hers. She could wait for him, or leave him a note, but she decided to do neither. She knew this was her fight, and involving anyone else would simply endanger their lives as well.

She waited for the bus, pacing back and forth by the sign, wearing sunglasses and one of Fenton's sweatshirts with the hood over her hair to hopefully disguise herself from anyone who could recognize her. When she saw the bus appear around the corner, she had a powerful wave of emotion hit her. *I'm going to die. I'm walking to my death, this is the day. This could be it for me.* She swallowed hard, strangely comforted by the fact if she were to die, it would be on her terms, trying to protect her mother.

Not a mother by blood, but the only mother she ever knew. It wasn't even a question. If given the choice, she would die to protect her mother.

Chapter 31

"If she flees, they will find her and kill her."

Carter was busy working with her lab team when she noticed Fenton's name pop up on her cell phone.

"Fenton, what's up? Are you both still in Washington or have you headed out already off the grid?"

"Getting ready to go. Wanted to check in before we left. Has your team uncovered anything on the laptop or phone Scarlet gathered from Robin's locker yet?"

"No, no luck, yet. My team is having troubles with getting into both devices. She didn't use her typical passwords on these, and the level of security is more substantial on both. We will get into it eventually. It's just a matter of time," she replied evenly.

"I don't like this, Carter. We are working blind. There is a laptop and cell holding information that could be pivotal to this case and Scarlet's safety. What if there is essential material which will reveal Scarlet as a fraud? We have no knowledge of what is on the two devices. How do you expect me to keep her safe when I don't have all the information?" he huffed, and Carter had to bite back sour words lingering at the tip of her tongue.

"Fenton, I'm not expecting you to be a miracle worker. You did the best you could in Vegas. You went above and beyond helping us vet out everyone at the party and assisting in helping us transform Scarlet into Robin. We have to focus on what we can control, and if my team is able to hack into the cell and computer and we uncover something that will put her at risk, I promise you we will take the necessary measures to keep her safe. Plus, this part is on my team. Where I really need you is to keep her safe now and up to the trial. That is all we can do now, and we can't pull this mission simply because there could be unknown danger, because you and I both know, it doesn't matter how hard you prep an undercover asset, there is always an element of danger. I appreciate your concern, but I need you exuding confidence in this mission in front of Scarlet. We can't have her thinking anything is off kilter. Do you agree?" Carter asked in slow and even tones. She needed to lull him into agreement so she tried appealing to his sense of logic.

"Yes, I agree," he said reluctantly. Carter nodded wearily on the other end of the phone. She wanted to move away from this topic as quickly as possible because she had something much more pressing to discuss with him.

"I sent you a couple of files last night, the results from her psych evaluation. Did you have a chance to review?" Carter said.

"Yes."

"What did you think? What do you deduct from the findings?" Carter asked, already knowing his conclusions would be correct, but needing him to say the words so he would arrive at the solution she needed him to deploy.

"The results show a scared, but stable, young lady despite the pressures she is dealing with right now. That being said, she is someone who needs to feel supported and comforted in times of immense stress. She is depressed, understandably, in some instances bordering on manic. Without watchful observation, she could cross the line and become suicidal, or try to escape her situation by running away. It would help if she could get back into a normal routine. Reintroducing hobbies or safe activities she enjoys that would remind her of her life before all of this happened. It would give her a sense of control in what she perceives is now a world of chaos. Without stability or something to anchor her, after everything she has gone through, we risk losing her cooperation. If she flees, they will find her and kill her," he stated matter-of-factly, Carter sensed he chose his words carefully to sound more clinical than emotional.

"Well said. My thoughts exactly. Looks like the anchor will need to be you. She feels a bond with you since you rescued her that night at her apartment. I can see the way her face lights up for a second when you come into the room, despite your attempts to run her like a recruit in the army. You need to soften a bit toward her, Fenton. She has pinpointed you as someone she is willing to risk trusting, so you will need to get her to open up to you." There was silence on the phone.

"I need you to be the person she puts her complete confidence in, so when you ask her to do something she doesn't want to do in the future, she'll do it simply because *you* asked her to. It wouldn't hurt to bring a peace offering. Get some art supplies or whatever you think she would like. If she wants to paint, sculpt, hell she could make wind chimes for all I care, you need to be the one to bring it to her. You need to be the one in her mind who brings back some light to her world of darkness. Do what you need to get it done," Carter said.

"At what expense? I need to be tough on her and she has to understand everything that's at stake. I don't care if she thinks I'm too hard on her, if it keeps her safe at the end of the day. If I become her anchor, as you suggest, and with everything that implies, she could develop an emotional attachment to me. I don't want to do anything to cause her more pain. She has been through enough," he said, a sharp edge in his voice.

"Yeah, well think of all the pain the two powerful crime families are causing across the country as they push their drugs up and down the coasts, before you get on your moral high horse. Keep *that* in perspective, cowboy," she said in a snarky tone. She took a deep breath.

"Let me rephrase. I empathize with your hesitation about letting feelings get in the way. Let me ask you this though. Is it not already emotional for her? Her twin is killed in front of her eyes, her personal place of residence is invaded by a perpetrator wearing a cop uniform, and she's tortured with poison. Instead of facing a brutal outcome you were there to save her. Even though she owes her life to you, which is already a personal debt, she also witnessed the intruder fall to his death as he toppled out of the window of her home. Now she's witnessed a third death in Vegas after she was attacked in her hotel room. In my meager opinion, it is past the point of questioning whether this will be personal and emotional for her. She lost both of her parents, as well as her only sibling, and this case has ensured she won't be able to continue a relationship with her aunt, the only family she has left. She can't connect with friends, colleagues, her dream job, her passions, and is, for all practical purposes, living on an island removed from society as she once knew it." The silence hung heavy between them like a fog at night. She took a long breath and made sure the tone of her voice was sweet and soothing to help coax him to her side.

"If you, the person who saved her when there was no hope, the person who came into her life telling her she can make it out of this to the other side against all odds, can bring a little life back to her dismal reality, would that be such a horrible thing? If she felt she had someone in her corner, looking out for her, someone who cares what happens to her and cares about her happiness? If it gets her through this hell, a nightmare which has turned into her waking reality, then maybe it's worth whatever pain it will cause her tomorrow. I'm more concerned about getting her through tonight, then tomorrow, and the next day after that. Can you be her friend, her confidant, her angel, her whatever she needs you to be? Just to get the poor girl through the valley of shadows? Can you do that for me?" Carter pleaded. There was silence on the other end of the phone. She knew what she asked was not a small favor. She was asking him to become a chameleon for her case despite his thoughts or feelings on the matter, so her star witness and undercover asset stayed happy and sane.

"Okay, Carter. If you think that's best," he said. *Does he sound nervous?*

"Okay great. It needs to start here and now. She is dealing with dangerous people who almost killed her, playing a wicked charade, and we can't have her crumbling now. If she breaks, she needs you to be the glue that can put her back together. You're sure you're up for that?" Carter asked, breaking him away from his thoughts.

"I'll get her through this, you've got my word," he said softly. *Perfect.* Carter smiled proudly, like a baseball coach sending in the closer at the last inning of the game.

"I'm giving you a lot of rope on this, Fenton. Keep me posted on progress when you take her off the grid, I want to see how you're making strides to gain her complete and total trust. I will need that level of trust. *We* will need her trust going into the next phase of this plan. If anyone could get it done, I know you're the guy. I just care about the results. I think you two already have a connection, so just keep building on it."

"I hate to admit you're right Carter, but yes, I think I can get her to trust me. Fine, I'll do what I can."

"Don't worry about building the connection, Fenton. I know you can be likable when you need to be."

"Yeah, add that to the list of things keeping me up at night."

"Chin up, Fenton. I wouldn't have picked you if I didn't have complete faith in your abilities. Now get our girl out of D.C. and away from anyone who could find her. Be safe."

"Always." She heard a click on the other end of the phone, and Carter couldn't help but smile to herself.

Chapter 32

"Even the most ruthless of killers... can't kill a ghost."

Eleonora hummed to herself as she took a leisurely stroll around the property before finding her brother Luca. She was enjoying the view from the balcony of the vast mansion as she made a few phone calls. One particularly successful call was with Vinny, a top hitman in her arsenal of favorites. Vinny was not his real name, but a nickname after he made a reputation for blowing up cars so even the VIN number wasn't detectable once he was through, let alone the make or model of the vehicle. His craft was designing explosives used on cars, and his specialty was installing a dirty bomb in record time so while an unsuspecting person was in the store running a quick errand, he could slide under their car and effectively install a bomb which would explode after a certain number of miles. He typically would rearrange his schedule when his best employer called, and today was no exception. She even managed to convince him with a hefty fee to stay on call for her throughout the day.

She made her way into the mansion through the door on the

balcony, weaving her way through a couple of large rooms, used mainly for entertaining, before she found Luca in the study, hunched over papers and yelling into the end of his cellphone.

"I don't care if you don't know! I'm paying you to find out! Someone ordered the hit on Alonzo, and I need to know which dirty coward thought they could get away with killing my brother. On behalf of my father, I will *right this wrong*. Dig around the Durante's. This stinks of rival bad blood, but I want to be absolutely certain. Get it done, and no excuses. Don't call me until you have something." Luca hung up, a look of disgust on his face, which immediately lightened when he saw Eleonora walk into the room.

"Sister, I'm glad to see you. I could use a distraction right now." He smiled warmly at her. She pulled a long, dark strand of hair behind her ear, and plastered on a wide fake smile in response.

"Brother, I certainly hope I can provide a distraction for you, you look tense. I know this must be a terrible burden for you, trying to figure out who came after Alonzo. I hope I can help," she said.

"Oh, Eleonora, I wish you could help, but I don't see how. Thank you though. Perhaps making sure Father has everything he needs. Could you bring him some coffee, and make sure he is eating? Luckily, with all the good news I just gave Father, finding Alonzo's killer would only help to further solidify my role in this family. I know Father will be comforted by the fact the family is in my capable hands. I have a lot of work to do, and the police will come sniffing around due to Alonzo's death, but I can handle it. I think the Durantes might be behind this, but there isn't any buzz on the streets or anyone taking ownership of the hit. I'll have to drag it out of someone, maybe I can get someone to snitch," he said, as he looked out the window above the desk in the study, calculating his next move and forgetting Eleonora was standing in the room with him.

"I know this isn't the time, brother, but we talked about my role of aligning with you in this family. Have you given that any thought? I know I can take on more responsibility, and I would like more ownership in the family affairs." She tilted her head at him, already anticipating his answer, but needing to hear him seal his fate by confirming her suspicions.

"Eleonora, you're right. This isn't the best time. I think you are doing everything you should be doing right now. I appreciate your loyalty, and we can think about your future after all of this is settled. There are a lot of domestic responsibilities and I think you may be best suited for those right now. Patience, and don't worry, you will be taken care of by this family when I take the reins. I don't want to complicate matters at the moment by shifting responsibility, you understand?" Luca said. Eleonora gritted her teeth, but put on her most understanding face.

"You are right. That makes sense. We shouldn't complicate things right now, especially with the mess you are in right now with the whole Alonzo and Robin situation. I'll let you get back to work," Eleonora said, as she headed toward the door.

"Wait, what Robin situation are you referring to exactly?" Luca said, his interest piqued.

"I assumed you already knew. She was acting strange when we went shopping. She kept leaving to take phone calls, and seemed very ill at ease. I knew I shouldn't follow her outside, assuming she was talking to you on the phone, of course, but when I overheard some of her conversation, I was simply appalled. You must know all about it though, I mean, she is employed by you, and romantically ensnarled with you as well. Anything I tell you now would only be information you must surely already be privy to, due to your sources," Eleonora said. Luca looked frantic, and drew a ragged breath as he ran a shaky hand through his perfectly styled hair.

"Tell me anyway. I want to make sure I'm filling any gaps I may not already know." He swallowed hard and Eleonora smiled back sweetly. He was a decent liar, and a pompous blowhard to the end she thought to herself. He had to make it appear he was in control. He couldn't know any of this because she hatched this plan only a couple hours earlier. He had no way of knowing she pulled his strings to see him dance like a little puppet.

"If you're sure, I hate saying any of this, knowing how much you trusted her. All I can say is she was making plans to get on a plane. She was urgently trying to get away from here as fast as she could. She did arrange a meet with someone, she never said a name, but I heard her say she would bring the folder with all the information. She said it was payment for the work they did. I could only assume she was referring to the hit on Alonzo. It must be a member of the Durante organization. She is giving them back all of their private information in exchange for her life." Luca stiffened.

"She was apologizing profusely to them on the phone. Said they wouldn't regret it. I could only listen in for a while, but she did repeat the location of the meet. I can write it down for you. She also said something about our Costa Di Lago street office being bugged, so you should stop there first and check the office quickly before trying to confront them. If Father were to find out one of the offices we own was bugged due to *your lack of judgment*, he would kill you himself," she said the last words slowly, with measure, and she saw terror flash across her brother's face. *Good, I've got him right where I need him.*

"I'm sorry brother. The meet is in two hours, and gives you enough time to debug the office. I would park in the back if I were you so the security cameras don't catch you coming in. It will be our little secret you were there, and then you can whack them both in the alley. It is a perfect plan, but that's why you're going to drive this family to greatness. You do what needs to be done, and when necessary, you do what needs to be done personally, when there is no room for error. I can sleep well brother, knowing you won't let the people near you double-cross you, and knowing you're the type of man who isn't afraid of confrontation, just like Alonzo. You will prove to Father you have what it takes to be more of a leader than he ever could be. Gabriel Nero will have tears of joy when you call him to tell him you personally took care of the two people responsible for Alonzo's death, Robin and a Captain in the Durante crime family." She wrote down the address on a napkin, and passed it to her brother. A dark cloud covered his face as he took it.

"I better head out. I want to make sure I sweep the office for any possible devices before heading to the alley. If Father asks, tell him I had to run a quick errand for the family, and didn't want to disturb him during his time of grief. Will you do that for me, Eleonora?" He was shuffling papers around on the desk, half organizing the chaotic work space. A couple of papers fell to the floor in the whoosh of activity, but he didn't notice. He was too busy seeing red, thinking about the double-cross and the blood which would soon be on his hands. Revenge consumed him, as did the fear he made a huge mistake. Fear his father would find out.

"Of course, I will do that for you brother," she said, working hard to control her facial muscles, which threatened to break out in a wide grin at any moment. The Costa Di Lago office was located about forty minutes from the Las Vegas Strip. It was nestled by the Las Vegas Wash, a twelve-mile-long channel which fed excess water into Lake Mead. She knew Vinny could time the explosives so at the exact moment Luca drove out of the office back parking lot, taking the most direct route to the alley, he would drive on a remote patch of road with water on either side. At that exact moment, the car would ignite, causing it to explode in two separate blasts – one blast on the driver's side to kill Luca and cut off the ability to steer the vehicle so the car careened off the road on either side, and the second explosion to blow the car to bits, thrusting the vehicle into the Wash at the most remote point of the road. The water would wash over the burning hunks of metal to hide the death for a period of time. That was what Eleonora needed to make her plan succeed. She didn't want Luca's body found, at least not for a while. It all hinged on Luca going to the office first, where Vinny could place the bomb, and since Luca was convinced he had to debug the office, it would give Vinny more than enough time to do his worst. *This might be my most perfect plan yet. You're getting better at this Eleonora. With each kill, it becomes clearer what needs to be done.*

"Make sure, brother, you debug the office first. After you have two bodies on your hands, you won't have time to go back. Father won't care what you did for him if he finds out you allowed him to be compromised. Best case, you find they didn't hit the office yet, but it's best to play it safe. Then nothing will be in the way of our success. I'm so proud to be able to help, brother, and I'm excited for what is to come for this family." She held out her hand to him, and he took it, kissing the back of her hand as he looked her in the eyes.

"What would I do without my beautiful sister? You're concerned for me and I'm touched. I was thinking the same thing. Thanks for covering for me with Father. I am overwhelmed with joy I can count on your loyalty, Eleonora, above all others. I must go." He hurried out of the office. Eleonora could hear the soles of his dress shoes clicking on the marble floor, fainting into the distance, and eventually disappearing.

She immediately called Vinny, and confirmed the plans. She hummed to herself again, delicately twisting a piece of her long, dark hair around her fingertips.

Oh yes, Luca, you can count on my loyalty. A loyalty to family above all else. I see a lot of promise for the Neros, a family made stronger by the loss of Gabriel Nero's two sons. Out of the ashes of their deaths a new powerful leader will arise. The true leader's face won't be revealed, a leader who is immortal, because she will operate like a ghost in the wind. A leader who has more power than all of her foes, because even the most ruthless of killers...can't kill a ghost.

Chapter 33

"Things don't work out for people like you."

Fenton came back to the hotel in Washington, pleased he finally had all the supplies they would need at the lake house where he intended to bring Scarlet. He finished packing up his truck, and knocked at their adjoined door to tell Scarlet to finish getting ready. There was no answer.

Getting the extra key to her room, he unlocked the door, and found the room empty. She had an unpacked bag open in the corner, a stack of mail on the table, and her backpack was gone. He started investigating, looking around the room for a clue as to where she could be.

She knows better than to leave without me, even if she needed something last minute before we go into hiding. She knows the risks. Why would she disappear without letting me know?

He saw the opened note on the table, next to the Yellow pages. He read the note, his fists clenching with anger and fear. He saw her notes listing bus lines, but he had no idea of how much of a head start she had on him. *Scarlet, what have you done?* He wrote down the address, and rushed into his room. Some of his knives were gone from one of the bags he kept in the room. He pulled out another gun he put in his back holster, and a smaller pistol that fit around his ankle holder.

He rushed out the door, fully armed, and got into his truck. He peeled out of the parking lot, driving full speed in the direction of where he believed Scarlet headed. He didn't consider himself to be an overly religious man, but he took the time as he was driving at breakneck speeds to pray.

He prayed for the strength and the ability to do what needed to be done when he got there. He prayed for Scarlet, and most important of all, he prayed to God he wasn't too late.

Scarlet slowly turned the doorknob of the abandoned house. A hand came up from behind her, clenching tightly over her mouth. Another arm fastened firmly around her waist, wrapping around her body as she was pulled off the doorstep, and dragged to the nearby woods. The thought passed her mind, thinking one of the men who grabbed her Aunt Jo finally got her. In her mind, she was as good as dead.

When the firm hold on her finally loosened, she whirled around to confront her foe, and came face to face with Fenton.

"What are you doing here? You scared me to death!" she hissed, catching her breath from the moment of terror of being grabbed from behind as she was about to enter the house to try to save her aunt.

"I could ask *you* the *same thing*, Scarlet. You deliberately disobeyed me. You came here by yourself and didn't even tell me you were leaving. Leaving without me was *stupid*, Scarlet. Are you trying to get yourself killed? Are you trying to get *both of us killed*?" Fenton was fuming. His fiery eyes burned into Scarlet, his fists were clenched and his body rigid, ready to jump into action. It made his already formidable figure appear even larger to Scarlet.

"You were out when I got the letter. I couldn't tell you so I slipped out. *They have my aunt*, Fenton, and I'm not about to let anyone else die because of me."

"You should have come to me with this instead of trying to take care of it by yourself. You don't trust me at all, do you?" His heart was racing in his chest. It was a close call, too close, and he didn't like the terror the thought left sizzling in his veins.

"You don't even want to be here to begin with, Fenton. You can't stand me. This is a messy job you didn't want any part of from the beginning. Carter must have something on you, something on you she held over your head, so you would help me. You don't have to protect me anymore. Now you can live your life, and get away from me. Sorry I kept you here this long. It's obviously painful for you to be anywhere near me as you can't stand to look at me. Just admit this job is making you miserable, Fenton."

"Scarlet, I took this job because I *wanted* to take this job. I wanted to help you because I knew you were innocent of this whole mess. I took this job because I don't want to see someone like you get hurt from the evil that exists in this world. Yes, I'm working for Carter, but I could have just as easily walked away."

"You're lying to me, and you don't need to anymore. I fire you, or let you go, or whatever magic words I need to say to release you from this burden. Something about me gets under your skin, and you've wanted to run far away from this job the moment we met. Tell me now or I'm going into that house to get my Aunt Jo. Admit it," she said.

Fenton stared at her in disbelief. Her hands on her hips, her lips pouting out as she fumed.

Shit, even when she is pissed, she is beautiful. What are you going to say now, tough guy? You've gotten yourself into a real predicament.

Fenton sighed and scratched the back of his neck. He looked down at her again, and then paced a bit, then pulled her further into the cover of the thick forest.

"Sit, on that stump," he directed, and she did as she was told. She folded her arms in protest, looking up at him.

"You're wearing my sweatshirt," he mumbled.

"I just confronted you about your true feelings, the fact you despise me and this job, and that is all you have to say in response? I grabbed your precious sweatshirt? Fine, *sorry*, I'll take it off." She dropped her backpack and started peeling off the hooded sweatshirt when he stopped her.

"Keep it on. Why do you have to be so difficult *all the time*? I don't care about the sweatshirt, Scarlet. Listen, I don't know how to say this, so I'm just going to say it, okay? Bear with me here, this isn't my strong suit." He paced back and forth, hating himself for what he was about to admit, but he couldn't risk her running into that house without him. His skin was already crawling from the fact she was outside, exposed, and the men who took her aunt could be lurking behind any of the trees waiting for the right moment. He knew he had to get her out of there. He decided to come clean, and convince her to leave with him. He remembered what Carter said, he should do whatever it takes to get her to trust him so she'll listen. She needs someone to lean on, and it was time to pull emotions into the conversation.

"I don't hate you Scarlet. I do want to be here. Well, not *here* as in these woods because you ran away without telling me, but here as in... *anywhere you are* because I want to keep you safe. You may have gotten the impression I hate you, dislike you, and can't stand to be around you. I know you think that, because I've tried hard to make you think it, because it's easier, and because I need to overcorrect my feelings toward you. I was worried my feelings toward you were heading in the wrong direction, so I tried to correct that by keeping you at a distance. In hindsight, it may not have been the best way to handle the situation, and maybe we wouldn't be here today if I had handled things differently," Fenton said, shifting his weight onto his other foot and looking uncomfortable.

Scarlet narrowed her eyes toward him and said, "What do you mean you worried your feelings toward me were headed in the wrong direction? You mean, this was all an act? The annoyance, the curt responses, the fact you could *hardly look me in the eye*? That was all to get me to do what exactly? Did you want me to drive you away?" She looked hurt, and he flinched at her response.

"I was doing it to make sure I could do my job."

"Your job? That meant you had to become an ass whenever I was in the room? I don't have time for this, Fenton. I have to save my aunt."

"*Sit down, Scarlet,*" he said through clenched teeth. The thought of her running into the house by herself was almost too much to bear. She looked at him.

"I couldn't let you get close to me, because of my feelings toward you. From seeing you tied up in that chair, to talking with you while you were in the hospital room, scared out of your mind. I couldn't stop thinking about you, *okay*? *Fine*, you're getting it out of me. I never felt this way toward a client before, and it's driving me crazy. Your background, who you are, everything about you, everything that's happened to you...I have to fight the urge every day to take you in my arms, away from all of this, someplace where you can be safe and happy. You're *the perfect girl*, Scarlet. I mean you, not you transformed as Robin, *but you*." She took a step backward, her eyes wide.

"See, it's dangerous thoughts like that, that I'm trying to avoid. I don't have the luxury in this line of work to develop feelings toward someone I need to protect. It's unprofessional, and it clouds my judgment. I tried to stay disciplined when it came to you. I was trying everything I could to distance myself, but I've never been as scared in my whole life...as I was back there at the hotel when I found you had left. I kept thinking I lost you. I've been through a lot, but that was one of the worst feelings I've ever experienced. *I care about you*, Scarlet. I shouldn't care for you the way I do, but it's how I feel. Since I realized I was starting to feel that way, I've worked hard to correct those feelings. Okay?" he said, shoving his hands in his pockets.

She stared at him in shocked silence. He was intently looking at the ground as if he just admitted some horrible fault, and Scarlet came toward him. She grabbed his hand, rubbing the scar on the back with her thumb. She kissed it lightly, and electricity ran through him. It lit him up inside, like a light turning on within a dark tunnel. For a second, all he saw was her delicate features, those green eyes enveloping him, and everything else fell away. He moved his hand to the side of her face, and graced the contour of her jaw, tracing her skin with his fingers to the warmth of her neck. She closed her eyes for a moment, and then looked into his, and he felt as if the ground dropped beneath his feet.

"Fenton, you could have told me."

"Yeah, well it's not an easy thing to say, and if it weren't for you running away I would have probably never said it. Promise me, now I've bared this truth to you. Promise me you'll listen to what I'm asking you to do. Promise me you won't run away like that again. *You're going to kill me*, Scarlet, if you keep this up. I'm dropping the drill sergeant routine. This is just me, begging you to *let me do my job to keep you safe*." She closed her eyes tightly as she pulled in a deep breath.

"I promise. I don't want to hurt you."

"Now, this is one of these moments where I need you to listen to me. I can't have you go inside the house after your aunt, it's not safe. I am going to take a look around, and I need you to stay in the car." He started leading her by her hand through the woods to an opening where his truck waited off the main road as she protested to no avail.

"Stay here," he said firmly, locking the doors behind him. He snuck back to the house, finding a way to approach the dilapidated building while staying close to the ground. Peering into the window, he saw Aunt Jo tied up, but couldn't see anyone else in the house with her. Suddenly, he noticed the devices on the doors. *Shit. It's rigged.*

He headed back to the woods, pulling out his cell as he ran toward the truck, realizing the men who set this up must still be around waiting for the final results. He called Carter, and filled her in on the situation, and she said she would get the bomb squad out to the property. He dreaded telling Scarlet. He slid into the driver's side door and started the truck.

"What are you doing? We need to go in there! We can't leave my aunt!"

"I'm sorry Scarlet, but they have the whole placed rigged with explosives. I called Carter and she has the bomb squad heading over here now."

"Rigged with explosives? Stop the truck! *Stop the truck, Fenton!*" She opened the door while he was driving, causing him to slam on the brakes. She jumped out.

"Scarlet, stop!" he cursed as he threw the truck into park, and ran after her. He caught up to her, and grabbed her, throwing her effortlessly over his shoulder. She was kicking and pushing at him in protest, but stopped when she realized his iron grip wasn't going to let her go. He opened her side of the truck, placed her in the front seat, and strapped her in. Locking the door behind him as he shut her in, he got back into the driver's seat and set the truck in motion once again.

"I can't leave her, Fenton! Let me out! I'll never forgive you for this!" Scarlet screamed, as she clawed at her seatbelt and tried unlocking her door.

"Childproofed. All doors but the driver's seat, for situations just like this. You can't get out, Scarlet, so stop fighting. What would you do? Bust into the house? You could set off the explosives by mistake, which would kill not only your aunt, but both of us as well."

"Both of us? Let me out now, and I'll do it alone," she stammered.

"Have you heard anything I just told you? You're not leaving this truck, Scarlet, and you sure as hell are not going anywhere by yourself. I won't let you out of my sight. Do you understand? Hate me, if you need to, but I'm here to protect you. Even keeping you out in the woods with me as long as I did was a risky move. The men who are after you could be anywhere. Going after your aunt won't save her. We have experts coming to get her as we speak, who handle these situations. She is going to be okay, but anything we would have tried would only have put her in more peril. Do you understand?"

"I can't believe you made me leave her. The only family I have left, the only person who cares about me is in a room tied to a chair. She could die at any minute if those bombs go off, because of me. All because of me, and you prevented me from doing anything about it. How could you? What kind of person are you?" She bit back tears, a look of pure contempt for him on her face.

"I've done a lot of bad things in my life, but this isn't one of them. I care, Scarlet. Shit, *I care* about you. Killing yourself won't help your aunt and getting yourself hurt or worse won't make you feel any less guilty. I know you don't believe me, *but this isn't your fault,* Scarlet. Let me help your aunt, trust me. You may hate me now, and that is okay, but eventually, you will see this is for the best." Tears were streaming down her face. She looked out her window in silence, no longer fighting, but also unable to look at him.

He knew she may never forgive him. He told her how he felt, and it blew up in his face. He scolded himself for expecting anything different. He knew the job doesn't allow for a life. Plus, she knew nothing about him, his background or what he had to do for the job. He felt foolish for thinking he could end up with her, and the white picket fence. A happy ending doesn't exist for bodyguards. Her anger toward him hurt him like a knife wound, and he cursed himself for becoming emotionally entangled. It was the last time he would make the mistake of showing he cared, because it only ended in more pain. She needed a protector, not an emotional wreck.

Fenton continued to assure himself as they drove in tension-filled silence her contempt for him was a small price to pay for her safety. He knew her safety trumped every other consideration, but he felt the loss of her trust like a bullet, and it hurt him deeper than he would ever admit.

Chapter 34

"Isn't that what we spend a lifetime searching for?"

Carter stayed in close communication with Fenton, and the bomb squad successfully removed the devices from the abandoned house and escorted Aunt Jo back to the safety of her home at the vineyard with police protection stationed outside to keep watch. The police searched the area but did not find anyone suspicious near the house. With her Aunt out of harm's way, there was nothing stopping Fenton and Scarlet from disappearing off the grid for a while.

Fenton explained to Scarlet she would leave all technology behind, and he would only bring his small computer which allowed encrypted access to secure messaging sites, and a burner phone so they couldn't be tracked. The small hitch in the plan was he planned on taking her to a lake home he owned. To protect her identity and give her a credible cover, she would have to pretend to be his girlfriend to explain why he was bringing her there for an extended period of time so the neighbors wouldn't be suspicious. She agreed, because she didn't have a choice, but she made it clear to him she wasn't pleased.

She hadn't spoken to him, except basic, one-word responses, since the day he drove her away from her aunt. Even though she was now safe, Scarlet couldn't ignore the fact her Aunt Jo could have as easily died. She also wasn't allowed to talk to her aunt, a mandate from Carter, which she was still fuming about. She wasn't ready to forgive him yet, or herself, from putting her only family at risk.

They drove in complete silence further into the wilderness, on a dirt road looking as if it was completely forgotten by regular civilization. Grass was growing between the stones, and the unkempt path curved and broke into smaller pieces of road which would most likely deter many unwanted guests from continuing down the abandoned road.

The lane opened to another paved stretch leading up into the rolling hills with dense tree coverage. Scarlet slept a little on the ride, mentally exhausted from the events of the past several weeks, and was surprised when she finally opened her eyes again to find their vehicle approaching a gated community.

Fenton typed in a code on the massive silver box in front of the large metal gates, and the entryway opened for them to drive through. It was another hour until they pulled into the winding driveway with two houses on the property, and a little guest house nestled behind the two buildings leading to the water's edge where boats and jet skis were tied to a wooden dock. She shot a look over at Fenton, who was grinning ear to ear.

"I told you, secluded. Private. Hidden. I didn't lie, did I?" His excitement about his private spot warmed her cold feelings a little. She shook her head in response.

"Come on, Scarlet. You can be pissed at me, but maybe a couple of words here and there wouldn't kill you. Remember, our cover here at the lake house is we are a couple. I know the people who live next door, personally. I need a little effort from you, or are you trying to win an award for best supporting actress playing the role of the livid girlfriend?"

"This cover was your idea, remember? I didn't ask you to take me away from the farmhouse, and I didn't ask you to bring me here. I think I have a right to be upset."

"Sure, you can be upset with me for as long as you want. This is the only place I know where no one can find you, so can you humor me a little bit? I go back with Dale from next door a long time and I would appreciate some cooperation. *I'm asking nicely, Scarlet.* Can you just play along? You can go back to hating my guts when we leave here, deal?"

"Okay, fine. For Dale's sake, so I don't ruin their family's time up here, I'll play nice. Yeah, you didn't lie. A gated community, a small private lake hidden by miles of dense forest and winding roads, a path constructed to look like it was forgotten long ago to deter guests from venturing further. We are certainly in the middle of nowhere. Is this a lake house or did you take me to Fort Knox?" she mused.

"My job is security, remember, and this place is as secure as they come."

"Then maybe you can finally relax, Fenton."

He raised an eyebrow at her.

"I can tell you need some rest. You have permanent circles under your eyes, and the line that appears between your eyes when you get really angry or tense, it's back again. Don't get me wrong, you pull it off, it gives you this rugged scowl, but I know that isn't you." She pulled a piece of hair behind her ear, and looked at him.

"I know I haven't made your job easy in Las Vegas, or when I went after my aunt, okay? I'm admitting that piece. You really need to take care of yourself here, the stress is wearing on you, and it's obvious. It would be nice to see you get back to your old self again, especially in front of your friends. It will only help our cover. They need to see the carefree side of Fenton — not the drill sergeant side of you, but the guy I talked to in the woods. The guy I got to know in the hospital who lit up when he talked about his dad. It would be nice to see some of that light come back to your face. I'm worried about you," she said, her face flushing red as she vocalized her concern. He peered over at her, a sly smile spreading across his face.

"Worried about me, huh? You weren't talking to me an hour ago, so I'll take that as progress. I appreciate the concern, but I'm fine. I thought this was about getting you back to your old self? Helping you find Scarlet again, remember? Don't forget, I'm the one looking out for *you*. That's the arrangement." He gave her a wink.

"Okay tough guy, this house will do us both some good, how about that?" She grabbed her bags from the truck bed and followed behind him as he unlocked the door of the smaller ranch house. Opening the door, Scarlet caught a glimpse of large, spacious rooms with cathedral ceilings, and lots of sunlight pouring in from the vast windows.

"What do you think? Pretty nice, right? I come here between jobs, whenever I can. It's my home away from home," he said as Scarlet took a couple tentative steps into the cozy cabin.

"Pretty nice? It is like a little slice of heaven. The calmness of the lake, the quietness of the woods, the warm tones of the cabin. I can't imagine how you pull yourself away from here," she said. She noticed a large stuffed dog on the couch.

"I didn't take you as the stuffed animal kind of guy."

"Taylor, the little boy next door you'll meet, gave it to me when I first moved in. He knew I'd be here by myself, so he told me he has one just like it to keep him company when he is home alone." He turned slightly red while telling the story.

"Oh my goodness, that is the cutest thing. What a sweetheart."

"Yeah he's a pretty neat kid. Come on, I'll show you around."

Fenton gave her a tour showing off the immaculate kitchen and side bedrooms. It was more spacious than her apartment back in Virginia, and the couches and chairs were filled with comfy blankets which looked perfect for snuggling into with a good book. He had her drop her stuff in a small guest room, and after unpacking a few things, she headed back to the main family room which opened to the vast kitchen. Fenton started rummaging through the pantry checking on what food he already had stocked.

Turning toward the lake, she saw the trees bending in the wind. She let herself take in the beauty of the lake, clearing her mind, and suddenly the face of the man she killed flashed before her. She shook her head quickly to shake the image, and ran a trembling hand through her hair.

"Something wrong?" Fenton asked coming toward her. He put his hand on her shoulder, and her breath caught as she noticed how close he stood to her.

"Nothing. I'm fine. I just can't seem to shake Vegas."

"It is typical when going through a trauma to experience occasional flashbacks. You may have posttraumatic stress disorder. It is not uncommon after a violent attack. I hope the lake house helps. I think a change of scenery will do you good. Let me know if they continue, or if the frequency changes."

"Okay, I'm sure I will be fine. I think you are right. The change of scenery should help. Just like you said earlier, you don't have to worry about me while I'm here," she said, biting her lip. She sounded more confident than she felt.

"It is my job to worry. Let me know what else I can do to make this stay more comfortable for you, anything at all. I'm going to run into town this afternoon and pick up supplies for us. Can I grab you any tools for an art project? You're going to have plenty of downtime, which could help take your mind off everything."

"I do feel like I've gone a little crazy without anything to do. I have no outlet for the tangle of emotions and frustrations. I would love that, thank you." She admitted. He nodded, setting down a couple more bags.

"Do you have any hobbies you are passionate about?" she asked.

"One or two. Mine are boring though. I want to hear more about your art, I'm curious. We are away from everything else and there isn't Carter in another room, or the Neros around the corner. Have a seat. I want to hear about your artistic work. How did you discover your passion?" He motioned for her to sit down.

"You want to hear about this? Really?"

"Yes, why not? This is important to you. Tell me why you love it. Have you displayed your work before? Write down a list of the supplies you want, whatever you want, there are no limits. I'll pick it up all when I go into town."

"Wow, thank you. Okay, please stop me if I start to bore you. I have sold some of my pieces, but not many. I have some friends in the art world, and sometimes they let me display some of my pieces in their venue or when they have an exhibit."

"Sounds impressive."

"It's not that big of a deal, really. I only have pieces in small settings, and I have never had a large exhibit in my name. Nothing comes close to the euphoric feeling of having someone tell me a piece of *my* art brought them joy. At the museum where I used to work, there was this painting I would look at every day. It was called, *Girl on Bridge.* There was a longing there in her delicate features. I used to wonder if she was crossing the bridge to get to something wonderful in her life, but then I started to wonder if she felt stuck on that bridge, looking into a distant future which would never become reality. She was never coming or going, but she was looking for something. I was getting a job interview lined up, before this whole thing. My dream job. It's funny how things can start to go one way in life, but it can all change in an instant. Sometimes I lay awake at night, wondering if I'm that girl on the bridge..." She cut off, her voice choking on the emotion the memory of her past life. Fenton reached out his hand, and took hers in his own. She looked up at him, her eyes filled with tears which threatened to break free.

"This is temporary, Scarlet. You will have a future. You won't be stuck on the bridge. I promise." He peered into her emerald green eyes, and she smiled.

"I know, I know. It sounds silly, but that's what I like most about art. It connects with people at some basic level, speaking to a version of truth. It illuminates the lies and truths about this world, and it helps others appreciate and understand the human condition a little more. It's like a little bit of magic. Isn't that what we spend a lifetime searching for? Answers? Meaning? A reason for why we have to cross these bridges in our lives?"

"I think so, Scarlet. It's a beautiful idea."

"Now that we are here, away from everything else, I have to ask a question. Does everyone call you Fenton? Do you have a first name?" she asked.

"It's Lars. Lars Fenton."

"Lars? Really? A tough guy like you? I bet all the girls love that, it's like the character in a romance novel. What do people say when you finally tell them?"

"I don't know."

"What do you mean you don't know?"

"I never told anyone on a job before you," he said honestly. She paused for a moment, scanning his face, looking into his eyes to see if she believed him. His answer created a warmth near her heart. It helped make everything else feel a little less awful. She nodded slightly, and smiled.

Chapter 35

"What horrible secrets wait on the other side of this image?"

Carter was restless. She was back in her normal environment in Washington, working tirelessly under her Rudy Giuliani photo, but she wasn't getting the results she needed quick enough. Things were going sideways on the case, and fast. With Scarlet getting targeted, the integrity of the audio and visual compromised from a key uncover operation, and the inability to cleanly remove evidence from Robin's laptop and phone were starting to irritate her frayed nerves. Adding to that, the fact she had to answer for pulling the bomb squad into a deserted farmhouse to save Scarlet's aunt, was making the other department heads nervous that she didn't have this operation under control, which meant more internal scrutiny, which was the last thing she wanted at the moment. She felt powerless, and she hated that more than anything else. She had to get to the bottom of this mess and she could feel something was about to shift in the pit of her stomach. The trail had gone a little cold, but if she pushed hard enough, she could maybe jumpstart this investigation and get it back on track.

"Starr! Get in here, I need an update!" she yelled out her door, and Starr came in with Robin's laptop and started laying out her documents in front of Carter.

"I wish I had better news for you, boss, or more clarity. My team is telling me the integrity of the photos from Robin's computer was compromised from the laptop itself," Starr said.

"What do you mean?"

"The files were corrupted from the laptop. Someone wanted not only to destroy the evidence, but they knew enough to tamper with the source code of the files so even if we retrieved them, they wouldn't be whole. The team should have something for us within the hour, but we had to reassemble the code within these documents."

"You're telling me Robin had the knowledge to do that type of thing? Scarlet never referred to Robin as a computer genius."

"Well, she was able to get into the Durante's main computer system."

"That is because Darius fed her information and computer logins while he was drunk. He all but created a map for her from my understanding. That doesn't count as superb code acumen. I don't buy it. Something doesn't add up."

"If Robin didn't deliberately tamper with the files on her computer, then someone either broke into her laptop when she wasn't watching...or..." Starr paused. Carter shot a glance at her.

"A computer locked away securely in her locker at her office? I doubt she would take a corrupted laptop and hide it away. Either someone got to it before she put it in her locker, or someone got to it after we bagged it as evidence. That is what you were going to say," Carter exhaled slowly. *Fuck, a mole, fuck.* Carter closed her eyes tightly at the thought.

"I don't see any other options, boss," Starr said.

"Shit. I know they've got people on the inside everywhere, but within the highest ranks of the police? Within the FBI? Tell me when they get the pictures and files pieced back together again, and tell them to step on it. This is a rush, highest priority. No one sleeps until we figure out what is going on here," Carter said. Starr nodded and left the office.

Carter leaned against her desk, staring at the distorted images. *What were you hiding, Robin? What were you trying to tell us? What horrible secrets wait on the other side of this image?* She swallowed hard, the bloodhound in her wanted to have all the evidence in hand, but there was also a large part of her which dreaded what they would find.

Chapter 36

"She would let them burn."

Eleonora rose from her chair, sipping a lemonade. She looked at her wristwatch and knew Luca would be at the office rummaging through her father's belongings looking for bugs by now. She knew it was time for the second phase of her plan.

Eleonora walked into one of the lavish bathrooms at the family mansion, and looked at her dark, gypsy-like eyes in the large oval mirror. Her father was in a room with his captains discussing the plan for retaliation for Alonzo. If she wanted to interrupt the closed door meeting, she would need to make a convincing entrance.

She tilted her head, looking at her reflection tilt back in the mirror. She ran her hands under scalding hot water, and then rubbed her eyes furiously. Dark red circles appeared, her skin turned red and splotchy, and her makeup looked smudged. She liked the result, but she needed more. She needed them to feel her pain by the look on her face. She took a drop of soap, just a touch, and put a small amount in each eye. She felt the angry stinging from the strong soap. Her eyes welled with tears until the hot liquid flowed freely down her face. Her body was screaming for her to wash out the soap, and purge the liquid from searing her eyes, but she needed them watering when she walked into the room to confront her father, so she would let them burn.

She walked with purpose toward the heavy wooden doors of her father's personal office. She heard loud noises behind the door, and one of his soldiers stood at the entrance, arms folded across his bare chest. He was about to open his mouth to stop her, but one look at her face left him in stunned silence. Eleonora never showed emotion, and none of her father's associates had seen her cry, *ever*.

She brazenly busted through the heavy doors, all five men surrounding her father looked with anger at whatever intrusion they would meet, but the same stupefied expression hit them like it did the guard at the door when they looked at Eleonora's disheveled appearance. They were used to seeing her perfectly put together, and her stunning beauty was well known, but her beet red eyes and swollen face caused them all to freeze. She looked like something that had crawled out of a drain pipe, and the festering red of her watering eyes made her look like a creature from a horror film. She took their shocked silence as an invitation to speak.

"Father, I need to speak to you alone, now." Her tone was commanding, and her wild look made every man in the room not even think to object, and they all walked to the door in unison. Her father looked at her with bewilderment.

"Holy hell, Eleonora, what happened?" He held an arm out to her to sit down, and she did as her father asked.

"I have something to tell you, and you're not going to be pleased, but I feel it is my duty to tell you. I don't think it is a coincidence that Luca's girlfriend, at his behest, pulls in information on the Durante family and then Alonzo is hit. I heard Robin talking about running away with Luca. I overheard Robin talking with bankers on her cell, but I couldn't make sense of everything I heard. I believe the Durantes found out Robin was getting this information for Luca, so Luca made a deal with the Durantes. In exchange for Robin's life, he gave them Alonzo's. Alonzo was killed because of Luca's sloppiness and his loyalty to Robin above our family." She wiped away a couple tears from her eyes with shaky hands as she continued.

"I confronted Luca. I wanted him to tell me I was wrong, that I made a mistake, because I wouldn't believe my own brother would do such a thing. The way he reacted told me everything I needed to know. He became combative and he showed no remorse for his actions. I told him I was appalled he would choose some girl over the welfare of his own flesh and blood. I told him I was going to come to you, and tell you everything I knew. Then he slapped me, Father, and I fell to the floor. I think he would have killed me if he had the chance. That is when Manuele came to my rescue, thank goodness he got there in time. Manuele pulled a gun on Luca to get him off me, and he ran out of the house. I think he is going to grab Robin and go on the run. I'm guessing they are going to the airport. You should take his name off the will, take him off all of the family accounts, and freeze him out before he can take what isn't his. I'm so sorry to be the one to tell you, but he double-crossed all of us." Gabriel's fists were clenched at his sides, and he had a wild look in his eyes. Eleonora took a shaky breath.

"Your prized son Alonzo, the rightful heir to this family, is dead because of Luca. He couldn't stand how you fawned over Alonzo. His jealousy and greed drove him to this. If it wasn't for Manuele, I would be dead as well. Then you would have two children to grieve, not one. Manuele should be rewarded for his bravery, and loyalty to this family, and I hope you see me coming to you immediately with what I know is a sign of the same love and loyalty." Eleonora sat rigid in the chair, her burning eyes brimming over with scalding tears.

"I can't believe this, my own son! *My flesh and blood!*" Gabriel Nero looked like a caged lion, ready to rip apart the next person brave enough to come close.

"He will atone for these sins. I will find him and he will answer for all of this, every last bit." His hands shook as he took out his phone. Eleonora had to hide a quick smile. The story was a risky one, but without any other plausible explanation as to whom had a motive to kill Alonzo, the most unbelievable tale made the bizarre twist of events seem possible. With Luca out of the picture to defend himself, or refute the story, there would be no other explanation offered.

Eleonora knew she had done her job well, because all she needed to do was come up with a story that would answer one simple question: *Why else would Luca run, why would he and his car vanish without a trace?* Vinny had seen to that piece of the puzzle, and even if shards of metal were found days or weeks from now, it would be an easy story to sell that the Durantes wanted to clean up their end of the mess. The person who put the hit on Alonzo, the only one who could tie them back to the crime, was Luca.

Gabriel tried calling Luca again, and Eleonora hid her face in a mock sob. His fingers shaking in anger as his daughter wailed in the background, he was barely able to dial the phone with his unsteady hands, and twice it went right to voicemail.

Gabriel Nero screamed at his cellphone and picked up a beautifully painted Chinese vase from his desk, hurling it across the room. The vase smashed into the opposite wall, and shattered into tiny pieces. His captains came running in from outside the room, unsure of what they would find. They saw Eleonora with her head in her hands, as her father's chest was heaving over the broken bits of vase sprayed across the floor.

What Gabriel Nero didn't know, but what Eleonora suspected, was Luca didn't answer his cell phone because exactly five minutes earlier, his car sped along a deserted part of the highway where the rolling waters of the Las Vegas Wash lapped on both sides. A small bomb securely attached to the bottom of his vehicle first exploded under the driver's seat immediately killing Luca on impact, while a second blast caused the entire vehicle to erupt in flames.

The burning metal sunk slowly to the bottom of the river bed, where the pieces started floating in opposite directions. The smoldering metal was sinking, covered entirely by dark rolling waves.

Chapter 37

"Is this world really such an awful place we have to live in variations of the truth?"

When Scarlet had unpacked her meager belongings at the lake house, she found Fenton looking at a newspaper in the kitchen.

"Remind me again how you know Dale, and the whole backstory. I want to make sure I'm up to speed when I meet him and his family."

"When my dad died and my mom died shortly after in a car crash, I had no family left. I took what I thought was my best option. I went into the Marines and then the Secret Service. As a part of the Marines, I was on special mission, and was shot while protecting a buddy. After I recovered, they rehabbed me and groomed me for a Secret Service role primarily slotted for protection details. When I transitioned to the group, they taught me how to be invisible. I learned how to exist as a ghost, invisible to most in society, but the freedom from being a ghost comes with a hefty price tag. All friends, acquaintances, neighbors, and anyone aware of your existence before, is removed from your life. Typically, those with family find all of that difficult to give up, but since I didn't have family left, it made the transition a little easier. They had me cut ties with everyone, except for one buddy I ended up protecting on a mission, and what he knows of me is part of one of my cover aliases. The buddy was Dale. He was the only one I kept in my life. With most of my protection jobs, I need an alias. It makes it hard to keep personal relationships. Even with Dale, he knows what I choose to tell him. He thinks I'm a consultant for a security firm, which explains my travel and long absences. For a high level cover, it works perfectly. He doesn't ask too much, and I don't offer too much. He is my one and only friend. His wife Winnie is amazing, and they have Taylor."

"Wow, doesn't it get draining having to keep up a fake persona when you're with them?

"The key is to use as much truth as you can, and minimize the lies. As far as he knows, I went into consulting immediately after my recovery, which is a half-truth. You could call what I do, 'consulting' to a certain degree. I told him part of my background and history and a lot of it was true, so I don't have to keep track of too many detailed historical fictions."

"I still don't know if I would be able to keep so many secrets."

"How can anyone keep secrets? How can a cheating husband or wife keep their secret lives hidden? How can anyone keep debts, bank accounts, past lives, and mistakes a secret?" Scarlet shook her head.

"It is a matter of discipline. Anyone can do it with the right amount of discipline and planning. You have to know how to avoid the pitfalls and control the story. Think about anyone you know — what you know of them is what they choose to tell you. When people make mistakes and let down their guard is when a liar is caught."

"Then why are so many people found out?"

"Because they lack the level of discipline required. I never said it was easy. Most fail, but it can be done. With the right motivation, it can be done."

"What is your motivation, Fenton?"

"If I don't stay disciplined, then someone dies. Someone I swore to protect. If I were to fail, then the entire system put into place to protect innocent people, like the woman who testified at my dad's trial, becomes weaker and less stable. The protection agency only survives on its ability to protect people, and if that fails, the bad guys will win. There will be nothing left in their way to stop them. That is why I have one friend. We have history together and I know I can trust him."

"Is this world really such an awful place we have to live in variations of the truth?"

"You saw evil men kill your sister and come after you. You tell me."

Chapter 38

"Keep the lies rooted in truth."

Fenton introduced Scarlet as his girlfriend to Dale, his wife Winnie, a cheery brunette, and her ten-year-old son, Taylor. Scarlet got used to quiet days enjoying the sun, sitting by the dock, eating meals together, and laughing with Winnie. The guys would toss a football, entertain Taylor, explore the grounds, and go fishing. The nights were filled with bonfires and stories, drinks and comradery. She started to feel a part of something larger at the lake. A mini ecosystem, *a family*. She also started getting used to being Fenton's fake girlfriend while in front of the neighbors. She liked the way he looked at her, with his easy smile, as if they were sharing a private joke of the day. Even Winnie commented on their chemistry.

"I'm so happy to see Fenton finally happy. I wasn't sure he would find someone, being so private, but it's obvious by your connection you're the right person for him," Winnie said. Scarlet could only nod and smile.

On one such late afternoon, Scarlet watched Fenton help Taylor cast his line off the dock. She sat on the second floor patio of Dale and Winnie's home. She watched as their bright red bobbers made tiny splashes when they hit the water. The sun was still high in the sky, causing the shadows to appear like moving mimes on the wooden boards as the guys tried a new spot to cast their lines. She stayed on the second floor balcony leaning over for a while, observing him. His face seemed more relaxed, and his muscles were without their typical alerted strain.

She could tell he felt comfortable here, surrounded by nature and seclusion. Even though she knew he viewed the trees as a potential threat, a spot where someone could sneak up on their location, the miles of trees between their private spot along the water and any of the main roads provided its own type of protection. The gates protecting the property had cameras at all entrance points, and more were hidden beyond the typical entrances hanging from the trees, and hidden in spots no one would find, unless they knew where to look.

When they first arrived, he reviewed the blueprints with her to help make her feel comfortable and safe. He meticulously checked all of the vantage points of the cameras and grounds, and pored over the documents and layout to reassure her the location was safe and he wasn't making a mistake, he took every precaution, and he followed his disciplined plan of checking and rechecking every security measure to intercept any potential flaws to minimize the threat. He seemed relaxed there, in his element, yet she also knew at any moment, he could jump into action at the slightest feeling of something being wrong.

His calm demeanor was a reward for the painful diligence, but it was a surface level luxury, which did not reach the core of him. There was a piece still actively on duty, still actively working, still fully aware of his charge, and still ready to perform his job. He occasionally looked up at her, eyes squinting against the glare of the sunlight, always keeping a cautious eye on her and her movements. Every action was for one outcome, to protect her from any threat. Any delusion regarding their so-called vacation was not present within her mind. She knew what this was and she knew the reason they were there was solely to secure her protection. Any enjoyment or feeling they were living in a parallel "normal" universe together as a couple was simply a byproduct of the ruse they played to maintain the cover. Her mind told her these were cold hard truths she needed to accept, but her emotions betrayed her. Her heart caused her to feel something for him, seeing him laughing with Taylor as he baited their hooks. As she watched him relaxing on the dock, she felt a longing for normalcy and companionship — not with just anyone, but with him and not the forced type of companionship they were in today, but a closeness because he chose her, not because his duty demanded it.

It was folly to entertain these thoughts, to give life to them, and she knew it. But standing there looking down at him, capable and strong, caring and masculine; she couldn't help but wonder. Every once in a while, a flicker of something deep down and dangerous would pass through his gaze, and just as quickly as it came, it would be gone. The quiet smirk, the façade of the reserved soldier boy finally returned home, yet still adjusting, would be replaced with an innocence and rawness palpable to her. She wanted to reach out and touch his face in those moments, but she knew she couldn't — not unless they were in front of the others, pretending. She recalled his arms lightly around her waist the other day, pulling her closer, his soft lips kissing her cheek, holding her hand around the campfire, walking up to her to embrace her in a hug before lunch, lifting her slightly so her toes brushed the top of the long strands of grass, and asking her, with warmth in his eyes, if he could get her anything. Only in front of Dale and his family, in their world of pretend.

She told herself, as she stared at him, these conflicting emotions can only be expected of the circumstances. They were brought together like two figures blending together on canvas, beholden to the colors and shades of the paint on canvas and the emotions they provoked. It was only normal to try to grasp onto some fragment of ordinariness. It was only normal for her to wish she was in a different life, as if this canvas was her reality instead of a cover story, and most of all, she tried to convince herself it was only normal for her to yearn for him. She shuddered at the thought it wasn't Fenton that ignited these feelings but instead simply the bodyguard role he played. She needed to convince herself it wasn't his face, his hands, his muscles, his thoughts, his secrets, and his being she coveted. She told herself she would feel this for anyone in his place. Yet, as she stood watching him, she had to push her thoughts completely away for fear of coming to a conclusion the last *truth* she told herself was in fact a *lie*. If she was falling in love with *him*, independent of their circumstances, this was a much greater predicament she didn't want to entertain. She couldn't add another quandary to her already precarious situation. Either way, she knew these feelings interfered with the mission. The mission to stay alive, to not further complicate that which was already excessively complex, and not add additional burden to the impossible load they both carried.

She knew all these things to be true, but yet the truth thrashed against everything she wished deep in her heart, and her heart had created this impossible and dangerous hope. All hope which starts like that, born from the wreckage of crisis and pain, manages to flicker like a candle which can easily be snuffed out. The real danger is if the last candle were to blow out, there would be nothing left to hope for, and without hope, there is nothing left to stop the darkness from seeping inside.

Scarlet heard a noise behind her on the balcony, and turned.

"Sorry if I startled you, you looked deep in thought. Being at the lake can have that effect on some people. Mind if I join you out here?" asked Dale.

When she first turned to him, her face looked vacant, as if her thoughts carried her far away or deep within herself. Within a moment, a bashful smile came over her face as she looked down at her sandals in embarrassment.

"I didn't hear you approaching, yes, please join me. Not so much deep in thought as enjoying the moment of calm. I can't believe the lake is so peaceful. Hardly a ripple in sight."

"Yeah, it is my paradise on earth, that's for sure. I never expected early retirement, but if it had to happen, I don't mind it being in a place like this."

"Yes, Fenton mentioned a little bit about your retirement. How are you feeling now? Have you recovered?"

"Well, the interesting thing about traumatic brain injuries, is it takes years to fully recover in some cases. Luckily, my family has military roots and I come from a long line of land owners and real estate agents. This lake estate has been in the family for generations, and during World War II, my family decided to gate off the houses around the lake. Owning much of the land and property at that time, it was easy to buy out the others, and they turned this into a safe haven during the war. There are a lot of fun family stories of how generals and other important historical figures came to this location for strategy planning and seclusion."

"I can see why Fenton likes it here so much. Everything here is beautiful. It is nice he is able to rent the house next to yours. I can tell he enjoys being here."

"I owe him my life. I would give him whatever he asked for. I'm trying to get him to buy the property from me. I would like him to come out here more often than he does. I understand with his high-pressured job, it is hard to relax, but he often seems distracted when he is up here, perhaps *restless* is another way to put it. What makes you think he enjoys it?"

Scarlet thought to herself that she may be getting into dangerous territory. *What did Fenton tell me about lying? Try to pull in as much truth as possible?*

"The seclusion I think is what he enjoys the most. I think he likes to get away from everything. I know for a fact he absolutely appreciates and cherishes his time with you here, even though it may not always seem like it."

"I am glad to hear that Scarlet. I was happy to hear he was bringing someone with him this time. You seem to have a calming influence on him. He seems like a different guy up here this time." *How would a girlfriend respond in this situation?*

"I am glad I have a positive impact on him, but I feel much the same way you do. I don't always know if I'm bringing him the type of happiness he brings me. I feel sometimes like the past isn't the past for him. It follows him like a shadow wherever he goes. I would love to hear a little more about how you two met, and what he was like back then. If you are comfortable sharing, especially your time in the service together. I don't mean to pry though."

"Are you kidding? Every girlfriend in her right mind would ask the same question, especially with someone as guarded as Fenton. I was starting to wonder because you hadn't asked me for the dirt on him sooner." He nudged her playfully, and she felt she had succeeded in the ruse.

"You couldn't ask for a better soldier than Fenton. He has more discipline than anyone I have ever met. Fiercely loyal to his friends as well — I would walk into a burning building with him, I trust him that much. That being said, when I first met him, he wasn't the fresh-faced, dewy-eyed kid with dreams of grandeur heading into war like the rest of the recruits. He came already jaded and there was already darkness around his eyes, which I found out later possibly came from witnessing the death of his parents."

"The death of his parents, yes, that couldn't have been easy. I knew they had passed away, but I didn't know he witnessed their deaths. How did it happen?"

"A car accident. He was the only one who made it," he said. *He was also in the car accident? Huh, this is a different variation of the story.*

"There always was a darkness to him before, a darkness which takes over from seeing too much and doing too much, but with war and being a Marine, there are things that can't be unseen. The loss of fear and the necessary indifference to death creates a life sustained by always living on the razor's edge. It numbs the human side, and turns the best of men into machines, yet the irony is they have to be machines if they want to survive and do the job."

"Do you feel that way about your experience in the Marines as well, about your experience with war?"

"No. When Fenton saved me, I hadn't seen as much as he had. He had already been in the service for a while, already stationed in a variety of places, but he took me under his wing. What I witnessed and did was just a flash in time compared to his experience. I can still be happy, because I'm still a little green. One thing I'm sure of though from my time, is happiness only comes from the ignorance of not knowing what exists out there, of not being aware of what creeps in the dark. Those feelings sink into a person like cigarette smoke fades into clothing. It lingers well beyond the flavor of menthol on the tongue. Have you ever felt paralyzing fear before, Scarlet?"

"Yes," she said without thinking. "I mean I think I have, maybe once in my life."

"Well, someone like Fenton has already faced every fear they thought they had, and forged ahead. The slugs, the scabs, the garbage, the horror, the soulless, and the warped have been on his playground. That changes a person, can't help not to, but just as crashing waves can wear down a weathered dock, so too can the darkness wear down the sense of justice and the sense of right. What is repetitious in life becomes normalized. I was happy for him when he said he was getting out, when he was giving up being a career soldier, but working as a consultant for government security at the Pentagon can't be any easier." *Oh, a consultant for government security at the Pentagon? He really is the master of half-truths,* thought Scarlet.

"Dale, I appreciate all of this background, but how do you reach someone like that? Can they come back, come back from everything horrible they have seen and still live a fulfilling life?" she asked it as much for Fenton as she asked for herself.

"In my experience, those types of people will not form relationships easily, but they will fight to hell and back for the people they love and hold dear. It is easy to get used to not letting many people in, because it's a risk. Anyone and anything they love could be used against them, and they know it so they will push people away to forge ahead alone."

"What kind of life is that?" she whispered.

"One with a little less blood on their hands, I suppose. We have all seen it. The guys who end up disappearing, taken away by the government to fulfill some secret role or duty. They always seem to be the ones who never kept friends and were estranged from their families. You're going to think this is silly, but I always felt like Fenton could have been one of those guys. I know, that's crazy, and I'm sure glad he wasn't. He saved me from being tortured, captured by the enemy. They beat me within an inch of my life. He stormed in and took out the whole building, practically by himself. Later in the chopper, after he carried me to safety, he said something I will never forget. I didn't know him that well at that point. Sure we were buddies, but not especially close. He said, *Dale, you're going to survive this, and you and I are going to be best friends.* I thought he was just trying to keep my spirits up. I was convinced I was going to die, so I asked him why he thought we would be best friends. He said, *Because you can keep secrets, Dale. They would have killed you or stopped torturing you if you talked, but you didn't. I can trust you, and that is what I value most in friendship. So, you're going to survive this, and we are going to go to the cabin you keep talking about.* Just like that, he visited me every day when I was in rehab. He was shot while we were out there as well, so we recuperated together. The son of a gun was right. We did become best friends. Every year since then he comes out here and stays with me for a while. The rest is history." He took a swig from his beer, leaning over the railing, contemplative.

The conversation certainly painted a clearer picture of Fenton for Scarlet. He never mentioned the fact he rescued Dale from captivity where he was being tortured, but it made perfect sense why Dale was the only one he wasn't invisible to anymore. He picked the one guy who, if anything were to happen, wouldn't answer a single thing about Fenton. Plus, having military experience and being secluded practically on a compound, he was as safe as anyone could be and could handle himself if necessary. It was the perfect alignment, the only way it would work, and she was convinced in that moment no one else knew about the relationship. She would have been flattered Fenton even mentioned the fact he discretely kept one friendship from his past, but she realized the fact he trusted her with the knowledge was a necessary precaution. He had to bring her here, a place most didn't know existed, but there was still an element of trust in telling her. Then again, who would she tell, she was like him – she had lost the privilege of having friends.

"Winnie is amazing, and Taylor is cute as a button. You're blessed with an amazing family."

"Thank you," he eyed her suspiciously before continuing.

"I may be a little forward for asking this, but Winnie has chirped in my ear about it all afternoon seeing Fenton and Taylor play. Do you think you ever want a family some day?" His eyes sparkled with his light smile. She smiled back pleasantly, trying to reassure him she didn't mind being asked, but her smile didn't extend to her eyes to hide the thoughts flooding her mind. *Kids? A family? I think building a life is saved for the normal people, the people who are not chased through the daylight and forced to hide in the shadows. A family is for the people who can live their lives, not for those who have to live on the run and hide their identity. Why would I want to bring a child into this world, when the world I live in is filled with people who are soulless, consumed only by the evil that pours from their black hearts so all they see is blood and power? At one time maybe, but now... I don't exist here anymore. The sun little Taylor played in this afternoon doesn't shine on my world anymore. My world is filled with scorched earth, despair, and the memories of too many dead eyes staring up at me. I can try to forget them when I wake, but they return to me when I sleep. A child needs hope, love, and someone to assure them the scary boogey men can't reach them. I can't make those types of false promises. I can't wipe away their scared tears, because I know what is waiting for me outside my door. How could I take care of a child when I can't even take care of myself?*

The thoughts saddened her heart, more than she would care to admit, because to this point, she hadn't thought about how her sister changed her chances for a normal life. A normal life where kids are on the family Christmas card each year, going to soccer games, watching plays, going to recitals, watching the kids play in the yard with the dog, watching them get older, graduate from high school, pick a college and become something to the world, and go on to get married and have children of their own. Until Dale asked her directly if she wanted children, she hadn't thought those five steps ahead, but now the weight of it on her chest was heavy and smothering. She mustered all of her strength to simply stay on her feet, and keep her face calm, as she withered inside.

"I think one has to be in a certain place in their life to know when it is right to bring children into the world. I love kids, I do. Honestly, if that point comes into my life, I would feel very blessed to have children." She smiled, a faint smile, because inwardly she knew she didn't lie to Dale. She only told a half-truth, which is something she was learning more and more about since meeting Fenton.

Keep the lies rooted in truth — it is easier to keep track of all the falsehoods and it makes it easier to say it with a smile.

The days blurred into one another at the lake house. She felt like the whole scene was pulled from the reel of someone else's life. Fenton was working in the garden, digging holes to help Dale plant bright new shrubs. He playfully came up to her, and leaned over as she read along the water. He rested his arms around her neck, and pull a strand of her hair behind her ear. He would look over at her often, keeping her engaged and giving a quick wink or smile.

The afternoon was filled with small chores like pulling weeds from the property, gassing up the fishing boat, and freshening up the paint on a couple of window sills. She watched him as he masterfully worked on a broken fence post with Dale. Dirt stains were visible on his simple cotton tee which clung to every strained muscle. He lifted the bottom of his shirt carefully to wipe his brow, displaying tanned skin gleaming wet with perspiration under the heat of the sun. Scarlet ran a shaky hand through her hair, affected by the sight of him.

Dale laughed and joked with him, and she saw Fenton's face erupt in a full, unadulterated laugh. It was like the lake house re-lit the fire within him, and the warmth poured through his eyes and real smile. She had never seen him like this before. It disarmed her, and every protective look he shot her way made her swallow hard as she couldn't stop the blush from flushing her cheeks.

The lake house felt like a protective bubble, where nothing could touch her, and a false sense of security from the bright sun rays made her feel as if the light would surely banish any darkness to the corners of the earth. She sat on the porch, watching the men work, and felt at peace and wondering how long the beautiful moment would last.

Winnie and Dale brought out sandwiches and cold lemonade for lunch, and they all sat around a large wooden table between the properties to enjoy the meal together.

Fenton sat down next to Scarlet and kissed the back of her hand. She turned to nestle her chin into his arm as she gazed up at him. He peered into her eyes, a question forming in his gaze as he brushed a thumb over her slightly parted lips.

"You look flushed, are you staying cool? Do you need me to grab you some lemonade? Winnie just made some," he asked gently. *I must look flushed from watching him work. Am I that transparent?*

"I'm fine, thank you for asking. I should ask you the same question. You're working up quite a sweat."

"There is a lot of work to be done. I don't mind it though. Are you sure I can't get you anything?" She noticed Winnie look over at them from the picnic table. Scarlet stood slowly, and tugged at the bottom of Fenton's shirt pulling him close to her. She stood on tip toes, and gently kissed his perfectly-formed mouth. She lingered in the kiss, exploring his plump lips, letting it send energy throughout her body as her eyes closed. She was lost in the moment, transported to another place, where all she wanted was his touch. She had to force herself to pull away, and smile slowly when she noticed his eyes were wide with desire, as he placed his hand on the small of her back and grinned at her.

"I'm fine, Sweetie, really. Thanks for looking out for me, Fenton," she purred. He grinned back wickedly.

"Yum, who needs lemonade? You're all the sugar I need." She burst out laughing.

"Really, Fenton? Is that the line you used to use to get girls? Unreal. You're lucky I saved you from the single life." She heard Dale laugh as he overheard her comment, and Fenton winked at her as he tapped her butt playfully before turning to walk back toward the fence. She watched him walk away, admiring his broad shoulders and perfectly-formed butt accentuated by snug jeans. She had to reminder herself to breathe. She looked up at Winnie, who waved and smiled, and Scarlet waved back. It was an act put on for Dale and Winnie's sake, but the problem was, Scarlet didn't feel like she was acting.

Chapter 39

"We need our witness if we have any hope of saving this case."

Carter was grabbing a granola bar and coffee from the cafeteria when her phone buzzed. It was a text from Starr, which meant their team had finally uncovered the corrupted files either from the laptop or phone. She rushed to the elevator and began pressing the UP button repeatedly. The minutes waiting for an elevator, and then the ride up to the conference room, felt like an hour. She stormed out as soon as the doors opened and headed toward the main conference room with other staff members scrambling to the room as well. Starr, holding a folder, was walking briskly down the hall toward Carter.

"Where is Westbrook?" Carter called after her.

"He was hunting down another lead, not sure where he headed. We have the results from the phone and the laptop." Starr said, a smile appearing on her face from the victory. *Let's wait to see what the images show us first.*

"Okay, throw them up on the big screen. Tell me what we are

looking at here people," Carter barked, and her team fell into action, passing files to Starr with the summary of each item recovered.

"Okay, first we have the images from the cell phone. Here is a woman with Alonzo. Correct that, it's Alonzo with Eleonora. Okay great, our first photographic evidence of Eleonora in the family's activities. Here she is at the warehouse, okay, here she is with Manuele. Here is Manuele with some man, talking over dinner," Starr explained.

"Okay, let's run that face in the database, obviously Robin thought it was important to capture it on film, so let's find out who our mystery man is," Carter barked, and another task force team member ran out of the room to start running the search. Starr continued.

"Here is Eleonora at dinner with another man who we can't make out because his face is pixelated. Here she is kissing him. Okay, we have a romantic interest possibly. Here are the photos from the laptop, more of Eleonora and Manuele. There was one face we are still trying to recover, you see him here in this photo and then in another picture as well but we have to work on the facial reconstruction of that one and then run it through the system."

They went through a handful of other photos and documents. Images of trucks loaded with drugs, and key soldiers and family members linked to the Durante and Nero families. It was a gold mine of information and visuals which would only further solidify Carter's case against the families, but the key footage Carter needed had the images captured by Scarlet at the gala. They were still trying to repair those visuals to make it usable.

"Run all faces against the database. I need Scarlet and Fenton back here to weigh in on these pictures. They may be able to identify some of these people. Let's use the time and date stamp to tie these visuals to our own wiretaps and information we gathered from the street. Connect the dots people. We need to paint a full picture for the jury and these visuals will help us do it with the right context. Lots to do people, let's get moving," Carter ordered. Starr pulled Carter aside.

"One more thing, boss," Starr said. "I didn't want to mention it in front of the others. The corrupted video, from Scarlet's undercover assignment, used the same backdoor entrance to access the code as the laptop corruption."

"What does that mean, Starr? Speak English."

"My coders tell me it's like a signature. Using the same code or method to do things means there is a possibility the person who corrupted the files on Robin's computer also tampered with our video feed from the sting." Carter nodded slowly, letting the implication of her words sink in. *Mole, we've got a mole in the department. A mole from the inside doing the dirty work for the mob.*

"How sure are they about this?" she whispered to Starr.

"There is a high likelihood the work was done by the same person," Starr responded. Starr's cell started vibrating, and Carter nodded for her to take it. Carter pinched the bridge of her nose as she had a sudden, overwhelming headache. *This case is the headache.* She looked up, realizing she had to keep everything together for her staff. She glanced over at Starr, who had turned positively pale as she spoke in hushed tones into the receiver. She hung up, and looked as if she just seen a ghost.

"What is it, Starr?"

"That was Agent Westbrook. He was able to keep it quiet, so it won't hit the news or the papers. They found a piece of Luca's license plate, washed onto shore about forty minutes from the Strip. They think his car was blown up. Shards of glass and metal are up and down the water way buried in the current. Carter, they think *he was in the car* when it happened. A professional job they said, densely concentrated explosives, with a timer. Someone got to him, Carter. Luca Nero is dead."

Carter felt winded at the news, and hunched over holding onto the chair for support. *Luca Nero dead? There goes a huge part of this case, blown up. Who went after Scarlet if it wasn't Luca? What does this mean? First Robin, then Alonzo, and now Luca... this is going sideways on us and we need to pull them in.*

"Get me a secure message to Fenton. He's off the grid, so it's our only way to reach him," she ordered Starr. Carter then walked into the middle of the busy staff room to address the broader group with the latest news.

"Let's keep this under wraps, team. I don't know what this means, but it's not good for us. I hope to God we are not too late. Get them back here, *now*. Their safety is our main priority. We need our witness if we have any hope of saving this case," Carter commanded, and her staff sped into action.

Chapter 40

"I'll do anything to make it out of this alive."

Carlo Durante nervously flicked his cigarette out of his car window. *All I've been doing since that damn bomb didn't go off is driving. Driving until I get the call, the call I know is coming. Ugh, I could kill Pete.*

The two men didn't wait around at the abandoned house when they heard sirens. Carlo heard through his network the bomb squad had successfully dismantled both apparatuses at the abandoned location where the aunt was being held, and were evaluating the bomb maker's signature. He heard there were no deaths. His plan failed. He didn't know a lot about bombs, but he knew the types of components to make a bomb and the wiring were like fingerprints for the cops. *What if they know it's Percussion Pete? What if they have his work on file? If they squeeze him, that little rat might just talk.*

Carlo knew Pete was in over his head with gambling debts. He knew he wouldn't stand up against hard questioning and the threat of doing time. *I'm tempted to hunt him down right now and kill him, just to be safe*. Problem was, he couldn't find Pete. He was nowhere to be found, leaving Carlo to take the rap for not killing the girl.

His phone vibrated. *Pietro, the capo.* He let it go to voicemail, and listened to the message as his hands shook.

"Carlo, what's this I hear about a bomb squad going to the abandoned house? Is there any way to trace the bombs back to us? Now they have their stinking crew all over that property. You left the family open to more risk, Carlo. We need to talk. I need to bring you in to talk to Romeo on this one. Give me a call." Carlo's hand shook as he lit another cigarette and took a long sip from his flask. He thought back to the days when things weren't so complicated, back to when he and Darius ran the streets, instead of running from them.

I have to find a way out of this. That call from Pietro is no good for me. I'm as good as a dead man, and I'm not ready to die yet. I'm not ready for Darius to haunt my soul. I have to survive this, whatever it takes. I'll do anything to make it out of this alive... anything.

His mind set, he picked up his cell phone, and made the call he really didn't want to make.

Chapter 41

"Who said my life isn't beautiful?"

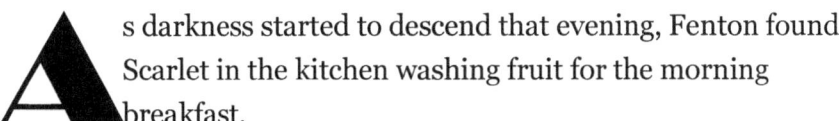s darkness started to descend that evening, Fenton found Scarlet in the kitchen washing fruit for the morning breakfast.

"Want to come out with me and light the candles on the dock? I just picked them up at the store. We used to use something similar when I first started coming out here. It gives a little bit of ambience for when we tell ghost stories around the bonfire later," he said.

"Sure, happy to help. That sounds incredible, can't wait to see it." Fenton guided her to the shed where they stored plenty of Mason jars with candles and citronella buckets to help keep the mosquitos at bay. They placed the candles up and down the dock, leading to the four seasons enclosed room just off their small house.

The four seasons room was the size of a little guest house, complete with a miniature wood fireplace and curtains which pulled around the glass windows for privacy. It was another memorable night.

Fenton told lively ghost stories, making big hand gestures, letting the curling flames cast shadows on his frame at the right moments to emphasis the scary parts. Taylor looked transfixed, while Dale and Winnie stifled giggles. Scarlet swallowed hard. She felt like she was looking at a normal family, a glimpse of what her life could be, if she was with someone like Fenton, if their lives were less dangerously tangled.

After she excused herself for the night, she went inside to grab a glass of water and saw them through the kitchen window packing up the chocolate bars and marshmallows from the s'mores. Dale and Winnie walked hand in hand behind Taylor who scampered ahead to their house on the hill. She took a couple of steps into the living room, waiting for Fenton. She wiped a few stray tears that peppered her cheeks. It wasn't sadness, but a wistful longing which settles once a person accepts that which they cannot have. Fenton walked into the kitchen, the box of Mason jar candles with him, and interrupted her thoughts.

"You're shivering. I can start a fire for us in the guest house if you like?" Fenton asked. She turned and nodded, surprised she didn't hear him come in. Scarlet followed him into the small, four seasons guest room, plopped on the couch, and hugged one of the soft pillows between her arms.

She watched him work as he created the fire with ease, and light the candles which he placed along the floor. The dancing flames cast a sheet of warmth on her legs, and the faint scent of vanilla wafted from the lit candles causing the whole room to glow in warm amber tones. She hugged the pillow a little closer, and felt compelled to clear her conscience.

"Fenton, we haven't talked about the night at the hotel and the situation with my aunt. I can't excuse my actions. I wasn't feeling like myself, and I'm sorry I put you in that type of situation. I also understand why you acted the way you did. I'm sorry." She bit her lip, and nervously scanned his face.

"Hey, you don't have to apologize to me, I understand." He stood from his crouched position by the fire, and took a seat next to her on the fluffy sofa cushions. He looked over at her, she blushed at his direct gaze, and he took her hand in his. Scarlet sucked in a quick breath at the contact of his warm hand. She felt a flutter in the pit of her stomach, and met his gaze again. She could see the reflection of the fire in his eyes, making it look like the heat was burning within him, which made his rugged features even sexier. She pulled her hand away self-consciously.

"I'm serious, Scarlet. I understand. There is nothing you need to feel bad about. You don't have to feel weird around me due to anything from the past. We've reached an understanding."

"Still, I had to say it. I know most would consider my situation to be dismal, at best. I would want to change a lot of what's happened to me as well, but one thing I wouldn't change for a second, is you. I should have trusted you earlier. I'm glad I've had a chance to meet you, Fenton. You're an incredible man, and I wish someday you can have a beautiful *normal* life at the lake, because after seeing you here, I think it suits you," she said. He chuckled softly.

"Who said my life isn't beautiful? I have you sitting next to me, don't I?" he said, tilting his head, and she punched him lightly on the shoulder, laughing.

"I'm serious, Scarlet, there is nowhere else I would rather be," he said, and the humor left his face. She swallowed hard.

"Not even Hawaii or someplace gorgeous? Someplace where you wouldn't have a care in the world?"

"I would rather be here, sitting next to you, helping *you* not have a care in the world. Plus, you're a pretty amazing fake girlfriend. I lucked out." Her eyes teared up. He smiled, a shy smile, and reached out to brush a tear from her cheek. She leaned into him, resting her head on his arm, the soft warm cotton of his shirt caressing her face, and he leaned down to kiss her forehead.

"You were quiet tonight at the fire. Anything you want to talk about?" he asked.

"I don't need to burden you with my thoughts. You have enough on your plate," she sniffled.

"Who said it's a burden? I like to listen and maybe I can make you feel better. I would like to try. I'm here to make sure you're okay, and that includes making you smile, if I can." He grinned down at her, and it ate her up inside. His charm and his endearing silent strength called to her. She took a deep breath.

"I know I said I wanted to feel like myself again, and bringing me here helped accomplish that, so thank you. The painting supplies have helped clear my mind, and you've done so much to make me feel comfortable here. I want to thank you for all of that. Yet, part of me wishes I was still pretending to be Robin, because I'm finding it's painful for me to feel normal again. Seeing you repairing fences around the property with Dale, and playing with Taylor – it's a snapshot of a life I will never be able to lead, and I have to accept I'm leaving all of that behind. The way Winnie and Dale are together, and the way you and I pretend to be here together. It makes me wish I could have a loving family. I *want* to have that." The last sentence came out as a whisper, the tears welling in her eyes again, and then streaming down her face. He wrapped a comforting arm around her shoulder.

"Look at me. I'm a blubbering mess!" She pulled back, but he caught her arm, pulling her closer.

"Don't be afraid to cry in front of me. Just because I carry a gun doesn't mean I'm a tough guy all the time." She rested her head on his shoulder with his arm securely around her as she curled next to him on the couch.

"Well, I wish I was tougher," she sniffled.

"You're not a mess, and you're going to be okay. You can have that life. Once you are in witness protection, things will go back to normal for you. No one will be able to find you, and you can start over again. You're an amazing woman and any guy would love to call you his own. Just wait, you'll see. I promise." His deep voice muffled into her hair as he continued to hold her close. She shook her head, and pulled herself away from him in frustration and stood up. She started to pace in front of the fire and wiped the back of her hand across her wet eyes.

"That's the problem, *that's the whole problem.* This witness protection thing. I won't feel protected. *You've ruined me, Fenton.* You've ruined me because I can't imagine ever feeling as safe with anyone as I feel with you. How can I give my heart to someone when I can't trust them like I trust you? I could find a movie star and I wouldn't want to be alone with him. Look at this romantic room, the fire is roaring, the vanilla candles are casting shadows on the wall, the stars are visible through the glass above us, and I can't think of anyone else I would want to be with in a room like this...ever. I can't think of another man's embrace, *but yours.* I think all this pretending has ruined me for other guys. Shit, I'm messed up." She stopped, gasping in little sobs as she leaned on the fireplace mantle.

Fenton rose from the sofa and approached her cautiously. He bent over slowly so his gaze was level with hers. He put both hands firmly on her shoulders.

"You are not *messed up.* It's normal to have these fears. I've been trained to keep you safe, so there is a sense of security that comes along with my being uniquely equipped to keep you from harm. You're not ruined. You're nervous you won't feel protected in your new life, but I assure you, once you get used to the new routine and identity, you won't be afraid."

"No, you're wrong. I won't feel as safe without you. I'm sorry, Fenton, I know you don't want me to say it. I know you don't want me to think it. I'm afraid...I'm afraid *it isn't just* your training. I'm scared it isn't simply your background..." she stopped speaking. His mouth was slightly agape in confusion as he was trying to calm her down, his attention solely focused on her. She swallowed hard, his steel gaze unsettling her at her core, and she felt a flip in her stomach as she realized her suspicions were true.

"Scarlet..." he prompted, still holding her arms. The smell of the rich wood burning to embers filled her senses, the room glowed. She could hardly think being this close to him, his supple lips inches from her own.

"I'm afraid it's you. It's you, Fenton. I'm nervous that no one will ever measure up...to you." She felt her knees buckling, the weight of her words terrifying her and the realization exciting her at the same time. The moment she said it, she knew it was true. He held her steady, his furrowed expression washing away.

"Well, shit, Scarlet. Is that all?" he asked, with a slight laugh.

"Is that all? What do you mean? It's horrible. *I like you.* All of this stupid pretending on top of seeing your face just before I think I'm about to breathe my last breath and you masterfully pull me out of the worst situations imaginable. Then, seeing you here in your element with your friends, and fixing fences masterfully. There is nothing *you can't do.* It's incredibly sexy. Then you build this amazing fire, the stars are shining above us, and you're wearing these shirts that just cling to every muscle you have. I mean, how do you even find shirts like that? It's enormously distracting. Geez, you make it tough on a girl. I thought my situation couldn't get worse but I've come to the worst possible realization: I've fallen for a guy who is *paid to protect me* and I'm going to be shoved into witness protection where I won't see anyone ever again. It sounds pathetic, right?" She let out another stifled sob, and Fenton burst out laughing as he pulled her in for a big bear hug.

She wrapped her hands around his broad back, feeling his powerful muscles beneath the cotton shirt. She fit perfectly within his embrace, like a puzzle piece. He rocked her in the hug, slowly back and forth, in front of the fire, his chuckles vibrating through her as she clung to him. He smelled of pine and fire, and something wonderfully clean mixed with the scent of pure *him*. She couldn't imagine anyone ever smelling as good, and it terrified her.

"I've never been accused of being too sexy before, I assure you," he said softly, and leaned back against the fireplace. Her arms remained entwined around her waist. He brushed a strand of her hair behind her ear, and wiped away a few more tears with the back of his finger. Then he leaned down, slowly, she arched her back expecting a kiss. Instead, she felt the warmth of his lips brush against her closed eyes. The warmth of his breath set her heart racing, and a tingling sensation down her spine. She sighed.

"Tell me this can't happen, tell me this is the worst thing ever, and we can move on," she said barely above a whisper. He put a hand under her chin and tilted her head slightly, her eyes still closed, and she felt his lips touch hers. She felt as if she were floating in his embrace, every sense on high alert as his kiss warmed her from the inside out. *Yum.* He pulled back from her, leaving her breathless and still clinging to the edge of his shirt.

"I'm not going to say it," he responded. Her eyes fluttered open, and saw his zealous gaze.

"I promise that is all I need to hear, Fenton."

"I can't say it, because it isn't true. Scarlet, I already admitted to my feelings and I'm not going to hide them from you, but I don't want you to worry about it getting in the way of the job."

"I'm not worried about that."

"Then why are you still crying?"

"Feeling this way about you makes me uncomfortable. I don't like to be vulnerable, and all I've been with you is vulnerable. I can't protect myself in Robin's world, and now I've confessed I may never be able to get close to someone else because of how I feel about you. I'm feeling exposed, and you're the one in control. After all of this, you're the one who can leave this situation unscathed. *You can leave me.* As easily as you came into my life, you could be gone. Nothing frightens you, nothing ruffles your feathers, and there is no visible chink in your armor. It's unsettling." She pulled away from him, and slumped onto the couch. She leaned back, looking up at cathedral ceiling made of glass. The night sky was peppered with flecks of light. The darkness of the night sky contrasted the hot warmth of the room. She heard Fenton sigh as he ran a hand through his hair and then sat down next to her.

"Look at me, Scarlet." She took a quick hand and wiped her face. Shame over her tears flushed her cheeks, and her lip trembled as she waited for his response. She pivoted on the couch, sitting cross-legged in front of him. He scooched her closer so one of her legs dangled over his, and clasped both of her hands in his own. He took a deep breath, rolled his neck side to side, and then leaned toward her looking directly in the eyes.

"Scarlet, you couldn't be more wrong. I can't leave this unscathed. I wasn't lying when I said if I could be anywhere right now, I would be here with you. I haven't brought anyone else here, ever. If there is any weakness I possess, it is my feelings for you. If I were smart, I would have left this case due to conflict of interest long ago. Yet, I couldn't do it even if I tried. The moment I met you, something about you affected me. I wanted this security job more than I've wanted any other job before. Not because of the money, not because of the circumstance, but because *of you*. I needed to *protect* you. I wanted to *know you.* It is hard for me to admit this, but from the first moment I laid eyes on you, I haven't been able to *stop thinking about you.* You are my Achilles heel, Scarlet. You are, because honestly, I would do anything for you. You expose me. You expose me by the way you make me feel, and the fact very dangerous people are after you terrifies me and I'm not the scaring kind. I'm not impenetrable. You can get to me. You alone *can get to me,*" his voice broke with his last sentence. His feelings were laid bare and the solemnness of his words solidified the honesty behind the emotion. She could see it on his face.

She had thought about that moment many times before, but nothing compared to being this close to him and hearing those words. The way he looked at her made her shiver. He looked at her as if she was the only woman in the world.

"You deserve someone better than me, though, Scarlet. I've done things in my past I'm not proud to admit. People have died by my hands, and I haven't been able to stop innocent people from getting hurt." His head fell with his admission of guilt. She felt him retreating from her despite standing beside her in the room. She grabbed his hand with the scar from grabbing the fake police officer who fell out of her bedroom window. She kissed the scar.

"You helped Dale, you stopped him from getting hurt. You've helped me. Like you told me, I have to believe in the sliding scale of judgement there has to be an understanding for people trying to do the right thing. I don't care what you've done. I care about who you are as a person, and I know Lars Fenton. Look at me, look me in the eye. You are a good man, Fenton. Your father would be nothing but proud of you and the person you've become." His eyes lifted to her, pain radiating behind his wounded gray eyes.

"Scarlet, I..."

"We both have things in our past, but that doesn't prevent us from having a promising future. Tell me the part again about how I get to you?" She said with a smirk and he chuckled.

"If I didn't break down into tears in front of you tonight, would you have ever told me all of this? All of those feelings? I didn't know to the extent…" she trailed off as she shook her head in disbelief.

"I didn't know you felt this way. Then tonight, when you admitted your fears, I knew I could stop your tears with a better understanding of my feelings. You've got me here, Scarlet. I'm all yours. I was yours the moment I walked through your door. I am who I am standing here before you, if you'll have me."

She leaned forward, cupping his face in her hands, and hungrily kissed him. She felt his lips part under her touch, and they both fell back against the soft cushions. She inhaled deeply. He smelled like cedar and fresh aftershave as she ran her hands through his hair. His hands securely held her waist as she quickly peeled off her shirt. He started to pull off his shirt, but her hands stopped him. Tugging at the soft fabric herself, she lingered over the ridges of his taut abs. He pulled his shirt off the rest of the way as she undid the buttons of his jeans. Tugging her hair, he reached up to pull her lips toward his and then flipped her around so he was on top of her on the couch. His hands roamed over her lace bra as he feverishly kissed her face, her neck, and the mounds of her heaving breasts.

As his hands moved lower, tracing her soft, supple curves and brushing a thumb over the flatness of her stomach, Scarlet's breath quickened. She let her hands explore his sculptured form, freely roaming over his chest, chiseled like a statue and gleaming in the firelight. She moved her hand down to his warm, pulsating shaft and felt his growing desire for her. He groaned a deep throaty noise making her insides tingle as he slipped his hand inside of her lacy panties and moved his fingers slowly and rhythmically between her legs.

She loved how he fervently touched her, his eyes wide with passion, devouring her as if all they had were that moment and her typical hesitations, modesty, and nerves, melted away because she was with him. She felt safer with him than ever before. Her body responded to every move he made, and she arched her back in ecstasy as he entered her. They moved in tandem, the flickering lights of the candle drawing pictures on their naked bodies. They made love like it was their last day on Earth, like they were the only two people in existence. Recognizing something in one another which took a lifetime of searching to find, their passion carried them into the twilight hours, until they curled up together, exhausted on the couch.

It amazed her that moments earlier she had felt the walls of her situation caving in. Now, she couldn't wipe the smile off her face. She couldn't remember the last time she was *this happy*. She wished the night would never end.

She promised herself as she lay in the dwindling candlelight she wouldn't let the pressures of the world outside those walls dampen her spirits. She would allow herself to feel blissfully content, wrapped in the arms of a man unlike any other she had ever met, until the harsh morning sun stole away the moment. She fell asleep nestled next to him, the sound of his heartbeat lulling her to sleep under the star-spattered night sky.

Chapter 42

"You have seen the monster on the other side of the mirror."

Scarlet lay next to Fenton in the quiet four seasons room, with the morning sun shining through the light curtains and across the bed, painting a stream of light on Fenton's face. She almost felt like a normal couple —a couple who would find this spot by the lake romantic and secluded, off the beaten path and peaceful, instead of as a haven from crime lords trying to silence her like they silenced Robin.

Robin. Full of life and spontaneous, Robin. She would have been able to handle this situation, thought Scarlet dismally. Robin was the right twin for this task of working with Kelly Carter, and for toying with dangerous criminals with itchy trigger fingers. This was Robin's scene, not hers, but it was apparent even her sister couldn't handle the façade.

She looked over at Fenton's resting form, his face peaceful and still, the light from the windows dancing across his lips and brow. The blankets were across his waist, exposing his defined chest and arms. She noticed the distinctive marks of scars, healed and jagged over his deeply-tanned skin. The sun at the lake house had bronzed him to perfection. She inched closer, studying the marks. Some were faded red gashes, while others were slightly raised markings as if they were healed wounds from a knife or something sharp. When she studied the faded scars, she wondered how the scenarios unfolded for each injury. Was he on a job? Was he protecting someone like her? She wondered if they still hurt him, if he experienced lingering pain. She frowned at the thought. There was a long, jagged line near his heart that particularly interested her, it looked like whatever happened, he was extremely lucky it wasn't a direct hit.

She reached out, and made sure he was still fast asleep before tracing the protruding scar with her finger. The angry scar started near his collarbone and ended by his heart, and she followed it lightly with her fingertip, intrigued by his numerous markings.

Fenton flinched, grabbing Scarlet's wrist, freezing her hand securely in his grasp, his eyes wide and aware assessing the threat. She noticed him visibly relax when he recognized her face, his movements were more on instinct and training than anything else. She could tell he was embarrassed by his instant defensive reaction, and he loosened his grip, turning her wrist over to kiss the back of her hand.

"You startled me," he said, letting go of her hand and sinking back against the bundle of blankets they turned into a bed. She looked at her wrist briefly, distinctive red marks forming from his tight enclosed fist.

"Geez, I'm sorry, Scarlet. Did I hurt you?" He propped himself up on his elbow, gently reaching out to pull her hand toward him to investigate the marks forming as a replica of a tightly-closed-fingered hold. He kissed her hand lightly. The sensation of his lips lingered on the back of her hand. It reminded her of last night, and she blushed.

His face was just inches from her own and he looked up at her wide-eyed and concerned, ashamed of his own strength. She was drawn into his gaze and she knew he was the only one truly concerned for her. He was the only one close to her in her life now, and he was certainly the only one who understood her and everything she had been through. His gaze held it all – understanding, acceptance, trust, faith, but most of all, his gaze promised protection. She leaned even closer, her eyes moving from his gray-flecked stare, to his perfectly-formed luscious lips. She closed her eyes and kissed him lightly, her eyes flickering back open and gauging his reaction. He smiled at her, a sleepy gaze, and kissed her lips lightly again.

She felt an overwhelming sense of fondness for him in that moment. She felt his past and her present create a bond of understanding, and a wave of emotion came over her. She looked at him and thought he was a lovely person with an intense light within him who simply ended up in dark situations. The fact he still shined, despite all he must have seen and done, transfixed Scarlet. She wanted to take a mental snapshot of this point in time when they understood each other's honest and ugly truths. She had never found him more attractive than in that instant. He smiled again, and she rested her hand on his chest.

"What?" she asked with a smirk.

"I just realized, when I wake up, I want to see your face next to me."

"Yum, I like that. Does it concern you that you feel that way toward me?"

"I'm tired of analyzing and re-analyzing these feelings. We can't tell our heart what to feel, right? We can't stop our mind from wandering to what it wants. We can't change what invades our dreams. We can't change what causes our blood to course feverishly through our veins. We can't sway what makes us feel calm or at ease.

317

When I see your smile, it cuts through my darkest thoughts and I can forget everything else for a while. I don't have to constantly hide myself from you. You have seen the monster on the other side of the mirror, and you didn't look away."

"That is because you're no monster. I have seen monsters, I have felt monsters, and you are nothing like them."

"I kill just like they do."

"You kill so that others may live, and you kill to protect. The motives are vastly different. You kill, even though you don't want to, but you know you need to. They kill for the power, they kill for the taste of blood, they kill to build their reputation, they kill because they believe they should have whatever they want in this life and will stop at nothing to get it. You couldn't be like them if you tried, even at what you consider to be your worst. I see the real you in your eyes. I see where you have to go deep inside to do what you do, but it doesn't make you any less good." She reached out and touched his hair, gently. His eyes peered into hers as she continued.

"If anything, you're better than most of us. You risk everything for a job with few rewards. You tirelessly work to achieve what few others have the strength and discipline to achieve. You have to go deep into the shadows, to the worst recesses of people's nightmares, because that is where the evil lives. Yet, you remain steadfast to your honor code, you remain steadfast to pursuing good, and that makes you better than the rest of us — better in every way."

"God, you've got me hooked." he murmured as he leaned over to kiss her.

"Good, now time to get up. I hear Taylor out on the dock. We should be social, like normal people right?"

"Yeah, like normal people." He winked. They gathered their clothes to pretend to be people with no other care in the world besides what type of bait to use on the other end of the fishing pole. It felt good, even if it was just pretend.

Hours later that day, Scarlet was laughing by the water as Taylor did cannonballs off the dock. Dale was trimming a couple of trees up the hill, and Winnie was putting out lunch on the patio table. She saw Fenton walk toward her, and a smile came across her face.

Then she saw his expression.

She knew immediately something was wrong. She got out of her patio chair, and walked toward him. He grabbed her hands, a pained expression hiding behind his eyes.

"Come inside with me, Scarlet," he said softly, and she followed without saying a word. Once inside, with the patio door securely shut, he turned toward her.

"I'm sorry, but we have to leave."

"Now?" she whispered.

"Yes."

"What's going on? You're scaring me." She hugged herself with her arms.

"You said you would always trust me, right? I need you to trust me now. I'm not going to let anything happen to you. I don't want to freak you out, but I think you deserve to know what is going on. Carter just called and she needs us back in D.C. right away. Luca Nero is dead." He put a hand on her arm, as she started to tremble.

"Luca... is dead? That means he wasn't the one who sent the Confectionist to get me? Someone had him killed, the same person who tried to have me killed, and they are still out there? Waiting?" She felt like she was going to pass out and she clutched the edge of the countertop. Fenton pulled her toward him, enveloping her in a warm hug.

"I told you, I won't let anything happen to you. We don't know anything yet. Carter has some images she wants us to look at which they recovered from your sister's laptop and phone. We are hoping the missing links will start to come into focus. We are going to figure out who is behind this, I promise." She sighed and closed her eyes tightly as he pulled her closer. She wanted to remain like this, by the lake, safe in his arms, forever, yet she knew it was simply another pretty picture in her mind which could never come true.

"Fenton, I'm scared," she said, barely above a whisper. He pulled her to arm's length and bent over so his face was even with hers.

"I know, and things will have to get a little worse before they get better, but then they will get better. We have to go through some of this to get to a better place. You want this to all be over, right? View this as the next step to ending this whole nightmare. I'll let you in on a little secret. We all get scared, even in my line of work, but for me, it helps if I close my eyes and think of one of my favorite places. Next time you feel you're scared, just close your eyes and think of this lake house. Think of the tall gates, thick trees, water to protect the property on every side, a house impossible to penetrate, and a little slice of heaven where you can be at peace. Think of this place and you'll start to feel better. It's what I always do." He smiled at her, and kissed her gently on her lips. A warmth lingered after the kiss, cloaking her with the memory of him and arousing the electricity he ignited inside her. She opened her eyes, and smiled back as she gazed at his face.

"I'll explain to Dale, don't worry about that. You ready to do this?" he asked, and she nodded.

"Thanks for bringing me here, Fenton. It was nice being happy for a change." She swallowed hard, and he bowed his head for a moment. His eyes looked a little brighter than normal, but he gave her a slight smile.

"Yeah, me too." They stood there in the kitchen in silence, two broken people acknowledging the fact they had to leave a place where they were finally feeling whole again. The heaviness of what their leaving meant hung between them, until finally Fenton left to explain their sudden departure to Dale.

Scarlet wiped a couple of stray tears from her eyes and went to pack her bags to get ready to leave a place she had grown to love and head back into the waking nightmare she thought she had left behind.

Chapter 43

"You can't bullshit a bullshitter."

Carter was pacing the floor, sipping coffee with bits of grounds floating at the top, but she guzzled it anyway. She was going on a couple of hours sleep for the last two nights and caffeine was the only thing that allowed her to power through. She saw Fenton open the glass double doors for Scarlet, and she felt like she could breathe again. Having her main asset under the same roof again helped make her feel the case was salvageable.

"Good to see you two. I'm glad you're back in town. Right this way, we have the conference room set up for you," Carter said. She was never one for small talk, but she heard Scarlet whisper to Fenton *I wish I could say the same* under her breath. Carter smirked.

She noticed Fenton pull out a chair for Scarlet. *Not only has he softened, but he is chivalrous now, too.*

"We were able to recover these images from your sister's laptop and phone. We are running facial recognition on each face we can't identify, but wanted to see if either of you recognize anyone from the party. There are also a few more images we are trying to reconstruct. I'll let you know when we have something. Anything strike a chord?" She clicked through the images pausing momentarily on each one. As Fenton and Scarlet stared at the screen intently, Carter was watching their micro expressions and body language. They could have a subconscious response before they realized what they saw. She noticed Fenton's eyes squint, and she went back to the last image.

"Get anything from this one?" It was an image of Manuele having lunch with an unknown male. With the image resting on the screen, she heard Scarlet gasp. She was about to say something when Fenton jumped in.

"Yes, the man with Manuele Nero is the man we know as the Confectionist. He's the man I killed in the hotel when he came after Scarlet." Scarlet shot him a look, but remained quiet.

"Okay good, do you think Manuele was behind this? I thought he was the drunk in the family, a disappointment, the son the family tries to hide?"

"Yeah, a drunk protected by his sister," Fenton said, his jaw was clenched and he looked like he was ready to jump out of his chair at the memory of the scuffle at the hotel.

"He is Eleonora's pet project from everything Luca told me," Scarlet said. Carter bent over her laptop to filter out all of the photos with just Eleonora in them. They started to notice a pattern with Eleonora, especially when Alonzo or Luca were in the shot with her. A disgruntled expression would show on her face in the candid shots when she either walked behind them or stood outside the circle of men talking. She paused on the photos of Eleonora kissing an unknown male.

"Wait, back up a second," Scarlet said. Carter moved a photo back.

"What do you see, Scarlet?"

"That man, not the man she is kissing, but the one outside the café keeping watch. I recognize him."

"From where? The party?" Fenton asked.

"No... from the night my sister was murdered. He was the one who took the photo of me. He was with a larger man. I am almost ninety percent sure."

"Your sister was killed by soldiers in the Durante crime family so why would the daughter of Gabriel Nero be in the same place, let alone same building, with someone from the Durante clan? Not only that, but someone important enough to have a guard standing at the front entrance?" Carter said. Her mind was a garbled mess from caffeine and lack of sleep.

"What if we've been looking in the wrong direction this whole time? It wasn't Luca behind this, or Manuele, but Eleonora? Eleonora is our guy, so to speak. What if she is the brains behind these hits?" Fenton stood from his chair and moved to the projector screen.

"Wait. Go back to the other photos. See? She meets with Manuele, time and date stamped the day before he meets with the Confectionist. We know the Confectionist was the hit man hired to kill Scarlet. We don't see him with any of the members of the Nero family except Manuele, who we know is a washed-up drunkard the family tries to hide. Everyone except Eleonora. She is almost always with him, otherwise he is off running errands, most likely at her behest. Now, it appears she has ties to the Durante family as well. It's got to be her," Fenton said, pacing around the front of the room. He grabbed his sunglasses off his head and tapped them on the table.

"Great. The one person in the family we have the least amount of intelligence on. I need to bring this to trial, Fenton. This isn't enough," Carter scowled. Fenton continued to tap his glasses on the table.

Tap...tap... like tap dancing. It sounds like a little army of tap dancers in my head. Tap dancers... that is what I need in this case, a little tap dance routine of my own to save this disaster of a case and bring it through to the finale. Wait a second... that's it...

"I've got an idea. Fenton, can I see you in my office please?" Carter said, smiling the first real smile in weeks. She noticed Scarlet glance at Fenton, worry spreading across her face, and then she saw him wink at her as he left the room.

That's right, trust in Fenton. I'll get him to do my little dance and then he'll get you to join in. We will be in lockstep in no time, heading toward a conviction which even would make Rudy Giuliani proud.

"No way. No way, Carter. There is no way she will agree to this, because it's reckless and a bad idea. You understand me? This *isn't an option*, it's off the table. I don't know how many different ways I can say no, absolutely not." Fenton rose from the chair in Carter's office in frustration, after hearing Carter's idea. He was pacing the room, shooting daggers into Carter with his eyes. She remained expressionless, leaning back in her chair with her arms crossed. Her eyes following him around the room.

"This is the way it has to be. You want something from me only I can provide you. You told me you wanted out of this life, completely out, with nothing tying you to your past. You want a new identity so you can be a normal Joe on the street? Well, I can make that happen. If you want the reward, you have to deliver the goods. I need Scarlet to go back in undercover to smoke out Eleonora. We need her, Fenton. She needs to get Eleonora to talk and she is the best one to do it. You want your outcome? Then get me mine."

"I'm not going to put Scarlet in danger. I don't care anymore. I'll walk away from our deal."

"You can't walk away from our deal. I doubt you would leave your little starlet to fend for herself. She impersonated her sister, two rival crime families are out to get her, and she needs safe transport into witness protection. You're the only one qualified to keep her safe, and that is why I know you won't walk away. You can't bullshit a bullshitter. Poker just isn't your game."

"You've taken this too far. Who else needs to die before you shut down this operation? Let her disappear, let me hand her off to witness protection, let's end this. She did everything you asked."

"Except this, this is my last ask, Fenton. We can get this done. We need to get this done."

"No deal." Fenton gritted his teeth and Carter scowled back at him. She carefully rose from her seat and sat at the edge of her desk. Rubbing her hands together, she thought of a new plan.

"How about this? I position this to Scarlet, and you help me convince her this is the right move. If she agrees, we can work out where she gets to walk away from this whole thing on the spot. You get what you want. It's a win across the board, but I need you in there helping me get it done."

"What do you mean, she gets to walk away?"

"We suit her up with a bulletproof vest and we play the angle maybe she was working against Luca. We get our best sharpshooter from the team to plug her at the end of the conversation. Eleonora thinks she is dead and we cart her away in the ambulance, after we get our confession, of course. Scarlet isn't dead, thanks to the vest, but you can transition her directly into witness protection. That ensures no one in their right mind will keep looking for her. We can offer her a level of peace that wasn't available before. The type of peace she thought she had lost forever. People don't hunt down a dead person, that's a fact. Don't you want to be her hero? Isn't this what she desires more than anything else? A chance at a real life, not looking over her shoulder? Then you get to walk away with exactly what you asked for from the beginning. It's a good plan, Fenton, and my final offer. Get her to agree or I do it alone. You have to decide if we move forward with or without you." Carter studied his face, she knew the look. The slow realization she holds all the cards, the crushing reality there isn't anything left to leverage against her. He was too easy — when he cares, he cares too much. It was a trait they didn't share.

"Okay. I don't like it, but I agree it gives her the best chance at a normal life. I'll do what I can, but if she doesn't agree, I'm not going to force it."

"Your objection is noted and I think you're wrong. You *will* force it, because you know what's best for her. Let's go in there." Carter nodded at him, and started back toward the conference room with Fenton trailing behind.

"Starr, get me the file we talked about, the one for Scarlet," Carter yelled over her shoulder at Agent Starr, who quickly grabbed the folder and followed them in. Scarlet started to get out of her seat, but Carter motioned her to sit back down.

"Here's the deal. We need you to go back undercover. We need you to confront Eleonora and get her to talk. We need to bring a case against her, and you're our best shot," Carter said matter-of-factly.

"What? No, I thought I was done. Eleonora is the one who sent someone to *kill me*. Why on earth would I face her again? Why would she ever agree to see me?" Scarlet glanced at Fenton, a lot of shock across her face, but Fenton remained stoic.

"We have Luca's recordings. Eleonora doesn't know with one

hundred percent certainty her hit on him worked, the wreckage of his car is well underwater by now. The proof has sunk. We lucked out someone got lost on the road, and called in the suspicious chunk of metal smoldering and we got the partial license plate match. We can splice together his recording to leave her a message with Luca's voice making it sound like he is still alive, and then you show up instead of Luca. She will believe anything we tell her at that point. It's the element of surprise. This can work." Carter scanned Scarlet's face, who looked unconvinced.

"Scarlet, how do you think your father died?" Carter continued, taking a different approach.

"He was drinking and alone at night. He fell over a guard rail, and fell to his death. What does that have to do with anything?"

"They ruled it a suicide didn't they?"

"Yes, but I never believed that." Scarlet crossed her arms. Carter leaned across the table, pushing the folder toward Scarlet.

"What if I told you neither of those scenarios are true? What if I told you the Nero family was behind your father's death?"

"I would say that's impossible."

Carter flipped open the file, showing a picture of Scarlet's father sitting with Manuele and another soldier in the Nero clan. The soldier was wearing a light gray suitcoat with silver horseshoe cufflinks.

"See this image? Your father is smoking a cigarette with a young Alonzo and Manuele Nero and a high-ranking soldier in the family business. Later the same day, notice the time and date stamp, we have this image from a satellite of your father walking with a man with a gray suitcoat with silver horseshoe cufflinks. That is about six hundred feet from where your father fell to his death. The evidence is circumstantial at best, since we can't prove beyond a reasonable doubt it's the same man, but you and I both know the truth looking at these images. There is no doubt in my mind Alonzo and Manuele had your father killed. Who uses Manuele as their errand boy? Think, Scarlet. Eleonora killed your father, and you're telling me you're going to let her walk away to sip her wine and vacation at the French Riviera in the summertime? She took away the only parent you had left. Then, Robin finds herself completely alone in debt to the Neros because of dear old dad, and she turns to a life of crime. That's how she got connected to Luca — she owed him your father's debts. Eleonora played an integral part in the death of everyone close to you. That doesn't bother you, *just a little bit*?" Carter tilted her head as she emphasized the last three words.

"How dare you drag my sister back into this mess?"

"Tell me I'm off base. Tell me I'm full of shit. You can't. You cannot say that, because you know everything I'm telling you is rooted in fact. Question is, are you willing to do what it takes to make her pay? You have the chance every other victim out there dreams about. You have a chance to make this right."

"I'm not a victim." Scarlet was battling back tears.

"Then prove it to me. Go undercover and get our girl." Carter kept her intense gaze squarely upon Scarlet's face. Scarlet turned toward Fenton.

"Do you think it is the right move?" she asked.

"I think this gives you the best way out. We can set it up so we fake your death, once we have Eleonora's confession, she will think you are dead. There would be no reason for anyone to try to find you again. You would be safe in witness protection," His face remained expressionless, but he spoke tenderly toward her, and her face softened with his words. Carter stifled a smile, but she was satisfied Fenton played his part.

"Okay, let's do it. When do we leave?" Scarlet said. The tears were gone from her eyes and replaced by a hardness, a hardness that comes from accepting the fear and moving forward anyway. Carter started barking orders to her staff.

"Splice up audio from Luca's recordings. Call Eleonora and set up the meet. She won't be able to refuse a face to face from her brother back from the dead.

After finalizing the details, Carter pulled Fenton aside.

"I follow through on my promises. You want out of this game right? You delivered. Scarlet is going to participate. Once the mission is done, I'll get you the new identification we discussed as well as your final payment. You will have a new life. My team will set you up with a background as boring as the next average Joe on the street and you can hole up in whatever small piss ant town you want to. Then we are square, right?"

"Yep, then we are square. What background are you going to give me?"

"Sales rep. One of the most common jobs in the world, plus, it will help explain your early retirement. You worked for a startup company which went public in a big way. It's an easy cover."

"Thanks, Carter."

"Anytime. Send me pictures of whatever beach you end up at. I can't see you being the relaxed type, but I've seen crazier things." Carter squeezed his shoulder, and walked out. Scarlet was standing outside the door.

"Can I talk with you, quick?" she asked.

"Sure, step into my office. I can grab Fenton."

"Ah, no. Just you and me is fine," she said timidly. Carter's eyebrows rose in surprise. Across the room, one of her agents yelled her name.

"Hey Carter, you're going to want to take this call. You wouldn't believe it. A guy named Carlo called the cops. It ties into your case." Carter nodded.

"Hold them on the line, one second. I have to finish this up quick. You want to talk to me, Scarlet? You got it, right this way," Carter said. She led the way to her office and shut the door. *Well, this is going to be good.*

"What can I do for you?" she asked Scarlet, and held her breath. *I'll give you anything you want, Scarlet, as long as it's something I'm willing to give.*

Chapter 44

"If you want something done right, sometimes you have to do it yourself."

Eleonora was getting used to the idea of power and all of her father's soldiers looked at her differently since she told the news about Luca to her father. She was now one of his last children, and the only one he could trust. Plus, she managed to elevate Manuele in the process. Her plan was coming together beautifully.

She noticed her cell vibrate from an unknown number and she let it go to voicemail. She didn't have time for random strangers calling her by mistake. She had a family to control, and soon nothing would stand in the way of her father relinquishing all control to Manuele and then her plan would be complete. She heard the familiar ping from her voicemail and checked it. The moment the voice on the other end of the line registered in her mind, her blood ran cold. She dropped the phone, and it bounced on the hard polished floors of their family mansion.

It was Luca's voice on the other end. Her dead brother. The

brother she thought she had sent careening off the road and violently crashing into the hungry waters of the river. He was asking to meet her. He said he was off the grid, unsure of who to trust. He said someone was after him, and he didn't have a car. That meant he was alive, surviving the blast somehow, and could ruin everything for her. She started calling some of her most loyal soldiers, the ones she kept on the side for just such an occasion. She would meet her brother and emphasize with him someone was out to kill them all.

She would make sure it was their last conversation. She couldn't have someone like Luca running around, not after she just got him out of the picture. *If you want something done right, sometimes you have to do it yourself.*

Chapter 45

"You don't know what you're saying."

"**N**o matter what happens to me, if I get her to talk, their voices will be recorded so Carter will be able to prosecute them with or without my direct testimony, right?" Scarlet asked Fenton nervously.

"Yes, faking your death will ensure you won't be there for the trial. You will be far away from here at that point. Are you nervous? You don't have to worry about that, the tape should be enough."

"Did Carter promise you something, for working with me? I overheard some of your conversation. Tell me the truth, Fenton." Fenton's eyes clouded at her question.

"It started that way, but you have to believe me, I don't care about my part of the deal. I told her I wouldn't put you in danger. I don't care if she can't get me a new identity so I can walk away from the undercover life. I wanted out and this was going to be my last job, Scarlet. I'm done, and it was part of the bargain for taking this case, but it was never the main reason. I couldn't stand the thought of something happening to you. I knew I was the only one who could protect you in this case, so I took the job. Please believe me." He took her hands into his own. She tilted her head at him, scanning his eyes, looking for the lie but saw none.

"I believe you, and it doesn't matter anymore. Listen to me carefully, Fenton. I want to make sure we are on the same page. I told Carter I will only do the undercover operation if you're not on the scene. You have to stay in the surveillance van. She agreed."

"What? What are you saying? I'm not going to let you go in there alone." He was furious, looking at her soft features, shocking him with her words.

"It's already decided. If something goes wrong when I go back in, don't come in and get me, no matter what. Even if it means you let me die there, I want you to do it. Don't come in after me."

"Scarlet, you don't know what you're saying. You're under a lot of stress right now."

"I do. I do know what I'm saying, Fenton. I know exactly what I'm saying. I don't want you to get involved no matter what. I don't care if it means I die. I don't care. You have a life to live after this mess, and I want to make sure you have the chance to live it," she said it quietly, softly, wondering if it would feel different to hear those words hit her lips, but she felt nothing.

"Scarlet, I don't want to ever hear you say that again."

"Fenton, I'm being serious, I don't know if I can live with what I've seen, with what I have done. You can still walk away from this when it's all done. You can still go to the cabin in the summers, retire and find a nice girl with whom to start a life. You have things waiting for you on the other side if you want them and I don't. It will be better this way."

"Scarlet, this is insane. Everything is going to be fine."

"I don't want you on site. You can stay with the other agents or in the van. I don't want you in the field on this. Okay? That is my one request."

"It's my job. If something goes sideways, I need to be there."

"No, you don't. You get your freedom after this. You get to walk away with a new identity, with a new life. I don't want anything to mess that up. It's my only demand. I won't do this if you're there, so either you have to explain to Carter why I've pulled out or you let me go in alone."

"Scarlet, I..."

"There is no use debating me. It's non-negotiable. You can hate me if you want, but at least now I know you'll be safe."

"I can't hate you, Scarlet, I care too much. Why do you have to be so difficult?"

"I learned from the best." She smiled at him. She held his hand briefly, but the agents came to pull her away to get her ready to fly to Vegas for her last undercover operation.

Chapter 46

"Sorry, sweetheart. You're just not that special."

The meet was set and picked strategically by Carter and her team to give them the best coverage, and to allow for the best shot at Scarlet when it was time. Carter explained Agent Westbrook would be the one pulling the trigger.

"Don't worry Scarlet, it's like we discussed. You get Eleonora talking and, once we get her confession, or she starts to move, we'll shoot you in the vest. It will rupture the fake blood bag we have under the material. Eleonora, and everyone else associated with this case, will hear you died on the scene. Then you will be free of this whole mess, and won't have to testify in court. Remember the scripting we gave you. You'll be fine."

"Thanks and where will Fenton be?"

"He will be in the van a couple of blocks away, far from the action, just like you asked."

Scarlet was nervous, but she knew it was the only way out for her, to see this thing through to the end. They had surveillance cameras set up all over the open courtyard they used for the meet. They purposely set up random construction signs around some of the main entrances to the courtyard to deter innocent bystanders from approaching. Agents wearing civilian clothing were stationed at several access points to make sure only Eleonora came through. Once they saw her approaching, they motioned Scarlet into action.

Eleonora sauntered into the courtyard, and sat on a bench. Scarlet came around the corner, and Eleonora's face turned into a surprised grin.

"Well, isn't this a treat? I get a call from my dear brother, but his girlfriend shows up instead. How are you, Robin? Where's Luca?"

"I'm not going to tell you Eleonora. You tried to have him killed. He is on the way to meet with your father right now, and guess what? I'm the only one standing in the way of implicating you as your brother's killer to your father. What do you think about that?"

"On what grounds?" Her face flushed crimson as she bit her lower lip.

"Oh come on, Eleonora. Don't play coy with me. If you're honest with me right now, I might just show you mercy. I'm impressed. You tried having me killed, then Luca, but you succeeded with Alonzo. I have photos of you and Romeo Durante. Is he your boyfriend? I gave those pictures to Luca. I just need the truth from you, all of it, and then I call Luca and tell him to hold off."

"You're bluffing. Why would you do that for me, anyway? Let's say I tell you what you want to know. How would you convince him not to tell our father?" Eleonora crossed her arms, eyes darting around the open courtyard as she sat on the edge of the wooden bench.

"We don't want you dead. We want your help to bring down the Durantes. If you agree, and tell me how you planned all of this, I'll tell

Luca you're back on our side. We need you to help bring them down from the top. If Romeo is your boyfriend, you're directly connected with the underboss of that family. This means you know more about how to bring them down than I could ever find on some stupid computer. I want all the politicians' names, what committees they bribe, how they help the Durantes, everything. The way I see it, you agree to help Luca and me, or you die a painfully horrendous death at the hands of your own father. What's it going to be, Eleonora?" Eleonora paused, contemplating the offer, and scanning Scarlet's face to see if she could detect a lie. She narrowed her eyes.

"I was told by Romeo and my contacts within the Durante family you were killed, Robin. You were killed at their warehouse. I saw that locket in your purse and you looked different. Who are you? Who are you really?" Scarlet stiffened, pulling from her inner strength to keep her face confident and calm.

"Silly Eleonora. You also thought Luca was dead, and you sent someone to kill me at the hotel. Obviously, I'm not that easy to kill. I'm Robin, Robin Lilly Matthews. I'm Luca's girlfriend. You flatter me with your gullibility though. You think you're the only one who can play games? You think you're the only one who can fool people? Sorry, sweetheart. You're just not that special," Scarlet said with a wicked grin, and Eleonora's eyes widened in horror.

Eleonora swallowed hard, doubting everything she thought was true, and then began telling Scarlet everything: the political connections tied to the Durantes, her plan to kill Luca, how she killed Alonzo, her dealings with the Durantes, the family's business and how she could run the operation better than her father ever could. She even gave details on operations she felt her father messed up, giving Carter and her team valuable intel on the rest of his illegal operations. Eleonora spit out the words with obvious disdain as she twirled a long piece of hair between her manicured fingers.

"I mean, hiding cocaine in fish? Smuggling it in that way?

Come on, I could come up with something better in my sleep. The next shipment is due in this Friday, and I was going to be there with better ideas for the future. My father finally brings me into the family business, and now this, just when I was about to run the whole operation. What will Luca do with me now?" she asked timidly. Scarlet shook her head.

"I don't know, Eleonora. I guess time will tell." Scarlet knew her time was drawing near to an end. She got everything from Eleonora she came in to retrieve. She had to remind herself not to close her eyes when she heard the shot she knew was about to come.

Now was her chance to really live...through death.

Chapter 47

"I can make justice complete."

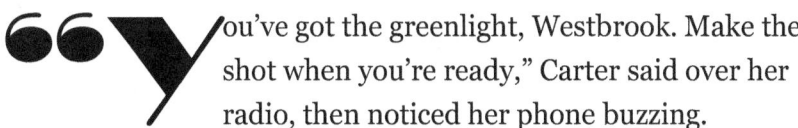ou've got the greenlight, Westbrook. Make the shot when you're ready," Carter said over her radio, then noticed her phone buzzing.

"Carter, where is your team?" Fenton's voice yelled frantically on the other end of the phone to Carter, who was a block away from Scarlet at the operation.

"What do you mean, where is my team? They are at the meet, where I am, what are you getting at?"

"We were able to clear up the blurry photo, Carter. I just got a call from the D.C. office. Who is supposed to take the shot at Scarlet?"

"Agent Westbrook. He is the best shot we've got. Who was in the photo? Talk to me Fenton."

"Call off the shot, Carter! Do it now! I'm on my way and I can fill you in," he growled into his cell phone receiver.

"I can't do that, Fenton. I've already given the order to shoot."

"No! Westbrook was the unknown in the photo! Westbrook was the mole all along. He's dirty. He was their inside man the whole time... he shot Alonzo. Manuele is a drunk, and Eleonora needed Westbrook to pull the trigger. Call it off, Carter! Carter?" Fenton's voice was just an echo now as Kelly Carter dropped her phone, its plastic case rattling against the pavement.

In the background on the other end of the receiver, Fenton heard shots fired.

Carter ran yelling into her radio and her full team converged on the scene right as Westbrook got off his shot. The commotion caused his aim to falter as Scarlet crumpled to the ground. Carter drew her gun and yelled at Westbrook to walk out in the open of the courtyard. The rest of the team ran in surrounding Eleonora, and dragged her away in handcuffs. Westbrook ran out into the courtyard behind Scarlet, pulling out a large knife and placing it to her neck yelling for the team to stand down as he used her body as a shield.

Carter yelled to one of the team members nearest to Scarlet. "Robin's been shot, she's bleeding out! We need to get her out of here!" The team member could tell by the urgency of Carter's voice it wasn't part of the staged scene. Crushing reality hit Carter seeing Westbrook's wild expression as he held the knife ready to finish the job, already covered in Scarlet's blood. *Westbrook didn't use blanks. The son of a bitch shot her with a real bullet above the vest. He shot to kill. He thought he could run in and pull Eleonora away before we got on the scene. He was so convinced the incriminating photo of him couldn't be recovered.*

She stood, gun drawn, over Westbrook, her hands shaking with rage. He stared wide- eyed at her while on his knees. Fenton came running onto the scene, drawing his gun at Carter when he saw

Westbrook's knife against Scarlet's throat.

"Carter, what are you doing? Put down the gun. Think of Scarlet," Fenton said evenly.

"You couldn't understand what this is like, Fenton, you couldn't understand this. I trusted him. I thought I knew him better than I knew my family...and then he shot the one person I brought him in to help protect." Westbrook looked wildly at Carter and Fenton.

"Try me. I know more about you than you may guess. I read your file. You lost a sister when you were very young. You blame yourself." She shook her head, and laughed ironically.

"So you read my file? Big deal. Then you know justice doesn't always punish the bad guys. You of all people should know that."

"You blame yourself for your sister's death? You were a small girl then. What could you have done?" Fenton motioned behind his back to Starr, who started moving behind the building to take a position to get a better shot at Westbrook. He kept a close eye on Scarlet, and he knew he had to get her out of there quickly.

"I should have done something, anything, to stop it. It was a neighbor who killed her, someone we trusted, just like I trusted Westbrook."

"Killing Westbrook won't bring back your sister. It isn't the justice you need, I promise. You have ambitions and career goals. This would ruin everything you have worked for, Carter."

"He ruined evidence, he purposely protected Eleonora and the family because he was one of them. For years he fooled me, and I want to make sure he can't fool anyone ever again. I can make justice complete." She licked her lips as she tightened her hold on the gun. Westbrook stared back at her impassively.

"I need to get Scarlet to a hospital, Carter. She is bleeding because Westbrook shot her, but he doesn't have to win. It isn't too late for her. My job is to protect her, Carter, and you're standing in my way. You have to stop protecting the dead and start protecting the living." He watched Scarlet's eyes flitter, her shirt stained red over the bulletproof vest. Westbrook glared at Fenton but his hand holding the knife shook slightly.

Fenton took another tentative step toward her and Westbrook's knife pressed harder against Scarlet's neck.

"Carter, how many bad guys have you put away? How many innocent lives have you saved in the name of your sister? You are strong because you survived and went on to make a difference. What you do matters, not what you *didn't* do. Make the choice now, make the choice to save the sister that survived. Give me the gun, Carter, give me the gun and let's end this," Fenton pleaded, and Carter slowly lowered her gun.

Fenton nodded, and Agent Starr who was inching out behind a building, saw Fenton's cue, and shot Westbrook in the leg without hesitation. Westbrook slumped to the ground holding his leg in agony causing him to drop his knife. Scarlet lay crumpled on the ground next to him.

Fenton didn't waste any time, scooping Scarlet up in his arms and cradling her against his body as he and Agent Starr raced to the closest police vehicle. He laid her in the back seat on his lap as he yelled to Agent Starr to floor it.

Sirens wailed as the police car raced toward the hospital. Lars Fenton held Scarlet in his arms in the backseat, her bouncy blond curls fell softly on her white shirt, now stained crimson. He could feel the liquid trickling down his pant leg, warm and damp from the gunshot wound. He couldn't get the metallic taste from his mouth. The smell of blood mixed with the lingering scent of ash and smoke filled the air from where the bullet ripped through her shirt. A wave of nausea hit him as he closed his eyes. *Keep it together Fenton, don't lose it now.*

Sunlight flooded the back of the police car, peppering the backseat with dancing shadows as the car raced faster. The shadows reminded him of their summer nights at the lake house and how the light danced from the licking flames of the campfire. It seemed like years ago now.

The silver bullet fragments embedded around her bulletproof vest occasionally caught the sunlight. The flashes of light blinded Fenton as he held her tightly against his chest. The bullet entered at the edge of her vest, angling into flesh near her arm. Only an expert marksman would know how to make the strategic shot.

"Is it over?" Scarlet whispered, the color draining from her face as her warm blood flowed over his hands like a quiet stream. He tried applying more pressure to the gunshot wound. *Too much blood, she is losing too much blood.* He blinked back tears, hot stinging tears, which felt foreign to him. He saw the innocence return to her features with her question. In that instant, she looked like the same girl he met only a few months ago. He remembered the first time he saw her, and the way she looked as she sat shivering in her apartment. He could see beyond the makeup expertly applied around her soft features. He could see beyond the strategic mask hiding a scared, young lady who once had the world in front of her.

Despite all the hours funneled into changing this woman into a completely different person, he was still able to see beyond the painstakingly rehearsed alter ego which fooled everyone else. With her lying in his arms he reflected on how they met. It crushed him to see her in pain and he remembered his oath to protect her.

"Hold on, we are getting you help, just hold on. I came as soon as I heard. I could have *stopped* this. It should be me lying here, not you," he said softly to her, and tenderly brushed a strand of hair away from her face. His hand was stained with blood that looked like war paint dried against his skin.

"No...I made you stay away," she gasped, and he held her tighter.

"Promise me... you'll go back...to the lake. Be... at peace there," she struggled to form the words. Her eyes lifted slowly with her remaining strength and she looked at him fondly, without restraint. The gaze held an incredible warmth, and it tore at his insides like the reopening of an old wound. He choked back a desperate cry of frustration, of injustice, as she fought against the looming unconsciousness which threatened to sweep her away.

"I won't go back to the lake without you. Do you understand me? Don't leave me now." He continued applying desperate pressure to the hole in her chest, praying in his mind to everything he held sacred. He made silent promises, negotiations, committing to become a better person. He swore he would quit the life if only she survived.

"Stay with me," he said forcefully, willing it into truth. Her eyelids flittered.

"Drive *faster*, dammit!" he growled at the Starr.

He lightly kissed her lips as he sealed his silent vow. The same lips that kept him up countless nights, the kiss he used to fight. He opened his eyes suddenly, realizing this time... she didn't kiss him back.

Chapter 48

"Truly an inspiration."

Carter's team issued arrests for many of the Durante and Nero family members. Her team used the years of surveillance they gathered on both families, but with Scarlet's undercover operation, they were able to bring in audio and video footage to help strengthen the case.

The charges included drug trafficking, illegal gambling, political corruption, extortion, kidnapping, fraud, murder for hire, bombing, racketeering, bribery, fraud, obstruction of justice, witness tampering, and money laundering.

Carter's team was there when the shipment of cocaine came in that Friday, hidden in stacks of fish. It was a record bust, hitting most of the major newspapers and news broadcasts across the country.

Carter was invited to a press conference with the Attorney General. She stood in front of a large board, depicting the Durante and Nero organizational structures. She answered questions about the evidence her team was able to gather and the charges they were bringing against the crime families.

After the press conference, a young, newly-recruited FBI agent, approached Carter.

"Congratulations. What a fantastic bust. You are truly an inspiration. Would you mind taking a quick photo with me? I would like to hang it in my work space. I'm new to the FBI, was just hired, and what you've accomplished is what I aspire to achieve in this agency." The young recruit smiled broadly as she shook Carter's hand.

Kelly Carter paused for a moment, looking at the excited gleam in the agent's eye. She nodded, and said she would be happy to take a photo. She posed with the new recruit for the camera, and she wouldn't admit it to anyone if they asked her, but she had tears of joy in her eyes.

Chapter 49

"I should have smelled it."

How are you feeling? You scared us out there," Carter said, a look of relief on her face. She sat in a chair next to the hospital bed where Scarlet lay with a sling around her arm.

"I've been better. Never had a hole through me before, and it's still pretty sore. I'll have my arm in a sling until it heals completely. Other than that, I'm just happy to be alive. I didn't know if I would make it. Where's Fenton? I was going to thank him for getting me out of there so quickly." *Tough kid. Asking about Fenton...hmm.*

"Sorry Scarlet, we transitioned you to the Marshals Service in the ambulance. The handoff with witness protection already took place. They have staff stationed outside your room, and as soon as you're well enough to leave, they are going to take you to your secure location. We finalized everything in the ambulance on the way over. We didn't expect you to be out cold for the discussion, but then again, we didn't plan for you to actually get shot. It was Agent Westbrook. He was working for the Neros on the inside. Fenton alerted me to it, and then against our pre-arranged orders, he almost got to you before the shot took place, but he was a couple of minutes too late. I should have seen it. I should have smelled it on Westbrook. Hell, I've worked with him for years. I'm sorry this happened. Believe me when I say I never apologize, ever, but in this case, I want to. I'm truly sorry."

"It's okay, Kelly. How could you have known? I mean Carter. Can I call you Kelly now?

"You can call me anything you want. You should know I don't let just anyone call me by my first name," Carter said, and Scarlet beamed.

"I'm glad I earned the privilege. Please know I don't blame you for Westbrook. How could you have known? Nothing was what it seemed in this case. It makes sense now, looking back. Westbrook brought me my mail before I went into hiding with Fenton, and the first letter on top was the trap to save my aunt."

"Yes, he was never told to deliver your mail. He went off the grid on that. He also was out of office when they found Luca's car, and he was pushing for a team to try to uncover evidence that a body was in the car at the time of the blast — most likely trying to verify the kill for Eleonora. He handled the laptop from your sister's locker and had access to her cell, as well as the footage from your undercover operation. He worked with Eleonora. He was trying to protect her by ruining evidence which could implicate her. He also volunteered to be the sharpshooter to fake your death at the final meet, knowing he would purposely botch the shot enough to send you to the hospital. If you didn't die from the wound, he probably would have sent someone to kill you at the hospital."

"Wow. What happens next?"

"Well, I am a woman of my word. I promised you I would let you see your Aunt Jo one last time. The Marshals Service agreed to help take you to see her quickly before you disappear. I'll take all of the evidence you helped us gather for the Durantes and Neros and we will take them to court. We have a solid case, finally, because of you. Carlo Durante even wants to make a deal with us. He will testify against the family, in exchange for protection. Guess he thought they were coming for him next and said he was a dead man walking anyway, and he chose life. This is a career case and I couldn't have asked for anything more. I never meant for you to get hurt, though. Please let me know if there is anything I can do to make it up to you."

"Actually, Kelly, this might be a weird request, but anyway could you see if Fenton would be willing to stick around? I feel I need to thank him for everything. I know he's officially done, but is there any way you could ask? Before I disappear forever?" Her eyes were wide, pleading.

"I'll see what I can do," Carter nodded, and a satisfied smile crossed her face.

Chapter 50

"You can't predict the future and you can't save everyone."

Scarlet felt flushed the moment she saw Fenton walk through the door of the waiting room. It was like the first time she saw him, confident and strong, with a heart of gold.

"I didn't think I'd see you again."

"You can't get rid of me that easily. They could tell me to pound sand, but I wasn't about to let you go away forever without saying goodbye. Now I even get the pleasure of escorting you. My lady," he said, holding his arm out for her, and she took it gladly as she leaned on him to avoid bumping her injured arm.

They talked in the car about Westbrook and the case Carter was going to bring against the Nero and Durante families. They talked about the lake house and Dale's family, and they talked about a lot of things that didn't matter because they wanted to avoid saying the things that did matter. They wanted to avoid talking about the things they couldn't change.

When they arrived at Aunt Jo's, Scarlet's jaw dropped at the site of the advanced security system.

"What is all of this? It looks like the security perimeter at the lake house. My aunt always left her door unlocked at night, and now look at this place — completely secured. Did you have something to do with this? I gave you her information, her location, and phone number when we first met. Did you arrange this?"

"I know some guys in the security game who owed me a favor. They gave me a great deal, and I knew it would be worth it. If she would have stayed inside, and hadn't fallen for the bait scheme, we would have avoided the whole bomb scare. Tough to think of everything though, and I knew she would be safe here before the trial. I hope you don't mind," he said bashfully, glancing at Scarlet from the corner of his eye, unsure of how she would react.

"Mind? Fenton, this is amazing. Add it to my list of things for which I'm grateful for since I met you. Saving my life back there, protecting my aunt, just being you, helping me maintain my sanity through this whole thing, and for giving me the best lake experience I could have ever asked for. I never once felt afraid when I was there with you. I want you to know that." She squeezed his hand, and he gave her a quick smile, relief flooding his face.

Once they were safely inside the gates, two vehicles filled with Marshals and agents pulled in behind them. Fenton opened the door for Scarlet when they were safely parked in her aunt's familiar winding driveway. Scarlet sat frozen in her seat, looking up at the slate blue, two-story house she knew would be for the last time. As she sat clutching the edge of the front seat, peering at the house through the window, Fenton gently touched her arm, breaking her from the spell.

"Are you okay, Scarlet?" he said softly, his eyes squinting as he tried to wipe the pained expression from his face. He couldn't put himself in her position exactly, but he was no stranger to loss. He knew what this was doing to her, and everything she had done to make this moment happen, despite how painful it would be once inside.

She looked pale and thin. The last few days were tough to get through, and the road ahead wouldn't be easier, at least, not for a while. From everyone he helped get safely into witness protection, they eventually felt more comfortable in their new normal. He knew this because he would ask his internal contacts how they were doing whenever they crossed paths, which, in his line of work, was fairly often. Scarlet nodded as she closed her eyes briefly, taking a deep breath.

"Okay, stay close to me as we get to the main door. I want us to get inside as quickly as possible in case anyone is watching. I called ahead. There are agents inside and she is expecting us."

"You talked to my aunt today?" She sounded surprised, and curious.

"Yes, we talk every once in a while. Are you ready?"

She nodded and stayed close to his side as they got to the front door. Agent Starr was already inside, having secured the area, and opened the door for them as they approached.

"She's in the kitchen, Scarlet. Fenton already filled her in on as much as we could. You only have a short time. I'll be here, and there is another agent out back. Wanted to give you some privacy though, so you should be able to say what you want to say before you go. Carter passes along her sincere thanks. This is your reward for your end of the bargain, and even though she couldn't be here today, she wishes you all the best." Agent Starr squeezed Scarlet's shoulder, and Scarlet swallowed hard as she followed Fenton into the kitchen.

Scarlet's eyes started to sting as she saw her aunt's familiar long, dark hair graying at the temples. As she rose Scarlet's mouth opened in surprise as Aunt Jo rose to hug Fenton. He seemed equally as surprised. Scarlet immediately wondered how many phone calls the two of them had leading up to this moment, and why he hadn't mentioned ever talking with her before.

Her aunt's eyes were already wet, and she hugged Fenton like she *knew* him, she hugged him as if he was family, holding him tight and whispering something into his ear. He said something soft in reply, and she leaned back with her hands on both of his arms, looking into his face with an expression of gratitude and admiration, and then hugged him once more. Scarlet's breath came in disjointed puffs. She felt strange witnessing what was certainly a private moment between the two of them, but she felt her heart warmed by the sight, despite the confusing circumstances. Two of the most special people in her life, connecting in some mysterious, but powerful way and it added a perplexing element to an already emotional situation.

Her aunt squeezed Fenton's hand, mouthing *thank you*, and he bowed his head in acknowledgement. He turned toward Scarlet, as she wondered what was exchanged between them.

"I'll give you two some privacy, I'll just be in the next room if you need anything, okay?" Scarlet smiled at him gratefully and nodded. Aunt Jo rushed to Scarlet, and hugged her.

It was the type of embrace which happens when two people feel it is their last time to say goodbye, like two shipwrecked souls starting to sink and they cling to each other as if it might prevent them from drowning.

"Hush child, it's okay, you're okay, you're my baby and everything is going to be okay. Say it, I want you to say it to me, tell me you're going to be okay. I need for you to believe it like I believe it."

"I'm going to be okay," Scarlet whispered the words while in the tight embrace. Aunt Jo pulled her to one of the seats at the kitchen table, and held her hands. Jo wiped away a few of the tears rolling down Scarlet's face.

"Aunt Jo, I've had to do some bad things to make sure I could see you this one last time. I wanted to call you, to tell you everything, but I couldn't. I need you to forgive me for those things. I can't tell you what they are, but I'm asking for your forgiveness."

"What you've gone through, it isn't fair. Everything you've been pulled into, everything you've seen and witnessed, and all the horror and tragedy. It isn't fair you had those things in your life. Don't think for a second I love you any less, or that anything has changed between us, because I know who you are in here," Aunt Jo said pointing to Scarlet's heart.

"I wish I could tell you everything that happened. Maybe I should have dug more into her past, and maybe I should have pressed her earlier when she evaded my questions. I could sense she was hiding things from me. I knew it, but I thought eventually she would trust me enough to tell me. Finally, on the night of her death, I followed her. I followed her that night into an alley where she went into a room with two men. I could have done more, I could have tried something, and maybe it wouldn't have turned out this way. Maybe we would both be here now, and none of this ugliness would have happened. I would still be clean, and not tainted by all of these things and then I wouldn't have to leave you, and say goodbye. I should have done something to prevent this. I'm so sorry."

"Honey, sweetie, listen to me. You can't live a life with these types of regrets, judging decisions you made in the moment, and expect to be happy. You did the best you could in the heat of the moment. Never apologize for that. You can't predict the future and you can't save everyone. I would rather say goodbye to my sweet girl, knowing you will have a life, than to see you buried and gone. You can't make a life and move forward if you're always looking back. You need to bury these thoughts with Robin, you understand? Otherwise, you will beat yourself up and the self-loathing will become a poison, ruining everything in front of you. You still have a future. Don't you worry about me. They can take you away from me and we may never see each other again, but they can't take away my unconditional and never-ending love for you. You will always be my daughter, and your mother would be so proud of you." Aunt Jo hugged Scarlet again, and Scarlet let herself sob quietly into her aunt's comforting embrace. Agent Starr knocked on the doorframe.

"I'm sorry, Scarlet, but you only have five minutes left and you need to say your final goodbyes now. I'll be waiting near the entrance when you're done."

Scarlet looked into her aunt's face, trying to memorize her features to lock away in her mind. She wanted it burned into her permanent memory bank, so on holidays and cold nights, she could think of her aunt's warm face. She looked over every inch, each laugh line and wrinkle, and her aunt smiled as if she understood the unspoken moment.

"I don't want to say goodbye, Aunt Jo," Scarlet whispered.

"Then don't, don't say goodbye child. Don't say goodbye. You will always have me in your life, because I will live in your memory and in your heart. I'm not leaving you, I would never leave you, child. You will always have me and I will always be thinking of you."

Fenton appeared in the doorway, his hands shoved deep in his pockets. He looked miserable, like he didn't want to have to be the one to tell her it was time to leave her aunt forever. A grim line formed on his face, and his shoulders and arms tensed with apprehension.

"I'll get the car ready, Scarlet, and meet you back at the door." Jo gave him one more hug, and then he left the room. Scarlet grabbed her bag and got up from her aunt's comfy kitchen chair, where growing up she had spent afternoons coloring. It was the same kitchen table where she would talk to her aunt about boys and do her homework. Too many memories were in this house, and in this kitchen, and it was ripping her to pieces to have to physically walk out the door one last time. As she started to walk toward the hallway, her aunt grabbed her hand.

"You know how I know you are going to be okay, Scarlet? Fenton promised me. He promised me you would be *just fine*, better than fine, and so far, he has come through on all of his promises. That's how I know you're going to be better than just okay, Scarlet, because I know you're going to have a wonderful life."

Scarlet looked up at Aunt Jo through eyes laden with tears, a look of confusion and amazement spreading across her face. She didn't understand what her aunt meant, she wasn't sure where this unusual certainty was coming from tied to Fenton, but seeing her aunt positively peaceful in what she believed to be the truth, left Scarlet finally feeling genuinely comforted by her aunt's words.

She hugged her aunt for the last time in the doorway of her childhood home, and was shielded by Fenton as they quickly made their way to the safety of his vehicle. He had the door opened for her and they pulled out of the driveway. She debated turning in her seat to look at the house as it disappeared from view, but she decided against it. She didn't want to see the house fade into the distance, she didn't want to see it dissipate into the fog, and she didn't want to see herself moving farther and farther away from the only parent she ever knew and loved. She decided to look straight ahead.

Fenton reached over across the console and grabbed Scarlet's hand. They drove together in silence, the bodyguard and the girl who had no family or place to call home, hand in hand. Scarlet looked over at Fenton. Her eyes glimmered with tears.

It was enough that he was simply sitting there next to her. She was grateful, and it was enough for her to feel closure.

It would have to be enough for the both of them.

Fenton pulled into a deserted parking lot, the other vehicles pulling in behind them.

"This is it. The Marshals Service already has your bags in their vehicle. They will take you on from here, into your new life. Remember everything I told you. You may need to change your appearance a bit – dye the hair, get a tattoo, that type of thing. The Durantes and Neros think you're dead, but in case you ever ran into someone…"

"Fenton, I don't know what to say. I feel like there is so much left unsaid between us, but we don't have the time. We *never had the time.*"

"I know, I know, Scarlet. You don't have to say anything."

"I think… no, *I know…* your Dad would be incredibly proud of you and everything you've done. Don't ever think differently, okay? You're *a good man*, Fenton. I never doubted it for a minute, and I don't think you should doubt it anymore either." She grabbed his hand with her free hand, and turned toward him in the front seat.

"I'm glad you were my last assignment. Saved the best for last, I guess, but part of me also wishes you were my worst client, it would make things easier somehow." He shook his head.

"I got you something, Scarlet." He pulled a large, fluffy stuffed dog from the backseat.

"Remember how Taylor gave me my stuffed dog when I moved in next door? Told me it helped him when he was alone? Helped him to not be afraid? Well, I thought you could use one. Don't open the card though until you're completely settled within your new life, okay?"

"Thanks Fenton, I'll cherish it."

She watched him drive away, his dark truck headed in the opposite direction, and a piece of her drove away with him. She hugged the stuffed dog. She named the stuffed animal Lars, and then she blinked back tears.

Three months later, Scarlet was starting to feel settled in her new life. The Marshals Service was long gone and she was now a brunette with bangs, with a Chinese symbol tattooed on her wrist. It was a tattoo which meant something to her. The dog sat perched in a spot where she could see it often, and finally one day, she was able to bring herself to opening the envelope Fenton gave her.

Scarlet, I wish you all the happiness in the world. You deserve it. You always could see the best in me. I hope when you look at your stuffed puppy, you don't feel scared being by yourself. Taylor was right. It helps. There is something inside the animal carefully hidden from view, waiting for when you're ready to find it. We will always have the lake house. Please know, you stole my heart the moment we met. No matter what happens, no one can take away the memories. We get to keep our memories forever. Love, Lars.

Scarlet wiped away her tears. She could hardly think straight, overwhelmed by the message. *Wait, there is something inside the stuffed animal? Hidden away so the Marshals wouldn't find it, knowing I wouldn't look at the note until I was far away from my old life?*

She looked all over the fuzzy creature for a secret compartment and finally found a button under his long fur that popped open the bottom of the stuffed dog. Inside was a clear bag containing a burner phone and another letter.

In case you still feel the same, and you don't want this to be the end for us...this time you get to make the decision. Throw the phone away or you can call me. Ask for Trent.

There was a number written on the bottom of the paper. A cell phone number, along with the burner phone and charger.

She took a deep breath. *In case I feel the same, and don't want this to be the end for us?* He was giving her a way to contact him. After months of shedding old skin, and learning how to not look over her shoulder while walking down the street, did she really want to connect with someone who reminded her of all the old pain?

She closed her eyes, and hugged Lars close to her body. She remembered what the Marshals said, she was to have no contact with anyone from her past. Fenton was breaking the rule by hiding away a burner cell phone as a means of contacting him. She took a deep breath.

Forgive me.

Chapter 51

"Sick of you? Now that's something I can't imagine."

The phone rang.

"May I speak with Trent please?"

That was how the conversation started. Two people sharing a sordid past, connecting again with new names and new identities. He recognized her voice.

"You decided to call," he said.

"How could I not?" she said.

"Can I see you?" he asked. She shared her address with him and he was only a couple of hours away from her. Her stomach was in knots as she waited for him to arrive at her door. The moment she saw him standing in front of her again, the nervousness melted away. She immediately felt safe seeing him, and it warmed her from the inside out. He had a worn army duffle bag in his hand as he stood casually on her step, eyeing her up and down.

"Dark hair, I like it. A tattoo as well? Wow, you actually listened to me this time," he said with a wicked grin and she laughed.

"I wasn't that bad before, was I? I always listened to you. Well, most of the time anyway."

"What does the tattoo mean?"

"It says Truthful Liars in Chinese. It reminds me I can be true to myself, and who I am, even though I have to live in a lie."

"I like that. I guess that makes two of us. You don't ever have to lie to me, though, I know who you are."

"I know, just everyone else. You thinking about sticking around these parts?"

"The lake house is only a couple of hours from here. If you're not sick of me, I think that could be our home away from home. I told you I wouldn't go back there without you, and I meant it. I also said you would have a wonderful life after all of this. I promised your Aunt Jo."

"Sick of you? Now that's something I can't imagine. You think I will be able to see Aunt Jo again?"

"Dale told me there might be a little house on the other side of the lake going up for sale. You think she might be in the market to buy? It's a gated community, perfect for secrets."

"You know, she just might. I can't believe you are here. I thought I would never see you again. You led me to believe I would be on my own the minute I left you."

"Okay, so I lied a little. You blame me?" His boyish grin made her laugh.

"No, I like you too much to blame you." She smiled at him and grabbed his hand to pull him inside. She brought both hands to his face, pulling him in for a long kiss leaving both of them breathless.

The End

Acknowledgements

I want to thank all of my family and friends whose love and encouragement are a blessing in my life.

To my lovely beta ladies and my good friends, Sue and MJ, thank you for everything. Sue, special thanks for your help with the book design, couldn't have done it without you.

To my editor, Michelle, thank you for your fantastic attention to detail and all of your help with this project. You made the editing process fun. Thank you Gloria for your keen eye, I appreciate all of your help and guidance.

Thanks to the great support network of inspirational women in my writing groups, RWA and WOW. I always walk away from those meetings feeling renewed.

I also want to extend a thanks to everyone who allowed me to talk about my novel, offering insight and motivation. Your enthusiasm for my project helps more than you know. Hope you find it as much fun to read as it was to write.